Praise for Michael Bishop's
THE SACERDOTAL OWL
AND THREE OTHER LONG TALES

"Bishop's illustrious career spans more than four decades, and this collection gathers four longer stories that showcase his talent for plumbing the depths of the human experience through science fiction. . . . Both startling and intimate, this collection captures Bishop's understanding of the human need to raise complicated questions and seek answers outside one's self. Fans will appreciate having these familiar favorites in one place, and newcomers will find it an excellent introduction to the richness of Bishop's fiction."
—*Publishers Weekly*

"Michael Bishop is a genuine original. These four stories explore the unexpected ramifications of faith—Mayan, Buddhist, Christian, and technological—in ways that no one else has, or could. Startling, funny, profound, and always marvelously detailed, Bishop's fiction creates unfamiliar worlds that we somehow recognize as ours, as us. A unique gem."
—Nancy Kress, author of *If Tomorrow Comes*

"In *The Sacerdotal Owl*, Michael Bishop delivers four wondrous, surprising novellas: We encounter a freakish, Lovecraftian Mayan sacrifice; a child on a gen-ship proclaimed to be the Dalai Lama's latest incarnation; an alien mantid who may well be the Second Coming, if not the actual First (and rendered, no less, in the chapter and verse of a gospel); and a tale 10,000 years in the future on a colonized world, where plays and acting are banned, so that only the dead, reanimated, may perform without penalty. Powerful, whimsical, horrific, and often slyly hilarious, this is Michael Bishop giving a command performance. We are royally entertained."
—Gregory Frost, author of *Lord Tohpet*

"Where else but in a Michael Bishop story would Central American guerillas make an uneasy alliance with ancient gods, or a reluctant Dalai Lama come of age on an interstellar transport, or a half-mad visionary reanimate the dead to perform in plays that hint at secret history, or a leftover alien messiah descend from the stars to proselytize humanity? Michael Bishop has the gift for creating realms where the landscape of body and spirit are firmly intertwined, each supporting and enhancing the other, so that the resulting tale resonates with the reader through cascading levels of wonder."
—Jane Lindskold, author of *Asphodel*

THE SACERDOTAL OWL

and Three Other Long Tales

THE SACERDOTAL OWL

and Three Other Long Tales of Calamity, Pilgrimage, and Atonement

MICHAEL BISHOP

KUDZU PLANET
· PRODUCTIONS ·
BONNEY LAKE WA

**THE SACERDOTAL OWL AND THREE OTHER LONG TALES
...OF CALAMITY, PILGRIMAGE, AND ATONEMENT**
A Fairwood Press/Kudzu Planet Productions Book
August 2018

First Trade Paper Edition

Fairwood Press
21528 104th Street Court East
Bonney Lake, WA   98391
www.fairwoodpress.com

Cover images © 2018 Getty Images
Cover and book design by Patrick Swenson

Kudzu Planet Productions
an imprint of Fairwood Press

ISBN13: 978-1-933846-72-9
Fairwood/Kudzu Planet Productions Trade Edition: August 2018
Printed in the United States of America

ACKNOWLEDGMENTS

"The Sacerdotal Owl" copyright © 2003 by Michael Bishop; first published by KaCSFFS Press in *13 Horrors*, edited by Brian A. Hopkins; reprinted in *Weird Tales*, edited by George Scithers and Darrell Schweitzer, March-April 2004.

And Strange at Ecbatan the Trees copyright © 1976 by Michael Bishop first appeared in a considerably different version from Harper & Row, March 1976; reprinted as *Beneath the Shattered Moons* by DAW Books, June 1977; reprinted in a Tor Double Novel with James Tiptree, Jr.'s *The Color of Neanderthal Eyes* by Tom Doherty Associates, January 1990.

"To the Land of Snow" copyright © 2012 by Michael Bishop; first published by Baen Books as "Twenty Lights to 'The Land of Snow'" in *Going Interstellar*, edited by Les Johnson and Jack McDevitt, June 2012; reprinted in *The Year's Best Science Fiction: Thirtieth Annual Collection*, by St. Martin's Griffin, edited by Gardner R. Dozois, July 2013.

"The Gospel According to Gamaliel Crucis; or, The Astrogator's Testimony" copyright © 1983 by Davis Publications for *Isaac Asimov's SF Magazine*, edited by Shawna McCarthy, November 1983; reprinted in author's collection *Close Encounters with the Deity*, from Peachtree Publishers, Ltd., August 1986; the version herein contains a host of revisions that make it the author's preferred text of this particular "long tale." But the same, in different degrees, holds true for each featured story here.

Grateful acknowledgment is made to Houghton Mifflin Company for permission to reprint lines from "You, Andrew Marvell" from *Collected Poems of Archibald MacLeish 1917-1952* by Archibald MacLeish.

for Jeri,

for a universe of more than good reasons

CONTENTS

ONE-RHYME SONNET ON THE MUTABILITY OF HUMAN FAITH

Muni Ben-Ami (1876-1942)

Adapted from the Hebrew (Micah) and the Yiddish (Muni Ben-Ami) by A. H. H. Lipscombe

> *Alas! I am a harvester of dying fruit,*
> *A drinker of the dregs of bitter wine,*
> *When nothing springs from the land to eat. . . .*
> *The good have left our holy earth;*
> *Not one saint clings to the altar horns.*
> *A bloodthirsty remnant slaughters its own,*
> *And even the young poison their begetters.*
> *—Micah 7:1-2*

Through unending wastes of heat-buckled clay,
   We pilgrims stagger on our dire way.
We grub up raw roots and choke down cracked hay,
   Petition old landlords, and sometimes slay
Their run-amok chickens, which every curst day
   We rend in secret or in starved fury flay
To red gobs, then bend to God, our hearts a-splay,
   And with ash-coated tongues pretend to pray.

Like penury, greed, or that pus-oozing stray,
   Hunger—whate'er we do—dyes our eyes gray;
It sweeps our taut guts like a hot soldiers' bay
   Emptied of tenants by their own lethal play.
Walking each wadi, struck numb with dismay,
   Here plod we pilgrims on our dire way.

THE SACERDOTAL OWL

Lace Kurlansky rode ashore with twelve others from the passenger ship *Novia Rosa*. She had worked before in Mexico and Honduras with her archaeologist fiancé Cabot Chessman, but she had never before visited the guerilla-besieged Central American country of Guacamayo, and her anxiety level soared as the tender neared the ramshackle coastal settlement of Dos Perros, entryway to the jungle in which Cabot directed a team excavating the ruins of the ancient Maya city of Chibal. Owing to its befuddling civil war, few foreigners landed in Guacamayo, and those who did pretty much clung to the government-controlled eastern coast and its hot white beaches. Dos Perros and the green jungle strangling its terrace-set adobe shops and homes, all with tin, thatch, or terracotta-tile roofs, intensified Lace's foreboding.

A town called Two Dogs, she thought, shaking her head.

Like all her fellow passengers, she had come by sea because, a year ago, a rebel with a shoulder-braced missile launcher had nearly downed an airliner landing outside the Ciudad de Guacamayo airport, the only one in the country with runways long enough for passenger jets. And Cabot wanted her to marry him here—not in the capital, or even in Dos Perros, but in the holy sanctum of a temple atop the highest pyramid in Chibal, as if they were latter-day avatars of long-dead Maya nobles imploring Xaman Ek, god of the North Star, to sanctify their union.

Pressing her hands between her knees, Lace chuckled bleakly. Her folks thought her both daft and unfilial, while her sisters regarded Cabot as an egomaniacal Svengali. Most of her friends called her a self-destructive romantic but wished her well, as did her closest colleagues at Vanderbilt.

Now, with the jungle advancing like a voracious beast, Lace marveled that she had agreed to Cabot's ill-advised program, fearful that her family had already pegged the whole wonky arrangement.

"Business or pleasure?" said a gray lounge-singer type sitting next to her in the gently awash tender.

"I'm not sure," Lace said.

"Anyone meeting you?"

"My fiancé." If that news failed to discourage further talk, she could always show him her silver tongue stud.

The man arched his eyebrows. "Then you should *get* sure as soon as you can." And smiled to soften the rebuke.

Disembarking with the others, Lace wobbled down the pier toward a bald, baggy-suited official checking passports. He waved her on, but halted a passenger as pot-bellied and swarthy as himself. Cabot did not appear among the family members, business folks, and natives crowding the esplanade. Lace's anxiety mounted toward a mild, unfocused panic.

"Cabot!" she yelled. *"Cabot!"*

Many people looked, but a slender young Guacamayan man carrying a strap-on bamboo tray of hand-carved mahogany idols and rainforest animals stalked along the cordon separating arrivals from locals, never releasing her gaze. She tried glancing aside, but the certainty that *he* hadn't looked away compelled her to check out his relentless tracking sidle. When they met at the end of the pier, he lifted for her approval a small wooden owl. In less than a minute, he had bridged to her—psychically, anyway—and his classic Indian features and thin sweat-glazed arms impressed themselves indelibly on her awareness.

"You want this," he said. "Only ten dollars, American." He had a musical voice and spoke Spanish with a queer, touching formality.

She shook her head. She wanted Cabot, and surcease from worry. Around them, other vendors—importunate peasants, although she did not begrudge them their efforts to earn a living—accosted the arrivals, showed their goods, and in some cases haggled over prices.

Lace, still searching, pushed on. The thin bronze man paced her steps, not with a crude aggression but a dogged cheerfulness that, despite her unease, began to have its effect. She liked his pygmy owl of slick mahogany. One of its wings seemed to hold a shield with a quasi-human face, and a splinter-like dart pierced its body diagonally from ear-horn to claw.

"Lord of the Night," the fellow said, turning the owl in his fist. "Messenger to the spirit world. Eight dollars, U.S.—a marvelous deal."

"Two-fifty," Lace offered. You never paid what the natives first asked, a custom acknowledged in this one's impromptu price cut. When he seized her hand and wrapped her fingers around the owl, she remarked him more closely.

He swayed a little, as if expecting her to run. The top of his head rose only to her chin. His lack of height, along with his back-slanting brow and full berry lips, identified him as a Maya of the regional Tunkuluchú. He was neither mestizo nor pardo, but a full-blooded Mesoamerican of ancient stock. Here in the sun, he exuded no special mystery or nobility (in every society, most citizens are commoners), just a mild desperation in the raw capitalist pursuit of his daily bread. At his throat he wore a frayed string from which dangled an obsidian pendant showing an aged paddler god with a stingray spine through his nose. (Body piercing has long historical roots.)

Lace recognized this fetish as one of the two canoe-paddling gods who carried dead kings to the spirit world. The Old Stingray God symbolized day, while his partner, the Old Jaguar God, represented night—polar opposites framing a fundamental unity. Between the collars of the huckster's well-made but grubby white shirt, this ebony icon shone against his yam-brown skin.

"Five dollars," he said after a moment. "No less."

"What do you want for the pendant?" With the head of his mahogany owl, Lace tapped the stingray-god fetish.

"I don't sell the pendant, ever," he said. "Five dollars for the owl."

"Three," Lace countered.

"Look at the craftsmanship, the delicacy. I implore you, señorita, five dollars, or you stab me to the heart."

This phrasing stabbed her to her own. The owl anointed her palm with a sweet-smelling arboreal oil, and it did have delicacy—as well as intricacy and the intercessory agency of a faultless eye. But she had no need for a carven owl, no matter how fine, and Cabot still hadn't showed.

"How do you call yourself?" Lace asked the man.

"Chac," he said.

"Ah, like the rain god."

"Yes. But many visitors mishear and call me Jack."

"And your last name?"

Chac squinted—less in suspicion, Lace thought, than in wonder that she cared to pursue the matter, given her agitation, which he had obviously already noted. At length, though, he said, "Sañudo, señorita."

"Ah." Lace did not say aloud that his surname meant "furious." He did not seem furious, only anxious to complete a sale. Clearly, he needed the money. Trawling Dos Perros for sympathetic tourists had no doubt proved harder and harder with the worsening guerrilla conflict.

"Four dollars," Chac Sañudo said. "Four is nothing. Four is mere pennies for hours of tender labor."

But she would not budge. Cabot may have suckered her, but this Maya boy—he was barely a man, if a man at all—would *not* do so. Shrugging, Chac took her three grimy bills, stuffed them into his khaki pants, and moved along to an elderly gringa who might prove more biddable. Lace looked after him almost regretfully and then turned her gaze on the port.

It was bigger than a village, smaller than a city, climbing in ragged terraces away from the miracle of the sea and sprawling at its edges toward a jungle that cramped it into a bright isolate bowl. Lace shook a cellular phone from her bag, to call the village near Chibal where Cabot and his team bought supplies and collected mail. The Nokia did not activate. It showed no power bars and no inclination to trump the technological gap rendering it useless. Only an idiot would have hauled it all the way from Nashville to Guacamayo. . . .

"Cabot!" she yelled. "You didn't check your calendar, did you? You went gaga in some stinking tomb and never came up for air!"

Jamming the phone back into her bag, she ignored the glances of passersby—and attuned her ear to the egregious jumpy snarl issuing from a nearby store, a noise like a leaf blower and a lawn-mower engine jockeying for supremacy. Lace crossed the street and entered the shop, where the snarl almost deafened her. The men inside, all with rolled shirtsleeves and sweaty faces, turned to her, one grasping a chainsaw as if about to rip the shop's counter in two.

Other chainsaws hung from the walls or rested on makeshift shelves like so many transmogrified bicycle parts. The emporium specialized in this item, and Lace figured that its owner legally outfitted rogue settlers who would travel inland and illegally attack the rainforest to clear *milpas*—maize fields—both for the timber and the hope of growing crops that would keep their families, and their ambitions, alive. And so they achieved the needful at the expense of tomorrow, a Faustian self-annihilation.

The man holding the chainsaw swung it toward Lace—mock-threateningly, she realized, but she had already reached the street when its snarling ceased and he shouted, *"Forgive me, pretty one, come back!"* The others stupidly guffawed.

A pox on you all, Lace thought. Then she recalled Honduran stelae—

monuments that the Maya called "tree-stones"—showing death figures with black spots, signifying decomposition, on their two-dimensional faces and bodies. Guacamayo belonged to Guacamayans, and if they wanted to risk government fines or even slaughter by guerillas, or to denude the countryside of mahogany and other precious hardwoods, who was she to gainsay this wish or to lambaste it as selfish or shortsighted? Let Cabot do those things.

And as far as "shortsighted" went, what about Cabot's failure to foresee today's boondoggle? He had his faults, including arrogance, overwork, and bouts of irritating intellectual distraction, but Lace could always count on him to do what he said. Cabot was reliable. He took pride in his reliability.

So why hadn't he shown? And what was she supposed to do, now that he hadn't? His team had no auxiliary personnel or contacts in Dos Perros, and the two of them had not even agreed on a hotel lobby or a bar to meet in if a mix-up derailed their rendezvous. Thoughtless—unforgivably so.

Lace explored the settlement, eventually hiking up a dirt alley to a terrace given over to ferns, flowers, lopsided shanties, and a five-peseta pension. At this motel-like structure, the Hotel Llama del Bosque ("Call of the Wild"), with cinderblock walls, thatched porticoes, and a rusted tin roof, she rented a room from a mestizo woman whose adolescent son carried her bag to her door. He flirted with big liquid eyes but succeeded only in cracking her up. He then indignantly stashed away her tip and strode barefoot back to his mama's office-cum-boudoir.

There was nothing to bind Lace to her room—no TV, no mini fridge, no reading material but matchbooks and a Gideon Bible. The electricity fueling the lights leaked a diluted mustard glow, and the heat was so brain-broiling that even a lobotomized guest would have wanted her skull heaped to the brim with ice cubes.

Lace freshened up with a washcloth and a lipstick re-do and walked back down to the esplanade. At a bar called Macanudo ("magnificent," "the best"), happy hour began at seven, and you could buy beer and Cuba Libres for sixty cents U.S. Even these prices limited the clientele to civil servants, army officers, a few brash tourists, and rainforest impresarios who had slashed and burned enough of the besieged jungle, through bribery and guile, to bribe and beguile again.

Did any of these people know Cabot? Could any of them tell her how to reach Chibal? Or did her fiancé lie wounded, if not dead, somewhere between the domain of the insurgent Tunkuluchuob and the outskirts of Dos

Perros? Lace sat at a table under a groaning ceiling fan nursing a rum and no-name cola—she knew it wasn't Coke—fretting these matters as if fret would fix them.

A barmaid scuttled over, and Lace dug into her bag for money. "When you're done," the barmaid said and scurried away. Lace's fingers closed not on coins, but on Chac Sañudo's mysterious owl.

As soon as she had it, Chac Sañudo himself appeared at the bar, moving with his goods tray as he had moved along the dock. He showed the patrons clay jaguars, onyx chess pieces, and a figure of Ixtab, goddess of suicide, a noose about her throat and her knotty wooden skin spotted black.

A customer with purple sweat circles under his arms tried to slap this figure from Chac's hand, but Chac pulled it back and edged around a table toward some less irritable patrons. An army officer bought a laughing wide-hipped woman a necklace, but this sale seemed the summit of Chac's luck.

Shoulders slumped, he continued scanning the crowd for buyers. Inevitably, his gaze fell on Lace. She beckoned him over, as if hailing an irksome cousin, and he placed his tray on her table before sitting.

"Hello, señorita. Are you here alone?"

"Why are you still working?" Lace rejoined. "Don't you have family?"

"I'm still working *because* I have family—my mother, a young sister, two little brothers. We all must eat."

"A family of five?" She could not nerve up to ask about Chac's father.

"A family of *eight*. I also have a twin and two older brothers, who were drafted seven years ago. They've never returned."

After that, he answered no more questions. Nor did he try to sell her anything from his tray. Instead, he asked questions—about her solitary presence in the Macanudo, her reasons for coming to Guacamayo, her plans to reunite with her no-show American fiancé, and what she'd do if something terrible had befallen Señor-Doctor Chessman, the archaeologist. Lace retorted that nothing terrible had befallen Cabot, who would surely arrive in the morning to check the guest lists of the hotels and to bring their nightmarish accidental separation to an end.

Chac fingered the stingray-god pendant on his dirty string. Even in this nocturnal temple to booze, dance, and piped-in music (a mind-fucking mix of flamenco and hip-hop), the figure symbolized day. It did not quite hypnotize Lace, but it obsessed her as a talisman of her anxiety and of Chac's allegiance to a strangeness at odds with his daytime normality. She wanted to buy the fetish, but he didn't want to sell it, and she had no right to badger him. After all, he had many other curios in his tray from which to choose an alternative.

"Don't you have a pendant of the Old Jaguar God?" Lace asked, thinking that the stingray god's partner would do if she couldn't buy *this* figure. Both meant bloodletting, spirit voyage, and death.

"My twin wears it," Chac said.

"And where is he?"

"Among the Tunkuluchú rebels." Chac offered this perilous declaration without lowering his voice or checking for eavesdroppers. (Lace thought, If Chac's twin has joined the guerillas, why hasn't Chac?) He laid his small hand on her wrist. "If you want to go to Chibal, I will escort you—for a nominal sum."

He actually, quite confidently, said *nominal*.

Fifty dollars. Talk about nominal. Lace converted her U.S. money into pesetas and remitted the absurdly low fee in advance.

The next morning, however, in the dining room where the Llama del Bosque's proprietress served breakfast, Lace learned from a CNN broadcast that a regiment of the Tunkuluchuob had captured Chibal. They had taken the archaeologists there hostage and packed the main pyramid's temple and the underground tombs with explosives. They threatened to blow up the whole complex if President Leopoldo Fuentes did not release a notorious guerilla leader now in custody in Ciudad de Guacamayo. They also demanded an accounting of the country's "disappeared"—priests, anthropologists, social workers, labor leaders, journalists, and the family members of known rebel combatants, including many children.

Such a blast would destroy irreplaceable Maya treasures—a major chunk of the Tunkuluchuob's own heritage—but it would also rob Fuentes of tourist revenues and political face. The rebels conceded their desperation, but stressed that the President's ruthlessness had eclipsed every reasonable peaceful option. They couldn't possibly lay down their arms before the implementation of even one reform, and they had exhausted all tolerance for Fuentes' intransigent arrogance and cruelty.

Chac picked up Lace on a battered motorcycle, with a jury-rigged sidecar, that looked as if it might have last seen action in Italy during the First

World War. He did not say how he had come by this vehicle, but Lace felt sure that he had borrowed it from a local outfitter. At her feet in the sidecar, three gasoline tins (which Chac had filled at her expense) confirmed her in this view. They climbed the hill behind Dos Perros, clattering like a chorus of ill-repaired chainsaws, and raced for hours along a jungle-pent two-rut road that jiggled her eyes, bruised her butt, and squeezed her kidneys like acid-drenched sponges. They passed some peasants walking single file, several coffee plantations, and a rattletrap truck hauling raw new furniture. They could not talk. Lace could scarcely even signal her need to stop.

Finally, Chac pulled over and helped her from the sidecar. After vanishing into the jungle, ruing her folly in undertaking this trip, she clutched her knees to keep from toppling backward as she peed. When she wobbled back to the road, Chac handed her a warm beer and a banana leaf wrapping a bean-filled tortilla. Squatting like natives, they ate and drank. Lace peppered Chac with questions, many of which she had already asked and a few that had occurred to her during their precipitous ride.

How long would the trip to Chibal take? Would government troops or guerillas try to stop them? Would the Tunkuluchú rebels kill them? Could they hope to approach the temple complex if insurgents had indeed captured it? Would news reporters reach the site before them? Could they buy gasoline if they—?

Chac touched her face with a fingertip and let it linger on her skin. "You worry too much, Señorita Kurlansky. Peace."

"I've just realized that I have no idea what I'm doing—what *we're* doing. How does a person summon peace from chaos?"

After setting his beer between his sandaled feet and wiping his hands, Chac took a folded sheet of paper from his shirt pocket. "I would like to read you something. Will you hear?"

"What is it?"

Chac ignored this question. He faced her, the paper at chest level, too close to his body for him to read. Even so, he declared, " 'The Sacerdotal Owl' by Chac-Xib-Chac Sañudo," and began to recite what Lace soon recognized as a poem of heavy strangeness and heat:

> *"A white girl in a white waterspout of a blouse*
> *whirled across my sight in a hurricane of longings,*
> *the reddest of which—like a marlin's gills, or a Mayan sunset,*

or a harlot's midnight lips, if not vein-true love—
I packed into my heart with the invisible hands of my poverty.
How, lovely girl, may I long for you?

"As the owl longs—in his fierce nocturnal melancholy—
for his most elusive prey, applying
the lustful clairvoyant mirrors of cold orange eyes,
the calipers of remorseless legs and talons, the heartfelt
focus of untiring wing-borne hunger,
and a sense of hearing so acute that the toenails of a vole
mincing through a bale of virgin cotton are to him
the oceanic bellows of a cyclone."

"Did a famous relative of yours write that?" Lace broke in. "It seems to make an oblique reference to our meeting on the pier."

Chac stared at her briefly, unhelpfully, before resuming:

"You bought a fist-sized wooden owl,
or, rather, stole it—just as you clawed from me
the scarlet chambers of my Tunkuluchú heart,
the tempests of longing laved in my hot blood,
and all my foolish dread of death.

"Now, I swear, our messenger to his spirit twin,
flown from my threshold heart to yours,
will bind us in grief-imbued mahogany,
pinion and polish us in his sap-fed flesh,
and we will melt, my storm-tormented girl,
to be cherished forever by all the reddest gods of Mayadom,
immortal slayers of the little mice of envy—
gods together, you and I, in the indignant memory
of the sacerdotal owl."

Chac, who had never once glanced at the poem in his hands, folded it back up and returned it to his shirt pocket. *"Selah,"* he said, like a Hebrew priest marking the end of a transgressive psalm.

"You wrote that," Lace said.

A wistful shadow crossed Chac's lips. Lace experienced alternating strokes of terror and tenderness, but finished eating and climbed back into the sidecar with a sense that Chac Sañudo knew what he was doing, although she did not.

By evening they had reached Las Orquídeas de la Virgen (The Orchids of the Virgin), the village nearest Chibal and so by necessity every tourist's headquarters. This hamlet made Dos Perros look cosmopolitan, but it did have cobblestone streets, a pair of cheap hotels, and a modern plaza with a concrete fountain memorializing the ascension of Leopoldo Fuentes to the presidency. Soldiers wearing shiny patent-leather tricornes and carrying submachine guns patrolled the town, and journalists from dozens of news outlets had arrived, although not in the numbers that Lace had feared. Moreover, because most tourists had left, you could get a room without bumping elbows with the news hawks. So, to save time and money, she and Chac took only one room in the Hotel Llovedizo on Xibalba Boulevard.

Privately, Lace acknowledged that she no longer much cared what happened to either Cabot or Chibal. This was shameful. But she had fallen in love with Chac Sañudo. He powered her pulse beats, filled her eyes, and nettled her loins. He had cloaked her in the diaphanous mantilla of his passion and so ensorcelled her. He had won her with a mahogany owl, a dignified solicitude, and a love poem—no, a *sex* poem—disguised as a paean to the Sacerdotal Owl of Chibal. In short, he had seduced her to a state of sensual dependency, and she had fallen.

In the lounge of the Hotel Llovedizo, they heard that government troops were negotiating with a rebel commander, and that journalists and curiosity seekers alike had no sanction to visit Chibal. They ate roast beef, black beans, salsa-smothered rice, and fried plantains, knocking back—at Chac's bidding, at Chac's expense—shot after shot of a fermented *balche* made from local honeys and philodendron bark. Chac assured Lace, who had grown indifferent, that he'd get her to Chibal anyway. No one, in fact, could stop him from doing so.

The lounge seemed to fill with clear oxygenated water, a breathable medium that supported quetzals, jaguars, emerald tree boas, spider monkeys, electric-green butterflies, and both human diners and apelike Guacamayan troops. Everyone moved as if impeded by an omnipresent translucent gel.

But I'm not drunk, Lace thought. I'm . . . *lucidly inebriated.*

The food, the balche, and the aphrodisiac peril of the hostage situation at Chibal worked both to lull and to arouse Lace. She made Chac recite his poem again, which he did from memory, then asked him to take her to their second-floor room and rock her to sleep. She hoped for a climax that undercut neither her sense of erotic drowning nor her allegiance to this new reality.

"Very well," Chac said. "Come."

They departed the lounge in a series of slow-motion steps that Lace observed as if from overhead. When they climbed the narrow carpeted stairs, they resembled salmon leaping dreamily from one waterfall level to another. And when they entered their room, with its rippled aqua linoleum and its green water-lily-patterned wallpaper, she swam to Chac and pulled off his shirt like a rescuer divesting a drowning man of his waterlogged garments. Chac returned the favor, and they rolled onto the bed so that his stingray-god fetish slapped her between the breasts as he rowed them on and on, without predictability or relent. His tongue probed her mouth, caressing the silver stud that she had inserted in it after having it pierced as a gift to Cabot, and as another show of independence for her bewildered parents.

At length, Lace slept. Once, she opened her eyes and felt the empty spot beside her, but, after seeing Chac silhouetted naked at the aquarium-like room's one seaweed-draped window, dove into sleep again, releasing the ballast of her anxiousness until she hovered bodilessly in the sustaining amnion of her dreams. The stamped-tin ceiling had no dimension, only a flat transparency through which the Mesoamerican stars glinted like sunfish scales.

The next time she awoke, this ceiling eclipsed those stars and she could neither move nor clearly see. Her body had the weight of limestone. A male figure—Chac, she presumed—knelt above her, stretching the foreskin of his penis out over her belly and repeatedly perforating it with a pinlike instrument. Drops of blood fell from this self-mutilation, scalding her flesh like candle wax. She couldn't wipe the drops aside or cry out a protest.

To be cherished forever by all the reddest gods of Mayadom, she thought.

Finally, Chac thrust the stingray spine—now she recognized it—into the mattress and leaned forward, still dripping from his figlike member, to gaze at her less like a lover than a surgeon. The coldness of his look half-panicked her. Then he touched her cheek and placed his moist lips on her fretful mouth. Her panic dissolved.

Mama, Daddy, she imagined saying, let me introduce you to the Tunkuluchú poet, Chac Sañudo, my beloved, my betrothed. . . .

As her betrothed leaned back, the obsidian pendant at his throat caught a ricochet of light, and her fear flooded back. The pendant depicted a paddling figure wearing a jaguar helmet and a jaguar ear—the Old Jaguar God, a night symbol, a ferryman of kings to the death realm of Xibalba.

Thoughtlessly, Lace reached for it. What had happened to the Old Stingray God? Or had Chac changed it from a mere ornament to a bloodletting tool? Her lover seized her hand and rotated it back to the mattress. "Shhh," he told her. "Sleep."

What could she do but obey?

As a member of the Vanderbilt swimming team, Cabot Chessman had specialized in the butterfly. With long golden arms and the torso of an obsessive ex-asthmatic (in other words, of a health-freak weightlifter), he had won prizes as a solo swimmer and as a participant in four-part medley relays.

Lace, accompanied by a girlfriend smitten with a teammate of Cabot's, went to a meet in the natatorium and gawked at this youthful blond Abe Lincoln clone. She spent the afternoon ogling his every movement, from his dolphin kick in the events that he so clearly dominated to his towel-flipping shenanigans during the long waits between the echoing-gunshot starts. Afterward, she met him, and he was older than his teammates, a graduate student who still had athletic eligibility, and who had decided to test it despite the rigor of his class work.

What a catch—like a gold-medal Olympian and a Nobel Prize-winning scientist incarnate in one lanky frame. Lace admired him. She liked that monetary gain figured less prominently in his career aims than did uncovering facts about humanity that would enrich its self-knowledge. Indeed, he had an idealistic naïveté akin to hers, for Lace had committed to a social-work major. But Cabot's idealism, along with a single-mindedness bordering on vainglory, did not endear him to the Kurlanskys, who still could not figure out Lace's refusal to go into computer engineering or business administration, much less the idiot defiance implicit in her tongue piercing. What would the newlywed Chessmans use for money? Stolen Mayan artifacts? Enormous all-you-can-eat platters of academic prestige?

But they had dated anyway. After Cabot earned his doctorate and accepted an assistant professorship of Mesoamerican Studies at Southern Methodist University, Lace paid her way to join him on two archaeological expeditions on which he served as chief lieutenant, first in the limestone hills of Yucatán, the Puuc, and later in Honduras at Copán. Cabot always exuded a quasi-distracted air, as if only the past and its artifacts held any reality for him, but Lace liked even this crotchet in him.

At a *cenote* (a limestone sinkhole fed by the water table, into which the Maya threw sacrifices ranging from jade ear-flares to stoic royal captives) in the northwestern Yucatán, Lace and Cabot shed their bush clothes and went skinny-dipping like skylarking teenagers. In the crystalline pool, with its inky cobalt bottom, Cabot wrapped Lace in his eel-like arms and pledged eternal fealty.

Eternal, Lace murmurs, lying abed in the Hotel Llovedizo. What does that mean? That you won't abandon me until my first gray hair?

No, Cabot replies, smiling. That you'll *never* be shut of me.

Never?

Cabot says: Like the faithful husband in that Mískito Indian myth, 'The Dead Wife,' I'll cling to you until you die and then escort your soul to Mother Scorpion. Even in a wasteland of ghosts, I'll protect you.

What a minute, Lace says. Who the hell is this Mother Scorpion?

The spirit of the afterlife. For some tribes it was Ah Puch, god of death. For the Maya who lived around Chibal in Guacamayo, that spirit was Tunku-luchú, the Sacerdotal Owl. One day I hope to lead an expedition there.

All the glyphs of Ah Puch I've ever seen, Lace says, depict him as a skeletal old coot with plague spots. And if Mother *Scorpion* presides over death, nobody would ever bother to ask, Death, where is thy sting?

I guess not, Cabot says, holding her tighter in the uncanny blue water.

So if you plan to escort my soul to the afterlife, take me to the Sacerdotal Owl—he sounds like a pussycat in comparison to Ah Puch and Mother Scorpion.

Owls are predators, Lace. Their beaks and talons can ravage.

I don't care, Lace says. Take me to the owl. (After all, she thinks, what can such a silly promise really cost you?)

I promise, Cabot obliges.

Now ravage—ravish—me yourself, you ruins-fixated galoot.

Now?

Sure. Before Davis and Lundquist show up to wash their sweaty clothes.

Cabot obliges again, there in the cobalt-blue stillness of both the cenote and her room in the Hotel Llovedizo.

Chibal was still not truly a tourist site. Visitors came only at the sufferance of the Fuentes regime and the university-based archaeologists working there. Chibal had no paved roads in, no visitor center, no camping areas, and no brochures touting its scenic wonders or its historical-cultural import. You reached it by hiking into the rainforest and using the faux-Mayan stelae set out at half-hidden intervals as landmarks. You packed in your own food and water, and you always left word in Las Orquídeas that you planned to return on such-and-such a day.

Given the hostage crisis, the defense minister forbad unauthorized treks to Chibal, and *all* treks were unauthorized. Reporters gathered at the police station, in hotel lobbies, and at a fancy bar called the Maya Royal. Theoretically, armed soldiers kept them from sneaking off into the jungle in quest of scoops, but persistent rumors held that a famous North American TV newsman had already slipped the quarantine.

Chac, who had never heard of this person, led Lace half a mile into the jungle before she fully awoke. Golden light streamed through the canopy, the palms, and the orchids cascading from giant ferns like flamboyant alien polyps. Bromeliads with two-gallon reservoirs perched on the rungs of monkey ladders and in the crotches of an *árbol de ajo*, or garlic tree, with a base the size of a small-town bandbox.

In this honey-hued light, Lace grabbed Chac's pendant and studied it. Seeing the Old Stingray God both relieved and puzzled her.

"What?" Chac said, touching her bottom lip.

"Did you forsake me last night?"

"Briefly. To scout the soldiers' positions and our best way in."

"I dreamed your twin with the jaguar-god pendant visited me."

Chac's eyes caught fire. "What did he do?"

"He ravished me. Later, he pierced his foreskin." Lace inhaled. "And dripped blood on my stomach."

Chac mulled this news dispassionately. "This morning, when you got up, did his blood still mark you?"

No, the blood had vanished. Lace asked if his twin had hoped to open a portal to the spirit world via his bloodletting. Chac said yes, but added that the absence of blood most likely meant that she had dreamt a harmless dream—nothing that would alter her life in the daytime world.

Fear, sharp and cold as an ice-skate blade, slid down Lace's spine. "Chac," she said, "let me see your cock." She had no idea what to do if his foreskin showed signs of piercing, but she could not take another step without knowing if his rebel twin had taken his place, however briefly.

Frowning, Chac unbuttoned his fly and eased his penis out. It neither shrank from Lace's touch nor engorged, and she admired this show of self-possession in so young a man. She also took heart from the organ's lack of puncture wounds. Only a nightmare had violated her last night.

"What's your brother's name?"

"Ex-Xib-Chac," Chac said, pronouncing the first two names *Esh-Sheeb*.

"Yet another Chac?"

"His name means 'Black Man Chac,' mine 'Red Man Chac.' But from our births, everyone called my brother Zafado."

" 'Impudent'? 'Shameless'?"

"Yes. He has always behaved so."

"Then you disapprove of his association with the rebel Tunkuluchuob?"

Chac disapproved of the bringers of premature death, whose number included both the Guacamayan army and the Indian guerillas. He believed in the sacred old gods—most of them—and in the gospel of Christ as embodied in his self-sacrifice on a dwarf variety of World Tree. The Cross and the World Tree linked the natural and the supernatural dimensions, as did physical love. Immediately, his face turned from yam-brown to reddish mahogany, and he cupped Lace's chin in his palm as if touching her might restore his equanimity.

"If you like," he said, "I'll take you back to Las Orquídeas."

Lace mulled this offer. If she loved Chac rather than Cabot, and if proceeding might deliver both Chac and her to disaster, why proceed? Well, she had pledged her troth—what a ridiculous word—to Cabot, and a situation beyond his influence, not his bastardly fickleness, had kept him from meeting her in Dos Perros. Besides, if Cabot could vow to escort her soul to the afterlife after she died, how could she deny him the solace of her presence while *he* still lived?

"No," Lace said. "Let's go on."

*

A harassing drone came through the ferns, lianas, and stiletto-spiked tree boles along their careful inward march. This drone had an insectile quality, but also a vibrato that heightened its irreality.

"Chainsaws," Lace said.

"Yes. More bringers of early death."

"The settlers will burn the trees to grow beans and maize in the soil that the ash has enriched," Lace recited.

Chac grimaced. Slash-and-burn agriculture depleted the soil's fertility in three or four years, but the settlers would simply creep deeper into the rainforest and make new swathes of destruction. Even the location-revealing buzzing of their saws failed to deter them. They posted guards. They terrorized or killed accidental intruders. They bribed or co-opted officials charged with enforcing the law. The army could send them packing, of course, but the army had the rebel Tunkuluchuob to contend with.

"A person could get rich," Lace said, "by inventing a chainsaw silencer."

At that moment, a patrol of silent men in camouflage (government special forces, Lace surmised) stepped forth pointing submachine guns. Under cover of the chainsaw snarl and probably with the aid of U.S. Ranger training, they had emerged soundlessly. Not even Chac had heard them. Despite Lace's fear that the soldiers would question and then kill them, their meeting ended peaceably. They were hunting rebels, and once Chac convinced them that, at the behest of the district governor, he was taking the fiancée of W. Cabot Chessman to Chibal for a negotiating session, the patrol leader scratched a map on the laterite floor with a twig, showing a better way in, and vanished with his team into the tangled understory.

Lace and Chac walked on through the jungle corridors and scents, its grotesque growths and beauties, conscious that other creatures—beasts or men—stirred within it and that they must take care not to stumble upon a boa constrictor or a balche-drugged human being with a bad chemical jones for bloodshed. Now and then a helicopter passed overhead, clattering. At length, Chac squatted and pointed through the foliage at Chibal's central complex.

A palace, four temples, two rows of tumbled columns, and the notorious Pyramid of the Owl, whose hieroglyphic staircase rivaled that at Copán, seized Lace's eye like the diorama inside a View-Master. A host of stelae thrust up among these structures, as if the city's architects had landscaped it with stones instead of shrubbery.

What a sense of metaphor the ancient Tunkuluchuob had! Every structure had a real-world counterpart. The pyramids stood for mountains, the temples atop them for caves, the history-engraved stelae for trees, and all the various doors for portals—in the Mayas' minds, *real* ones—to the spirit world. Cabot had promised that if they wed in the bloodletting sanctum of the temple atop the Pyramid of the Owl, under the tree growing up through the pyramid from a limestone sinkhole at the center of the structure's rubble-paved base, both God and the mountain-dwelling deities who had presided over Chibal's daily life would bless their union forever.

Armed guerillas in tattered uniforms occupied the plaza, huddling in old looters' trenches, behind gravel piles, or between crude walls of dirt and sticks. The walls put Lace in mind of the revetments that the Maya of Dos Pilas, in the Petexbatún forest of northern Guatemala, had thrown up circa AD 760, just before Dos Pilas fell to warriors from Tamarindito and the whole loose-jointed empire of Ruler 4 collapsed at his default capital of Aguateca.

Maybe *these* rebels were also doomed. Maybe they paid homage to their doom by threatening to blow up Chibal, whose excavation and development might one day lead Guacamayo to prosperity. Or maybe they realized that if prosperity flirted, it would not court them, but instead the right-wing cronies of Fuentes and all the foreign capitalists underwriting his regime. Here, at least, Lace heard no helicopters, for the guerillas had many nasty weapons, including a portable missile launcher.

"Come," Chac said. "Let's find your fiancé."

Lace clutched his shirt. "Won't they kill us?"

"Zafado's brother? And Zafado's brother's friend? No—at least not at first." Downplaying her fear, he pulled her through the tattered ferns to the edge of the clearing. Her heart hammered. In the heavy jungle mugginess, her whole body radiated a shameful sweltering terror.

When they stepped into the clearing, brown wraiths with contraband rifles and submachine guns surrounded them. Instead of prodding them at gunpoint, however, the rebels put them at the center of a protective ring and walked them across the great plaza toward the Pyramid of the Owl.

Because the ruins of Chibal were too dear to obliterate entirely, the rebels had no realistic worry of an assault from gunships or mortars. But military sharpshooters in the jungle posed a danger (despite Commander Ah Katun's warning that losing even one rebel to sniper fire would trigger the destruction of Chibal), and their guards stayed alert to this threat.

All seven of these rebels had mistaken Chac for his twin Zafado. Nor had Chac tried to disabuse them of the error. Their mistake implied that Chac and Zafado were identical twins, who could lie with Lace without her distinguishing between them, and that Zafado had either left Chibal or hidden himself.

As they neared the Pyramid of the Owl, this puzzle resolved itself. At the top of the broken hieroglyphic stairway, Cabot emerged from a portal in the boxlike limestone temple. Two other men also came out, Commander Ah Katun, whose fatigue hat sported an iridescent blue-green quetzal feather identifying him as the rebels' leader, and Chac's twin, Zafado, who looked so much like Chac that Lace glanced at Chac to make sure that he had not teleported up there.

Like a baroque leafy pagoda, the crown of a huge oak thrust through the temple's roof and spread its canopy, shading the temple, its apron, the men upon it, and the upper third of the stairway. Lace had never seen anything like this lofty growth at any other set of Maya ruins. But, with her lover at her elbow and her fiancé on the pyramid's summit, she endured a frisson of déjà vu.

Well, why not? Chibal reminded her of Palenque, Yaxchilán, and Copán, all of which she had visited within the past few years. But *Cabot* looked different. He towered over the Indians with him, as she would have expected, but he wore a bamboo breastplate with an obsidian medallion at its center, a loincloth, and calf bands with braided tassels. His body was both tawny and leprous—brown at arms and throat, white everywhere else. He clutched a stave, or spear, and a small circular shield.

"Lace!" he cried. *"Come up! Come up!"*

Their guards peeled away, leaving Lace and Chac exposed at the bottom of the pyramid. The guards split into two groups, advanced to the stairway's outer edges, and began to climb, leaving the middle section open for Chac and Lace's ascent. Both balked at this opportunity.

"Cabot's never gone ancient-native before," Lace said. "What's going on?"

Chac nodded her upward. "Let's see."

They mounted the tall steps, each so copiously chiseled with costumed warriors and Maya dates that Lace felt as if she were climbing another *katun*, or twenty-year cycle, into the Chibalec past. Her vulnerability seemed total. She would either lose her balance or a sniper would pick her and Chac off (along with the Tunkuluchuob on either side of them) like a shooting gallery patron potting rusty metal ducks. Her parents had warned her that this might happen . . . sort of.

The jungle and other nearby pyramids seemed to rise too, as did dark but silver-threaded clouds on the horizon. Near the summit, shade from the oak spiraling up from the city's pyramid-pent cenote began to fringe her shoulders. A breeze cooled her sweat-damp clothing.

Cabot reached down and pulled her up the last two steps. Chac followed, without help, and nodded at Zafado, who mirrored him like a bookend. Commander Ah Katun, whose name derived from one of the Maya gods of war, bowed like a courtier—but his squat body, bristly nose hairs, and rank philodendron-leaf fatigues sabotaged the godly image that he hoped to project. Also, he had painted raccoon-like circles around his eyes and black lightning bolts on his cheeks.

Lace held Cabot off, resisting his efforts to embrace her until he could no longer assume that she regarded him lovingly after their separation.

"Lace, I *couldn't* come to Dos Perros. These guys wouldn't let me."

"Where's Lundquist?" Lace said. "And the rest of your team?"

Cabot gestured at the limestone temple behind them. "I guess they didn't like my throwing in with the rebels. Commander Ah Katun had them bound and marched up here as captives."

Before Lace could internalize the enormity of this news, Chac stepped toward Zafado and said, "Let the hostages go. Disarm the explosives with which you've mined Chibal."

Zafado glanced at Commander Ah Katun, who nodded. Then, swiftly, Zafado seized the fetish at Chac's throat, broke it loose, and shoved Chac down the hieroglyphic stairs.

Chac cried out and fell. He tumbled from step to step, lacerating or bruising his flesh, plunging toward the bottom of the pyramid as if in slow motion—a nightmarish reversal of the dreamy leaping that he had performed with Lace on the stairs in the Hotel Llovedizo.

Lace's mouth opened, and she stepped back from the precipice. Cain and Abel in Guacamayo. The twin with the Old Jaguar God pendant had slain the twin with the Old Stingray God fetish.

Now she, too, would die. She had experienced this gut-scouring certainty twice before—in a Hyundai rolling on a slick Tennessee road, and later in a confrontation with a coked-up ex-con in an Atlanta parking lot. She had survived those close calls, but this one—murder just having had its bloody template manufactured before her eyes—she would not escape, and the wisdom of Lane and Melba Kurlansky struck her now with all its prophetic admonitory power.

Lace wet her jeans and fell to her knees, devastated by her disobedience and folly. Aloud, she pled for mercy.

"Be quiet!" Commander Ah Katun barked. "Silence yourself!"

Cabot helped her rise. "It's all right," he told her. "Saving the city demands both ritual and sacrifice."

"Fuck the city," Lace whispered. "A man has just died."

Lightning flashed. Thunder walked. The clouds amassing in every compass quarter fused into a broad slate vault. A cargo of rain cracked this vault and poured out on Chibal. It pelted the temple, the pyramids, the stelae, and the rebels' frail makeshift barricades. It washed down the stairs in leaping crimson-brown combers. It baptized her lover's corpse and rattled the forest. It mocked Lace's tears.

"Now you must wed," Zafado told Cabot. He said other stuff, but Lace, clad in bridal rain and drenched to the marrow, could deduce only that he and Commander Ah Katun believed that Cabot's and her union—the marriage of two gringos!—would open a portal to the spirit world and impel an irresistible outpouring of Tunkuluchú allies. These zombie warriors would rout the soldiers of Leopoldo Fuentes and restore to Guacamayo the long-forgotten reign of the Sacerdotal Owl.

It was crazy. It reminded Lace of the self-deluding program of the Ghost Dance warriors of the North American Plains, who believed their mad dances would summon herd upon herd of white buffalo from the Rocky Mountains and so halt the juggernaut of European settlement. But Guacamayo had existed as a state for almost two centuries, and the civilization that the commander proposed to revive had collapsed eleven hundred years ago. Madness.

The rain slackened, but its runoff still plunged from step to step.

"Come with me." Cabot looked stupid in his Maya getup, his blond hair plastered to his brow. He held his shield and his spear in one hand so that his other could draw her into the temple, upon whose sides Death Serpent bas-reliefs and Spirit Monster masks glowered poisonously.

Zafado sidled into their path.

Lace looked into his face—the face of one recently beloved—and said, "You murdered your brother, you filthy little shit."

"I killed a worthless poet. Chac loved a tyrant more than his own people."

"Not true," Lace said. "And you've slain a part of yourself."

Zafado laughed, as if she were a lobotomy candidate, and turned to Commander Ah Katun, who said, "Bring out the archaeologists."

Under rebel guard, Hap Lundquist and other members of the team limped from the temple, their lips or eyebrows pierced, their bare chests and ragged pants stained a candid reddish-brown. All had scarlet markings—colored ink—on their left breasts, as if a guerilla had prepared them, symbolically, for the surgical removal of their hearts. In fact, Cabot's team had received exactly the sort of treatment, short of heart extraction and beheading, that royal captives could expect in the old Maya wars.

"Hap!" Lace said, reaching toward Lundquist.

Lundquist's gaze flicked over her, but he kept his chin down and trudged to the edge of the high courtyard. He was stifled, dismayed, an enervated husk. The others—Newman, Tapscott, Balcavage, and Villaurrutia, the "rat man" who wriggled through tunnels into the tombs of Maya kings—had fared no better. Lundquist could not even summon the will to spit in Cabot's face, and his hopelessness meant that he knew as well as Lace that Commander Ah Katun planned to kill them. If anything, her arrival at Chibal had hastened this outcome.

"Let them go!" Lace cried. "Don't hurt them!"

But drizzle continued to slant, and Cabot maneuvered her into the temple like a cop manhandling a suspect into a patrol car.

Helplessly, Lace glanced back and saw Zafado hurl Hap Lundquist down the stairway of the Pyramid of the Owl. Then Zafado yanked Newman forward. No one screamed, but the sound of Lundquist's body bumping from step to step resonated even in the echo-muffling drizzle. . . .

The inside of the temple astonished Lace. It loomed larger in every direction than she figured possible. The Tunkuluchú oak reaching down through its floor to the hidden cenote, and up through the wide-cloven roof, shivered in place, filling the temple with ceaseless leaf music. Even so, a four-sided altar featuring high-relief sculptures of every Chibalec king also bulked inside this sanctuary, enclosing the oak's trunk. There were also censers, benches, flower stands, door panels, priestly implements (including stingray spines and blood-collecting basins), and figure-bearing columns of frangible dirty-saffron plaster—history in hieroglyphs.

Dried blood freckled the paving and the lower portions of the walls. Fresh blood glistened almost everywhere, sickeningly.

Knowing who had shed it, Lace took Cabot's arm.

Zafado entered and said, "You, too, must let blood." He approached her with one of the clay offering bowls, which brimmed with strips of beaten-bark paper, like outsized confetti from a manila packet. He thrust this bowl into her arms. Cabot pushed down on her shoulders until she had knelt in front of the western altar, the towering liana-wrapped oak behind her. Then he, too, knelt.

"You don't need to puncture her tongue," he told Zafado. "Lace, show him."

But Zafado seized Lace's chin, forced her jaw down, and yanked her tongue into view. The silver stud at its center glowed like a tiny Christmas-tree bulb. Chac's brother unscrewed and pocketed this stud.

"I told you she was the one," Cabot said.

Shut up, Lace thought. Just shut up. There in the Guacamayan tropics she felt as cold and brittle as an icicle dagger.

Zafado took off his jaguar-god fetish, paired it with Chac's stingray-god fetish, and swung them crisscrossing before her eyes. Lace's consciousness split and swung, just like the obsidian canoe-paddlers, so that she leapt to a psychic terrace high above her own nerve tips.

"The hole needs enlarging," Zafado said. "Hunab Ku, Itzamná, and Ix-chel, bless this new piercing."

He put his own necklace back on, pocketed Chac's pendant, and jabbed a large stingray spine through the slit in her tongue, twisting his wrist as he did so. Blood filled Lace's mouth and dribbled down her chin. But the assault did not hurt, and she raised the bowl in her arms to catch the sacred redness and to stain the brown strips of paper that the Tunkuluchuob would eventu-ally burn in a censer, to create a lovely odor for the Lords of Xibalba. From the bowl holding this paper, Zafado dragged two feet of rope punctuated at intervals with thorns.

"Take this," he said. "Finish your task."

Already entranced, Lace threaded this rope through the bottom of her tongue and pulled it out the upper side, meanwhile feeding the rope back into the bowl and bleeding into the paper. Cabot, she knew, regarded her slow disgorgement of the thorny rope with admiration and gratitude.

Resentment welled in Lace, but no hatred. Her fear of dying trotted away like a feisty peccary. I'm a mess, she thought, a doomed and apathetic mess. And this thought released a toxin into the waters of her aplomb. Febrile and swaying, she rose anyway and dropped the now dangling rope all the way into the bowl. Zafado pulled it out again and flipped its ends about his wrists so that it sort of cuffed him. With his foot, he nudged a basket full of paper strips toward the kneeling Cabot.

"Now you, Señor Chessman."

Outside the temple, several of the Maya chanted in Tunkuluchú. They had done so throughout her bloodletting, Lace realized, and this eerie song merely continued their earlier chant.

Cabot removed his loincloth. Then, much as in her dream in the Hotel Llovedizo, he squatted, spread his thighs above the basket, and jabbed the upper skin of his penis—once, twice, three times. He slipped a strip of paper from the basket through the hole nearest his groin. Then he did two more piercings, laced them with paper, and let these festoons incarnadine the tan strips in the basket.

Lace hardly bothered to watch. In her mind, if nowhere else, she had eloped to Disney World, Nepal, or Callisto, places more solidly real.

Zafado, still rope-cuffed, picked up both bowl and basket and carried them to a censer. He filled it with stained paper, the bloody rope, and a mixture of maize kernels and tree resin. Commander Ah Katun appeared and lit the censer with a foul-smelling stogie. The paper flared and ignited the other fuel. Smoke rose in sweetly acrid curls through the cenote-rooted oak inside the sanctuary altars. Cabot, wobbling, climbed to his feet. Lace tried to steady him.

"Are we married now?" she asked Zafado.

"Have you seen the owl god Tunkuluchú, gringa?"

"No," Lace confessed.

"Then you're not married yet. Come, both of you." And Zafado led them into a deeper temple room—maybe, Lace realized, to have their hearts sliced out and set before the owl god as an offering.

*

In the temple's innermost sanctum, beyond the northern altar, a knee-high censer resembling a humanoid owl burned red strips from earlier bloodlettings, probably those of Cabot's team members. Lace and Cabot faced the censer and the upper trunk of the oak whose extruded green crown capped the temple, protecting it from rain but allowing leaf-puzzle glimpses of sky.

Brackish smoke curled up through the tree and diffused in wisps through the sanctum. Fumes from the smoke assaulted Lace's nostrils and massaged the membranes of her lungs.

Twelve of Commander Ah Katun's soldiers had crowded in, but no longer wore the boots and bandoliers of latter-day guerillas. Along with Zafado and their commander, they wavered on the edges of Lace's vision wearing white capes pinned at the neck with red spondylus shells, flower-patterned skirts with calf bands, or just loincloths and high-backed sandals. Arrayed along the walls, they had no more meat than ghosts; their chants sounded like the mewling of starving jaguar babies.

Cabot clutched one end of a fresh thorn-embedded rope, and Lace the other. Her consciousness had fragmented, and in one part of it she recalled the funeral of a friend of Cabot's, a swim-team member who had burned to death in a house fire. A priest at that funeral swung a censer whose bitter miasma drifted into the eyes and lungs of everyone present, a foul evangel of the inescapability of death. And she had floated away on those fumes, into a pocket of her mind where marriage to Cabot plucked Mother Scorpion's sting and garlanded their days with concerts, wines, foreign films, jokes, travel, and well-behaved children.

Now they were *actually* marrying, and Mother Scorpion had scuttled up the great oak to preside at their vow exchange. Lace gripped her owl pendant in her free hand and wept—for the fumes in her eyes, for the poor immolated swimmer, for the lost Chac Sañudo, for the slain archaeologists, for Cabot, for Guacamayo's destruction, and for the standing peril to Chibal.

Floating away on these fumes, now she saw not Mother Scorpion, who did not really belong there, but the Sacerdotal Owl, who did.

A conch-shell trumpet sounded, and the chanting of the guerillas both intensified and faded off into inconsequence.

The Sacerdotal Owl—priest, messenger, and lord—clung to the oak in the guise of a man-sized epiphytic orchid, high above the floor where Lace and Cabot gripped the bloodletting rope and peered up in bemused awe. The orchid owl swayed out over their heads, the wide lavender petals of its wings fastened to the liana behind it, its silver breast emitting a vanilla-like fragrance that cut through the censer-smoke stink, annealing Lace and Cabot to their perplexity.

You are all predators, the orchid owl said, *parasitic fungi plundering the dead and the living alike.*

Vines twisting about the vine supporting the owl began to spiral slowly about the World Tree's trunk, without dislodging the god. They moved like barber-pole stripes, or the threads of propeller screws. They hauled into view purple or silver fruits the size of basketballs, the enormous meat-colored blossoms of a plant that Lace knew to grow only in northern Sumatra, and the head of Edwin L. Shay, the television anchorman who had gone missing from Las Orquídeas de la Virgen. His head moved on an upward left-to-right slant on a liana snaking along under the unmoving Nike-like body of the imperious orchid owl.

"Edwin L. Shay!" Lace said.

"In the five-year insurgency against the regime of President Leopoldo Fuentes," said Shay's head in its orotund broadcaster's voice, *"the Tunkuluchú rebels rarely take a backseat, in either sadistic cunning or applied brutality, to the U.S.-advised troops of the government."* The head spoke fluently in Spanish.

"You lie!" said Commander Ah Katun.

The head lowered its bruised-looking eyelids. *"Do you really think I don't know who decapitated me?"* And it glided on upward, slantwise—on around the trunk of the World Tree. All the other migrating lianas continued to writhe and twine, pulling strange fleshy growths into, and out of, view.

A curse on all your factions, said the orchid owl in a voice like smoke. *Descend, Lace Kurlansky, to the waters of Xibalba.*

In the smoke of the owl-shaped censer, before the swaying body of the orchid owl, the big jawless head of a Maya warrior—perhaps a Maya king—took changing and changeable shape. Scrolls of smoke, symbolizing blood, poured from its mouth, and the vacant whirlpools of its eyes throbbed with the pinks, indigos, and umbers of unnamable rainforest blossoms.

Go down, said this smoky Maya king.

Descend, Lace Kurlansky, said the owl on the bole of the oak.

Lace pocketed her owl talisman and released her end of the thorny rope. Cabot, wearing only his bloodstained loincloth and tasseled calf bands, looked at her as if he no longer recognized her, which, she understood, he most likely did not.

Cabot belonged to a faction that Tunkuluchú, the messenger owl, had cursed, just as Commander Ah Katun and Zafado belonged to another, just as Leopoldo Fuentes and his soldiers belonged to a third, and just as Lace belonged to a fourth. But some quality in Lace, maybe her unaccountable love for Chac Sañudo, had registered in the orchid owl in the ritual of her bloodletting, and so this god, the living spirit of the Tunkuluchú dead, had set her apart . . . for ruin or salvation.

Bloody of mouth, throat, breast, and arms, Lace jumped onto the carven altar of Chibalec kings. Then, like a gecko spread-eagling itself on an adobe wall, she seized the trunk of the great oak. Her fingers found handholds of bark and vine, her sneakers sought their own footholds, and she shinnied down through the flue of the four fitted sides of the altar toward the cenote in the abyss.

Tuning forks of lightning crackled overhead, and a columnar draft of cold air rose from the springs over which the Tunkuluchuob of another age—of several other ages—had built the Pyramid of the Owl. As she shinnied, some of the vines wrapping the oak started to corkscrew again, spiraling down rather than up, but without rotating either the orchid owl or the head of Edwin L. Shay back into her ken.

"Lace!" Cabot called. "Lace, wait for me!"

Apparently, the smoke in the wedding sanctum had paralyzed everyone but Lace and Cabot, who emulated Lace's jumps. Soon he was descending through the epiphytic blossoms after her, the soles of his feet flopping from bough to bough like pink mullets. Below, reflections of rainforest lightning scribbled the surface of the cenote inside the base of the pyramid—but only at the pool's far edges, which Lace could barely see while peering down through the blossoms and vines.

"Lace, wait!" A distinct note of desperation sang in this plea.

"Cabot, you signed Hap Lundquist's death warrant—his and Chac's and all your unsuspecting friends'!"

"I did it to save Chibal!"

"Bullshit," Lace said. "'We had to destroy the village to save it.' That's the sort of idiot thinking that kept the Vietnam War running so long." It had a sad, ironic relevance here in Guacamayo, too, Lace realized. Or it could, if she bought into Cabot's perfidious madness.

Cabot was an athlete, and he could swim like an Olympian, but Lace had more nimbleness out of the water than he, and a sixth sense about tree shinnying that allowed her to quickly outdistance him. She passed the second highest level in the pyramid, and then the third, observing that each royal chamber or tomb was filled with stone carvings, priestly paraphernalia, and murals of historic conflicts or the doings of Maya gods. The riprap between strata consisted of rubble from earlier versions of the pyramid—so that the shaft surrounding the World Tree gave vivid glimpses into the sequential architectural approach of the pyramid's builders.

"Lace, please slow down!" Cabot's plea—the cry of a man trapped in a high prison tower.

Lace pressed her body against the oak's trunk, passing through various thick foliage clusters to keep Cabot from seeing her. Now she glanced up. Twenty feet above her, Cabot hooked his knees over a woody liana and leaned out in the apparent hope of cantilevering a clear view of her. The weight of his own torso yanked his legs from the natural trellis, and, grasping and flailing, he slipped and tumbled through the shaft calling her name: *"Laaaaaaaaaaace!"*

His body, white and brown, supple and gangly, flashed past and careened on down to the lightning-scrawled cenote, which it struck with a sound little sharper than that of a ballpoint plashing into a commode. This echo reverberated, and Lace closed her eyes, having already watched Cabot slice himself on the oak's epiphytic growths as he flailed past. Now it seemed likely that, smacking the water at the tree's base, he had broken his spine.

My God, Lace thought. (And she could not say whether she was apostrophizing Christ or Tunkuluchú.) In a mere hour or less, both her Maya lover and her Anglo-Saxon fiancé had fallen to their deaths. It was horrible. It was funny. How often did a gal have a good-looking guy fall head over heels for her? Today, horribly, hilariously, two times too many. Ha-ha.

Lace swallowed a salty clot of her own blood, ground her teeth, and resumed her meticulous descent. She completed it in what she estimated as only twenty-five or thirty minutes and then hung out over the cenote like a kid at a hidden swimming hole reaching for a tire swing.

Now and again, droplets fell into the pool from the bromeliads and liana blossoms scabbed to the World Tree and from the rainy sky miles above, but they dropped without violence or reverb. And so the pool exuded a dim serenity reminiscent of old museums, empty movie theaters.

What now? The vines hugging the great oak had long ago ceased to corkscrew about its trunk, and Tunkuluchú, the orchid-owl god, remained atop the tree, too far away to praise, scold, or instruct her.

Then Lace heard Chac whisper, "*And we will melt, my storm-tormented girl, / to be cherished forever by all the reddest gods of Mayadom.*'"

She looked about. A peal of thunder, or an explosion, made the cenote tremble, but from so far away—farther away than the orchid owl at the top of the World Tree—that it did not tremble long. However, only twenty feet from the massive base of the oak to which Lace clung, a supine body burst from the waters, arching its back and floating with its arms spread, its legs dangling out of view, and its hair undulating around its head like a spun-gold halo.

Cabot, of course. Kaput. A victim of either impact trauma or drowning. Here in the Chibalec netherworld, his body thrummed with a mythic import that Lace could not readily decode. Did it mean that excavating Chibal was no longer a profitable enterprise? That the rebellion of the Tunkuluchuob had failed? That Fuentes' soldiers had called off their operations? That her old life was dead?

Holding to a nublike branch, Lace eased into the water, so illusorily like dark plum gelatin. She dog-paddled to Cabot, seized his arm, and pulled him back to the tree. Three red strips of paper still festooned his penis, which bobbed impotently in the blond nest of his groin. The sight moved Lace to a throat-constricting pity. What had happened to him? How had the antique dead grown to mean more to him than his own persnickety comrades?

"*He stole their lives,*" Chac said inside her head, "'*just as you clawed from me / the scarlet chambers of my Tunkuluchú heart, / the tempests of longing laved in my hot blood, / and all my foolish dread of death.*'"

"Chac?" Clinging to the oak and her dead fiancé's arm, Lace searched for her dead lover. She extended her toes, immersing herself to her chin. The cenote's bottom lay deeper than she could reach. How long could she tread water beside a drowned man and a tree whose roots might stretch to the planet's very core?

"*Here,*" Chac said. "*Look to the east.*"

Frustration clamped Lace like a shrinking garment. "Which way is east?" Dos Perros lay east of Chibal, of course, but the Tunkuluchú netherworld seemed a demesne without compass points or borders.

"*Here, señorita, here.*"

From the plum-colored dark beyond Cabot's body, a canoe glided toward Lace over the plummy waters of the cenote, which she had thought contained by the lower portions of the pyramid's walls. You could not build a pyramid on water, after all, any more than you could throw a shadow without a light source. Whatever the truth of these supposings, however, the canoe vectored in, and in it sat two figures with paddles, the nearer a humanoid avatar of the orchid owl she had seen earlier, the farther her dead lover Chac.

Gazing across Cabot's leprous belly, Lace gawked at this apparition. The orchid-owl paddler was no doubt an Indian in the mask and plumage of an owl, and the paddler whom she had taken for Chac was surely just a man who resembled him. The costumed paddler dipped and pushed with a lovely ritual grace, and the Chac look-alike behind him aped his actions on the canoe's other side.

Reflections of lightning drew fleeting wiring-diagram arabesques in the waters around the canoe, and a series of thunderclaps—if not explosions—shuddered the World Tree, the waters, and the notional inner walls of the pyramid.

Lace feared electrocution, drowning, being cudgeled to death by dislodged stones. None of these fates befell her, but strange repercussive tides buffeted her body from side to side, as they did Cabot's, and she felt as she imagined Londoners must have felt in subways and basements during the Blitz, if those subways and basements had been flooded by the Thames. Her every nerve had gone numb.

Literally abreast of Cabot, the canoe halted, and the man in the orchid-owl getup spoke in a familiar smoky voice: "Kiss him."

"What?" Lace shook her wet cap of hair. "Who?"

"Your husband. The dead interloper. Kiss him."

"He's not my—"

"Don't quibble with me, *gringa*. Kiss him."

The owl god's eyes looked real, not like costume-jewelry stand-ins. Meanwhile, his plumage appeared more feathery than floral, and hence more lifelike than that of the orchid owl atop the World Tree. Lace looked past him at the Chac look-alike, who gave her a wincing sort of smile. This smile underscored his identity as the Chac with whom she had fallen in love. It soon reshaped itself and stayed, as an emblem of bashful favor, maybe even encouragement.

Lace hooked Cabot's neck, pulled him to her, and placed her trembling mouth on his cold one. When he did not respond—and she had not expected him to—she used her tongue to prise his lips apart, then she fed her tongue into the breathless cavity, like an intrusive oyster, and let it linger until even his corpse could taste the blood spicing it. She withdrew reluctantly, retreating to the base of the oak, shivering like a shipwreck victim.

Cabot's body swelled at the chest, thrashing from side to side as it had done after the thunderclaps or explosions. Then it ceased thrashing and floated more or less calmly on the shaken pool. Twitching, its sightless eyes shed their milky glaze. Lace had the giddy sense of having resurrected Cabot with her kiss. This feeling intensified when he pulled himself upright with a few instinctive finning motions of his hands. The swimmer in him automatically reactivating.

"Cabot!"

The Sacerdotal Owl spoke over his shoulder to Chac, who eased the canoe about so that he could gaff Cabot harmlessly with his paddle. Cabot lifted a hand in alarm or protest, but did not struggle against this minor indignity—given everything else that had happened—and even seemed to cooperate when Chac reached down to haul him into the canoe, now tilting perilously near the water.

So when the humanoid owl god, whose wings sheathed arms not unlike Cabot's, flapped up out of the canoe, disclosing feathered pantaloons where Lace had expected to see human legs, and talons where she had expected sandals, she coughed in amazement as the spirit of Tunkuluchú gripped Cabot's shoulders, lifted him bodily out of the cenote, and set him with Chac's help into the center of the canoe.

Cabot got to his knees by himself and vomited twinkling gouts of blood, bile, and water over the vessel's side. The owl flew disciplined circles overhead until Cabot had purged himself of all earthly nourishment and taint. Then it hovered a moment, fanning the cenote with lustrous silver-gray wings, before quietly peeling off and rocketing into the dark.

Once the owl had flown, Cabot knee-walked to its place in the canoe and took the abandoned paddle. He had not spoken a word since his resurrection, and Lace intuited from his ten-mile stare and his bruised lips that he would not speak again in this region of the netherworld.

"Come," Chac said, reaching out to her. "Let us conduct you the rest of the way. I'll help you in."

"But where would you take me?"

"Someplace better, *mi prometida*."

"Better than this?" Lace punched the cenote with a tightly clenched fist. "Better than immersion in the blood of Chibalec kings?"

"Absolutely." Irony confounded Chac. "Please, Señorita Lace—take my hand."

What option did she have? Cabot and Chac, working together, bumped the canoe nearer, pinning her between it and the World Tree. One option, of course, was climbing back up the tree to the temple, but she doubted her strength and resolve. She reached for Chac's hand, seeing for the first time that a large stingray spine passed through his head on a sharp diagonal. Its points emerged from his throat and the back of his skull, but he disregarded them. Before she could recoil from him, Chac landed her asprawl in the canoe, although not without cushioning her entry with his arm. The canoe bucked wildly, but Cabot went on sitting stone still, spaced out, unperturbed.

"Go," Chac told him. "Paddle."

Lace righted herself between the two men, gripping the sides of the canoe as if clinging fast would protect her from any assault. Cabot and Chac paddled, in rhythmic alternating tandem, and their canoe surged away from the tree on a downward slant like that of the stingray spine through Chac's head.

The canoe submerged. Dark plum water streamed around Lace's head, shoulders, and back until she had gone totally under, along with the zombie paddlers and the canoe itself. But Lace did not gag on the influx or find her vision occluded by the purple water or distorted by refraction. Nor, apparently, did Cabot or Chac.

They glided along as if soaring in a crystal vacuum rather than forging through an impeding liquid, and the neon gars and see-through eels finning about them seemed more bird- than fishlike. Water had become air, the cenote an underground cavern, and the pyramid above them a mirage. Water lilies floated at different levels around their canoe, while far below the wraiths of Maya boys and men competed in a vast sunken ball court, their bodies etched by ultraviolet shadow and glowing purple pinstripes identifying their actions as long past, historic, spent.

Lace looked behind her. "For God's sake, Chac, what's going on?"

Chac pointed—not at the water lilies, the airborne fish, or the ball players, but beyond the players at a gateway arch, like one Lace had seen in the

Yucatán, opening into a royal garden. Cabot and Chac paddled over the ball court and the sunken cityscape around it as if planning to steer between the arch's hieroglyph-rich walls into an honest-to-God Tunkuluchú paradise. Many of the hieroglyphs represented the Sacerdotal Owl in different stances of authority, and the royal garden through the arch, unlike the ultraviolet nightmare of the ball court and its players, glistened with the daylight colors of the living world that Lace had always revered.

Thunder walked, the air in Xibalba shuddered, and huge carven stones began to fall. Every gleaming purple and silver player in the ball court looked up. Every player raised the back of his wrist to his brow and held it there in what Lace recognized as the immemorial Maya death gesture. Even the dead enjoyed flashing this gesture. Even the dead, Shakespeare and Donne notwithstanding, could die again. And the stones plunging from the indistinct firmament seemed guided by some doubtful intelligence to make sure that these helpless dead suffered a redundant annihilation.

Lace covered her head while Cabot and Chac paddled harder toward the gateway on a low gray hill now a hundred meters distant. The falling stones, some as large as residential propane tanks, some no bigger than bricks, clattered down, ricocheting off one another like meteorites, striking the spectral city and its ghostly denizens with dust-raising clouts, and whizzing past the three canoeing fugitives from latter-day Chibal in roentgen-charged torrents.

It's only a matter of time before we're hit, Lace thought, cowering away from the implacable barrage. And of course she was right.

In the dispensary tent near Las Orquídeas de la Virgen, a town too small for a hospital, Delmira Xisto gazed down on her patient with something other than clinical detachment. She had volunteered to track the progress of the wounded and the injured, and this petite but supple American—her body a map of bruises, her face a swollen acorn squash—was finally waking up. Would she first ask, "Where am I?" or "Who are you?" or "When may I go home?" Eventually, she'd ask all these questions, but the *order* in which a patient spoke them betrayed the true state of her mind.

"How many people died?" said the American woman, reaching for the hem of her caregiver's linen jacket.

Delmira took the patient's hand and smoothed its back with her own. "Too many, Miss Kurlansky."

The patient pulled away and scrambled to a sitting position from which to survey the tent and its inhabitants. She squinted at the cots around hers and then into Delmira's face. Obviously, she was surprised to find herself in this tent of makeshift treatment and problematic recovery.

"Did Cabot Chessman die?" she asked. "Did Chac Sañudo?"

"Yes, the North American archaeologist died, and so did all his friends." Delmira consulted a clipboard. "And the second person you named—also dead."

"Thrown down the stairs," Miss Kurlansky said. "Everybody but Cabot—thrown down the stairs. Cabot fell from the World Tree into Xibalba."

Delmira mulled this odd assertion. "You should lie down again. You should rest a while and then eat something."

"How long have you been watching over me?"

"Two and a half days. Rescuers dragged you from the primary Chibalec temple, which had dropped into the plaza."

Miss Kurlansky stared at Delmira as if she had proclaimed President Fuentes an unparalleled world philanthropist, or an adult male jaguar the ideal family pet. "I don't understand," she said.

"When he learned that the Tunkuluchuob were murdering their hostages, Fuentes authorized mortar assaults and sent in gunships. Government forces reduced the ruins to ruins." Delmira chuckled ruefully—*reduced the ruins to ruins.* Did powerful men enjoy destroying things so much that the devastation of other's dreams registered with them as a constructive achievement?

"Chibal is gone?" Miss Kurlansky said.

"Even less extant than before. But its destruction saved you. The guerillas would have killed you had the government's attacks not stopped them."

"If the temple of the Pyramid of the Owl dropped into the plaza, *luck* saved me, señora—sheer unadulterated luck."

"Yes," Delmira admitted. "And Chibal is gone. The ancient Tunkuluchuob have suffered their second death—probably an incurable one." (As if you could cure death, or as if anyone of faith would want to.)

Miss Kurlansky swung her feet to the duckboard floor. "Where's my stuff?"

"You had only your torn clothes, señorita, and a mahogany charm from one of our native carvers." Delmira fetched this talisman from a cardboard box and handed it to the patient.

The young American woman squeezed the charm—an owl with a dart through its body and a small man-faced shield on one of its wings—and squeezed and squeezed and squeezed it until her knuckles whitened and a teardrop burst from her eye like a faultless organic diamond.

Lace stayed in the dispensary tent another day. Most of those receiving treatment, she learned, were Guacamayan grunts tagged by friendly fire or falling debris within the old city's plaza. All the guerillas (a young lieutenant with a raffish pencil-thin mustache like Zorro's told her) had died—including, presumably, Commander Ah Katun and Chac Sañudo's bloodthirsty twin, Zafado.

Fortunately—if you could use that word without incurring the wrath of Yahweh or Hunab Ku—the men in Lace's tent had suffered such serious injuries that they could not even begin to think of ogling, joking with, or propositioning her. In fact, she insisted on helping Delmira Xisto sponge-bathe the hurt soldiers, spoon-feed them banana mash and soft-boiled eggs, even counsel and encourage them while sitting next to their cots on an up-turned ammo crate.

Lace Kurlansky, the Florence Nightingale of Las Orquídeas de la Virgen.

Nearby tents quartered soldiers less severely wounded and even some smock-clad orderlies in an ever-jovial frame of mind. They had set up a flea market of collapsible tables and oaken folding chairs in a clearing on the edge of the jungle. Here, they traded watches, bracelets, dog-tag necklaces, painkillers, fake-silk fans with bamboo struts, cuts of howler-monkey meat, and caged pygmy owls. The number of people patronizing this market sometimes seemed larger than the population of Las Orquídeas, and it was always a raucous affront to the dispensary as a quiet haven for battlefield casualties. Lace hiked through it on the morning of her fourth and last day in Guacamayo, desultorily evaluating the junk on display and ineffectually repressing her pain.

At a distance of thirty feet, near a trestle table made of plywood and two battered sawhorses, she caught sight of Chac—except that it couldn't be Chac, it had to be Zafado, wearing a tray of carven doodads and haranguing the crowd in his singsong hawker's patter to buy from him and to keep his family from starving. The sight of him paralyzed Lace. He threaded his way among the shoppers and the tables, selling items at a healthy clip, moving ever nearer.

Lace could see the Old Jaguar God pendant hanging from a dirty string around his neck and the bruised-looking hollows under his eyes, which she briefly assumed he had created with grease paint or mascara. No, they were real, but they did almost nothing to counteract the air of dapper nonchalance that he projected, an attitude that drew people to him and lightened their pockets.

Then Zafado saw Lace. His eyes flashed, like sparkplugs in a dark adobe garage, and he smiled at her. When he smiled, he parted his lips, and when he parted his lips, a tiny silver beacon lit the surface of his tongue and rayed across the market to dazzle and disorient her.

Lace dropped her gaze and reeled, flailing and half off-balance, toward the haven of her dispensary tent. As she retreated, a familiar growl-and-rattle rose from the jungle, increasing in volume until she could no longer hear the voices of the crowd or the baffled hydraulics of her heart.

For Brian A. Hopkins, who handed me the seed.

AND STRANGE AT ECBATAN THE TREES

And strange at Ecbatan the trees
Take leaf by leaf the evening strange
—Archibald MacLeish

PART ONE

i

I went with the old man because Our Shathra Anna's foremost minister had bade me watch his every move. For ten days I had been at the old man's side, and uncomplainingly, though not very congenially (though this was changing), he had accepted my presence. The old man's name was Gabriel Elk. He was sixty-three years old and universally acknowledged a genius, perhaps the only bona fide one in all of Ongladred, indeed on all of our ruthlessly harsh planet, Mansueceria.

And on the night with which this account begins, Gabriel Elk and I were going into Lunn, our capital, to buy a dead masker.

The city lay before us as ominously quiescent as an unstruck gong. I had been living—these past ten days—with Gabriel Elk, his wife, Bethel, and his son, Gareth, at Stonelore, the neuro-theatre he had built nearly seven kilometers outside of Lunn. Now we were coming back into the city under the cold light of the Shattered Moons, and I was glad to see Lunn's majestic squalor again, the unbroken rows of four-story dwellings, the canyonlike alleys, the ever-visible lemon sheen of the dome under which Our Shathra Anna resides and toward which nearly all the dirty alleys lead: the Atarite Palace. As an aide to Chancellor Blaine, as a minor doer of the sort of work Our Shathra may not sully her hands with, I was going home again, even though Gabriel Elk and I would not set foot within several city squares of the domed palace. We had pointed ourselves toward the poor—the Mansuecerian *people*, as Elk would say—and our route funneled us through torch-lit sidestreets.

We walked our horses, their hooves clacking, their eyes round with a mute claustrophobia, their nostrils aquiver with the acrid smells of city-pent humanity. But we met no one in the streets. It was the time of the Halcyon Panic (hence, my assignment to Elk, whom the Magi feared as a potential demagogue), and at night everyone stayed docilely indoors—everyone but those with state business and, of course, the maddeningly uncoercible Gabriel Elk, who had come on business of his own.

"Do you know where we are?" I asked, a bite in my voice.

He halted his shaggy animal to look at me. The old man's eyes were a pale green, his face as heavy as carven marble, the jowls giving way only slightly to his sixty-three years. Great white sideburns framed his cheeks, and his hair fell in bearish curls over his forehead and neck. "On Earth my sixty-three years would be seventy-five," he'd told me at our first meeting, but he carried himself with an intractable agelessness. In this alleyway in Lunn, he looked like a statue that has willed its limbs to move and broken out of stone into life.

"I do indeed, Ingram. This city was mine long before you entered either the service of Our Shathra or the elitist gangs of Chancellor Blaine. Some say the Chancellor got his roan tooth by sucking blood up through it, and, from what I see, a bit of that blood is yours, Master Marley. You're as bumptious and ticky as a person of power."

"I work for persons of power, Sayati Elk." Against Blaine's wishes, Our Shathra Anna had given Elk the title *sayati* in his fifty-sixth year, after the construction of Stonelore and the presentation of the first series of neuro-dramas. In the seven succeeding years, Blaine and the Council of the Magi had agitated quietly for the revocation of his royal dispensation to assemble the people and for the nationalization of the formidable power complex that he had built in the upland arena.

"So you do, Ingram, so you do. And in your own way you also are a person of power."

"I do what I must—to insure that the Halcyon Panic doesn't break out roaring in the throats of our within-doors maskers."

"And I do what I must, Ingram, to insure that when the 'maskers' come out to Stonelore they perceive an order in things that the universe and the Magi of Ongladred don't always choose to grant them. The order is there, it inheres, and I'm the man who reveals it to them."

The Shattered Moons moved in a yellow band beyond the in-leaning rooftops, a monochrome rainbow in the night sky. Only the brightest stars were visible behind it, and it was hard to imagine that Ongladred was an island besieged, that the culture we had twice before built up over six thousand years as colonists on Mansueceria was in danger of collapsing again, collapsing completely.

My voice echoed in the silent street: "And so to give the maskers order, you've come tonight to buy a dead man."

"Not exactly, Ingram. I've come to buy a dead woman, a beautiful girl killed by reivers. And the order I try to give the Mansuecerians, the gentles, is a glimpse of the order inhering outside themselves—for inwardly they're disciplined, Ingram, they're more serene, more in control of the animal in themselves than you or I. Only artists have to rage, artists and rulers."

"Our rulers don't rage, Sayati Elk."

"No, they simmer, Ingram. The worse for them." His horse, a woolly beast, lifted its head and whickered. The old man pulled the horse's head down and began walking again. The stones rang. Shadows wrapped themselves around us like voluted capes. "My sense of direction rarely fails," he said after a while. "Look there."

We had come to a side-canyon, a narrow crevice between two rows of maskers'-houses perpendicular to the alley by which, on the city's southeastern outskirts, we had originally entered Lunn. There was no room for our horses here. But I looked where Elk was pointing and saw a green-gowned figure on a third-story balcony on the lefthand side of the alley, a figure stooping beneath a pair of conical lanterns to see us. But for this solitary revenant and those two lanterns, the alley was unhaunted, dark, and coldly daunting.

The Halcyon Panic had begun to play in me; I wanted no part of Sayati Elk's sinister purchase of a dead girl.

"Come on, Ingram," he said. "We'll tie our horses here." He wrapped the reins of his animal around a stone gutter-spout; I did likewise. Our footfalls reverberating in the night air, we walked through the alley between the maskers'-houses. There was a balcony across from the one on which the stooping figure stood, and it seemed to me that it would require very little effort to step from the lefthand balcony to the righthand one, three stories' worth of darkness gaping beneath that step.

"Who's up there?" I asked.

"Josu Lief, the father of the dead girl. Or so I'd guess."

The man on the balcony called out. Before he did so, I hadn't been certain that he was a man; the gown had confused me. It was mourning garb. Under him now, I saw that the gown and his shaved head—he was newly bald—

were his only concessions to "grief." The Mansuecerians are immune to it, genetically serene, philosophically spartan.

"Sayati Elk?" Gentleman Lief called out. Then: "Please come up, both of you." A serene, if spartan, voice.

We entered the bleak doorway and climbed the corkscrewing stairs. We let Josu Lief usher us into a three-room flat where the rest of his brood, dressed in forest-green mourning gowns and sitting in a candlelit central chamber, awaited us. There were introductions. Lief's wife wore her hair cut short, as did the two female children. Josu and his young son were bald from the razor. They accepted the news that I was a minor official of Our Shathra Anna's oligarchy with utter blandness; they were maskers, and I was a nouveau Atarite, programmed to rule. Gabriel Elk had sprung from such folk, but differently, as a throwback in whom the primeval aggressions still roiled, threatening eruption. The old man spanned a chasm between the Lief family and me.

"Where's Bronwen?" he asked.

"This way," Gentleman Lief said, and led us from the central chamber into a sleeping room where six pallets rested on the floor. The girl lay on the pallet on which she had undoubtedly slept while alive: Bronwen Lief, eldest daughter of these anonymous maskers. One family amid a city full of similar families, all of them debeasted, shaped in their genes toward a civilizing harmony. On them had been founded the state of Ongladred; only rulers and artists raged, and we Atarites so seldom as to suggest an innate serenity akin to that of the maskers.

"Will you accept my price?" Elk asked Lief.

"I accept it, Sayati Elk."

"Good. I've already credited the money to you. It's there for your use. Three days from now, bring your family to Stonelore."

"And she will perform?"

"A special performance, for the Lief family and some privileged others. Not a neuro-drama, but a kind of reading."

"Will she later act in the dramas?"

"So I hope."

The three of us studied the dead Bronwen Lief—Josu with an expression predictably neutral, in which shone neither pride nor remorse nor pity nor anything paternal in a strictly Atarite sense; Gabriel Elk with quiet appreciation; and I, the outsider, with an awareness of terrible loss. For

Bronwen Lief, arranged on her pallet in her white death-gown, evoked a catalogue of lovely names: Helen, Guinevere, Ligeia. Although beautiful, her young face nonetheless hinted at the ability to betray. In a Mansuecerian, a masker, that look disconcerted, it slept in the corners of her mouth like an incongruous smirk, an anomaly of character. As a dirt-runner, I had long ago learned to recognize such telltale glimmerings under people's false, placid exteriors, but Bronwen was a masker girl, and a corpse, and the candlelight made her flesh resemble porcelain.

Sayati Elk said: "I'm very pleased, Gentleman Lief. She's beautiful; she's what I'd hoped for."

"Our thanks, sir."

I said: "How did she die, exactly?"

The two older men turned their faces toward me. Josu Lief, I saw, could not have been more than forty. Even with a shaved head he was a handsome man, with full lips and dark eyes. "I have told our friends, in a fall. But there's more, as Sayati Elk knows. Last night she went with a young man, the one selected for her, to see the bonfires by the eastern channel, the bonfires holding off the sloak—"

"You let them go?" I said. "At this time?"

"Bronwen did as she wished. I could neither permit nor hinder her, ever. She had a good life, Master Marley."

"And a short one. What happened on the coast with her young man?"

"Laird and she walked the rocks, looking at the Angromain Archipelago where your renegade ancestors kill each other and catch fish, Master Marley. They was thinking on the cycle of the sloak and the barbarians way out to sea there. Bronwen's young man says they spoke of the bonfires on the beach and of living to oldsters in Lunn, such stuff as that. Then they saw an empty boat, just a pinnace, beached in a rocky place between two of the bonfires. No sooner had they saw it than they heard voices, men speaking in accents not of Ongladred. The men surprised them, a party of three or four thick-bearded Pelagans on a raid of some sort. The Pelagans ran at them, pushed Bronwen and young Laird from the rocks, and leapt to the sand. It was a short drop, Laird says, but Bronwen . . . she twisted her neck. Laird fell into a gravelly place and broke his leg. He shouted so that the bonfire tenders on both sides come running, you know, but it was too late. Out to sea the Pelagans went, oaring it like fiends—and Bronwen was dead. So she came home to us, and we dressed her like you see, in her death-gown."

"And Laird?" Gabriel Elk asked.

"He's on the mend, I'd wager."

ii

We went back into the apartment's central chamber. The women sat on straightbacked chairs, working on patterned quilts in their laps. Lief's son, his own bald head shining, was on the floor marking a piece of paper with a stylus; he looked about five. "At least your boy won't be called up," Elk said. When the Halcyon Panic broke, military service for men between the ages of fifteen and fifty would be obligatory . . . unless one were an Atarite, and in some cases even then. I knew that inductions had already begun. Josu Lief confirmed me in my knowledge.

"They tapped me two days ago," he said. "I go in five days."

And he would, too. Docilely, he would take off his mourning gown, don a warrior's breeches, and cover his bald noggin with a leather cap. Then off to the Lunn garrison for assignment. The masker, the gentle, would become a soldier—pacific in his innermost soul, but ruthlessly obedient in war.

"Then Gareth will be touched soon, too," Elk said, and genius or no he could not keep the regret out of his enormous, furrowed brow. Unlike the serene Gentleman Lief's, his feelings toward his children—his child rather, now his only son—ran deeper than stoic affection. After all, Gabriel Elk was a mistake, an artist; in every endeavor he raged, harkening to a gong inaudible to maskers and Atarites alike.

We sat down. Gentlewoman Lief left her chair, went to a cabinet in the kitchen, and returned with three cups of *haoma*. This is a mildly intoxicating drink distilled from the bullcap fungus and banned at court. Maskers believe that it induces righteousness and piety rather than drunkenness. Curious, I sipped what was given me. At once sweet and tart, the haoma seemed to transfuse warmth through the lining of my stomach, into my veins and marrow, like a flow of heated blood. While Gabriel Elk and Gendeman Lief talked, I nodded and tried to heed their words.

"When will the Halcyon Panic break?" the old man asked.

"Not yet, Sayati Elk, not yet."

"Your neighbors?"

"They continue calm. They talk of the sloak, and of the Pelagans, and even of the rupturing of the sun—but no one screams in his sleep, no one's yammering of Ongladred's death. Our Shathra Anna watches over us. She's a wise-eyed lady, wise in her watching."

Gentlewoman Lief smiled at her husband, the girls continued sewing, the boy colored his scrap of paper without heeding his father's visitors at all. At court, a young official's death would have kept us from secular activity for at least a day or two. Here, it required all my haoma-ridden powers to remember that Bronwen lay dead in the next room. Haoma. No doubt Josu Lief had had the examining physician administer an undiluted extract of the principal drug in this beverage to his daughter's corpse, as a stopgap preservative. And here I was, embalming myself in a maskers' drink. Bronwen's face, her wistfully smiling face, floated into my mind and sight. I gripped my chair.

Unaffected, Gabriel Elk stood. The others in the room began rising, too. I heard Josu Lief say, "Do you want me to bring her out to Stonelore tomorrow, Sayati Elk?"

"Have you a blanket?"

"I've just finished this quilt," Lief's wife said. "You may take it, if you like. For Bronwen."

"Good. I'll wrap her in it, and Ingram and I will take her now. There's no need in your carrying her out to us tomorrow, Josu."

I was standing now. Someone took the cup out of my hands. Josu left the room. He returned with his daughter wrapped in the quilt. I noticed that the silken quilt, a series of cream-colored squares, was embroidered about its hem with blue flowers, a kind that grow prolifically on the cliffs above the Angromain Channel. Bronwen's face was not covered; her black hair fell over Josu Lief's supporting forearm. Lief gave her into the arms of Gabriel Elk, even though by rights I ought to have been the one to carry her.

"Remember," the old man said. "Come three days from now." Then, turning to me: "Ingram, let's go." I hurried to door and opened it for the heavy-laden old codger. The stairwell yawned beneath us. The family, but for Lief's son, crowded into the opening. I stood with my back pressed against the open door, cold seeping up at us from the street.

"The Light stay with you," Gentlewoman Lief told Elk, "and the Lie die." That was their religion, all of it, conveyed in two gently spoken imperatives. The woman said nothing to her dead child, though I half expected her to. The girl had gone to the Abode of Song—despite the fact that maskers never sing during their lifetimes. Singing is an activity that lies outside their stoic code; indeed, outside their very natures.

Gabriel Elk teetered on the stairs. I looked back into the Liefs' main sitting room. There stood the five-year-old boy with a piece of paper dangling from his hand. He quirked his blond, boyishly thin eyebrows.

"Goodbye, Bronwen," he said.

I reeled toward the stairwell, grabbed the railing there, and clumped groggily down the steps behind the old man and the dead girl he carried. In the cold street we found our horses and rode toward Stonelore and Elk's rock-capped residence. Bronwen Lief, wrapped in a quilt embroidered with blue flowers, lay doubled over the philosopher/playwright's saddle, wedged between the pommel and his paunch, deprived of dignity. Lunn faded behind us, and the Shattered Moons danced. Our horses climbed powerfully into the dark of the countryside. Immersed in wind, my head began to clear.

iii

Even though Stonelore lay seven kilometers beyond Lunn, to the southeast, it was easily accessible by a road running from the capital to the fishing village of Mershead on the Angromain Channel. In the spring, the maskers set up produce stalls and vanity booths along this road, and did a good business among the travelers and fishermen going between Lunn and Mershead. Since it was in the spring that Elk presented his three neuro-dramas of the year, he had no difficulty attracting maskers to fill his circular stone amphitheatre. But, on the night we rode back from Lunn with Bronwen Lief over Elk's saddle, the equinox was still a good Mansuecerian month away, so the Mershead Road was deserted but for a company of lately inducted maskers, carrying antiquated Yorkley rifles, marching toward the beaches. (The Halcyon Panic had had its subtle grip on Ongladred for the whole of that winter.) A few of these men hailed us as we rode by, then the darkness loomed up again, and abruptly Elk goaded his horse off the road and into unmarked country—a stony shortcut to his home in the rocks.

The ground, topped with short grass, seemed to swell up beneath us, the horizons to expand. I imagined that at any moment we would ride into peril; our horses would plunge from the sea-fronting cliffs, the withdrawing tides would carry us to the barren archipelagoes where our enemies lived out their hatred for us. But, instead, the horizons tautened again as chunks and blocks of stone began to rise up around us.

Finally, we rode into the rock-walled upland arena in which the Stonelore amphitheatre lurked. The amphitheatre shone palely under the Shattered Moons, its broad plastic cap gleaming dully. To the left of the amphitheatre rested the energy unit that provided the power for both Elk's house and the animation of the delicately programmed actors in his neuro-dramas. It squatted in the dark like an outsized toadstool.

In Lunn, a similar but differently constituted unit powered the heating and cooling systems in Our Shathra Anna's palace, as well as the glass flambeaux in the corridors and bedchambers. Solvent from his early literary activities, wealthy from his share of booty taken from the Pelagans during the mid-century skirmishes in which he'd served as a commander, Elk had bought the components of this unit with his own funds; then he'd engineered its design and construction, engaged in covert talks with a Pelagan minister, and acquired enough fissionable material to keep Stonelore running for three hundred years. Later, he had admitted—openly—making a reciprocal arrangement with a representative of the barbarians that Ongladred had successfully held at bay during the undeclared, midcentury hostilities.

Those days had fled. Elk, long past the age of conscription, lived and worked beyond the means or the capabilities of the citizens whom his work "enlightened." Only Our Shathra Anna and the richest of Atarites could challenge his lifestyle. Several days before, I had asked him about this.

"How can you, one of the people, justify the way you live, Sayati Elk?"

"I needn't *justify* anything, Ingram. Our Shathra Anna gave me the title by which you address me, and Stonelore sprang up around me as the result of the efforts of my hands and mind. I dwell here, but I don't look upon a single pebble of this site as 'property.'"

I laughed. "You're a caretaker, only?"

"No, I'm a creator. Transient as they are, Stonelore and the neuro-dramas are my gift to the civilization of Ongladred."

"A civilization now threatened," I pointed out.

"Exactly, Ingram. So I create the harder. A social order promoting social order, and nothing more, isn't civilization at all, but a machine for maintaining the status quo. The Mansuecerians live as they must, the Atarite Court rules as it must—but I have to give shape to voices and forms lying outside your experience or muffled so close to you that you're blind to them."

"Why? In these times, to what purpose?"

"So that you may experience them. And so that I may live." He started to say more, but bit his heavy lip and turned aside.

We guided our horses to the right of the amphitheatre and dismounted in front of the house carven out of the rear wall of the upland arena: Grotto House. Gareth, Elk's son, came out to greet us; he took the horses and led them to shelter in a stable down from Grotto House. (The stable was an anomaly, made entirely of wood, and virtually invisible from the environs of the amphitheatre.) Holding Bronwen, I watched the boy go. He was sixteen or so, very nearly the child of his father's dotage—except that Elk was a long way from senile garrulity. He fought to contain his natural affection for the boy.

Gareth was his parents' last child. Two older sons had died in separate accidents, one drowning in the Angromain Channel, the other apparently the victim of a thief or Pelagan raiders, much like the dead girl in my arms. This was years ago. A daughter lived in Lunn, married to a masker with no more fire in him than any other of their kind. She did not care to venture out to Stonelore. As for Gareth, he had his father's heavy face, and he was trying to grow a beard. It was coming out thin, red, and sorrowful, but he persisted in his standing refusal to shave. Verily, he had some of his father's spark and had already shown himself skillful at hacking boulders into strange, sinuous shapes. Sculptures, he called them, though it was often hard to tell of what. He said they were supposed to be trees, symbols of the possibilities of growth.

"Come inside," Gabriel Elk said. "Before you drop her."

My arms *had* begun to ache. We passed through a wrought-iron gate that blocked the entrance to Grotto House, a gate with old Spanish scrollwork in the iron. Then I followed the old man into the rock house's foyer. Illuminated panels made every wall glow. Two rough corridors led out of the foyer to right and left. "Where do you want her?" I asked.

"In the programming room."

Bethel Elk came out of the righthand corridor to greet us. She took her husband's hand and nodded at me. She stood as tall as I, her arms bare in a pale-yellow gown. With no self-consciousness, she wore a wire brace for additional support for her back, which, long ago, she had injured in a fall. She was a Mansuecerian, but it was rumored that her father had been an Atarite. How else account for the saucy cast in her eye, a look heightened rather than dampened by her age?

"The girl's beautiful," she said.

"Aye," Elk said. "So I bought her. Now if Master Marley will escort her down to the programming room—"

"Tonight?" the woman rebuked him. "Let her lie in a bedchamber."

"I must work tonight," Elk said. "Haomycin doesn't last long, my lady, and we have company in three days. Go on, Ingram."

"Surely," I said, "you can begin in the morning and still get done."

Elk grinned, his sideburns flaring away from his smile like white wings. "Ingram's on orders to watch me, but he's too tired to do it. Don't worry, Ingram, I'm won't sneak off while you sleep and file for citizenship among the Pelagans. Take Bronwen down the hall. Then go to bed."

"Fine," I said. Alone, I went down the left-hand corridor to its end, then halted in front of the elevator there. The door slid open. I stepped in. Humming, the elevator dropped us three or four meters to the programming room.

I carried Bronwen Lief into this chamber, placed her on a table, opened her silken quilt, and gawped at her gowned body and noncommittal lips. Still, the ability to betray remained there yet; in death as well as in life, she could betray. In the programming room, amid support consoles, minicomputers, oscilloscopes, and Elk's privately engineered neural-surrogate equipment, I associated Bronwen Lief with everything that then menaced Ongladred's civilization: the barbarians of the Angromain Archipelago, the mythical sloak, Elk's own wayward genius. And, damn me for thinking it, even the inflexibility of Atarite rule. Somehow Bronwen Lief carried all these things within her and so embodied all the intangibles of the Halcyon Panic.

Weary, I left the programming room, found my own bedchamber on the upper level, and slept until the sun was high.

iv

All the next day I saw nothing of Gabriel Elk. However, a tunnel ran from the programming room to the comp-center beneath the Stonelore amphitheatre, and I was sure the old man, laboring alone, was preparing both the corpse of Bronwen Lief and the comptroller room itself for the special performance two evenings hence. I was of Our Shathra Anna's intelligence service, the Eyes and Ears of the Court, but I'd begun to trust Elk—indeed, to respect

him. He was too busy, too unconcerned with our petty preoccupations to try
to elude me.

At midday I threaded my way through the rocks to the stable. In the
barren paddock, I found Gareth and the Elk family ostler, a middle-aged
masker named Robin Coigns. He had been sleeping when we arrived from
Lunn the previous evening, and Elk had chosen not to disturb him. Gareth,
as usual, was chiseling at a block of stone on a split-rail table, and Robin was
grooming Gabriel's horse, pulling out long strands of kinky sorrel hair. The
other animal stood beneath the wooden awning, eating.

I entered the paddock. "Hello, Horsesweat," I said to Robin.

Blandly, the ostler grinned. Gareth, chiseling, merely nodded. His chisel
glinted in the anemic sun. Splinters flew away from his gloved hands. This
statue, this "tree," would turn out as twisty as any he'd ever made. I shielded
my eyes and looked into the sun, into feeble old Maz.

"Well, Robin," I said. "What do you think? Is Maz going to go nova and
blow up in Ongladred's skies? Everything else imaginable is supposed to
happen when the Panic breaks."

"Maz won't blow," Robin said. "I'd expect the sloak first."

"You believe in the sloak?"

"It's been ver-i-fied, hasn't it, Master Marley?"

"Postulated, not verified."

"Well, Our Shathra Anna says there's geological evi-dence."

"Some." The gullibility of maskers always amused me.

Gareth looked up from his work. "I believe in the sloak," he said. His
wide face glistened with sweat; his patchy beard limned his jaw with a moist,
plastered ruddiness. "And Father believes in it. As Robin says, there's evidence
to support its existence—at least in theory."

"In theory," I said. I had heard all the arguments before. *Sloak* was the
masker name for an apparently chimerical sea creature that no one had ever
seen. No one had ever seen it because it dwelled kilometers off the coast
of Ongladred, on the bottom of the ocean floor as a millimicron-thin
membrane of otherwise immense proportions cloaking the sea floor all the
way to Mansueceria's equator, where the planet's waters supposedly became
too warm for so sensitive a beast. Legend had it that the sloak, which moved
in slow, oddly peristaltic undulations, thickened itself consciously every two
thousand years and pulled its bulk over the entire surface of our island. Then,
like a big dappled eye, it lay basking, breathing, for a year or more, in the dull

sunlight of our world—after which it returned to the marbled green depths of the Suthward Trench.

An unhurried, rhythmical departure, no doubt.

"Two previous civilizations on Ongladred died," Gareth said. "Died at the height of their glory; died without suffering human conquest. And Father says that it wasn't so terribly long ago—during or after the creature's last cycle—that the Angromain Archipelagoes were settled by fleeing Atarites. Only enough people survived on Ongladred to begin again. Ours is the third civilization of colonists so threatened, Master Marley."

"The sloak is an explanation only if you have no other," I said. "There's firmer evidence for two periods of mild glaciation. Why not accept those things as the means of destruction you're looking for, Gareth?"

"Glaciation from the south!" the boy said. "Why accept the illogical? I prefer the sloak, Robin's sloak."

"The sloak it was," Robin said. "The sloak it was."

"And if the cycle holds true," Gareth said, "this is the year." With his chisel, he made chips of stone fly.

"The more immediate threat to Ongladred is human, Gareth—the Pelagans. They're real, they're greedy, and they've finally begun to demonstrate the unity to defeat us. Before, their own divisiveness kept them manageable."

"Ten thousand years ago, on Earth, the threat was always human," the boy said, furiously chiseling. Then he halted, looked over the block of stone on the table, fixed me with his blue-green eyes. "And you, Master Marley, see a threat even in my father. That's why you've come to Stonelore. That's why we bed and feed you, one of the Eyes and Ears of Our Shathra."

"I do what I must." Clearly, I had used these same words a hundred times before. Ingram Marley, a dirt-runner, a spy with no cover. Robin Coigns finished grooming Gabriel Elk's horse and led it under the shelter. He began pulling the wire comb down the flank of the other animal, tactfully out of earshot. Aswim in a welter of ambiguous loyalties, I watched him.

"As does my father," Gareth said. "He also does what he must, but you've placed him among the potential dangers to Ongladred. In fact, he embodies the culmination of what our civilization should stand for. Does the Atarite Court know what it's doing, Master Marley?"

"Do you question Our Shathra Anna?" I was ashamed to frame this subtlety-free response, but not knowing what else to say, I resorted to the tactics of intimidation.

"Not Our Shathra Anna. She alone among you may understand what my father represents. It's Chancellor Blaine and the Magi of the Atarite Court whose wisdom seems to me suspect, Master Marley."

"How suspect, Gareth?" Then I asked him something else, to prevent him from answering my first question. "Will you disobey your conscription chit when it comes, as it surely will?"

"If Ongladred requires men to defend her, I will aid in her defense." The boy was indignant. "My father fought for this island, and so will I. I, too, am an Elk, Master Marley."

"Your father's a man of influence. Will he let you go?"

"He'd have to, wouldn't he? In everything, he obeys our laws. Besides, if he attempted to hinder me, I would not be stopped, I'd go without his consent." The boy's stare fell away from me, a gratifying respite.

Robin Coigns came back, his currying unfinished. He sat on a bale of fodder between Gareth and me; while I leaned on the paddock rail. Robin said, "They say all civi-li-zations die, Master Marley. It's the nature of things. En-tro-py, everything running down. But I believe, one way or the other, it can be fought. So I'll fight it, too."

Apparently, he had heard the last part of our conversation. "Are you of induction age, too, Horsesweat?" I asked.

"Forty-nine," he said. "I'll go with Master Gareth. The top and the bottom of their numbers, we'll be. Youth and sa-gassa-ty."

Gareth laughed. I did too.

"Oh, I'm not worried a' tall," the ostler went on. "My father always said that at the third coming of the sloak, the Parfects would return. To watch over us, you know. They dropped us here six thousand years ago, he said, and they'd come back if things went too swackers, as they're starting to do now. Why, it's my opinion, Master Marley, that the Parfects are cruising a ship out there among the Shattered Moons now, orb-it-ing, you know—watching over us Mansuecerians, the People Accustomed to the Hand. And maybe over you ruling Atarites, too, for governing us good like you have."

"Comforting notions, Horsesweat. But I fear your sloak and the hoped-for return of the Parfects are cut from the same mythical cloth. They cancel each other out. We're left with the Pelagan threat, and no mitigating circumstances."

"And don't forget the peril posed by my father," Gareth said.

My grin faded, even as I realized that Gabriel Elk's son was baiting me, prolonging the moment of uneasy jocularity that Robin Coigns had given us. In the same spirit I said, "I won't. You keep reminding me. The children of geniuses ought to slit their throats as soon as they're cognizant of their heritage—a gash in the Adam's apple. Elsewise, they soon take themselves much too seriously."

"You don't like my stone work, Master Marley? My trees?"

"You'd be better off petrifying driftwood. Wouldn't take so long, and the results would pretty much coincide."

"That's a hit," Robin Coigns said. "That's a hit."

Eventually, we all ambled back through the garden of rocks to Grotto House. Bethel gave us haoma, biscuits, and jerky for a midday meal, and sat down to eat with us herself. It was the first time since I had been there that she had served haoma. The old man did not appear; it was doubtful that he had slept that night. I thought for a moment of Bronwen Lief, of her disquieting beauty. Then I put her out of my mind to enjoy the company of the Elks and Robin Coigns, the company and the food. The haoma began to work in me as it had done the night before in Lunn.

Afterwards, I excused myself and retired to my bedchamber for a nap. I didn't see Gabriel Elk at all for the remainder of that day. Nor did I see him the next. Nor the next—until late afternoon.

V

The Magi at the Atarite Court had determined that if we on Mansueceria converted our system of time-keeping into Earthly terms, it would be the year 12,500 A.D.—a broad approximation. We measured time not in this long-ago-discarded way, but in terms of how many Mansuecerian years had passed in the reign of our current shathra. The winter and spring of the Halcyon Panic were preternatural seasons in the Year 35 of Our Shathra Anna, and ensconced in the Elk home at Stonelore I wondered how many more years she would reign. I hoped it would be many, for she was an estimable woman.

As Robin Coigns had said on the morning after Elk's and my return from Lunn, there had been colonists on Mansueceria for six thousand of our years. We had been brought from Earth in starships conceived and constructed by a neo-human species whom our earliest records had always referred to as the Parfects—principally because Earth's last men had considered them free of all human vices, cleansed of the quasi-mythical taint of Original Sin. It was the Parfects who had saved mankind from ultimate extermination in the terra-cotta city of Windfall Last in the Carib Sea; who had redeemed us genetically, providing for two contrasting but complementary types of human entity (the stoically disciplined Mansuecerians, or "maskers," and the more aggressive, more emotional Atarites); and who had then delivered this population of half a million to the rugged heartland of Ongladred, on a planet more than eight hundred light-years from Earth. Another chance. Yet another chance, in an isolation even more splendid than that the ambient sea had insured at Windfall Last. Then, the early records and later legends unanimously agreed, the Parfects had left us, gone back to turn all of Earth into the gardens of Adam's first paradise. As for orphaned humanity, it had the rocks of Ongladred—and another chance.

And for six thousand years, despite two major collapses, we had held ourselves entire. More, we had managed, with few exceptions, to maintain our genetic heritage as well, the People Accustomed to the Hand and the People Touched by Fire alike. Together, we had survived. Now Atarite barbarians from the sea-blasted, storm-scoured archipelagoes in the Angromain Sea threatened all we had built together, and there were rumors in the land of the coming of the slow, ravening sloak and the imminent explosion of woe-beset Maz. It was the Year of the Halcyon Panic, as well as Year 35 of Our Shathra Anna, and a self-conscious calm prevailed.

Late in the afternoon of the third day after our return from Lunn, Gabriel Elk emerged from his seclusion and greeted me in the open courtyard at the center of his house. My ankles crossed, I had been sitting on a stone bench watching Maz descend the fiery sky. "How have you been faring, Ingram?" Elk said. His green eyes looked frosted, his unkempt winged sideburns drooped, and I could at last discern the heretofore muted resemblance between him and Gareth. Yes, for the first time, I saw it clearly.

"Well," I told him. "And you? Have you finished?"

"I had to finish. Tonight the Liefs are coming, Ingram, with others."

"What others, sir?"

"Be patient, and see." He stood rigidly before me, casting his long shadow over both the flagstones and my legs, then turned and reentered the house. I had to pull myself up and follow. Uneasily, I sensed all the diverse strands of my anxiety getting ready to knot together.

We had no supper that evening, shared no haoma. Bethel met her husband in the foyer, took his hand, nodded vaguely at me. Then we left Grotto House and walked across the sandy arena that Stonelore's amphitheatre totally dominated. Instead of entering Stonelore, however, we took up sentry positions in one of the natural doorways in the rock wall overlooking the Mershead Road. The wind blew balloons of sand out over the grass, Gabriel and Bethel talked in low voices, and I waited, simply waited.

At last the Liefs came, man and wife, distant figures walking on the low road. They had just traversed the seven kilometers from Lunn. Even after we saw them, it took a while for them to reach us. Maz had set, and when they arrived, the five of us stood in the twilight like liquid ghosts.

"Hello, Josu," Gabriel Elk said. "Welcome, Rhia. Tonight you'll see your daughter given a kind of life again. Bethel will take you into Stonelore and show you your seats. I'll follow in a while. There are others whom I am pledged to greet."

The Liefs departed with Bethel in the grim dusk, toward the amphitheatre. When I looked after them, Stonelore's broad circular cap gleamed a soft yellow-orange. In response to my questioning look, Elk said, "Gareth's in the comptroller room. Tonight, he does my work." We turned again to the Mershead Road. Overhead, the Shattered Moons were scarcely visible, as milky as a thousand clumsily shaped pearls floating between Ongladred's strong rock and the heavens' washed-out stars.

At last we saw the vehicles on the roadway, and I knew that our visitors were Our Shathra Anna, her Chancellor, and some Atarite retainers—guardsmen. Two chariots preceded Our Shathra's equipage, and torches burned in the hands of the chariot riders. The sound of the horses' hooves grew steadily beneath the low moan of the wind, and Gabriel Elk and I watched as the chariots separated from Our Shathra's carriage and circled off in different directions, one halting about fifty meters from the gate in the rocks, the other surely taking up guard on the other side of the arena. The equipage, though, proceeded us on up, black and silent, its matched horses caparisoned and haughty.

Elk, waving his arms, directed the vehicle to the steps at the base of the amphitheatre. Robin Coigns had appeared from the darkness to help our eminent visitors disembark and to show the coachman where he might shelter both himself and his horses during the neuro-performance.

"Sayati Elk," Our Shathra Anna said.

The old man bowed, as did I. The carriage drew away from us. Arngrim

Blaine, a tall, ascetic-looking man in his sixtieth year, smiled at us. Even in the failing light his roan tooth was visible, a translucent reddish-black canine pointing upward like a knife. Long ago he had had it scrimshawed with his initials (it was rumored), but over the years these had either faded or worn away (if they ever existed). He was a well-meaning but narrow-principled man. "Hello, Ingram," he said. "Sayati Elk. I'm happy enough to greet you, but not at all certain this trip was merited. Stonelore has always seemed a frivolous waste to me, and now more than ever."

"Arngrim has no taste for the arts," Our Shathra said. She wore a black cloak that fastened at her neck. Although she smiled, there were deep gray circles under her eyes.

"Neither did Cyaxares of Mede," the Chancellor said. "Nor Walpole of Augustan England. Besides, Ongladred wasn't made for art."

Our Shathra said, "With which man do you compare yourself, Arngrim— the Median king or the English minister?"

"The minister, Lady. The other would be presumptuous." He bowed.

"Art is an enrichment granted those cultures deserving it," the creator of Stonelore said. "Or inflicted on those attempting to repress it."

Our Shathra looked at Gabriel Elk. When she spoke, her tone was liltingly sharp. "Blaine is irritated because he can't rule in all things. Most of all, he can't rule me. I've come to see your entertainment, Gabriel, because I may not be able to come again."

"The season's dangers ought to have dissuaded us from coming tonight," Blaine said. "Two chariots! An inadequate guard, Lady."

"Then I love the lady for the dangers that she's passed," Gabriel Elk said. "And I welcome you both. Let's go inside." He did *not* bow; his gallantry derived from conviction. Taking Our Shathra Anna's arm, he escorted the lady up the stairs to the illuminated portal of the amphitheatre. Chancellor Blaine and I trailed them up the steps, two serving-men, each as much a dirt-runner as the other—a situation that I found gratifyingly amusing.

Two of Gareth Elk's tree sculptures flanked the wide door.

Inside, Elk led us to a glass booth on the theatre's highest circular tier, a booth reserved for Atarites and Atarite retainers. The top of the booth was open, and even though we were on Stonelore's uppermost level, the ceiling arched over us like a small sky, utterly out of reach. Our velvet-upholstered wingback chairs allowed us to look comfortably down into the neuro-pit. Across from us, in the preliminary dark, we could make out Bethel Elk and the Liefs sitting poised and expectant on their own stone tier. Otherwise, Stonelore was empty—sentient, immense, and brooding. Gabriel Elk had infused it with something of his own character.

"Those are my actress's parents," he said. "I felt that they should be here, too, if they wished to come."

"Of course," Our Shathra said.

"I hope," Blaine said, "that they're maskers in every sense, inured to false emotions and resigned to their daughter's death. This sort of thing can undermine even the stolidest personality, Sayati Elk."

"It hasn't yet, Chancellor. This evening, a reading only. The neuro-drama undermines nothing. It offers release, purgation, for a folk manufactured to think they don't require it, but subliminally craving it in any case. The neuro-drama illuminates our oneness, strengthening the social order you represent."

"When it's comprehensible, I suppose," the Chancellor replied. "Mostly, at Stonelore, it drains energy reserves." It was not hard to admire the roan-toothed old pragmatist: even genius left him unabashed, wittily clawing.

Gabriel Elk glowered. "The reserves are mine, not the state's. And the drain is hardly substantive since the law does not permit human actors. Stonelore is a compromise with that law, Chancellor Blaine—a law of Atarite urging that you capably championed before the Magi. Perhaps you remember?"

"I do, Sayati Elk, very well."

Our Shathra Anna leaned forward in her engulfing chair. "May we begin now, Worthies? These differences are from tired old arguments and I've come for smart entertainment, not debate."

"Certainly, Lady." Elk left the booth.

Chancellor Blaine turned to me. "Well, Ingram, what can you say for yourself? It seems you've been enjoying a holiday at Stonelore."

"Shame," Our Shathra said. "You wanted him to come out here, Arngrim. Now you scold him for doing your bidding."

I said, "Listen, I don't think that old man is a threat to Ongladred. He'll precipitate no early break in the maskers' steadfastness, Chancellor—nor will the neuro-dramas planned for after the equinox."

Blaine asked, "What *does* Sayati Elk have planned?"

"I don't know," I admitted. "I'm not even sure what we'll see this evening, but Gabriel Elk's neither a fool nor an apostate."

"Thirteen days out here, Ingram, and you still don't know what the man's planning. You're arguing from faith." Blaine's roan tooth seemed to slash at me. "When the Halcyon Panic breaks, when the maskers give themselves over to fear, misdirected anger, and other inutile emotions, you'll find Ongladred's biggest fool and darkest apostate coexisting in the same skin, Master Marley: *yours!*" The Chancellor's lips drew together firmly, hiding the red-black canine.

"Melodrama," Our Shathra said. "Your own fears betray you into fustian, Arngrim."

"I hope so, Lady," Blaine said, quickly calm again. "But I see no reason to court disaster. The neuro-drama is a folly, a corruption of masker and Atarite mores, that I can't comprehend your fondness for. In times like these, Lady, your protection of it—forgive me—seems virtually perverse." He regarded me again. "In the meantime, Ingram, I think your mission at Stonelore is effectively at an end. Tonight you'll come back to Lunn with us."

"Very well," I said.

vi

Suddenly the neuro-theatre was plunged into impenetrable darkness. There was music: one stringed instrument playing mournfully. The sound—not loud, but resonant and golden—seemed to issue from everywhere at once. "At last," I heard Our Shathra's voice say, "the *folly* commences." Then a battery of bright lights threw their stinging yellow glare into the sunken arena of the neuro-pit, Sayati Elk's "stage." Even yet, however, the blackness obliterated everything else in the Stonelore amphitheatre. We could not see Elk's wife and Bronwen's parents on the tier opposite ours.

Then Gabriel Elk stepped into the light. As he spoke, he turned so that all in the theatre could hear him, even the phantom maskers whom he apparently imagined to be in the tiers above him. His foreshortened body, his enormous hands, his upturned, expressive face all had a sharpness of focus intensified out of the realm of nature. Ageless he was, ageless and transcendent. Turning slowly, he spoke, and, without amplification, his voice struck us like a wave breaking. "My performer tonight is the corpse of Bronwen Lief, a girl killed by the Pelagans four days ago. I bow to her parents, for letting me buy her." He bowed to them. "What she will perform is not of my composition; indeed, it is not even of our tongue, and I've decided to let her speak it as its ancient poet, now forgotten, set it to paper. The strangeness of the language will be no stranger than the strangeness of our times. Finally, all languages are vehicles for the same remorseless, unending reaching out—even to the moment of humanity's extinction."

On that word, he walked out of the neuro-pit, into the ambient dark. But did not return to our booth.

We were left staring into the neuro-pit, where a section of the floor about three meters in diameter withdrew into the bowels of the amphitheatre. When it returned on its pneumatic lift, Bronwen Lief was standing on it—her supple body clad in a white Etruscan stola, her eyes reflecting back at us the disquieting glaze of her deadness. The music began again, livelier now but still mournful. Just as the girl had no soul, the music now had no body. Its thin plucked notes slipped away into the air. Perhaps Elk intended for the music and the girl to complete each other, to make a whole person out of an empty shell and a disembodied noise. I had no idea. This was my first performance of any sort at Stonelore: Arngrim Blaine enforced his own prejudices among the Eyes and Ears of Our Shathra Anna, and except for my assignment to Elk as a dirt-runner, I might never have encountered the old sayati's special brand of "enlightenment."

The performance itself both bewildered and moved me. I saw a corpse behave as no living masker ever had, even under Atarite command in war:

Bronwen Lief, a dead girl, danced.

Maskers never danced—nor did Atarites, even though the range of emotions conducive to dancing lay well within our psychological compass. The law did not permit it. For the same reason that dancing was against the law, living human beings were forbidden to access a stage and act.

As products of the Parfects' genetic engineering, the human population of our planet reflected their unanimous verdict as to what qualities a reasoning creature ought to have. Out of the maskers, the Parfects had bred avariciousness, aggressiveness, xenophobia, lust, and even a degree of the inclination to fear. At the same time, the Parfects had realized that survival on a new and hostile world depended, at least in part, on these very "vices." Hence, they had engineered a second, smaller group of colonists to guide and administer to the first; these were the original Atarites, people in whom the dangerous dross of the animal, the primeval recourse to fang and claw, still had some play—albeit subordinated now to the need to build, command, and protect.

The Parfects had even tried to program into our ancestors' genes the elementary knowledge that the two groups were dependent on each other; that the seemingly irresistible urge to interbreed would lead to ruin; that the similar tendency for the People Accustomed to the Hand and the People Touched by Fire to go their separate ways, to take their own evolutionary roads, would have to be subconsciously, even intuitively, fought. In this, the Parfects had perhaps shown the extent of their own limitations. Still, we'd managed to survive. Renegade Atarites had established themselves long ago on the islands of the Angromain Archipelago, and for several generations on Ongladred there had been more liaisons between ruler and ruled than were wise (my own grandparents were an example). However, even perilously menaced, our civilization stood.

In Gabriel Elk's neuro-theatre, the dead Bronwen Lief went through the motions of a choreography programmed into her but seemingly motivated from within, from a human source. Of course, that source was Sayati Elk (and Gareth, too, for he directed some of her movements from the comptroller room). The old man had turned technology into a kind of aesthetic, trying to infuse spirit into what was at base a mechanical operation—not because he wanted to, but because he had to. The neuro-theatre was a compromise with the laws of Ongladred, a compromise that Elk could not have been entirely happy with. I was moved by Bronwen's dance because her programmer had come so close to accomplishing the impossible. She moved with genuine grace. Her garment followed the flow of her limbs like a ghost counterpointing her motions. But, in reality, it was Gabriel Elk's vision, his need to communicate, that danced there under the withering brightness of Stonelore's lamps.

Bronwen Lief was the vessel into which he had poured both vision and need. Because she was a corpse.

The law said that no human being could act, that no human being could essay any sort of performance contrary to Mansuecerian nature. For uniformity's sake, the law included Atarites. The relatively high incidence of interbreeding between the two groups during the last century had made the law seem reasonable to many. An actor, after all, is one who continually assumes roles requiring her to abase or repudiate, if only momentarily, the genetic characteristics given to her by the Parfects. One becomes something other than oneself. Drama derives from conflict and emotion—excessive and aberrant emotion, according to men like Chancellor Blaine. In a society like Ongladred's, these men felt, such "artificial" emotions posed a very real danger to the persons acting them out; the audience for these spectacles was also in some danger of corruption, but a few of Our Shathra Anna's most influential Magi had deterred the closing of the neuro-theatre by arguing that it could serve as a healthy outlet for the subconscious turmoil of the ordinary Mansuecerian. Or maybe this was a rationalization of Our Shathra Anna, who was a sympathizer, who enjoyed an occasional illicit entertainment. And so the issue of Stonelore balanced on the horns of the fuzzy moral ideologies of these two factions: One could attend the neuro-dramas, but one could not take part in them.

The dead, however, were exempt from this law. No stigma attached to the reanimation of corpses as actors. In Ongladred, we had developed a nearly callous disregard for death and the attendant luxuries of mourning, burial, and lingering memory—or at least the maskers had, out of both necessity and the hope for survival. Therefore, Sayati Elk reanimated the dead. He poured his vision and need into the only vessels the state would allow him, striving always to touch and transfigure. This he did for audiences that almost invariably sat mute and subdued to the end. That his audiences generally returned to be silently worked upon was his incentive to continue—that, and his obsession with a dream, and sometimes Our Shathra Anna's reaction, whether approval or pique.

Tonight she approved. "Beautiful," she said.

Mansuecerian dancer, Atarite applause—except that Arngrim Blaine made a sighing noise, shifting his thin body in its chair so that his lacy clothes rustled. I ignored him. Leaning forward, I tried to catch every nuance of Bronwen Lief's performance.

Then it ended, or at least this preliminary part of it did. She came out of her last graceful *pas seul* into an equally graceful walk. Then she stopped, turned her eyes up to her parents, faced in the direction of our booth, and looked up at us. They were still dead, those eyes, still empty and glasslike.

The lute continued to play.

When she spoke, her voice was deeper than seemed right, but melodious. The ancient language in which she spoke came naturally to her lips, mesmerizing us with its accents. We ignored our inability to understand and simply listened. From the voluminous dark, his voice following richly on each line that Bronwen delivered, Sayati Elk translated the forgotten poet's words.

The poem dealt with time, with the inevitable crumbling away of empires, and with the poet's awe in the face of their passing. It dealt, too, with the nearly meaningless prospect of his own death. A fluid poem with few pauses, and a headlong surge toward its final lines.

In Elk's translation we heard them:

> *And here face downward in the sun*
> *To feel how swift how secretly*
> *The shadow of the night comes on . . .*

Bronwen folded her hands and let her head fall to her breast. And that was all. The performance had ended. A dance and a reading, with little room for the sort of *emoting* that Chancellor Blaine so loathed. Elk had programmed the girl and cautioned Gareth to underplay the "entertainment"; in everything but the subject matter of the reading, he had aimed at conciliating my roan-toothed superior. Less than twenty minutes had passed since the dimming of Stonelore's house-lights and the flaring of the immense lamps around the neuro-pit.

Brevity had always impressed Arngrim Blaine.

vii

But afterward, in the tapestry-hung dining room of Grotto House, we discovered that the poem's subject had only impressed him negatively. Six of us sat about the great stone table, there, with places for two more. Those two were for Gabriel and Gareth, acting now as our stewards, moving between dining chamber and kitchen with platters of food and decanters of vintage haoma. A silent masker woman, the cook and scullery maid Maria, helped them. Our Shathra Anna and Bethel Elk sat at opposite ends of the table, each as queenly as the other. To the right of Our Shathra, Chancellor Blaine voiced his objections to the reading while the Liefs remained tactfully or humbly noncommittal.

He was saying, "I can only assume, Mistress Elk, that your husband chose that piece for its elegant pessimism. He must have had to rummage long and hard through your library—until he found an item whose shape and color suggested the defeatism of its contents. A tasteless choice, considering the dangers besetting us now." He sipped some haoma from his cup, a guilty illicit pleasure.

"Or an appropriate one," Bethel Elk said.

"No. He might as well broadcast propaganda for the Pelagans. What if this were given on the first night after the equinox. How would our maskers—" Blaine's lips tightened. "Forgive me. How would our *Mansuecerian* citizens react?"

"Why not ask the Liefs, Chancellor?" I said.

Husband and wife continued silent, Rhia smiling and Josu bland under his leather mourning cap.

Blaine continued: "You see, they can't yet formulate their reactions. But the effect of a presentation like the one we saw tonight is bound to be insidious, and most neuro-dramas are a thousand times more disquieting than Bronwen Lief's recital. Eventually, such 'entertainments' will wholly sabotage the people's faith in Our Shathra and the Atarite Court." In the glow of many candles, his roan tooth glinted with carnelian highlights.

Gabriel and Gareth came in with big baskets of potato bread, and Sayati Elk smiled at his wife.

Our Shathra Anna said, "Arngrim is maligning your choice of material, Gabriel. Says you'll sabotage Ongladred and me with barbarian propaganda."

The boy answered her. "Father will respond to that after we've eaten—if the Chancellor leaves anything for us." He and the old man went out again, and, surprisingly enough, Blaine smiled, albeit wanly.

Then the Elks, father and son, returned and took up their places at table with us. Gabriel spoke to the Liefs: "What did you think? Tell me how you felt seeing Bronwen as you saw her." Unlike Chancellor Blaine, he genuinely wanted their reactions, even to the point of preparing to take mental notes.

"I don't know, sir," Rhia said. "She wasn't our girl, that one down there."

"Her voice, it was different," Josu volunteered.

"Getting the voice right is hard," Gareth said. "We must coordinate the neural impulses from the electrodes in Broca's area of the brain with the programming of the lungs, vocal cords, and lips."

"Why don't you just use a recording?" Blaine asked. "It seems to me you've made things unduly complicated for yourselves, Sayati Elk."

Elk glanced at the Chancellor and then returned his gaze to Rhia and Josu. "Bronwen didn't sound like herself?" he asked.

Josu said, "No, sir. Not exactly—but it could've been that old sort of talk she spoke in."

"Maybe it was the talk," Rhia said. "That funny other tongue."

"Which supports my contention that your choice of material left much to be desired," Blaine said. "The language, Sayati Elk, alienated the Liefs from their reanimated daughter, and that moany business about every civilization crumpling into shadow certainly wasn't designed to send either Our Shathra Anna or me away from Stonelore whistling your praises. A bad choice—from a diplomatic point of view, if not an artistic one."

"It's spoiled your digestion, not mine," Our Shathra told Blaine.

Suddenly a stillness descended on the dining room of Grotto House. Eight people stared at one another over baskets of potato bread, decanters of haoma, and the silver platter of roast mutton and the bowls of bread pudding. A silence and a chill. Then Arngrim Blaine raised his cup and sipped. By this act, he directed our attention to him. Looking over the rim of his cup, he spoke to Gabriel.

"Is Ongladred going to die, Sayati Elk?"

"One day."

"Soon?"

"*Soon* is a relative term, Chancellor Blaine. On what scale do you wish me to apply it?"

"Bronwen Lief's performance in Stonelore suggested that collapse is inevitable. I'm guessing that you selected the piece out of some rational, therefore comprehensible motive? What motive? To frighten us? To warn us? To suggest that resistance to fate is foolhardy? What, Sayati Elk? As for my definition of *soon*, do you think Ongladred will die during our lifetimes?"

"It's conceivable."

"Is it inevitable?"

"Even its death isn't inevitable, Chancellor Blaine. Societies fall when their leaders fail."

A pause; a darker tension.

Blaine's mouth was agape, and a spittle filament lay across his discolored tooth. He sipped more haoma. Then he said, "Who do you see as failing first, Sayati Elk? The Atarite Court in Lunn or the wolfish Pelagan captains across the Angromain Channel?"

Gareth Elk, the son, said, "Whoever is least flexible, Chancellor Blaine; whoever is least adaptable." It was a thought that I'd had before, but never voiced. Blaine, though capable of a quick, witty range in conversation, was not otherwise known for his readiness to abandon old ways, old prejudices. The boy, I felt, had inadvertently given voice to our most basic fears about

Ongladred's time of trials—the suspicion, even among Atarites, that our leaders had lost or set aside the quality of vision.

Then Our Shathra Anna said, "We may have as much as a year before the Pelagans put us to the test, or as little as three months. Right now they're content for reivers and fear-strikers to harass, steal, and"—here she nodded at Rhia and Josu Lief—"murder when surprised in these pursuits. Invasion is not yet. We have some time to mobilize. Even so, Gabriel, you must remember one thing."

"Yes, Lady?" he said.

"That you must include yourself among that group of leaders who may fail or not fail in the attempt to preserve Ongladred."

"I, Lady?"

"Come, Gabriel. You're too old to play coy. Just as Arngrim and I are"—she inflected her next word sharply—"*political* leaders, you are an intellectual leader of our island."

Blaine smirked. "In other words, Sayati Elk, you have a responsibility nearly as great as ours."

"Sometimes," Bethel Elk said, "Gabriel views his efforts at Stonelore in a Promethean light. Against a hostile array of gods and vultures, he labors alone for the redemption and advancement of humanity."

"Oh, no," the old man protested, grinning. "Not alone. The gods and vultures I don't dispute, but I've always had help—you, Gareth, and lately even coy Master Marley there. The work's almost always been *intellectual*, though. I wouldn't presume to put my foot in *politics*."

The meal went better after that. I studied the ornate woolen tapestries on the walls; I enjoyed the haoma, the food, the less sensitive drift of our talk. It was hard to credit Stonelore's relative isolation from the Atarite Court, the warlike nature of the inhabitants of the windy archipelagoes, the nightmarish threat of a creature called the sloak. Candles flickered. The evening drew to a close, as did my own residence at Grotto House. Oddly, I regretted this fact; I didn't want to go back to Lunn.

Then Our Shathra Anna said, "Arngrim, you'd better tell the Elks of Gareth's conscription."

Talk again ceased.

Chancellor Blaine said, "The gist of it is that Gareth and your ostler—"

"Robin Coigns," Bethel said.

"Yes. Gareth and Gentleman Coigns must report to the Lunn garrison in two days. Our Shathra wished this message to come from me personally, Sayati Elk, not from an induction-runner."

"Two days!" Bethel said.

"That's skimpy notice," her husband added.

Our Shathra said, "The message was to have come a day or two ago, Mistress Elk, but we hoped hearing it from our lips would make the news less distressing. I am earnestly sorry the notice is not more, though."

Josu Lief put his arms on the table. "You'll report, Master Gareth, when I do, it seems."

"Fine by me," Gareth said. "The hardship's not mine, but Father's. He'll have to do virtually all the work in the neuro-theatre by himself. Mother can't work in the comptroller room. Her back won't let her."

Gareth's comment seemed a serendipitous cue for Chancellor Blaine, who quickly interjected: "Sayati Elk, we can offer you the command of a unit of recently inducted men—a naval unit—if you accept it now. You will hold it for a year, or until this crisis is past. Should you accept, spring performances at Stonelore will cease to be a problem for you, and Gareth's absence won't be felt here."

"Certainly it will," Bethel said.

Blaine qualified this comment: "I meant that your husband's work in the neuro-theatre wouldn't be impeded by his absence."

"Because there wouldn't be any work there," Gabriel Elk said. "I'd be captaining a contingent of young Mansuecerian seamen against the Pelagans—at age sixty-three. Stonelore would close."

"Regrettably," Blaine said.

"I refuse." Gabriel Elk turned to Our Shathra. "Lady, was this proposal of your own devising? Am I to understand that you wish me to close Stonelore and limp off to war?"

"You're far from limping, Gabriel. But no. The proposal originated with the Chancellor."

"Who knows," Blaine volunteered, "your intellectual leadership can be put to good military use. After all, survival depends on leadership."

"I refuse. I'm too old for conscription. Moreover, I've served."

"Our Shathra Anna," Gareth said, rising, "I'd like to go tell Robin."

"Please. Go ahead."

As the boy left, Gabriel Elk said, "Anyway, we've nearly finished. When you return to Lunn, Lady, I humbly request that you let Josu and Rhia share your coach. The roads warp into dangerous rivers at night."

Our Shathra agreed, and in another twenty minutes our entire company was outside, in the shadow of Grotto House, under the motionful brightness of the Shattered Moons. Stonelore's amphitheatre loomed before us like a huge round starship, promising us Earth. The air was cool. Gareth and Robin Coigns walked toward us across the upland arena, Our Shathra Anna's equipage rattling behind them like a circus cage of noisy blackbirds. Somehow, the equipage struck me as an evil artifact. Above the caparisoned horses, the driver snapped his long whip; apparently they had not been unbridled during the whole of the evening. A second time the driver snapped his whip, and a third.

In front of Grotto House, Josu Lief crumpled to his knees in the dust and then pitched forward on his face.

If I hadn't seen the spark of uncanny red in the rock spires opposite us, I would have thought that the man had fainted—but the three successive crackings of the carriage driver's whip had concealed the report of a rifle. The second shot had no such fortuitous cover, however, and the burst of fire from the rifle muzzle seemed terrifyingly brighter than the first one. The report and the ricochet totally deafened us.

"Get down!" someone cried. "Get back inside!"

I fell to the ground and rolled. I saw the three women—who had come out last—duck back into the deep well of Grotto House's entrance. Gabriel Elk and Arngrim Blaine scrambled into the rock garden to the entrance's right. I rolled again. On my stomach once more, I looked up. Gareth and Robin Coigns, caught in the open, ran for the protecting curve of the amphitheatre, the carriage rattling after them, horses whinnying.

Another bright spit of fire; another shot. Everything was noise and moving bodies. At last I found some cover for myself, a crevice on the side of Grotto House leading down to the stable.

"Gareth!" Gabriel Elk shouted. "Gareth!"

"Here, with Robin!" the boy replied from the portion of Stonelore's wall out of our hidden enemy's sight. "We're all of us whole."

viii

For once that evening, I sat alone with my thoughts, blood revving through my temples, roaring in my ears. The Shattered Moons buckled, flowed, shifted in their myriad orbits. I tilted my head back against the rough wall of my hiding place and watched.

I, Ingram Marley, dirt-runner and spy.

For three hours, I had been subsumed in the personalities of people more important, more powerful, than I. Now, through this violence, I had been given back to myself. I did not entirely appreciate this gift. Involuntarily, my shoulders pulled up against my neck, my palms flattened on cold stone.

How long did the lot of us have to live? If the armed men in the rocks had sneaked past Our Shathra Anna's chariot guard, who remained to save us? Only ourselves: Gabriel Elk and son, our effete Chancellor, Robin Coigns and the coachman, and one member of the Eyes and Ears of the Atarite Court. Stonelore and Grotto House lay too far away from either Lunn or the Mershead Road for us to count on reinforcements—although if the court party were too long in getting home, the Magi *would* dispatch a contingent of horsemen.

Two, three, four more shots sounded in Stonelore's arena. Could they be heard on the Mershead Road? Maybe. As dull, echoing *pings* over the sounds of wind and sea. I didn't imagine that anyone would follow them up.

Frozen in place, I felt my own impotence in the face of a reasonless, impersonal hostility. Then the hostility took on a human character: laughter sounded in the rocks opposite us. Gleeful, self-assertive laughter, which even the wind's erratic gusting could not drown.

Then two more shots, ricocheting away.

Then more laughter and a voice crying, "Ilk! Ilk! You surrender!" After which Elk, from his hiding place with Blaine, shouted an obscenity. There was then a disconcerting silence. No shots. No braying laughter.

Several minutes passed.

Finally the voice in the rocks started taunting us in a dialect at once lilting and guttural, a Pelagan dialect, one I'd never learned. Our attackers—how many murderers peered down on us?—were men from across the Angromain Channel, reivers, thieves, fear-strikers, danger-drinking barbarians. I thought of Josu Lief lying prone in front of Grotto House. In less than a week, these randomly shifting Pelagan agents had killed two members of the selfsame family. And one of them, drawing down on us with a stolen rifle (no doubt), was alternately laughing and spewing out streams of unintelligible invective.

After a time, I realized that this reiver was declaiming poetry, venomous couplets in his own tongue. He wanted Sayati Elk, Ongladred's sole literary giant, to suffer these insults in a form that mocked the old man's genius. And so he railed at us like an actor, disdainful both of Sayati Elk and of the Atarite law that had indirectly given rise to the neuro-theatre. More than likely, Chancellor Blaine was chewing his upper lip with chagrin, his roan tooth on the verge of breaking flesh. How must he feel, in a situation in which he was as powerless as I?

"Ilk! Ilk!" the reiver called, then spewed his nonsensical couplets.

For answer he got three bursts from a handgun and a bit of bravado from Arngrim Blaine. "You'd better get out while you can!" his thin voice shouted. "If you don't go now, you'll never make it!"

I couldn't see around the crevice containing me, I was afraid to look out— but apparently the old Chancellor had taken the handgun from beneath his cloak and fired in anger. Gabriel Elk, beside Blaine in the low rock garden, translated his message into the Pelagan dialect and added a severe-sounding message of his own. I knew then that my fear was greater than Chancellor Blaine's, that it was my weakness that had imagined *him* chewing *his* lip. I was afraid because we were pinned down in Stonelore's arena. Still, we were not automatically doomed to end up like old Lief, wavy pencils of blood outlining our chins and staining the ground.

Into my belt I'd slid a knife, a dagger with an ornate haft. Almost every Atarite or Atarite retainer carried one like it; mine, like most of the others, had never been used. I curled my fingers around its haft and edged away from the crevice's opening, my back still in contact with stone. Rock encased me. Then the crevice funneled out and the night sky flooded in on me. A tatter of wind slipped through a wind-worn hole in the granite passage, and later two separate, fancifully carven windows peered out on the narrow trail leading down to the stable. I pulled myself up and crawled through the larger of these.

On the trail, I ran.

Almost at once I came to the fenced-in paddock in front of the horses' shelter, a stable without walls. Despite the moons and the attenuated starlight, it was dark here; every shape appeared distorted, angular, unreal. Above me, in the Stonelore arena, more rifle fire barked. Echoes of hysterical laughter sounded, as did the mocking lilt and clack of the reiver's "poetry"—all of this noise incredibly tiny with distance. I was tempted to steal down the path, find my way to open country and tall grass, and circle back to Lunn. *To bring back help*, I said to myself repeatedly; *to bring back help.*

Instead, I opened the paddock gate and walked between bales of fodder that Robin Coigns had left out for his animals. Maybe he had come down here during our entertainments at Stonelore and Grotto House and carried a bale or two back to the arena for Our Shathra Anna's horses. If so, he had not returned to the paddock for a while.

One of the distorted shapes that I nearly stumbled over was not a bale of fodder; it was Gabriel Elk's own round-eyed wooly gelding. I knelt. A reiver had plunged his knife into the animal's breast and then ripped the blade upward toward its long muscled throat. The other horse, the one I had ridden to Lunn, had been dealt with similarly.

How many Pelagans had done this? What had happened to the chariot guard? Alone, I fervently wished myself back with the others.

The smell of recently spilled blood, warm and salty, commingled with that of dry fodder and the horses' last, scarcely cold droppings. These things daunted me. I trembled with nausea and night-chill. I heard Chancellor Blaine's handgun again; he could not have many shots left, unless he also wore a flush bandolier under his cloak.

Why had the Pelagans not placed men on both sides of the Stonelore arena? Had they done so, those of us emerging from Grotto House would have had little chance of getting back inside or to cover. Maybe we'd come out before they expected. Certainly, they'd been busy up until then. The chariot guard must have bought a little time for us. After slaughtering the guards and our horses (our transportation down from Elk's citadel), the reivers had crossed back to the other side to see what they could do with Coigns and the unsuspecting coachman. There could not be many of them; otherwise they'd have worked in several concerted, simultaneous assaults rather than in cautious stages. Like me, the Pelagans were amateurs—infinitely more daring and bloodthirsty maybe, but not inherently any more competent.

I stopped wondering. I stopped thinking.

If I managed to get onto the roof of the stable, I could pull myself from there to the top of the rock wall into which Elk had built Grotto House. The rock wall, though broken in a couple of spots, inscribed a rough lopsided circle around the Stonelore arena.

So I climbed. I stacked several bales of fodder and reached the stable's roof. Then I fought the wind and dizzying sky and clambered onto a rectangular ledge projecting out over the roof. From there, up to the rugged dentition of the rock wall itself. Using hands and feet alike, I edged my way between these granitic, Brobdingnagian teeth, through the unexpected drops, and over a few treacherous flat places—toward the chattering Pelagan who'd murdered Coigns' defenseless horses and the masker Josu Lief.

Something ancient had come awake in my blood. At one point, I realized that I was atop the roof of Grotto House. A useless realization. The rooms lay embedded in the stone under me like fossils buried in strata geologically unapproachable. The tapestries in the dining chamber; the electric wall panels in the foyer; the sound of women's voices. I wasn't a part of those things anymore; I was alone, skulking toward an indefinable but necessary end. The Shattered Moons accompanied me. Then, halfway around the wall I did something stupid: I stood full up and looked down into the arena.

Gareth and Coigns huddled beside the amphitheatre, Our Shathra Anna's equipage a tangle of reins and shadows and jittery horses in front of them. The ostler and Elk's son were gesticulating madly at the coachman, who had slumped down in front of his seat, keeping his head low. As I watched, they managed to attract his attention and convey to him their plan.

Then, rapidly, these things happened: The coachman jumped nervously down from the equipage. He threw open the door on the side away from me. Gareth and Coigns rushed out from the wall and hurdled into the coach, which began rocking. The coachman, shielded by the amphitheatre, slapped at the flanks of the gaudily accoutred horses, shouted at them, tugged at bridles. First a lead animal, then one in the second rank, reared in their traces; then all four of them plunged forward together, yanking the carriage out of its irritable rocking: The coachman jumped back out of the way and sidled to safety along the base of the amphitheatre's wall.

Rattling and churning, the equipage jounced toward the opening by which the Liefs and the Court Party had originally entered the arena. The two men inside had not a bit of control over where it went or at what speed, they simply kept their heads down.

A reiver fired at the departing carriage. I saw him silhouetted on the wall's rim, upright among the rocks. We were almost on eye level with each other, though fortunately he never looked my way. Fascinated, I remained where I was. I thought I could see another Pelagan crouched beside the first, staying out of sight—the profile of a hawklike head.

Because of the intervening bulk of the amphitheatre, the man with the rifle had only a moment to stop the carriage, that moment when it burst into view again on the far side. But by then the matter was out of the reiver's hands. Although not in full control of the situation, Gareth and Coigns had escaped. Our Shathra's horses, ears flattened and manes floating, hurtled toward Mershead Road.

A shot from Arngrim Blaine's handgun reminded the armed Pelagan that he could not take aim with impunity. He slumped quickly out of sight, so quickly in fact that I thought he might be wounded.

I waited.

Several minutes dog-paddled by before the glibber of the two Pelagans began taunting Gabriel again. "Ilk! Ilk! You surrender! That coach going off, it means nothing!" Then the mocking couplets, a singsong of scorn. Arngrim Blaine responded; the old man translated, shouting words that carried a taunt of their own. Back and forth, this colloquy of deprecation.

No thinking, I told myself, moving again, *deeds only.*

In another ten minutes, I'd worked my way over a broken line of wall and back into the gnarled rock. The Pelagans' voices came to me more clearly. When the poet wasn't shouting mockery, I could hear their exchanged whispers and even one man's irregular breathing. At last I could see them. I hugged a rock spire behind their natural blind and tried to still my revving heart. Looking out over the grassy highlands surrounding Stonelore, I saw no sign of the chariot guard who had allegedly taken up his watch there. The Pelagans had so thoroughly dealt with him that the landscape must have cracked open and engulfed him, chariot and all.

No thinking! I leapt down into the reivers' blind. Blood pounded viciously behind my eyes, rudely insistent. A face turned toward me, a face unlike any I had seen in Ongladred. The Shattered Moons poured light over its features and over the whole of the shape squatting to its left. The shape to the left had the rifle. I saw its glinting barrel too late. That figure I should have attacked first—not this unarmed one, with its weird, glowering mask rising up out of its own off-balance surprise to confront me. I gripped the haft of my knife and felt the knife sweep in a fluid arc up to my ear, its blade quivering a forearm's length from the face beyond it. Then, wanting a less terrible portion of the Pelagan's anatomy for a target, I pulled my knife down into his face— stabbed once—then drew back as the reiver screamed, clutched his fearsome wound, and rolled away.

—*An image of dead horses flashed into my mind.*

My weapon clattered into the rocks.

As I had done just a few minutes before, I stood upright and exposed, stupid in my immobility. The other Pelagan, his odd face somehow managing an utterly incredulous expression, began to rise. He brought his rifle up, a rifle that had thrown off sparks and noise for over thirty minutes, and all I could do was remark the clumsiness of his effort and the way the barrel shone so prettily. Could that thing kill me?

Abruptly, a shadow eclipsed the second reiver, knocked the rifle out of his hands, and bobbed nimbly away. Robin Coigns, alias Horsesweat, had jumped into the blind and disarmed my would-be assassin.

A moment later Elk followed Coigns out of the darkness, and the three of us stood looking down on the disarmed Pelagan. The one I had stabbed lay to one side, dead or dying, his face mercifully twisted away from us.

No one spoke. The nearly peaceful sound of heavy breathing droned, beneath a misleading glut of peaceful white moonlight. I was empty of whatever had moved me so violently to this place. A malarial dizziness still ran through my blood, but the menace of infection had fled.

I looked at Robin Coigns, I looked at Gareth Elk, I looked at the disarmed Pelagan. They in turn regarded me.

ix

Back in the Stonelore arena, we tried to piece the situation together. Someone had wrapped poor Josu Lief in a blanket; the women inhabited Grotto House, Our Shathra and Bethel Elk senselessly comforting the dry-eyed, virtually unperturbed Rhia.

In the arena, I had my first real chance to look at the man we had captured. He was bound. Too, since he had proven annoyingly voluble on our trip back to the arena in Our Shathra's carriage, we had gagged him with his torn undertunic, as well as bound him with it. Now the Pelagan sat in the dirt beside the luminous amphitheatre while Coigns and the coachman calmed the horses, and the rest of us huddled beside the dusty equipage, assessing and reassessing.

"Look at him," Arngrim Blaine was saying. "He isn't a man. How can you argue he's a man?"

"Despite his looks," Elk said, "he's a man very much like you, Chancellor Blaine." He paused, to add sardonically: "Or me. But perhaps more like you since the people of the archipelagoes were all originally from Atarite stock, and I must confess a background predominantly Mansuecerian. Even so, Chancellor, the man's a human being, not an animal."

"Look at him, Sayati Elk! Look at him!"

I looked at the Pelagan captive. The Chancellor had overreacted, as I had overreacted to my first glimpse of the face of the reiver I killed. It was easy to see that our captive belonged to our species, although certain minor differences in physiognomy and anatomy made it easy to pretend that an evolutionary breach had occurred.

Sitting in the dust, his knees drawn up to his chin, his head balanced sullenly there, the reiver did look human. His dark eyes followed us with the same pupil-bright disdain with which a minor court official might regard a nouveau Atarite like Ingram Marley: I knew the look. It was made bearable now by the fact that he turned it on all of us—Gabriel, Gareth, Blaine, Coigns and the coachman, as well as me. In the Pelagan's eyes, *we* were the animals, creatures undeserving of the tribute *Human*. He lifted his head from his knees and threw it back against the amphitheatre wall.

These physical distinctions existed: The captive was darker than any of us; his hair hung straight and black, over his forehead and ears. His upper eyelids had a tuck, an epicanthic fold, Elk said. In fact, the old man told us that the Pelagan's appearance would have once been seen as a physical impariment. Contradicting this assessment, however, was the reiver's abundant body hair, a sparse, ravenlike down over hands, arms, and face, but so thin on his face that only the moonlight and my own proximity made it visible. On the man I had killed, this facial down had seemed more horrifying, the sort of animalization of human features that Blaine now insisted upon. Earthly Mongoloids, Elk averred, had very seldom had much hair on their faces and bodies.

Finally, our captive had a purplish patch of skin on his throat, distinctly visible now because his head was back.

"All the people of the Angromain Archipelagoes don't look like this one," Blaine said. "I've had rocky dealings with a few of them before."

"The man I killed had similar features," I said. "Face, body hair, all of it."

Gareth affirmed this. We'd left the dead man in the rocks, not wanting to sully Our Shathra's carriage any more than was needful. "He even had a mark on his throat like this one."

"From what I've heard and seen," Gabriel put in, "this type—this quasi-Mongoloid type—isn't at all uncommon in the archipelagoes now. I've had many dealings with the Pelagans, Chancellor—more often than even you, I'd imagine—and I've seen men resembling this one more than once. The Pelagans esteem men like him," nodding at him, "because they habitually behave with daring and great resourcefulness. Many like this one assume positions of leadership."

"Because he's both cruel and murderous?"

"Archipelago life is not entirely like life in Ongladred, Chancellor; values differ."

"Obviously."

"Few Asians fed into the final population of Windfall Last," I said. "Isn't that right?"

"Yes," Gabriel Elk said.

"Then why should a people who look like Asians—the eye tuck, the dark hair, the yellow-brown skin—suddenly manifest in the Angromain?"

"It hasn't been so sudden. It's been incremental, Ingram—though what the precise origins of people like these are, who knows? Maybe the Parfects slipped an Atarite heritage into the genes of some of those penultimate Asians in Windfall Last." Gabriel Elk, quite an engineer himself, here pronounced the word with a deliberate nasality. "The descendants of some of these folks were undoubtedly among the Atarites who fled Ongladred a millennium ago. Ironic, yes?"

"Ironic?" Blaine asked, visibly peeved.

"Many of the oldest Earth civilizations were Eastern. Now, out here, eight hundred light-years from our spawning place, Asian physical characteristics have asserted themselves again."

"Albeit altered," I said.

"Yes," the old man agreed. "Altered. As everything alters, as everything changes—except ourselves." Nobody replied to that; the comment had a self-consciously sagely ring to it that Elk usually avoided. Moreover, the Parfects' big experiment on Mansueceria didn't wholly support the concept of an unchanging and unchangeable human condition. Long ago, for our own good, we had been "engineered." No one could dispute that.

We had all begun to feel the length of the day, the late-evening cold, the after-numbness of fading shock. We moved about in the arena's dust; we watched Coigns and the coachman soothing the sweaty-flanked horses, currying them with rags, talking to them. We tried to shake ourselves back into reality with random gestures and banal resolutions.

The reivers had murdered the chariot guards, just as I had earlier assumed, and their horses had more than likely pulled the empty vehicles all the way back to Lunn. This was something none of us had yet come to grips with. As was the death of Josu Lief. Coigns put the dead masker, wrapped in a borrowed blanket, into the equipage—on the seat opposite to the one on which Blaine and Our Shathra Anna would ride.

Blaine raised no protest.

Then we all came back to our captive, the Angromain barbarian who had taken part in, maybe even masterminded, the night's surreal carnage. The women remained in Grotto House, waiting for us to do something, regal in their patience; at last, all our movements came to revolve around the sullen, insolently watchful Pelagan who had nearly killed me up on the rock wall.

Out of this uncertain numbness, Elk said, "Take out his gag."

The coachman did so, stepping away as soon as the cloth was free. A film passed over our captive's eyes, he shook, his body feebly radiating its weariness. And then the man began to curse. He cursed vehemently, moving his head from side to side against the wall.

Elk seized my arm and raised his voice over the man's belligerent cursing: "This is the other one, Ingram. No style and no subtlety. You killed the poet, the one with the hair, don't you know?"

"I knew afterward."

"Did that knowledge gladden you?"

"No." I yanked my arm away. "Why should I be glad? Why should I be glad, either way?"

The Pelagan stopped cursing, drawn to our disagreement.

Elk ignored him. The old man's eyes, amid leathery wrinkles, looked into mine with rapt, unsettling focus. "You shouldn't," he said softly. "You *shouldn't* be glad, Ingram. Forgive me."

"I don't know why I did what I did," I said. "I'd never killed a man before. Something happened."

"Forget that, Ingram," Elk said. He turned to his son. "He's run out of curses, Gareth. While he's quiet, oil his wound. But, first, clean it out."

The boy moved obediently, and Blaine said, "We needn't let our mercy overflow the cup, Sayati Elk." However, he didn't try to halt Gareth's bandaging of the captive.

That man clenched his teeth while Gareth worked at his shoulder, but kept his eyes suspiciously on the boy, sometimes letting them rove to our faces as well, where they seared their suspicion and disdain into our flesh. I tried to return the man's intermittent stares; in the attempt I noticed something utterly untoward and startling in his expression. The barbarian's mouth put me in mind of Bronwen's. The dead girl shared it with the archipelago-ite, a down-tugging of one corner of her lower lip. This evident tug flawed an otherwise lovely face.

For the Pelagan was comely. Because of his epicanthic fold, the darkness of his complexion, the hair on his hands, arms, and face, he was imposingly handsome—in a rugged, exotic way that few Ongladredans ever could be. But the set of his mouth! The set of his mouth sabotaged this alien handsomeness. That he should share such a flaw with Bronwen Lief, who had danced and declaimed as Elk had programmed her to, amazed me. In the upland cold, the wind moaning through the rocks, I stared at him.

Then the Pelagan's eyes caught mine, and I looked away.

Gareth had finished with him. "Are you going to take him back to Lunn in the coach?" he asked, pulling the captive to his feet.

Blaine said, "We have a dead man there already. The widow will ride with us, but I don't want Our Shathra exposed to the corpse's presence any longer than necessary; if possible, not at all. Ingram," turning to me, "I'd like you, young Elk here, and the ostler to walk the prisoner back to Lunn, if you would. We have no horses now but those on the carriage, and this man is too ill-disposed against us to bleed to death from his wounds on our trip back. I'm sorry to ask it, but I see no other good alternatives."

"Very well," I said. I didn't relish the walk, especially in the company of a man whose stare burned so piercingly.

Elk said, "Leave the prisoner here tonight, Blaine, and send someone back for him in the morning."

"No," Blaine said. "You may well have a secure place for him in Grotto House, but I want him back in Lunn immediately. I intend to have him questioned thoroughly about the activities of other reivers and the likelihood of a concerted invasion by the entire Angromain. When? Where? How? I don't want him to escape from your custody, Sayati Elk."

"I'm not sure I want Gareth and Coigns on the Mershead Road tonight," Elk said. "They've been conscripted, yes, but their service doesn't begin until the day after tomorrow. Why should I let them go? A night is a long time, and it may be an even longer time after Gareth enters Lunn garrison before Bethel and I see him again."

Blaine protested, "Ingram can't take this man back alone!"

"No," Elk said. "And I don't propose that Master Marley go alone."

Arngrim Blaine pulled his cloak tight over his throat, crushing the lace there. His lips parted. The carnelian tooth gleamed in the gap. He sensed some Elkian maneuver he would be powerless to avert. "Please, Sayati Elk, don't toy with me tonight. What is it you want?"

"Isn't it true that you intend to cut short Master Marley's scrutiny of me and Stonelore? That you're returning him to the palace?"

"That was my intention."

"Please let him stay."

"It was my impression you considered him a barely tolerable nuisance, sir. He's been here thirteen days eating your food, sleeping in your beds, an obvious agent of Our Shathra's Eyes and Ears—and tonight you tell me you want him to stay? Why? Please enlighten me."

"The why is immaterial, Chancellor. I propose to allow Gareth and Coigns to accompany Ingram and the prisoner *if* you send Ingram back to Stonelore on the day my son and the ostler report for duty—if not before."

"For how long?"

"Until Gareth and Coigns return."

Blaine looked at me with contempt. "You want to keep this indolent dirt-runner until the Halcyon Panic breaks, the Pelagans invade, the sloak crawls up, and Ongladred sinks into the Nathlin Trench? He's been on a long sabbatical already, Sayati Elk—idling, idling every minute."

"I'll have work for him. Never fear otherwise."

And so it was decided.

Our Shathra Anna and Rhia Lief climbed into the equipage with Arngrim Blaine, and the coachman galloped the tired horses through the Stonelore arena and down to the Mershead Road. Because there was no help for it, they went unguarded—although both the coachman and the Chancellor carried rifles across their laps.

As soon as they had left, Gareth, Coigns, and I set off with our Pelagan captive, whose renewed curses required us to gag him again. Blood had welled up through the bandage on his shoulder, but the man seemed none the worse for it. "See that he's treated humanely, Ingram," Bethel Elk said to me as we, too, prepared to leave.

"Aye," her husband echoed her. "See to it."

Down from the upland arena we went on stiff legs, Wind rippled the tall grasses. The Shattered Moons flew their shadows through the wind and careened among themselves like drunken soldiers. We reached Lunn well before dawn. Robin Coigns and Gareth Elk returned at once to Stonelore, refusing beds and breakfast at the Atarite Palace. I refused only breakfast and slept a terrestrial ice age, untroubled by any nightmares of the murder I had committed.

Later, I learned that representatives of the Magi had tortured the Pelagan captive, seeking information. The man died on the second day after our trek back from Stonelore. He died without imparting one nugget of intelligence—not his name, not his dead companion's name, not the Angromain island from which they had set out, not the purpose of their reiving. Nothing. Every torture he had endured, reviling his tormentors whenever he could summon breath to do so. A heroic performance, the representatives of the Magi said. I had slept through most of it, heedless of his suffering. What would the Elks ask me when I returned?

Several days after the captive's death, when I had firmly renewed my residence in Grotto House, three fishermen found a two-man boat nine kilometers north of Mershead. It had been hidden in a cave on the shoreline cliff faces; undoubtedly, it had belonged to the men who had attacked us, killed our horses, and murdered old Lief and the chariot guards. A two-man reiving party. Together they had come at least thirty kilometers, mostly at night, in an open boat. On the side of the boat, painted in a thick indigo pigment, was a cryptic glyph, which looked like this:

X

Gabriel Elk indeed had work for me. The state had taken Gareth from him, and the spring equinox drew inexorably nearer. With its approach came the beginning of his annual series of neuro-dramas. In preparation, he put me to a strenuous apprenticeship, for I would serve as Gareth's replacement in the comptroller room beneath Stonelore. That I had little aptitude for such work Gabriel Elk refused to concede. He had need of me.

So long as no more than three reanimated maskers took part in the action in the neuro-pit, the old man required no help. But when more actors moved into the sunken "stage" from below, another comptroller had to assist him. I was to be that person. During the concentrated weeks of my training, Elk permitted me very little time to myself. I learned everything about neuro-drama that he could impart and that I could absorb.

I learned that none of his compositions required more than six performers. When operating with a full cast, he controlled three corpses and I controlled three. Neural programming before each performance took care of facial expressions and speech only; the majority of the actors' movements we had to direct remotely from beneath the neuro-pit. Stamina was required because each drama adhered to rigid Aristotelian standards of unity, and we often held our swivel chairs—amid console banks, sweat-inducing light, and closed-circuit screens—for more than two hours at a stretch. An additional burden devolved upon us because the plays also implemented pantomimic elements from an Asian form called *Noh* drama; these poses and gestures demanded an agonizing, empathic monitoring. Also, we had to control Stonelore's lighting, the pneumatic lift in the center of the working area, and the synchronization of Elk's or other composers' musical scores with the action overhead.

A vivid memory of mine from that period centers on my introduction to the dead actors. This occurred on the second day after my return to Grotto House, at the beginning of my apprenticeship.

"Come, Ingram," Elk urged. "You must shed your innocence. We can't begin work until you've seen them."

Together we went by elevator from the main level of Grotto House down into the programming room—into the rock, into the realm of cybernetic miracles. But we did not stop there. Elk guided me through one crowded vault to a massive door opening on a tunnel leading to the Stonelore comptroller room.

The tunnel, the whole subterranean meta-complex, called up in me edgy sensations of *déjà vu*—and not because I had once carried Bronwen Lief into the programming room. No, I felt as if in some indefinable past incarnation I had denied the light and entered a secret underground mausoleum resembling this one, out of which I'd emerged as pale as a dead man. Red rays lit the tunnel, and we stood for a moment in its mouth looking at the sealed comptroller room. Then we walked a few meters to a door on the corridor's right-hand wall; here Elk admitted us to the crypt-like dormitory of many dead colleagues, cohorts in Ongladred's unique repertory company.

This room breathed ice upon us.

The corpses that Elk had bought lay in white plastic coffins, *preservators*, with crystalline lids. A rank of three such units on each side of the room, a narrow aisle in between. Each one had its own self-regulating cryostat. All shared linkage with a central system of liquid-oxygen storage tanks, and these ice-touched canisters ranged like bright, upended cannon barrels against the far wall. Or like organ pipes. *Yes*, I thought, *like organ pipes*. As if each sleeping actor were listening to cathedral music in the numb privacy of his own death, forevermore plugged into the tanks' silent anthems and the seethe of unendurable cold.

I looked into the unfrosted glass of a preservator at Bronwen Lief's face. Unchanged, she slept.

I moved down the aisle.

Through the crystalline lids the faces of four men and another woman peered up at me. The masker female appeared haggard, maybe diseased. The men offered a small cross-section of the male Mansuecerian population, two being youthful, one stout and middle-aged, the fourth wizened by six or seven decades of Ongladredan winters. The neuro-theater's players.

I looked back at Elk. He told me the names of the five performers new to me, reciting about each a litany of biographical information: birthplaces, families, jobs, achievements, failures, and, finally, manners of dying.

"Did you know any of them while they lived?" I asked.

"No." He looked at me and ambiguously sighed. "But I found out as much about them as I could over the winter. I bought them all this past winter—except for Bronwen. I had to wait for her."

"You buy every winter?"

"I have to. I burn them out, Ingram. One season at Stonelore burns them out, as life rarely gets the chance to do."

"Must you program them all before the season begins and then re-program them before each new play?"

"The ones with roles often need surgical adaptation, electrode implanting, neural grafting—the last of which lets us control our performers from beneath the amphitheatre. I work hard on the ones carrying the brunt of the dramatic situation, less hard on others. Sometimes, an actor will be masked, easing my preparatory burden. Sometimes, an actor or two won't have to speak. But the work's there, it exists. Your efforts here, Ingram, will be confined to the mechanics of immediate control, as were Gareth's. I won't even try to introduce you to the other. That's my task. My hands and mind are inured to its tedium."

"And when the season ends? What's gained? And our burnt-out players," sweeping an arm over their sleek, insidiously still coffins, "what of them?"

"Cremation. The funeral of Atarites, not Mansuecerians, for in the last days of their wild, posthumous lives, they will have behaved as do people touched by fire. A death they have—then a brief, intense second life here at Stonelore—and then a second, irrevocable death. After which we put their burnt-out bodies to the torch and their smoke curls up to Maz from our autumn bonfires."

I thought of the sloak, of fires burning on every beach, inlet, and strip of coast around Ongladred. What must those tiny pyres look like from above? If the Parfects were indeed orbiting our planet amid the Shattered Moons, wouldn't they recognize the bonfires as cries for help?

Standing in Elk's cryogenic locker, I shook the thought away. "But you, Sayati Elk," I said, returning to an old question, "what do you gain?"

His pale green eyes, combining ice and fire, lifted to mine. Then he turned and walked out of the chamber, forcing me to follow.

Materially, he gained very little.

On the nights when Elk and I sat in our cramped control niches beneath Stonelore, the Mansuecerians filing into the theatre and filling its concentric tiers always "paid" for their seats, not so much from economic obligation as from a ritualistic impulse to honor Sayati Elk. No one had to give anything, but nearly every masker made a donation of three or four mithras upon entering, dropping the small coins into a large-mouthed urn beside the theatre's inner doors. Elk fed this money back to the state, which taxed him mercilessly. Or else, in the autumn and winter, he used the small surpluses remaining to him to buy new actors and to acquire materials unavailable to most Ongladredans. Genius and madman, he was neither fish nor fowl, masker nor Atarite—he bridged the social order.

He bought materials and equipment from Atarites whose wealth, station, and access to the Old Knowledge had bestowed upon them the benefits of an incipient technology, for throughout his life Gabriel Elk had striven to assemble as many bits of the Old Knowledge as he could buy, extort, or cajole from those privileged to possess it. His library in Grotto House was a tribute to this effort: forty thousand microchips, meticulously catalogued, all facsimiles of those the Parfects had given humankind when they dropped us off, like so many unwanted curs, onto our rocky, gong-tormented planet. Twice the Old Knowledge had survived the dissolution of Ongladredan civilization; twice, foresighted men who had found one another in the ruins had partially restored it. Now Elk had his share of it, and his neuro-dramas both drew upon the Old Knowledge and remade it radically. So maybe this was one of the things that Sayati Elk gained from Stonelore, the satisfaction of an omnivorous mind communing across time and interstellar distance with its intellectual forebears. But that wasn't the whole of it. After all, the process had begun with Elk long before Stonelore, and it would have gone on until his death, in different manifestations, even if the amphitheatre had never been built.

Why, then, this agonizing reanimation of dead bodies, and all the sweat and emotional stridency of control? I had no answer.

One night, during the first week of the dramas, as Elk, helmeted and wired, directed the action in the neuro-pit, I leaned back in my chair and stared with bleary eyes at my console's central screen.

There the haggard old woman and the middle-aged man acted out their parts in Elk's *Agon*—life-sized figures projected as electrons through a cathode-ray tube and reassembled on the sensitized face of my receiver as tiny parodies of themselves. They hitched and spasmed on the screen, seemingly kilometers away, even of another universe. Thin and metallic, almost garbled, their voices eked through my headset, and the spectacle grew violent as the woman brandished a temple knife and shrilly cursed her adversary.

How was our audience reacting?

With no controlling to do for another fifty or sixty lines, I turned in my chair and saw Elk across the room, his shoulders pushing forward, his arms stretched like knotted cables over his console, fingers curled about eight different switches at once and ceaselessly shifting among them. The cord-trailing helmet he wore made him resemble a stocky, bellicose medusa.

Facing my console again, I made one of my cameras scan our audience. I watched the left-hand monitor over my comptroller unit. In Stonelore's darkness, the camera scanned by means of infrared floodlighting and a quartz-lens relay. Tier after tier of masker faces, rigid beneath the gaze of the camera, and because of the continuing conscription program many of the faces belonged to women, the elderly, and the very young. I halted the camera to bring a section of the audience into startling close-up.

On my flickering screen, I studied their facial expressions. A revelation dismayingly grim, not because the maskers appeared either stern or disapproving but because their eyes and mouths betrayed no emotion. They sat, just sat, merely sat, gazing down upon our actors and partaking of Elk's surcharged dramaturgy as if it had no more magic than an indifferent daydream. Faces rigid with blandness; eyes too wide-awake and attentive to suggest apathy, but so noncommittal as to be subhuman. Indeed, I began to feel that our audience wanted reanimating more than had our dead actors, the ones who now shadowed forth Elk's vision. The dead vicariously living through the dead, our audience seemed.

But I had to go to work again. My visor came down. The pneumatic lift hoisted another actor into the arena, this one a young man under my direction. My eyes turned from the lefthand monitor to the one in the center. Watching this, I let my hands direct the movements of my protégé's hands; I wandered into his mind, activated Elk's neural tweaking of the speech centers, and withdrew. My presence was now external, a transference of will conveyed by delicate mechanical means and the aching implementation of rote memory— mine. For twenty more minutes, I sweated (eventually manipulating Bronwen as well as the young masker) while Elk deployed every one of his corpses and kept them all hitching and spasming like the decrepit primitives they were supposed to represent: a *tour de force* of comptrolling. Then *Agon* was over.

Wearily, I tilted back. My left-hand screen showed that one closed-circuit camera was still scanning our audience, relaying their images into the comptroller room as they sat unmoving and likely unmoved in the rising houselights. Again, that infuriating omnipresent expressionlessness!

Finally, they stood and, chattering softly or saying nothing at all, filed out of Stonelore into the night, a regiment of automatons. Then, the amphitheatre felt no more quiet than it had while they occupied it. I turned to Elk, who had laid his helmet aside and swiveled toward me.

"Three nights in a row, Sayati Elk. Are they always like that?"

"Yes. Often." Sweat matted his sideburns, and their lower portions curled moistly over his cheeks. With narrowed and red-rimmed eyes, he looked very old that night, every one of his sixty-three years.

"So, you're telling me, we can expect a response no more lively than what we've had these last three nights?"

Stony-gazed, Elk imperceptibly nodded.

"A brigade of automatons," I said. "Blaine's conscripted almost every man of fighting age, but we attract a brigade of automatons—several brigades—

from Lunn, Brechtlin, and Mershead. The come to Stonelore every night."

"Different ones on different nights, Ingram. And they're not, as you would style them, *automatons*."

"How judge a masker except on the basis of its behavior, Sayati Elk?"

"With the People Accustomed to the Hand, one must judge on the basis of *significant*, not just conspicuous, behavior."

I shook my head. "I don't understand, Sayati Elk; I've sweated through this with you three times and still don't understand why you do it. The money is nothing, and the maskers file out every evening as if they've just wanted a warm place to sit for two hours. It demoralizes me, sir, it guts me of purpose and initiative. Whereas you . . ." At a loss, I stuck.

"Whereas," Elk said, "I notice that they return, Ingram. No one forces them to come, but they come back—performance after performance in the spring and summer, year after year."

He stood up. "They always come back," he reiterated.

We then went about the task of securing the comptroller room and caring for our feverish performers. I worked wordlessly, only half-comprehending what he had told me and listlessly ignorant of what he had left out. We spent a lot of time pushing the mobile preservators up and down the tunnel. Later I slept, dreamlessly, only to awake anticipating a fresh new evening in the comptroller room. For, as usual, Stonelore would be full.

xi

Meantime, during the fifteen straight presentations of *Agon*, events in the outside world threatened to break in and force us out of our isolation.

The far northern coasts of Ongladred, four hundred kilometers from Lunn, had begun to suffer the first of many Pelagan naval assaults. From what we heard, these were not the hit-and-run tactics of foolhardy reivers operating singly and apparently at whim, but the early strikes of a nation testing its full-scale capacities for war. Usually, one or two large Pelagan vessels slipped through the draperies of night and wind-whipped spray to fire their cannons at a coastal village and the small ships at anchor there. The bonfires scintillating jewel-like at intervals along the coast to hold off the sloak did little but illuminate the barbarians' targets and betray the simple people who had set them.

Prows like dragons, sails like reptilian wings, banners like streaming serpents' tongues, witnesses said. Then, having wrought their sudden destruction, these ships vanished back into the night and the mocking sea wind.

But the little fishing village of Nogos, we heard, had not escaped so easily; the Pelagans had come ashore, killed most of its people in their beds, abducted maybe twenty more citizens, and fled seaward. The next day, several fishermen from south of Nogos found bodies floating in their fishing grounds; most of the corpses had been mutilated by boarnoses (shark-like creatures infesting the iciest waters of the Angromain Run). But one morning later, two or three more bodies washed up on the tide near Thumbre.

Because of their latitude and their remove from the main islands of the Angromain Archipelago, folks in the north of Ongladred had believed themselves safe from such brutality. The Atarite Court in Lunn had agreed; most of the state's forces had taken positions bordering our southern and eastern coasts, and not only because Chancellor Blaine wished to preserve Lunn over any other Ongladredan city. No. Lunn was vulnerable, that was all. And so the greatest portion of our navy lay just off the coasts where our ground troops had encamped, a defensive barrier against the Pelagan fleet. Reivers had penetrated the barrier at night, yes, but Blaine reasoned that they would have real trouble sneaking a hundred large warships past us. Now, it seemed, the Pelagans would not even try. Instead, they would sail their dragon vessels east from their own islands, away from Ongladred, circle toward polar ice, and fall upon us from the White Sea and the multicolored Angromain Run.

Two days after the devastation of Nogos, four after the first hit-and-run raids on other villages, Our Shathra Anna ordered a reprisal, dispatching seven of our galleons to strike swiftly, heavily, at Orcland, the largest island of the Angromain group and the suspected seat of the newly centralized Pelagan government.

At Stonelore, Elk and I had been readying the ninth performance of *Agon*. We worked in total ignorance of what was happening some seventy kilometers out to sea. Later we learned:

The reprisal strike had failed.

Several ships of the Pelagan fleet had intercepted our galleons more than an hour from the Orcland shore. Firing without warning, they had sunk three Ongladredan raiders, captured a ship, crippled two more, and sent the cripples limping home in the wake of our only unscathed galleon. Our enemies, it seemed, had strength, resourcefulness, and a well-developed plan to establish themselves, eventually, as masters of Ongladred.

That much we learned; little more.

By and large, Gabriel Elk ignored these developments, although on two or three occasions I managed to draw him into brief, unrevealing discussions. The only link he and Bethel recognized between themselves and the fortunes of the state was their son, Gareth. He and Coigns had been assigned away from the Lunn garrison to the infantry forces of Pavan Nils Barrow, now encamped outside the northern coastal city of Thumbre. Bethel, from all external appearances, saw this link as much more significant than Elk did; she feared for Gareth, but also feared for Field-Pavan Barrow and the people of Firthshir Province. One day she faced me stiffly, her back held erect by her brace.

"Ingram, do you think the Pelagans will land up there?"

"I don't know. But for a few reivers, they've shown real reluctance to test us down here—if that tells us anything. But the raids on Nogos and other northern villages must mean *something*, Lady Bethel."

"It's almost summer now, but it's still cold there, very like winter."

"Yes. Or very early spring."

"Gareth and Coigns have blankets and woolen coats. I hope the others are as luckily equipped." Abruptly, she left me where I sat, in Grotto House's open courtyard, absorbing the warmth of pale Maz.

During the days, Gabriel Elk left me to my own devices.

He spent most of his time reworking the lyric passages of the dramas he had composed over the winter. A little time, he spent in the programming room, forecasting the methods and equipment he would use in preparing actors for new roles. As soon as *Agon* ended, the mechanical work would begin. In the interval, he focused on perfecting the odes and a rhymed variety of stichomythia in which he often had his characters speak, parrying epigram with epigram. All I got from him was that his next two dramas completed a trilogy whose subject was "human suffering and achievement." Whereupon he grinned. First, *Agon*. Then the plays *Anabasis in Spring* and *Omega Thwarted*. The titles meant nothing to me, but Elk did let me know that the trilogy represented a new direction in his work. All I could do was nod. I had neither seen nor read these fresh neuro-dramas.

Now, as he revised *Anabasis in Spring*, I wandered about Grotto House thinking on the frivolity of *enlightening* the masker population of Lunn,

Brechdin, and Mershead while the villages of Firthshir Province burned. An enlightened masker, as far as I could see, behaved no differently from one who dwelt in deadpan ignorance. Then our fifteen reps of *Agon* concluded, and our island was growing into summer—real summer—with meadow flowers nodding yellow and blue heads among the dull upland grasses. Fifteen days we had. Then Elk and I would return to the rending, gray world of the comptroller room.

Our fifteen days off did not constitute a vacation. Although we did get to see the anaita-roses fluttering—and the little blue flowers whose name I never learned (but remembered from Rhia Lief's embroidery)—and to feel the southerly sea wind, the *maloob*, blow like invisible velvet over our skins, these respites were rare. While Elk readied corpses, I readied myself. That preparation consisted of reading *Anabasis in Spring* and studying its diagram-laden companion, a Manual of Control. This last was a bleak booklet in Elk's own tiny longhand. Like some of the flowers around Stonelore, the ink (I recall) was violet.

As summer came on, so did the rumor and the fact of Pelagan hostility. On one of these days between dramas, during new preparations, I found Elk in Grotto House's dining room and sat down beside him. "I'm afraid I'm beginning to be of Chancellor Blaine's persuasion, Sayati Elk. What we're doing, how do we justify it? I can appreciate the aesthetic experience of the neuro-dramas, or at least I can before the tedium of comptrolling blunts my nerves—but too much is happening beyond Stonelore, things of genuine moment, for me to rest easy here. I'd like to go back to Lunn, sir, to the Atarite Palace."

"Oh?" Elk leaned back in his heavy wooden chair. "What would you do there, volunteer for a seaman's post?"

"As a member of court, even as a fairly obscure dirt-runner, I'm—"

"—exempt from such demeaning service. I know, Ingram. So what'll you do while 'things of genuine moment' confront your countrymen?"

"Whatever Our Shathra and Chancellor Blaine require of me."

"Ah, duty; a fine sentiment, Master Marley." It'd been a while since he'd slapped me with "Master Marley." "For now, because Gareth's been taken from me, they require *you* to serve *Ongladred* by aiding *me*."

I heard these heavy stresses. "The two are equivalent, I suppose?"

"No, no, Ingram. I suffer from no such delusion. Besides, Arngrim Blaine doesn't equate the two. To keep you here, I intimidated him."

"Then we're back to my original question. If my service to you isn't really service to Ongladred, why do we nearly kill ourselves for an audience whose only response is to return as listless as it left? What are we *doing*?" I had to pin the old man down.

"Service is of different types, Ingram, and some types lie outside the stagnant pale of nationalism and duty. This is one such type. What we're doing, though, I won't try to tell you, for I'm a selfish old man, Ingram. *Selfish* and *old*, those are the key words. And if I'm deluded at all, it may be in assuming my selfishness a nobler service to Ongladred than would be a dutiful renunciation of my self. At least for now. This, like all things, may change."

And so we ignored the continuing depredations in the north; we forgot the fragrance of the anaita-roses, the freshness of the maloob blowing inland across a summer ocean.

Here is a summary of that time: The Ongladredan fleet overextended itself trying to set a defensive line across the coasts of Firthshir, Vestacs, and Eenlich provinces; Elk and I, near the end of our fifteen-day preparation period, gave up big chunks of sleep time, courting exhaustion. Galleons burned. My morale sank. Rumors of impending invasion reached us via the tinkers and trades-boys who often stopped at Grotto House. In my sleep, I saw Stonelore filling with maskers who wore, under vacant faces, tunics thus emblazoned:

Then, with only token resistance, the Pelagans landed an army of eight thousand men in Eenlich; on the evening of that day, Elk opened Stonelore for the first performance of *Anabasis in Spring*. Just as the Angromain barbarians had committed themselves in the north, we too had gone past the point of abjuration. Two improbable enterprises had been set in motion, the Pelagans' and ours.

"How like you the title of my play now?" Elk asked me. "I'm a prophet in my own land, unhonored and indifferent to my neglect. The Pelagans, your erstwhile brothers, quasi-Atarites, march upon us. And my play predicts it."

"Pillars crumble. People die. And we—"

"—*fiddle*. Is that the word you're looking for? Remember this, Ingram: Gareth's up there in Firthshir, with Barrow's forces."

I turned away. So he was aware, coldly aware of the situation. Why, then, our singlemindedness in putting on a neuro-drama, in running corpses through an intricate, unreal series of events? Apparently, Elk had his own satisfactions; I had only the sweat. My back to the old man, I looked at the left-hand monitor.

Our audience was filing in.

"People die," Elk said, talking to the back of my head. "But not these. They still live." I could feel his eyes fixed on my monitor. Together we watched the audience come in: women, children, old men, cripples of every conceivable sort: the bent, the legless, the scarred, the humpbacked, even the blind. All of them People Accustomed to the Hand, maskers who had come to Stonelore for undivulged reasons of their own.

Then Elk swiveled, faced his own control console, signaled that we were about to begin. I put on my helmet, turned a dial, and plunged the amphitheatre into darkness. The sweat, the sweat of comptrolling.

And that night Elk and I, working begrudgingly together, orchestrated a fine performance of *Anabasis in Spring*. The poetry came through my headset; the alternating grace and clumsiness of our actors poured into me like haoma. I was a part of Elk's poetry, a part of our actors' movement. The sweat of comptrolling turned into the sweat of participation.

In the neuro-pit above us, two dead men discuss the cycle of the sloak; I am both dead men, two young soldiers. Then the corpse of the haggard woman enters, now inhabited by Gabriel Elk. She is masked like a demon, enormous and dreadful in spite of her tiny bones and frail gestures. To the soldiers, she is an apparition, a minion of hidden powers. In a long, image-crowded speech, she tells them the sloak is real, that it does the bidding not of its own protoplasmic desires but of a watchful intelligence external to itself—an intelligence vastly more alive than Humanity's but different in kind. She dances while she speaks, and her huge, one-eyed mask seems to float between her upraised arms like a kite to which her thin, twisting body is the knotted tail. As the accompaniment of tabor and flute grows more insistent, her head—her leering mask—threatens to pull her aloft, lift her into soaring flight. But the music stops, her speech ends, and she plunges into death's eternal underworld. The two soldiers whom I inhabit stare after her in awe and consternation.

That scene, even in the observation of *Elk's* comptrolling, wrung me of energy. And there were other such scenes.

Anabasis in Spring dealt not only with the threat of the sloak, but also with the problems of command in an army always on the march. It was not prophecy, as Elk had said it was, because one could not help feeling that the sloak and the army in this neuro-drama existed in a totally distinct realm of experience, another world; everything was distanced, set at a remove—in spite of which the actions and feelings of the characters had an uncanny immediacy.

Still, though overwhelmed by the poetry and the detail Elk had lavished on this spectacle, I knew that it wasn't real. What relation did it have to reality? To the sloak and to the Pelagan forces? The genuine sloak, the true invaders? So absolutely powerful in Stonelore, Elk and I were ironically powerless in the face of these threatening certainties. Was Elk withdrawing into prophecy, abandoning the real for the sake of artificial order and contrived significance? He had said no. He had said that I ought to remember the dilemma of his son, which he had not forgotten either—which he could *not* forget.

Wrung out, I pushed my visor back and remembered nothing, thought nothing. The sweat of comptrolling, the sweat of participation, lay dry on my skin. Elk stood behind me, his big hand on my shoulder. Together we watched the maskers file out: the women, the children, the old men, the crippled and the deformed. Their faces mirrored the dullness of the underside of a leaf; their eyes were the wicks of guttered candles. Only a few of them talked.

"Nothing," I said. "Nothing."

We presented *Anabasis in Spring* on three more evenings. Then stopped—but not because of this lack of any discernible response. No. Events intervened, events and Our Shathra Anna. Against history and royalty, Gabriel Elk ultimately had no more resources than did a poor masker. And, on the following morning, history and royalty came to Grotto House in the person of Chancellor Arngrim Blaine.

PART TWO

xii

His roan tooth oddly like a miniature tusk, Chancellor Blaine said, "The Halcyon Panic has broken, Sayati Elk. And your neuro-dramas have been instrumental in destroying our citizenry's calm." Like ripening bruises, anger lay under the planes of his thin face.

"Obviously you haven't come to a neuro-drama this year," I said. We were sitting in Elk's quiet little study on the main level of Grotto House; the room held leather-bound books—not microchips, but books. Both Gabriel and Bethel Elk sat with us, in adjacent, scrupulously carven chairs.

Bethel said, "The people know about events in Firthshir, don't they?"

"They do, ma'am."

"How, then, can you blame their distress—the breaking of the panic, as you call it—on Gabriel's plays, not a one of which you've seen in its entirety? The Lief girl's performance doesn't count."

"Because things have come to a head far too soon; the misdirected rage the young women of Lunn have shown these last two days comes well ahead of schedule. It defies the computations of the Magi."

Gabriel Elk said, "But then again, Chancellor Blaine, the Pelagan invasion has also taken place sooner than the Magi expected."

"And the rage of young Mansuecerian women, the wives of our soldiers and seamen," Lady Bethel said, "has been growing for ages—since well before the Magi decreed the existence of a 'Halcyon Panic.' It's the product of a long-ingrained and often aggravated sense of helplessness, which *I* feel too."

"I don't doubt that. However, Our Shathra—who is also a woman, as I shouldn't have to remind you—says that the 'sense of helplessness' you allude to need not reveal itself in hysteria and acts of vandalism."

"Our Shathra Anna's experience has hardly been typical."

A chill descended upon the study, a dust of invisible snow sifting out of the air. We were all as separate as corpses in sealed, sound-muffling preservators. Who would resurrect us?

I looked at Blaine, sitting cross-legged opposite me. He had dressed not as the Chancellor of Ongladred, nor even as a member of the Atarite Court, but like a mildly successful masker tradesman. Two young guards had accompanied him, posing as his sons. All these precautions had grown out of his wish to prevent a visit as disastrous as Our Shathra Anna's last one. And yet the Chancellor had come in person, as himself. He had not sent a representative.

Coolly he said, "Two days ago—the day after your newest production had opened, Sayati Elk—a group of women left Lunn, marched out Mershead Road, and began turning over vegetable booths and fish stalls. But only those tended by masker tradesmen exempted from military service or by minor Atarite officials. Nothing could stop these angry lasses."

"Then," Elk said, laughing, "you might have chosen a wiser disguise."

Blaine ignored this. "That night a pack of children—turned loose by their mamas, no doubt—ran into the boulevard beneath my offices and began chanting a litany to Maz, asking Him to blow Himself up and Ongladred, too, so that we might at least die in the light." The Chancellor offered a wan satiric smile. "We had no success catching the children or driving them away; the ones the guards did catch were quickly replaced by others, all crying together, 'Maz, Maz, destroy us in light. Preserve us from the slime of the sloak and the knives of barbarians. Let the Lie die.' A litany drummed into them by furious women."

"Your sleep was spoiled," Bethel Elk commiserated.

"Oh, that episode has its amusing aspects; I'm not blind to them. But that same night some hysterical person, or group of persons, lit a row of dwellings on Lunn's southwestern outskirts afire. The houses burned, and several people died, including children, Mistress Elk. A violet pall of smoke hung over the rooftops, quite lurid under the Shattered Moons, I assure you. And yesterday the wail of keening women issued from every house from dawn until long after nightfall, a wide lamentation the likes of which I've never heard in Lunn. Then yesterday—since the keening by no means ends the matter—a procession of *old* women, as many as two hundred, walked all the way from Lunn to Brechtlin, on the point opposite Mershead, and disrobed on the beaches. After that, they waded into the sea until their strength failed and they drowned. These were widows, unmarried women, grandmothers. None of the Mansuecerian population tried to stop them. That they be left alone seemed the unspoken desire of even their relatives. We sent a few Atarite guards to turn them back, but the women would not be reasoned with—and simple coercion failed, from want of enough men to restrain them. Into the water they went, naked pathetic creatures obeying a hysteria beyond comprehension. Even now they are being buried, the known and the unidentifiable washed-ashore corpses alike. And these things—the arson, the keening, the suicides—betoken the depth of our citizenry's fear."

A different kind of silence entered then. Arngrim Blaine had reasserted his dignity. The four of us sat there, self-conscious, in its palpable aura. At last Bethel said, "And you believe that *Agon* and *Anabasis in Spring* are responsible for these dire responses, Chancellor?"

"In part, yes."

"I'd like to think you are right," Elk said.

"May I ask why?" said the Chancellor, clearly pained.

"Certainly. Everyone requires a degree of power, no matter how minute."

"Of this sort? Power to cause suicides and provoke arson?"

"If one is weak, yes. However, I am not weak, and that's not what I need in the way of power. I see in these behaviors—this hysteria—the potential for something constructive, a germ of constructiveness that I would like to think my neuro-dramas help nourish. In all the negative acts of these last three days there runs a thin, affirmative thread."

"Very thin." The Chancellor's lips hardly parted.

I said, "The best explanation for this behavior is not the neuro-dramas, but the news from Firthshir."

"That figures prominently," Blaine said. "I don't dismiss it. In fact, I ought to note that the Pelagan forces have pushed out of Firthshir into Eenlich Province, driving Field-Pavan Barrow's army before them." He paused. "There's no word of casualties. As far as I know, Gareth and Coigns still live. On that point I can say no more, for I know no more.

"Messages have described the retreats as 'strategic,' but we are in fact losing ground daily. Fields are being burned, early crops ruined, farm animals slaughtered, and villages overrun and then abandoned. The enemy supplies itself at our expense. This is changing, though. A runner from Pavan Barrow reports that our folk destroy any goods that may be useful to the Pelagans. The procedure now is burn and fall back, burn and fall back. We want to force the barbarians to be dependent on their own supply lines—in the hope that we can establish an unmoving front and interdict at sea, destroy their own naval logistics system. But their troops receive reinforcements almost three times a week, and we estimate an invading army of almost twenty thousand. If they continue to advance at twelve to fifteen kilometers a day, they will soon reach Lunn, and Ongladred will fall."

"Why have you come to Stonelore to tell us these things?" Bethel asked. "Surely, Chancellor, you don't hold the neuro-dramas responsible for the Pelagan invasion?"

"No, Mistress Elk, I don't." He turned to her husband. "Do you remember the talk we had here at Grotto House after Bronwen's recital, before the reivers murdered her father?"

"I do. You don't plan to offer me the command of a Mansuecerian vessel again, do you?"

"No. That's not the portion of the talk I'm referring to."

"Then which?"

"You and Gareth argued strongly that societies fail when their leaders fail. You cited inflexibility as the most dangerous sin of command."

"Yes, I remember."

"And do you remember that Our Shathra told you that one day you'd have to include yourself among Ongladred's leaders?"

"Yes, that too—more or less. But we also made a distinction between intellectual and political leadership."

I almost laughed, but Blaine was maneuvering craftily, as if born to the Socratic method. Fascinated, I watched him do so. Elk, his hands on his knees, was also a man ensnared in spite of himself.

"Distinctions such as that blur," the Chancellor said, "when the enemy puts boots on our own soil. See me here before you," spreading his hands self-deprecatingly, "I'm trying to bend. Our Shathra bids me remind you that in these times we must all bend, especially the leaders among us. If you feel Ongladred is worth saving, for its own virtues or in preference to the barbaric code that would supplant ours, you too must bend, Sayati Elk. You must—"

"Stonelore will immediately close, Chancellor."

And Blaine stopped talking, cut off in mid-harangue. I, too, was surprised; Elk had said nothing to me about discontinuing the neuro-dramas. He had not even hinted at it. Of course, he had only just decided himself, it was his

own preemptive strike—a way to regain the initiative. And yet he struck out
of belief, not from wounded pride or insecurity; that his decision nonplussed
the Chancellor merely increased his cold delight in affirming a conviction.
Elk leaned back; his hands lifted from his knees.

"Good," Blaine said. "That was easier than I expected."

"I don't do it to please you, but because Ongladred is threatened and I am
no fool. I had hoped that Field-Pavan Barrow and our ships in the channel
would save me such a decision, but that's past recall now—a dead hope. The
news you've brought tonight, Chancellor, wounds and frightens me, a man
almost too inured to pain and too old to get very frightened anymore. And
for that reason, Stonelore closes."

"But what else does the Chancellor wish?" Lady Bethel asked. "Will you
place Gabriel in command of a galleon?"

"No. That would be too little, Mistress Elk, a misapplication of talents.
Our Shathra wants something more."

"A weapon," Gabriel Elk said.

Again. Blaine looked surprised, almost incredulous. He uncrossed his
legs and set them straight out before him. "Yes," he said. "An unconventional
weapon, something that can be developed in twenty days or less, easily
transported, and deployed in the field."

Elk laughed, a sardonic yawp. I started, so unexpected was it. Then he
folded his hands in his lap and assessed them like a sculptor taking mental
notes. "A weapon," he mused.

"That's principally why we want Stonelore closed," Blaine said, "so you
can devote time to this project—although I believe that secondary benefits
will accrue, the foremost among them being the return to calm of Lunn's
populace. Our Shathra Anna wishes you to begin at once. Will you?"

"Why not put your Atarite scientists to work on this, Chancellor? They
have the Old Knowledge, the materials, the technological capacity—or at
least its potential." Elk clasped his hands. "Why trek out here to ask me to
accomplish this pretty little enormity?"

"We have the technological capacity to do all you've done, Sayati Elk.
We also have the materials, the physical resources. It's the psychic capacity
that we lack. Were it not for this inhibition, an inhibition programmed
into us by the Parfects thousands of years ago, the People Touched by Fire
would have created self-propelled carts, atomic-driven ships, mechanized
communication systems, vehicles that fly—all these we would have developed

long ago. The knowledge is there, but we don't let ourselves use it. We are inhibited, psychically inhibited, and even our recognition of this fact doesn't cure us, Sayati Elk. In this case, self-awareness *isn't* power. We've heated and lighted the Atarite palace, and a number of Atarite lords have done the same with the houses on their estates—but beyond that we haven't ventured, we haven't *wanted* to venture. What you have done at Stonelore and Grotto House doesn't confound our intellects, it confounds our sense of propriety, mocking something innate and immovable in our natures. And so we've come to you, sir. Those are our reasons. Understand?"

"Yes. I'm an aberration."

"That's a pejorative I would not have used. Please don't attribute it to me. What I mean is that you're not inhibited in the way of either those Accustomed to the Hand or those Touched by Fire. Your aggressiveness is intellectual as well as physical."

I said, "You're Ongladred's superman, sir, Zoroaster's *übermensch*."

Ignoring this, Elk said, "The Parfects re-created Man in a strange, divided image, Chancellor Blaine. They didn't want us killing ourselves, but they didn't want us dying, either. Mansuecerians. Atarites. A divided people struggling as one to subdue Ongladred. Then, a thousand years ago, we divided again, and what the Parfects tried to provide against is happening once more. We're killing one another, but, even as we do, we excuse ourselves on the grounds that it isn't yet genocide, the extinction of the species. Neither the Pelagans nor the ruling order in Ongladred has essayed a genocidal weapon; something in our shared unconscious won't allow the attempt. And yet today, Chancellor, you ask me to commit myself to the development of the first such horror on the road to just that end, the power to destroy utterly, without mercy or discrimination."

"Because you have the skill," Blaine said. "And the temperament."

"The *temperament!*" Lady Bethel cried.

"Why, yes. The temperament that conceived and raised the miracle of Stonelore out of the dust of this upland arena."

"Come now, Chancellor. Your language apotheosizes Gabriel."

"Its intention is the opposite. It's because Sayati Elk is more 'human' than we that we ask this of him."

"My difference from those in the Atarite Court," Elk said, "is not so great that it frees me from the scruples of our shared unconscious."

Arngrim Blaine pulled his tradesman's clothes together, smoothed out the wrinkles in his breeches, and stood. "Then I'll tell Our Shathra that although Stonelore is closing, you cannot bring yourself to do something no Atarite will attempt." I was impressed by Blaine's fairness; he might have said something as self-serving and crass as "cannot bring yourself to save Ongladred," but he had refrained. Conscience had prevailed.

"Sit down," Elk said. "Tell Our Shathra Anna that in twenty days—with the help of Atarite lords who can supply me with information and materials—I will deliver what she wishes."

Blaine sat back down. "You have the complete cooperation of the court, Sayati Elk."

"Then I must also have your promise to return the weapons to me when we have defeated the Pelagans. The weapons will be small and deadly—but in themselves will fall mercifully short of any doomsday weapon. Still, I want your word that after our victory, the weapons will come back to me—without fail."

"You have it, Sayati Elk."

"Then let's stop talking and have a drink. Ingram, please serve us."

I got up and went down the hall to the kitchen. I could not believe that the evening would not find Elk and me helmeted, wired, and perspiring in our swivel chairs. Before returning to the study, I had a solitary sip of haoma and let several scenes of *Anabasis in Spring* play through my mind. I would never see them again, except in my imagination. Somehow, that struck me—for reasons I refused to deeply consider—as a poignant loss.

That evening, we turned away a crowd of masker women, kids, and old men, saying that we had closed the amphitheatre. Unprotesting, they re-trod the upland grasses, tramped down to the Mershead Road, and returned in virtual lockstep to their homes, to tell their friends the news.

xiii

The next day Gabriel Elk began work. He used the facilities in the programming room under Grotto House. Bethel handled the correspondence that the project required, writing letters in her small, looping hand and sealing them with purple wax and the impress of Chancellor Blaine's ring. I carried the letters. To the homes of the landed Atarites, to the offices of our scientists, I rode. Always I returned to Grotto House; and soon wagons of materials—chemicals, metals, precious stones, boxed unknowables—began rattling up into the dusty arena and dropping off their cargoes. Often, men whom I didn't know arrived with stern or expressionless faces, vanished into the programming room, stayed a day or two, then emerged and departed, not to be seen at Grotto House again. Ten days passed. If not for the Pelagan invasion, I thought, we would have just concluded our second neuro-drama and begun preparations for the third.

Omega Thwarted. Appropriate title. I'd not even read the play, had no idea what sort of end it would mark to Elk's trilogy or which corpses he had hoped would carry the burden of its theme. For now, they all lay inviolately frozen in their preservators, darkness and ice weaving about them a smoky, blue shroud. In my dreams, their cold faces grew fine, web-like coverings of hair, their eyes all narrowing—until each one strangely resembled the reivers who had attacked us so many nights ago. I then awoke to our nightmare in the north.

Field-Pavan Barrow's forces had begun to slow the Pelagan advance— but the countryside through which they retreated, burning what our people had built or planted, stretched off to the White Sea like a desert of ash. So our runners said. Firthshir, Eenlich, and Vestacs provinces had all transmogrified into the Fields of Astivihad—diseased deathscapes in which charred tree trunks and unfilled graves lay desolate and no birds broke the silence with their songs. At sea, several more of our galleons had been sunk, and even in Lunn we could feel the breaths of an animalish people, hot and rank, on our faces. The enemy was only a little more than a hundred kilometers away, momentarily stalled. Or so our runners told us and so we hoped. . . .

The fighting continued. Even young Atarite men were going to the front (those who could command were already there), and, at any hour, I expected to hear my own summons. At times I wished for it, so futile and ignoble did my own privileged role seem. What was Elk doing? Though I slept in his house, I seldom could talk to him. At the front, there would be continuous conversation of a lethal kind, the bass imperatives of cannon and the high-pitched yawping of rifles. Old, damn-near falling-to-pieces Yorkley rifles.

What kind of advantage would Elk's handiwork give us?

On the sixteenth day after Arngrim Blaine's second visit to Stonelore, two empty, closed wagons arrived at the arena. Elk directing, we spent the morning and all afternoon toting equipment out of the programming room to the wagons. Up and down in the elevator, back and forth through the stone corridor. I worked with four masker menials, ill-formed men who had not been inducted; I struggled to preserve my dignity before them, sometimes attempting to lift more than I was able. Not long past, hadn't I come from these people?

Elk and I rode horseback (on creatures sent by the Atarite Court, animals that Elk eventually bought outright) beside the wagons on our way to Lunn. At sunset, we reached the Atarite Palace and drove through the cobbled court to its white-stone recreation building. Here we unloaded our materials, setting them up in the vast athletic hall exactly as Elk told us. Once, in passing, the old man said, "Your fire-touched friends will have to forego their genteel pellet-ball and fencing for a day or two, Ingram."

The hall was fiercely lit, electric torches rippled with the energy coursing into them, and the palace (as far as I could tell, outside, from its draped windows) was almost dark by comparison—as if the recreation hall were draining some of its power away. Before we finished unloading, Arngrim Blaine came out of the palace and approached the hall; he approached with two of the men who had been to Grotto House during the early stages of Elk's work. For the first time, their faces wore looks of ill-disguised excitement.

The wagons rattled away. In the shadow between two great buildings, we five men conferred. Blaine said, "Master Gordon and Sayati Snow have told me nothing about this enterprise, Gabriel, except that it progresses. Does it?"

"No further, I hope, than it has already."

"What have you made?"

"A photon-director, which I've developed, not made. The Old Knowledge preserved for us by the Parfects contains raw, deliberately cryptic 'descriptions' of the instrument and an abstract of its theory, including a list of applications, all of which are benign, from precision measurement to healing retinal lesions."

"Then ... ?"

"Don't fear, Chancellor. I haven't been working these last sixteen days to create a machine of mercy. The Parfects told us nothing at all about how to kill one another by such a device. But the information's there for minds astute enough to see it." Elk spoke as if each word scalded him. "Astute enough," he reiterated. "And *flexible* enough. In times such as these, flexibility is a cardinal virtue."

"And genius," the Chancellor said, sensitive to Elk's tone. And between Blaine's parted lips, the carnelian gleam of his little tusk, a knife of discolored bone. And then his lips wetly joined.

"Genius is a hag that flies in the heart," Elk said. "This was different, this was a toad, squatting there."

"But it works?"

"It works. Master Gordon and Sayati Snow will demonstrate it for you in the morning, Chancellor. At first light."

"They know how to operate this . . . *photon-director?*"

"Yes. And they aided me immeasurably in their construction—there are three, you see. Three photon-directors. Apparently, the Atarite inhibition against conceiving and developing an advanced weapon doesn't extend to mechanical matters like assembly and use, Chancellor."

"It's been told that I have Pelagan ancestors," said Sayati Snow, a man of my own age, a mathematician and abstruse theorist. His smile startled me.

"And I," Master Gordon said, not smiling, "don't like being ruled by enzyme tags, plastic viruses, rebuilt chromosomes, or any such. So I help with this." Gordon was an artisan, a dark, stocky man with violet eyes.

"At first light, then," Blaine said. He led the others to their rooms in the palace, and I found my gloomy bachelor quarters, deserted now since long before spring (with the exception of the nights I'd spent there after bringing the Pelagan captive in from Stonelore), two rooms in the low building opposite the recreation hall. Amid its odors of musty quilts and stale air, I slept.

At first light, Gordon and Snow demonstrated one of the photon-directors in the hall. Elk stood aside, with the Chancellor and me, and watched. While his terrible streamlined machine burned holes of various shapes and sizes in several distinct target materials against one wall of the building, Elk held forth:

"The old name was laser," he said. "Oddly enough, it was built on Earth *after* the weapon that twice—in Holocausts A and B—leveled the civilizations of our ancestors. That the Parfects chose to hint at its existence suggests that they looked upon it as a device chiefly beneficial. *Necessarily*," he said, making the word sound evil, "we will pervert it to our own ends."

Sayati Snow triggered the device and a beam of ghastly red light shot through the hall to burn a hole in a cuirassed effigy suspended from the ceiling. Gordon turned a small wheel on the side of the machine's casing and manually directed the beam to inscribe a valentine on the cuirass' left breastplate. When he had finished, a heart-shaped plug of bronze smouldered there. For a long time the plug did not fall, as if the metal did not realize that it had been severed from its own curved matrix, the torso of a hay-filled warrior. This inscription the photon-director made *without* setting the straw man afire. Then, realizing its separateness from the cuirass around it, the plug fell and rang hollowly on the stone floor. Then Sayati Snow triggered the device again and a brief stream of ruby light ignited the effigy, which burned madly, and the breastplate, no longer supported, dropped to the floor with a hot clang of its own. Elk, Blaine, and I could still feel the heat the machine had generated and the scalding backwind of the ruined dummy.

Then, after a time, Blaine: "And these will save us?"

"Unless the Pelagans are more cunning monsters than we," Elk said. "So please send Master Gordon and Sayati Snow, with photon-directors, to the front. Post each man on a flank of Pavan Barrow's line of defense. Ingram and I, with the third device, will board a warship to the northern run—to halt the barbarians' supply fleet."

"Why not a direct assault on Orcland and the Pelagan capital?" Chancellor Blaine asked. "That would be surer than trying to intercept the supply fleet in the White Sea fogs. With one vessel and a dubious weapon."

"Far from dubious, Chancellor. I'm requesting two escort ships in addition to the man-o'-war carrying the machine itself. As for the *lasers*, they're to be used only defensively."

"And returned to you?"

"And returned to me."

"Very well, Sayati Elk."

That afternoon, accompanied by a guard of Atarite retainers, Gordon and Snow left Lunn for the northern provinces. Elk and I rode in an unguarded wagon to the port of Brechtlin and there, as two old masker stevedores carried our boxed weapon aboard the warship *Paradise*, watched the landward gulls flashing wings in the day's last light. Then a sailor pointed out to us the stretch of beach where the wives, widows, grandmothers, and spinsters from Lunn had waded into the uncaring water and drowned themselves.

xiv

We sailed in the morning. Around the southeastern cape of Ongladred we went, passing the village of Mershead and picking up an escort of two armed galleons. The weather was good, a late maloob blew from the south, and our sails bellied out like linen-shirted paunches. For fifty kilometers, we followed Ongladred's coast, staying within the line of defensive warships positioned ten kilometers off the land at intervals permitting each captain to see the vessels on his flanks; then we swept out into the Angromain Channel and journeyed northward as a trinity of solitary freelancers, glorified reivers, our task the crippling of our enemy's supply lines, a task we would have to perform amid an archipelago not of rocky, knife-edged islands but of shiny, tabular icebergs, all perilously in movement. Through the Angromain Run we sailed, into the cliff-littered White Sea.

On this trip, Elk taught me how to aim, activate, and control the beam of the photon-director, which we had mounted on the raised forward deck of the *Paradise*. I spent two hours one afternoon burning holes in the improvised sails of a dinghy being dragged at a safe distance behind one of our escort vessels; then I sank the dinghy, setting both its sails and hull ablaze. The sailors on the *Sea Drake* cut the boat's tow line and waved cheerily at me. I may have grinned. The maskers at Stonelore had never reacted with half the effusiveness of the seamen; not once. Those on the *Mandragora*, our other escort, fired a cannon. How much more powerful than this could one feel, I wondered.

"Good, Ingram," Elk said. "Soon you'll deploy against the Pelagans."

"Me? Why not you, Sayati Elk?"

"I've done enough, Ingram. This is for you."

We did not talk about how Snow and Gordon were faring, nor about how the forces of Field-Pavan Barrow were acquitting themselves. These were things beyond our control. We hoped only that the Pelagans had not altered their manner of supplying their own forces and that we could intercept them in the White Sea. And, although we did not talk about the land war, it was not hard to see that Elk often thought of it. In more than one sense, his blood struggled in that conflict, striving to honor itself and to pulse for its nation— even though Elk and his son were driven more by abstract ideals than by any zealous nationalism.

The wind continued brisk, and, on our third evening at sea, we entered

the southernmost reach of the Angromain Run, that corridor of indigo-
and vermilion-shot water between Ongladred's northern coast and the
overarching scorpion's tail of the barbarian archipelago. Most of these islands
are little more than rocks, and uninhabited. Of our voyage into this region,
I principally recall the bitterness of the night air and, off to port, the small,
pearl-like fires burning on the coast. These were intermittently visible when
a jut of land, like the nub of a giant finger, poked out accusingly from our
nation's usually unobtrusive shore. Parallel to Firthshir Province's eastern
coast, we saw no more fires. The enemy had let them go out—apparently, they
didn't fear the sloak, or had forgotten about it, or (the most likely alternative)
had too few men to keep the fires going.

But even without the coastal bonfires, the *Paradise* sailed on a mirror
surface of rich dark light; the Shattered Moons lit the Angromain Run as if
it were a floor of marble and swirled the icy water with deeper indigos, more
elusive vermilions. Was it really true that in the wake of the Pelagan advance
our country was becoming a gutted ash pit? At sea, it didn't seem possible;
the moonlight had an aurora-like brilliance and the very air sparkled. At
night I spent as much time as I could abovedecks, just to see these things—
the immemorial wheeling of stars, water, and curdled satellites.

"The moons are brighter out here," I told Elk on that night.

"Several of them are decoys," he said.

"How do you know that, sir?"

"The Parfects carried us here six thousand years ago, eight hundred light-
years from Earth. One of the Shattered Moons, perhaps the minutest shard,
is an instrument of observation, data-accumulation, and relay—the Eyes and
Ears of the neo-humans who sought to re-engineer their own progenitors.
Humanity was given genes for morality. You and I are integers in a modestly
cosmic experiment, Ingram, and so the Parfects have a small vested interest
in us—they would have wanted to see how their experiment turned out and
made provision for monitoring this hemisphere of Mansueceria, at least."

"But how do you—?"

"There's more. They would have wanted a way to interfere in our affairs,
to alter the balance of historical forces in Ongladred. Their satellites among
the Shattered Moons also fulfill those purposes."

"Robin Coigns once said he thought the Parfects would return to repair
our botched world at the sloak's third coming. Surely, you don't believe that."

"No. One property we can't lease out is the equivocal terrain of our fates."

"An epigram," I said. with a cruel inflection that surprised even me.

"If you like, Ingram. But true for all that. In spite of the Parfects, we're alone, and also accountable."

"But these instruments in the sky, the Eyes and Ears of the Parfects, how can you be so certain they exists? What proof have you?"

Elk, looking into the scrolling, night-darkened sails, grinned like a sly boy. "Faith. Simple faith, Ingram." And retreated to his own private cabin.

On our fourth morning, we rode the White Sea, traveling northwest out of the Angromain Run. Because we had no idea into which of the many fjords at the top of Ongladred the Pelagans were running supplies, our small fleet stood well out to sea and waited. Eventually, our enemy's hideous ships must sweep down the arc of the Angromain's scorpion's tail and show themselves—or else, for want of provisions, they would soon have fed their hunger on ash and gunpowder. Several kilometers from the coast, we tacked about and faced to the east, our three vessels now strategically placed to cover the wide, white mouth of water out of which the Pelagan ships must sail, dragon-prowed and sinister. Evil was the word I thought, knowing that Elk would have smiled at my meager imagination.

We had nothing to do but wait. Nothing but wait and watch the icebergs drift down from Mansueceria's polar cap, like hermetically sealed, buoyant cities of crystal. Or like imperturbable monsters of glass. We saw five icebergs on our first day of waiting, none so close that it posed a danger to the *Paradise* but all near enough to incite wonder. The closest to us had inlets and firths like an island, although its sides rose up from the water so steeply that none of these afforded a landing place; an eerie sucking noise roared in the iceberg caves as the sea rushed in, and a reverberant echo trailed each guttural cry. The ice itself was a thousand different colors, mostly shades of blue that purpled the water beneath the iceberg and, as evening drew on, turned the sky behind it a brittle cobalt. Maz went down early; but not before this nearest leviathan calved, groaning thunderously as her birth pangs tore the berg apart. Another night to wait, but our first night to worry about striking the progeny of a fecund, multicolored ice-creature. Captain Chant had seen service in the White Sea before, and so we survived the night.

The fifth morning hailed us with cottony fog banks, all rolling down from the archipelago's last few islands. The *Sea Drake* and *Mandragora* disappeared, faded off into the thickening gauze—like phantoms becoming invisible once more. Thus enshrouded, we were made a bobbing universe to ourselves. Now we feared the icebergs would demolish us or, worse, the Pelagans would glide past us in the murk. Again, we could only wait, muffled in hanging fog. Maz was a wan dream on the other side of our anxiety, and fog dropped down from the masts and spars like a ghostly moss. Then night fell, a night that sealed us into ourselves. All that reminded us of the worlds beyond our own was the intermittent ringing of the *Sea Drake*'s and the *Mandragora*'s ships' bells. These notes, blurred by the fog, drifted to us like parachutes of iron sound. Where did they come from? How did they reach us? And then I realized that the *Paradise* had a bellman of its own, that he was on the forward deck (by Elk's canvas-covered machine), and that our bell, too sometimes sent out peals of hollow warning.

"Aren't we just giving ourselves away?" I asked a masker seaman on the *Paradise*'s main deck.

"Oh, the bell. Perhaps. But it's better than banging against our sister ships, and the Pelagans have likely ceased to run, to let the soup blow off. They've got fellows with passable heads, too, you know."

I said: "Our bells won't keep the icebergs off. The bergs don't listen."

"If we bump we bump, sir. It may mean giving up a sail or two, but we'll pull her by. So, too, the *Drake* and the *Mandragora*."

His confidence was pleasant but not contagious. I went belowdecks and tried to sleep.

XV

On the sixth morning the fog began to shred—into a series of staggered curtains, some standing open, some closed but for a hairline of blue where sea and sky parted them. Our sister ships became visible again. Ahead, still partially veiled, the mouth of White Sea water from which our enemy must come. Feebly, Maz was parting the veils, the stretch of predatory sea once curtained.

A voice cried: "Dragons floating! Six in flight!"

Elk appeared, wrapped in furs. Sailors hustled on the *Paradise*'s decks.

Paralyzed, I watched, watched everything.

In a crush of bodies, Elk halted, twisted his gaze toward me, and said, "Up here, Ingram!" He strode through the swarming men, a distinct and preeminent figure, and climbed to the forward deck. His stocky form teetered above me, vanished. Then it reappeared at the ladder head, gazing down on me—though I couldn't see his eyes, just the light falling over his shoulders and through his akimbo arms. "Ingram, get up here, damn you! Is all the fog in your head now?" In only a moment, I had scrambled to my master's side.

Looking forward over our prow, I saw nothing but twinkling water and, off to our left, one iceberg. No others were visible, only this one rectangular block with a length several times that of our ship's. It loomed just out of our intended course. Another cry from aloft: "Dragons floating! Six in flight!" And I wondered if the man up there weren't simply reading his own apprehensions into the facets of this solitary iceberg. Maybe the dragons floated solely in his mind.

"There," Elk said, pointing, and I saw the first sail.

It rose up out of the White Sea like the wings of a pelagic, half-frozen pterodactyl, crisp, crimson-brown. Fog scattered as these wings beat through. The prow beneath the vessel's sail was carven into the shape of a horned, reptilian head . . . like that of a fire-lizard or an ancient Earth saurian.

Exact identification did not matter. The impression was that of a ship's having emerged hungry from a long sleep in the cold sea. Now the monster was hunting, and the only prey in its path was the galleon on whose forward deck I stood. One by one, five more sails breasted the horizon, popped into view as if propelled upward from the White Sea's bottom. We saw them, they saw us. And these new Pelagan ships rode as hideously festooned as the first, bright banners streaming above their blood-dyed sails.

On the *Paradise*, orders to the crew. Elk tenderly and quickly drew the mantle of padded canvas off the photon-director, and it hit me that I was going to operate the machine, trigger it, control the intensity and direction of its scorching needle-flare. More orders! From where? From whom? Elk said something to me, bumped me into place. My gloved hands seized the device's obscenely neutral-looking controls, a curved trigger and a simple metal wheel. Out in front of me, water like frozen milk, one blue-green berg drifting toward us several hundred meters away, and the distance-dwindled but still terrifying Pelagan warships. The only fog I saw now was sidelong, every wispy curtain drawn into the wings of our theatre of battle. Inside my heavy gloves, my hands ran with sweat.

"Are we in range?" I managed, my words atremble with two distinct kinds of cold, my voice hoarse as if from shouting.

Elk said, "Only a target beneath the horizon is safe, Ingram."

"Do I fire?"

"Did you hear Captain Chant?"

I looked at Elk under his fur cap, at his iceberg-green eyes, at the snowy sideburns standing away from his cheeks. Why was he talking to me? Quietly, guardedly, he was saying, "Captain Chant wants you to wait, to see if they'll turn now that they've seen us, turn and run." *Was this true?*

Absently, I said, "I never heard that order."

From aft, a megaphoned command: "Fire, Master Marley. COMMENCE FIRING!" The order echoed aloft, and the immense northern sea swallowed the echo. Elk pushed me away from the machine and pinioned my arms.

"Captain Chant, I've decided that this man will fire at my word! At no word but my own!" Then he shoved me back into place. My hands gravitated to the laser's controls—and I was keen to the rippling of the highest foresails. My gums burned with the otherworldly chill, my ears throbbed, and the *Paradise* seemed frozen by Sayati Elk's legal, but irregular, usurpation of Captain Chant's command role. No one moved. Captain Chant's megaphone was stilled.

The Pelagans' supply fleet had indeed begun to turn—but not from fear or surprise. Two dragon-prowed ships maneuvered away from the other four, to the west. The remainder kept running toward us, but with their starboard hulls slightly open to us, cutting across the wind. Like ours, the ships were all three-masted, but their sails differed in being serrated and ornamented. Each topgallant bore the yin-yang symbol that Elk had once said our enemies had appropriated from legendary Cathay. I stared as ships and sails alike buffeted toward us.

"Do you know what to do, Ingram?"

I did. I could tear cloth with the photon-director, or burn clean holes, or set lacerating fires, or incinerate men on deck, or shear off mastheads, or open ragged vents beneath the ships' water lines. What could I not do?

—Turn the barbarians back with a shouted word or a wave of the hand. No hope of either of those, of course. So, instead, I would use Elk's re-created device to funnel all my frustration and rage.

"For Maz's sake, Sayati Elk," Captain Chant called from the pilot's deck, "let the young master fire!"

"Stay your hand," Elk whispered fiercely in my ear.

Numb, I obeyed, and a puff of smoke appeared as if by magic on the starboard side of the foremost Pelagan vessel. Momentarily, I feared that I had accidentally triggered my weapon. The puff of smoke tattered into greasy threads and blew away; a roar followed, pinched-sounding at this distance. Then, about fifty meters out to sea, a spout of water kicked up in front of the *Paradise*; air and water vibrated with the shock, as if someone had poured liquid mercury into my ears, it was that painfully deafening. Another puff of smoke, followed rapidly by another; two muted barks in succession; then the shock of impact as the milky sea broke under the burdens of Pelagan cannon shot and water spiraled up in two separate fountains off our bow. Individual drops glistened in the midmorning air, miniature prisms tracing their own kaleidoscopic parabolas of descent. Altogether numb, I could only watch.

"Sayati Elk," Captain Chant shouted, "let him fire!"

"Fire, then," Elk said in my ear.

I pulled the trigger with my gloved finger, then released it. The machine's needle-flare blazed over the White Sea, a radiant, resilient thread snapping from one point to another—as if its light had originated at the target and then simply reeled the instantaneous beam out of the machine's tubular throat: *Fffffthup!* An obscene, rapid sucking. After, the air seemed changed—but the beam shot past the enemy warship and was mysteriously absorbed by the charged air. Had my hands thrown this ray-like lightning, this gone-astray miracle of fire? Bursts of smoke formed and dissolved on the sides of two of the Pelagan warships. Spray kicked across the bow of the *Paradise*, the noise eerily oppressive, water leaping to our high deck, drenching everything with lashing fallout.

"Again, Ingram!" Elk shouted. "Again!"

I swiveled the laser on its mount, pressed the trigger, held it back with all my will. Rage, frustration, bewilderment, longing for power, impotence, hatred, pride—these and more spun from me in the swift embodiment of the photon-tube's luminous, ruby ray. Almost blinded, I swiveled the machine, turned the wheel controlling the beam, and, teeth clamped, willed the disintegration of all that was not Ingram Marley.

I stitched the sails of the first Pelagan ship with fire, I sheared off all three masts above their topgallants, I scorched a line of black piping along the middle of its starboard hull. Water drops clung to my lashes, tears of half-frozen spray, and the red lambency of my emotions streaming through the tube of the photon device was mirrored excruciatingly in these tiny beads of ice.

The cannon on the first Pelagan ship ceased firing; no more puffballs of smoke. Aboard the *Paradise*, men screaming, shrieking like the winter ghost-wind, their full-voiced terror ludicrously out of phase with the placidity of the northern sea. On the enemy ship, the splintering crack of wood; cut mastheads toppling, catching, and finally tearing through the adjacent sails to crash on the warship's decks, crushing men and equipment alike. The hull of the Pelagan ship was filling with water, ineluctably beginning to sink—sails hanging and aflame, every banner scorched away, the dragon-prow glaring balefully out of one burnt-through eye and nodding ever seaward. Finally I released the trigger and stopped swiveling the photon tube.

The booming of cannon growled over the water again, this time from the *Mandragora*, which lay behind us and over a hundred meters to our right. A hollow booming, full of antiquated fury. Spray geysered up in front of the enemy vessel that I'd already demolished, a line of dancing punctuation marks. They added nothing to the unequivocal statement of the photon-director.

"They're jumping," Elk said. "The Pelagan seamen who still can, Ingram, are jumping. They won't last ten minutes in the White Sea. If that long." Elk did not look at me, but at the sinking warship. "If that long," he repeated.

I remembered something. "Where's the *Sea Drake*?"

"There." He gestured to port. "Those two warships that split from the main contingent are bearing down on her, trying to use that iceberg as a screen between her and us." They were moving west, but because of our position, I had to look north to see them. Already they had hid behind the berg's striated, azure-and-rose cliffs and were cannonading the *Sea Drake*—a noisy, echoing barrage. At the same time, the three remaining vessels assaulting us and our other companion continued to come on, undeterred by the demolition of their leader or the ungodly shrieking of crewmen. They made no effort to pick up the overboarded sailors; the Pelagans knew what Gabriel Elk knew: they were dead men. Three warships, then, bearing down on us as their two fellow vessels attacked the *Sea Drake*.

Captain Chant was shouting orders again; masker seamen scrambled about frantically on the *Paradise*'s main deck.

I was drained, trembling. "What now, Sayati Elk?"

"Hit the ones closing in on us, Ingram. I see nothing else for it."

Swiveling the photon-director, I aimed at the Pelagan vessel negotiating its way toward us from behind the wreckage of the first. In ten minutes, it was reduced to a smoldering shell, masts down, hull precisely ignited.

More men struggled in the water. Smoke trailed away to the north like a tattered banner. Even through my gloves, I could feel the heat coming off the casing of Elk's machine. Inside my fur clothes, my body was all a-sweat. My face felt hot—but in my eyelashes, those frozen beads in which I saw the distorted reflections of the scene before me! No longer did I fire out of rage, frustration, or hate; cold resolve sustained me, that and Sayati Elk's droning, even perfunctory encouragement. For these things, I had created mortifying wreckage.

"Now the third, Ingram; now the third."

I slew the third ship, even though it had finally begun to turn away from us. Its captain had seen enough. No doubt he died with a terror in his heart more dreadful than that his painted sails and grotesque dragon-prow had ever provoked in his enemies.

The fourth Pelagan warship fled. Successfully.

"Let it go, Ingram. Someone must carry word back to the Archipelago, back to Orcland."

Off to port, to the northwest, the *Sea Drake* was suffering the methodical onslaught of the barbarian ships shielded by the now seemingly immobile iceberg. Their cannonade continued. The booming was almost melodic, deep and sweet. We already knew, though, that the *Sea Drake* would not survive the encounter; its foremast and several of its staysails had fallen, and she was returning fire rarely, a tacit acknowledgment of her doom. Neither the *Paradise* nor the *Mandragora* had taken a direct hit.

"Can you help her?" Captain Chant shouted.

"Can we?" I asked.

"If you burn through that berg, Ingram, if you split it up and give yourself an aisle to your targets."

"Can I do that?"

"Probably not. I don't know. It may be too big."

Again, I swiveled the laser. Again, I adjusted the intensity and width of its beam, allowing for maximums in both. Again, I pulled the trigger back and held it in place. At once the berg erupted in a volcanic billowing of steam, white clouds pouring over its table-top and sweeping off like thin gas. Hissing and creaking accompanied this eruption.

When I finally released the trigger, the photon-director had done little more than bore an uneven tunnel whose depth I couldn't gauge. Ships fell to this weapon more readily than did the calves of Mansueceria's polar cap.

Still—with time—I might have won through. We just lacked time. . . .

The *Sea Drake*, capsizing into a foam scarcely whiter than the surrounding sea, slid out of sight; gently she went, incredibly gently. If her crewmen were screaming, we could not hear them. Maskers often die without a sigh of protest, and the officers of Ongladred, the Atarite elite, must ape their stoicism, even in death. We watched our sister ship go down, sliding with broken but commanding dignity into the indigo-riven deeps. And all on the *Paradise* were silent, stilled by our comrades' last end.

"Wait for the bastards," Elk told me. "Wait for them, Ingram, until they have to pull out." Fetched up with the *Mandragora*, we waited for the Pelagan renegades to sail out from behind the berg. I am sure they knew we were waiting, that they had seen what we'd done to the rest of their fleet.

A half-hour passed, then forty-five minutes. And when the barbarian ships came out, they emerged from opposite sides of the azure-and-rose ice plateau, cannons booming, their captains apparently determined that one crew would sacrifice itself for the other. The water was pockmarked with shot, deliquescent with spray.

"Incinerate them," Gabriel Elk said flatly.

Working on one ship and then the other, I did just that. I alternated until both went down, blackened husks crumbling into ash on the waters. We escaped damage. After, Elk stalked away from me, descended to the main deck, strode the length of the ship, and without a word to anyone ducked into the passageway leading to his cabin. After, sinking ruins; a flotsam of boards, boxes, and men bent like shrimp-things, bobbing hopelessly; and smoke curling and dissolving above it all. After, the photon-director. On its swivel: a slender, one-eyed beast no more remorseful than the snake that strikes and soon after sleeps. I covered it with a bolt of canvas. That way I could continue to look at it.

I looked at it for a long time.

xvi

That evening as we sailed southward, the sky still smoking behind us and the *Mandragora*'s masts and sails silhouetted against all that brownish flame, I went belowdecks and rapped at Elk's cabin door. He hadn't been seen after our victory over the Pelagans, never having joined Chant and the other

Atarite seaman in the officers' mess. "It's open," Elk called in his flattest voice. He sat on a stool in the middle of the cramped room, while a middle-aged masker leaned over him with a razor. A basin of sudsy water rested on the writing board next to Elk's bunk. The masker, a thin eyebrow-less fellow, was shaving Elk. When I entered, he nodded at me and went back to work.

"This is Gnot," Elk said. "Yukio Gnot. He's a barber as well as a yard-trimmer and buntline-tender."

I squeezed in and sat on the cabin's narrow bunk, a sort of wall cot. The skinny masker bowed, holding his razor extended gallantly out behind him. He recited, "*I am Gnot, the man / You think I am,*" and resumed work a second time, altogether humorlessly; indeed, with deadpan seriousness.

Elk was wrapped to the throat in a khaki-colored apron, his face partially lathered, unnaturally pink where Gnot had already shaved. Then I noticed a pair of heavy shears and barber Gnot's soap-filled basin resting atop the writing board beside me. What did all this mean?

For a time, Elk in his khaki tent, Gnot expertly ignoring the sway of the ship, and I exiled from the intimacy of shaver and shaved, we listened to the groanings of the *Paradise*. Between its groans sounded the almost frictionless scraping of Gnot's razor, as if the blade were also scraping my skull's wet inner wall. Would no one speak? And then, Elk:

"Sorry I deserted you, Ingram. Sorry I made you do what I made you do."

"You did desert me, didn't you?"

"Yes. Just as I deserted myself after closing Stonelore—and made that horrid thing up there." His eyes looked deckwards.

"That was for a cause, sir. But what about this morning's desertion? What prompted that?"

"A quest for my own sanity, Ingram. As the gold-hearted beauty of the Stews once said, 'It's nothing personal, Master, nothing personal a' tall.' But I regret the desertion mightily for what it must seem to imply."

"Why does Gentleman Gnot shave you at this hour?"

"An ablution of sorts," pursing his mouth as Gnot scraped at the whiskers near his Adam's apple. "Maybe I should be bled clean. Say, friend Yukio, an extra mithra if you go neatly into the jugular."

Gnot stepped back. "There's nothing neat about that operation, Sayati Elk. As for the mithra, I'm Gnot for nothing and all's for Gnot in this barbering. You owe me nothing, for all the pleasure's mine." It was patter, amusing but sadly hollow. Then the man leaned over Elk again, his browless eyes vulnerable and nude—like ripe, peeled grapes. His hands flashed expertly. Then I saw that he had shaven away the old man's sideburns.

I said, "Gentleman Gnot, was that requested?"

Elk's sidelong glance showed the whites of his eyeballs like small quarter moons. "I've requested it all, Ingram—jaw, cheeks, and skull."

"The masker mourning cap?" I said. "But what for?"

"For today."

"Sir, you aren't one of the People Accustomed to the Hand, and you've suffered no loss of kin. Did you sit for this when your two elder sons died?"

"I didn't, Ingram—because I'm not a Mansuecerian, though born of them; their customs aren't mine. But today I revive the custom of the mourning cap. Why? Because I mourn and cannot express it, the expression of it's gone out of me, all of it out. Today was a day I relearned everything but its expression, Ingram, and so I turned to Gentleman Gnot for help. I'm no longer young, I'm nearing death, in fact—but I've never understood the element of affirmation that may exist in mourning, though I know that it *does* exist.

"Atarite mourning always struck me as defeatist; the Mansuecerian, as cold and ritualized. But today—a day I made myself—requires this atonement at least. Already an odd feeling flows in, behind Good Barber Gnot's fashioning of my cap. The outside will teach the inside. What say you to that, Ingram?"

"Nothing. Nonsense from Our Genius."

"Exhibitionist nonsense?"

"Your words, your doubts."

Elk shifted under the khaki cloth. The wall candles flickered, and the cabin filled with interlocking shadows, most pooling and ebbing around the two men in the center of the room. Delicately, Yukio Gnot wiped the lather from Elk's face; he was at once naked, as if newborn. Would I have recognized Elk had I not seen the transformation?

"I'm a dramatist and poet," he told, or scolded, me: "Introspection and exhibitionism have been my trades. No doubts whatever in that, Ingram. But this that I do now has nothing to do with my trades. It has to do with my humanity, my mortality. How the world interprets it, I little care."

He nodded at Gnot and said, "Proceed."

Gnot took the shears off the writing board (I had to move my feet for him) and began sclip-sclipping at Elk's massive head, and ring-curled, silver-white hair tumbled over the blades like wool. Satyr's wool, I thought, for Elk was smiling cryptically. Like the parings of old dreams, his hair fell. In the shadow-filled cabin it almost floated, each curl a fleck of time, of coil-wound chronology, cut and discarded. Individual hairs clung to the drab bib or laced the floor with their frightening dead beauty. Awe seized me. This was something more than a simple barbering: I thought of the Parfects, of the Pelagan reiver I'd slain, of denatured animals and the resurrected performers of Stonelore. A sense of elation; a sense of loss. Elk's hair kept curling from the blade, white as ash.

When Gnot had finished, he lathered Elk's shorn head, stropped his razor, and scraped at the stubble. "Harvest time," Elk said. He sat perfectly still under the masker's hands. Then, the scraping concluded, Gnot laid the shears aside and washed Elk's liver-spotted skull. Strangely, Elk did not look ludicrous—maybe because his baldness did not shine like a tunic button, but more probably because his tortoise-like features already radiated humor at their own expense.

"Done, Sayati Elk. You needn't pay me. I'm Gnot for nothing."

"I'd rather, Gnot," Gabriel Elk said, shaking the apron out on the floor. He then fetched out a handful of coins for the masker.

Grinning, Gnot bowed "Oh, Sayati Elk, that's amusing how you put that. So very witty, sir."

"I'm doubled over with laughter," I said. "Tied up in a Gnot."

"Oh, Master Marley," Gnot said. "You, too. All's for Gnot, it is."

Disgusted, I let my gaze slide from the barber to a point just over his head.

"I'll clean up, Gnot," Elk said. "Don't feel obligated for that, too. You're a seaman and a barber, not a mercenary in the broom brigade."

"Oh, no. I must do it, you know." Gnot took a tiny horsehair brush from the inside of his jacket, knelt, and swept the fallen hair into the barber's apron, which he had spread out as a receptacle for hair, dust, and any other oddments he could rake up. Speedily done, he pulled the four corners of the apron in and tied them off as best he could, careful not to spill either dirt or severed curls. He slung the resulting bag over his shoulder, bowed to Elk, and bowed to me.

"Take a few of those shavings," I said, "and paste on some eyebrows."

The masker, alerted to something unkind in my tone, stared at me in utter incomprehension, his nonexistent eyebrows quizzically raised. Elk opened the cabin door and released him into the dark cramped hall.

"Thank you, Yukio," he said. "You're a good and skillful man. Let's hope we find our country and families safe when we put in at Brechtlin."

"Yes, Sayati Elk. Let's so hope."

Elk returned to the cabin. He sat down opposite me, pulling his stool around as he sat. His naked, gravely humorous face was as unfamiliar as a map of Austernmere, the Brobdingnagian continent sprawling across over a quarter of Mansueceria's southern hemisphere. The naked, unfamiliar face looked at me, simply looked at me.

At last I said, "Oh, that wasn't so bad, Sayati Elk. I've sunk five ships today, drowned nearly eight hundred men in an icy sea. Insulting Gentleman Gnot was one of my less murderous thrusts." I wanted to cry, but instead pulled in my bottom lip and tried to stare the old bastard down.

"A Mansuecerian, Ingram. A simple masker—"

"Why are you trying to shame me?"

"Oh no, Ingram, I don't mean to shame you, just to make clear that his shaving my head was my idea, not his. To explain that he speaks as he does because he's a simple man, almost innocent of education."

"But the banality, Sayati Elk, the endless banality of it." My eyes filled with wet candlelight, gems of melting color that washed the old man's unfamiliar face away. I couldn't control my shoulders. "*The terrible, utter banality . . .*"

Then the old man's lather-sour warmth engulfed me, his heavy arm and strong hand pulling me like a child into his side to sit beside him on the bunk next to my previous perch. The breath from his voice warmed my face. "It's a banality that touches us all, Ingram—and we all attempt to transcend it, however we can. Even Yukio Gnot. Even the maskers who file in to Stonelore." His huge hand squeezed my biceps. "But for pushing you to this, I'm sorry. I mourn for you, too, Ingram, I mourn for you, too."

"Will what we've done make a damned bit of difference?"

"That's hard to gauge."

"Won't the Pelagans send more ships, and more, and more?"

"One escaped today. That one will return to Orland, and the news its captain gives of his compatriots' watery deaths will soon be broadcast throughout the Archipelago, both as rumor and warning. Or so I hope."

I pulled away from Elk. In the melting-diamond light I found my feet and crossed to the door. "Goodnight, sir."

I left without waiting for a reply. Inside my fur-lined parka, my shoulders became a part of my body again, and I found my way to the forward deck. There I directed two masker seamen to take the photon-director off its mount and carry it to my cabin.

Under close-hauled sails, tarnished-tin stars, and windy shadow-pocked moons, they did so. Indeed, they put the machine on the floor in the center of my cabin. After they'd gone, I sat for a long time on the edge of my bunk looking at it. Then I extinguished my lamps, undressed, and lay down under several ragged quilts. Arranging them, I remembered from childhood a quilt with blue flowers embroidered over its silken squares.

The *Paradise* groaned, gently rocking. The shadow of the photon-director, the sinister bulk of its silhouette, drew my gaze again. I stared at it as if compelled to wrestle with the implications of its shape. I was past crying. I lay in the dark and relived that whole dreadful day, oh, eight or a thousand times.

Then I swam into dreamless nightmare, a series of floating images without correlatives....

xvii

On the morning that we rounded the southeastern cape of Ongladred, a strange thing happened. Captain Chant was wringing the very air for wind, so still was the day; our sails were expertly trimmed, the yards finically dressed, and we were sailing homeward—but only just. The *Paradise* rode the small listless whitecaps sluggishly, and the *Mandragora* had fallen back half a kilometer in our languid wake. Aloft, our banners only rarely fluttered.

Because the sailing along our island's coast was so poor, we rounded the Mershead Cape well out to sea—far enough out that land was no longer visible. Although we rocked now in waters lapping softly against uninvaded territory (the civilized heartland of our nation), only one or two ships of all of Ongladred's fleet sailed into view, both out of hailing distance. An odd morning, indeed; a subdued and lonely homecoming.

Gabriel Elk and I stood with Captain Chant and his helmsman on the pilot's deck. Maz shone with thin but elemental vigor, an unlikely sun to go nova, to explode us all back into primordial plasma. Therefore, none of us wore parkas or overtunics, but basked in a rare autumn mildness, wondering at the absence of wind and the tranquility of the sea.

"Where have all our ships gone, Sayati Elk?" I asked.

"On a day like this," Captain Chant said, "their captains would hope to be in harbor, to take stock and restock. Maybe they're there today."

"But we ought to see a few, as a precaution against the Pelagans."

"The Pelagans, Ingram," Elk said, "are defeated. Last night—and the night before—we saw bonfires on the coast. Having beat back one foe, our people are tending their anxieties about the sloak again. Like Captain Chant, I believe most of our ships to be in harbor."

"But the sloak," I said, "is no threat at all, merely a superstition."

"Perhaps not a superstition at all," Elk said.

Captain Chant's eyes caught mine, and their irises seemed to surround a question. And neither of us could speak.

Meanwhile, on the *Paradise*, sailors worked with insect-like efficiency keeping the sails open to whatever breath of wind they could smell or intuit in the air. We were bound for home, and only that mattered. The strange thing that happened that morning came too late to seem a wry comment on my refusal to see the sloak as a threat. Too much time had passed to italicize my words with irony. Or so I strove to believe.

This is what happened:

With no warning, the sea beneath us—and everywhere else around us, insofar as we could judge—began to heave and surge, surge and heave, lifting and dropping in large, vaguely peristaltic swells. Our masker seamen turned their incredulous faces to the skies, shouting, checking braces and halyards. Captain Chant roared unintelligible orders over their shouts and scufflings, his megaphone jutting out before him like a ritual trumpet. Officers on the other decks relayed each misheard order back and forth over the sailors' heads, and the whole ship trembled and jostled with split-struck confusion. Great slaps of water pounded our hull, as if a team of ocean-breathing giants—seaweed for beards, driftwood for bucklers—essayed a game of toss-the-blanket on the bottom of the Angromain Channel. The flap-and-fall of their monumentally water-logged blanket translated itself into the lift-and-plunge that the *Paradise* now experienced, into the running swells surrounding us. It had to be giants. For there was no wind, and our banners were still hardly billowing. Hence, this sea-quaking, this ferocious faulting, had to originate from *below* the surface. Even I knew that, even I intuited the odd nature of the channel's upset—and could do nothing but pray that the giants grow weary and desist. But, with Sayati Elk, I remained on deck, watching.

"The sloak!" I heard a voice cry out.

"Aye, the sloak!" in answer.

"The sloak it is!"

Grabbing Elk's arm, I shouted, "I don't believe that!"

"Then what do you believe?" he replied.

"That this is some kind of tidal anomaly!" I had to repeat my words, but I got Elk to face me.

"Ingram, I've never seen a tidal anomaly like this one!"

"How about sea-bottom volcanic activity?"

"Who can say, Ingram? Who can say?" He was reveling in the surge of the waters, the cries and scuffling of our sailors. Me, he more or less dismissed, for I could not question him while this untoward pounding made our bilge echo and our battered masts thrust and fall back. This oceanic phenomenon mocked us all; it battered with scorn our tender pride as sailors, and Elk, well, he laughed and drank it all in, every haughty wave.

I shouted, "Do you—do *you* believe it's the sloak?"

But he refused to hear me. Beside him on the pilot's deck, I waited for an immense mythical creature to capsize and drown us on a transcendently fair day. The masker seamen, hauling line and climbing, kept us afloat, and then, in a split-struck instant, the seas calmed and the *Paradise* settled into a gently bobbing sea scarcely even foam-flecked. The giants had wearied of blanket toss and gone on to more fastidious amusements.

—*Like subduing boarnoses to their clammy hands*, I thought. I could imagine the sleek, sharklike creatures undergoing training.

After we'd sailed for a time on this calm, I again forced my questions on the old man. We stayed abovedecks in the midmorning sun, nor far from Chant and his helmsman. "Was that the sloak, Sayati Elk? Not freak vulcanism or a tidal quirk, but a creature you and the maskers have christened the sloak?"

"I believe so, Ingram."

"Why do you believe that?"

"It's the only answer that works, the simplest and thus most likely."

"You really expect this gelatinous thing to snuff the coastal bonfires, haul itself across our island, and destroy Ongladred a third time?"

"Ingram, I am past expectation, past prophecy and vision. But I don't think Ongladred will be destroyed again. At least not by an entity as hugely out-of-nature as the sloak."

"If you believe in the thing, why not?"

"What we've just experienced, Ingram, was meant as caveat and warning, it was directed specifically at us aboard this ship and the men on shore who witnessed the phenomenon's batterings—the men of our nation."

"Caveat and warning," I said incredulously. "From whom? The sloak?"

"No, from those controlling it. It's a thing out-of-nature, an anomaly in its own right, a product of smug and juridic intelligence. It has no will of its own; it executes the judgments of this 'higher,' all-ruling intelligence and does so in the guise of an apocalyptic phenomenon. The sloak exists, Ingram, but it's a lie."

"I don't understand." But his argument was somehow familiar. I'd heard it before. In Stonelore. From a haggard woman in a neuro-drama.

"I'm speaking of the Parfects. The sloak is a quasi-organic biological construct that the Parfects have twice activated to pull us back from forbidden knowledge. For them, the Old Knowledge is the limit of what we may know; the sloak, the cruel weapon by which they fix the parameters of our knowledge. Once again, Ingram, we've begun to encroach on the boundaries of the permitted: We have used technology—proscribed technology—to kill. Hence this warning, one especially vivid to us on the *Paradise*, us wielders of stolen fire."

"Your reading, Sayati Elk, hardly seems the simplest and most likely. It's infinitely complicated."

"But the simplest explanation accounting for the arrogantly directed history of our island, Ingram, and by 'arrogantly directed' I don't wish to imply that we—Atarite and Mansuecerian alike—don't share in the shame of our failures and the simple pride of our glories, only that we're measured against an alien standard and made to suffer unduly for the squalid aspects of our nature—even though They have altered that!"

"Aren't you possibly seeking a scapegoat, sir?"

"I absolve humanity of nothing! Even so, I refuse to designate humanity the culprit here, as the Parfects decided six or seven thousand years ago it must be designated. I find that view abhorrent, as abhorrent as the utter denial of our guilt, for I also abhor the Parfects' self-excusing Sitting in Judgment."

"And if Humankind destroys itself?"

"We must be free to do so, even if we do it over and over until the last sterile coupling of the species. Or until we learn."

"And if we don't learn?"

"Then our viability as a species worthy of the cornucopian gifts of chaos has proved altogether too weak and we must die—cursing ourselves, mind you, and not that cruel but munificent chaos. Our passing must have the grandeur of tragedy. That much is evident, Ingram, that much is clear."

I looked away from his intent, naked face. Ahead, off to the right, the hazy blue line of Ongladred's southern coast had become visible; we had successfully rounded the cape. The ships in harbor at Mershead and Brechtlin must have had to endure the shock waves of the pounding we had ridden out at sea. Now, however, the clear sky and windless air mocked our memories. The planet basked.

"Could the sloak, whether natural or quasi-organic, cause an upheaval like the one we just survived, Sayati Elk? Legends have it that the thing's so thin its body has almost no width at all."

"The legends are legends, and even if true, the activation of the creature's biocybernetic consciousness from the Parfects' orbiter would spill enough energy to thicken the sloak's weirdly thin membrane and to stir up the sea in the process. Once drawn together to attack Ongladred, the sloak becomes as formidable a sea beast as any—either in Mansueceria's oceans or in Earth's."

"For everything, you have an answer." *Didn't Sayati Elk's resurrection of the dead for the purposes of his dramaturgy have a kind of parallel, a kind of affinity, with the Parfects' "activation" of the sloak?* (Assuming of course, that his hypothesis was correct.) That was a question that I didn't ask, but that I hoped to think about. There were many questions that I must think about in the days and years ahead.

"No, not answers, *theories*—all of which I strongly embrace, for they are better than all others. Moreover, they are mine." Elk said this without a hint of haughtiness. Still, I wanted to deflate him, to disabuse him of his own intricate but annoyingly logical theory.

And so I asked, "What about the two-thousand-year cycle of the sloak? Isn't that too regular for an expedient that you say is punitive? Does Humankind reach the brink of forbidden knowledge with so inhuman a precision every two thousand years?"

"The sloak has come only twice, even according to legend. How can we accurately compute its cycle? Besides, Ingram, this—the Year of the Halcyon Panic—is not the only year that we have predicted the return of the sloak, the destruction of the species. We are superstitious beings, who read numbers into everything. Eventually, our mystical numbers become the floor for a numinous science. Oh, it's beautiful and frightening, this becoming, one that always undoes itself to evolve again. The cycle of the sloak? It unites science and superstition by harmonizing their unique integrities through the mediation of numbers."

"Dear Maz," I said, "spare me the academic argle-bargle."

Elk threw his head back and laughed, with hearty abandon, as if his breath would puff our sails in the airless day and so billow us into Brechtlin's harbor—a galleon of heroes ready for gallons of haoma, a crew of gallant murderers hoping to drown their crime in the masker panacea.

Amazing to say, in one hour Captain Chant and his seamen, having wrung the air for its faintest stirring, took us into the recently wave-lashed but now quiet harbor, and, after fifteen days at sea, we disembarked upon native soil.

Behind us, a sky stippled with masts. Before us, a port, a road, and all of Ongladred. In the flush of this excitement, I forgot that I had incinerated nearly eight hundred enemy human beings—until, when I left the *Paradise*, I saw Yukio Gnot staring bemusedly after me.

xviii

Gabriel Elk and I rented a wagon in Brechtlin, had the photon-director loaded into it, and drove not to Lunn but along the coastal road toward Mershead. "The weapon is mine," he said, "I need not return it to Chancellor Blaine; he'll discover soon enough, without our telling him, that the *Paradise* is in harbor." It was dark when we reached Stonelore. Oddly, I felt that I had come home too; that this arena of rock and sand and artificial light belonged more certainly to me than did any of the tract on which the Atarite Palace sits.

Bethel and Robin Coigns met us in front of Grotto House. That there were only the two of them discomfited—nay, frightened—me. Bethel kissed her husband, then stepped back, her hands still on his shoulders, and said, "Gareth is dead, Gabriel." Then she ran her hand over her husband's head, backward from the brow. "Someone has told you already?"

"No. You are the first." He pulled the Lady to him, and they embraced—a calm and silent, but somehow expressive, embrace. Coigns and I stood apart, not so much excluded from this moment as incapable of comprehending its intensity. Then Elk drew his wife with him toward the house, she an extension of him, he an extension of her, and, together, one loving, reproachful whole.

"Ingram," he said, "Robin, come." We followed. Silently.

Later, in the arras-hung dining room, we talked—with the boy Gareth's almost tangible presence hovering in our words and breaths. The stone table sat between us like a funeral slab; the Atarite Palace and the provinces of Ongladred faded in our minds to ghostly grays on a battle chart. Before a single dead loved one, the concepts of civilization defended and honor reaffirmed dissolve into fume and drift away, like cannon smoke. Even with no one of my own to mourn, I knew that much. The knowledge had grown in me.

"He died four days ago," Robin Coigns told us. "Those machines that Sayati Snow and Master Gordon brought up to just below Firthshir turned it all around, the fighting, you know, and the Pelagans had retreated north, all the way through Vestacs and Eenlich. Your son was killed in the pursuit Field-Pavan Barrow ordered right after the machines turned 'em around. Then, when he sees they can still kill us, you know, while we're pursuing 'em, ole Barrow calls it off and we just let 'em run—but Gareth was already lost, Sayati Elk, along with a mess of others, all of them on-the-line fellows."

Lady Bethel sat with her hands in her lap, as regal in silken green as I had ever seen Our Shathra Anna. Elk kept his gaze down, apparently directing it at his big, rope-veined hands.

Then he said: "An irony, Robin. A part of my trade. A philosophical joke to pull on my creations. Which now comes home to haunt us."

Bethel Elk said, "Forget that, Gabriel. We must mourn awhile."

The old man looked at Robin Coigns. "Where's Gareth? Did they bury him in the north?"

"He's under, sir. In the tunnel 'twixt Grotto House and Stonelore."

"Here?"

"Aye, Sayati Elk."

"How?"

"He took a rifle ball in the throat, through the Adam's apple so his wind was cut; the ball lodged there, you see. It wasn't meant for me to be beside him then, I s'pose. Others came running and took me back, but by then our officers knew him for your son and called for haomycin to go into his blood so as to get him back here 'fore he stiffened. I was shunted off to one hand, Sayati Elk, and most near cried, watching 'em do what they had to. Gareth he lay in the midst of all this scramble, you know, bleeding the life all out and not seeing see me no more than if he was blind, his eyes gone back and his face as still as old milk. He got home afore me, Sayati Elk—*preserved*, sort of. They took him off that way, with nothing for me to do but watch. I near cried, sir."

"We put Gareth in a preservator, Gabriel," Bethel said.

"Which one? They were all full."

"They're empty now. Except for Gareth's and Bronwen's. After you left, I had some men come from Lunn to give the other dead ones their second funerals. They were burned, our actors, all together—in the place we always burn them—at summer's end. I couldn't leave them sleeping in heartless ice, Gabriel."

"Why did you spare the girl?"

"She was new—newer than the others. And I'd watched her dance."

"I want to see Gareth," Elk said.

"May I go with you?" I asked.

After an almost imperceptible pause, he said, "Please, Ingram."

We excused ourselves. Bethel and Coigns let us go without them. They had seen the boy, and they knew Elk's wish for what it was, a plea for one last intimate moment of communion. Maybe I was less sensitive than they, for I knew this, too, and should not have gone—but felt that he would have stopped me if my presence had threatened to throw up a wall between him and Gareth. I had to go with him, down into the programming room, the dark tunnel, the dormitory room for corpses. Sensing my need, Elk had said yes. And so we left the dining room, walked a hallway of luminous panels, and rode the elevator into the womb and bowels of Grotto House. My sense of going home grew more pronounced, more vital, more uncanny.

We arrived in the preservator room, among ranked coffins and upended tanks of lox. A faint musical seething hummed there. Our breaths took shape like dreamy sails; we had voyaged into a numinous place, a world whose deities were enshrined in ice and plastic. Four of the shrines rested empty, but in the two nearest the door, we found the daughter of Josu and Rhia Lief and the newly slain son of the Elks. These dead children had become numens of the preservator room, guardian spirits whose frozen youth mocked their guardianship. I stared through crystal at the young woman and then the young man—whose throat was swaddled in a beige cloth bandage. Bronwen Lief looked different. Her face was not a whit altered from the first time I'd seen her, back before the spring had come. But the smirk I'd read then in the twist of her mouth seemed not at all sinister now; it was not even a smirk, but a charming natural flaw, wholly human. As for Gareth, he looked no different at all—except that his sparse beard had sharpened to stubble. If Bethel had had him shaved before laying him to rest, then even in death his facial hair had gone on growing. So his corpse's features were fresh and youthful, but touched with the start of a prophetic mature weariness.

With frost-gloves, Elk adjusted the cryostat on Bronwen's preservator. With the cryostat he could take the temperature within each coffin up and down a limited scale of cold quite quickly, although the room itself remained at a constant 0° C. in case of separate cryostat malfunctions. As the temperature in Bronwen's unit rose toward that of the room, Elk leaned over his dead son to study his face. At length, he sighed. "He was growing into himself, Ingram. He was just on the verge of becoming the willow that the seed of him enshrined."

My hands, for warmth, were in my armpits. For the first time, I saw on the back of Gabriel Elk's mottled, naked skull an angry red gleam: a birthmark, a magenta discoloration to the right of and a little above the brain stem. Before I could stop myself, I had reached and touched that tiny mark. Elk turned slowly and looked at me. I retracted my hand, the image of the nevus clearly before me even though I had withdrawn my hand. Briefly, Elk's face was inscrutable. Then his eyes crinkled into Pelagan slits—a joy-etched but bewildered smile.

"Oh, that. When I was little, my father would brush my hair aside and tell me, 'You've been branded by the Evil One, by Ahriman himself.'"

I said, "It's like a little scorpion with its stinger raised."

"My father always told me of that nevus with a smile, as if joking, but he upset me more than he knew. Early on, I dreaded his touch—his reminder to me of something I knew was back there but couldn't see for myself. My father was a Mansuecerian, Ingram, a masker, and I knew I was somehow different from him. Growing up, I believed the difference lay in the scorpion mark, that it and only it set me apart from my family and everyone else."

"It probably made him uneasy, sir. It's nearly perfect, almost a tattoo."

"He told me that, too, Ingram—but not in those words. And when I reached puberty, I ceased resenting his reminders of the birthmark; I understood his uneasiness, his ill-expressed love. I knew what I was and how the differences in what we were did not finally matter. But I kept waiting for him to express—in some cleverly flamboyant way—the love he could not articulate." Elk rubbed the spot I'd touched. "Those are mostly good memories, Ingram, almost from another life, they recede so far into the past." He turned and disconnected a piece of the apparatus affixed to Bronwen Lief's coffin. Clearly, he had no intention of letting his memories overwhelm him. Then, as we'd done several times over the summer, he pulled the preservator on its coasterlike wheels out of its moorings and pushed it toward the door.

"What are you doing, sir?"

"Going back to work. Will you help?" In passing, he flipped me a pair of frost-gloves. I yanked them on, opened the door, and helped him push the rolling white deathbed through the tunnel and into the programming room. I could not believe that it was beginning again and had no idea how to react.

Once there, however, Elk told me, "Go upstairs and get some sleep. Take Gareth's room. I want you to have it."

"Sayati Elk, I can't tell Lady Bethel I'm taking her son's room."

"Tell her. She'll understand."

"Are you staying down here?"

"For a while. Go on. Go up. Go to bed."

Reluctantly, I rode the lift. Alone in the main hallway, I felt like a figure in a photographic negative, like the light-blackened obverse of myself. Then, in her silken green gown, Bethel Elk approached out of the sheen of the hallway's wall panels and restored color to the gray haze of Grotto House. I told her what her husband had told me to tell her. She nodded and led me to Gareth's room. The door slid open for me.

She said, "Go on, Ingram, and sleep well." The door closed behind me. Again, I felt like a black figure on a white ground—until I brushed a sensor and a flood of sunset-colored light reversed things again.

The room was just like the one I'd had before Gareth's death—except that at many spots about it, Gareth had displayed pieces of his idiosyncratic statuary. Sinuous trees carved out of stone, every piece a gnarled and leafless tree. I lifted the stone tree next to my bed. It was unfinished, almost as if the boy had realized that no matter how exemplary his vision or how expert his hands became, in execution his trees would always be petrified and dead before he could massage life into and thus finish them. Maybe he had given up on this kind of sculpting as if the mere attempt was a fool's game. Or maybe he had simply died too young to show the world the mature lineaments of his aborted potential.

A vast melancholy fell upon me. The stone tree in my hands may have been the last Gareth ever essayed. I set it aside and carefully stretched out across the bed of my bereaved hosts' dead son.

xix

The next day Arngrim Blaine appeared at Stonelore, an arrival that coincided with Robin Coigns' departure for Brechtlin in the wagon we had rented the previous afternoon. The ostler would return the wagon and ride back to us on the horse following the wagon on a short tether.

As Coigns left the upland arena, joggling on the wagon seat down the hillside, the Chancellor's equipage approached from Lunn. In a red billow, wagon and carriage passed each other. Only two Atarite guardsmen rode beside Blaine, and they did not venture into the arena with his ebony coach; instead, they halted and took up positions outside the rock wall, as had the charioteers on that night when Bronwen Lief danced and the reivers drew down on us from their blind. Had we learned nothing? But the war was over, I told myself, we had successfully beaten back the bringers of ruin. I had murdered a few myself.

"Welcome," Sayati Elk said when Chancellor Blaine stepped down from his coach. "Once again, we're honored."

The man with the roan tooth tilted his head and clasped Elk's hands in his own. "It's I who should welcome you, Sayati Elk. Welcome home to Ongladred. Your countrymen and your nation's rulers have proved to be more flexible than many"—the Chancellor gave me a look—"felt to be possible. Our Shathra Anna has fathomless reservoirs of flexibility; she ordered me to pay you a visit when it became clear you would not come into Lunn of your own volition."

"An inconvenience to you," Elk said, "for which I apologize."

As the three of us crossed the arena, walking slowly. I said, "Why exactly did she send you, Chancellor Blaine?"

After several steps, he replied, "To offer congratulations and condolences, Sayati Elk—tasks I undertake willingly. Don't speak of inconvenience. There is none, none whatever. I'm only sorry that your son's death diminishes the joy you must feel in your homecoming."

Shut-mouthed, Elk opened a wrought-iron gate across the foyer to Grotto House and led us inside. Lady Bethel joined us, and because the day was fair and unseasonably warm, we passed through the foyer to the house's open, central courtyard. All but Elk took up seats on stone benches. Elk stood with his back to us, his bald head absorbing rather than reflecting the sunlight. But the scorpion mark above his runneled nape focused my attention.

Elk said, "Robin tells me that Snow and Gordon swept the enemy before them with ease. And that we pursued our retreating enemy."

Blaine replied, "And Captain Chant tells me that Master Marley destroyed six Pelagan warships as if they were soap bubbles waiting for the lance."

"Five," I said.

"Was that pursuit necessary?" Bethel pointedly asked.

"Only Field-Pavan Barrow could say. I'm no tactician."

"Where are the photon-tubes that Snow and Gordon used?" Elk asked. "They must be returned, Chancellor, as stipulated in our agreement."

"In safekeeping at the Atarite Palace, Sayati Elk. Where is the one you and Master Marley used aboard the *Paradise*?"

"Beneath Grotto House. Coigns carried it down for me last night, and I removed its chemical power source." Elk faced us. The leaves of the blood lily behind him caught the sunlight, showing their velvet, crimson underbellies. "It's a disemboweled machine, Chancellor. Dead."

"Well, while it lived, it reveled. So be it."

This remark seemed inordinately tactless. I stood and walked a few paces down a stone path in the courtyard. Then I halted, still within speaking distance of the others. Around me gleamed blood lilies, fall azaleas, the hard yellow berries of the ahura-wood, the inner walls of Grotto House. The Elks and the Chancellor formed the points of a triangle that excluded me—until I realized that I had just extended the geometry of our disenchantment. I was a fourth point. I meant too.

"Surely, offering up congratulations and condolences," Elk said, "doesn't comprise the full purpose of your journey."

"Actually, it does. The only other thing Our Shathra asked me to do was to return Ingram to Lunn. He's handled his responsibilities capably, and we wish to reward him."

"Then let me stay here," I said.

Arngrim Blaine looked at me as at an impudent child. But for the carnelian flash of his tooth, his smile would have been fatherly. "A decision such as that is out of my hands, Ingram. Nor could Our Shathra Anna make it without knowing Sayati and Mistress Elk's feelings."

"Does Our Shathra Anna seek to reward me, too?" Elk asked.

"Certainly." The Chancellor's eyes blinked rapidly.

"Then I ask for what Ongladred owes me—a son. If Ingram wishes to stay here at Grotto House, we wish him to do so as our son."

Bethel said, "Grant Ingram his request, Chancellor Blaine, and you grant ours as well."

"Isn't Ingram a little old to be acquiring parents, Mistress Elk?"

"Indeed," she replied.

"Besides, it's not only for his personal qualities that I wish him to stay here," Elk put in. "A fortnight from now I intend to present a neuro-masque in the Stonelore amphitheatre, and Ingram will be of invaluable assistance to me in the comptroller room. Tell Our Shathra Anna that she is invited, that the masque will commemorate her reign in dance and song."

And so it happened, in that exchange of words, that I gave up my place in the Atarite Court, my status as a dirt-runner, my only partly executed duties as a member of the Eyes and Ears of Our Shathra Anna. As the Chancellor and Sayati Elk and Lady Bethel talked, my past fell away.

I looked up at Maz, conscious of the courtyard's fluttering colors, leaves peripherally afire with burnt red and smoky emerald, and of the wan circle of the sun shedding its summer scales down the sky. My past had fallen away, even that part of it encompassing my sojourn with the Elks. It had not disappeared; it lay at my feet like dead leaves or shed scales, and I could collapse into it or stride out of its alluring, brittle debris. I was still held, but the coils were off, the colors were golden.

The conversation of the others went on around me as I tried to tell the future in Maz' outlines, to adjust to the new skin that I still had no right to. The morning passed, and the afternoon, and somewhere in this evanescent progression the Chancellor bid us goodbye and left.

Before I could think what had happened, to all of us, I was in Gareth's bed again, hypnotized by the tangled shadow cast upon the wall by one of his carven stone trees. I couldn't sleep. My mind climbed the branches of that shadow. I lay ensnared in the flown, leafless day. Too many things had happened, but only I possessed any clue to their significance. Then, faint footfalls began to patter in the shadow's branches—an illusion. They were coming from the hallway, from the corridor outside my door. I lay listening to them even after they had gone. A long time later, I rose and left Gareth's room. Down the gray-lit corridor I walked, placing my feet in the shadows of footfalls that had preceded me.

I was in front of the elevator. I rode it down.

In the programming room, I found Elk bent over the corpse of his son, working with untrembling liver-spotted hands to turn the boy into an actor. As he worked, he talked . . . in a low, almost emotionless monotone whose very lack of coherence moved me.

Beside the table on which Gareth lay was the preservator I had seen him in the night before. It stood open and empty, like the casing of one of those fabled bombs that had so long ago virtually destroyed our spawning place, making our planet the home of a preemptive neo-human species that had exiled us, masker and Atarite, to the darkling islands of a northern sea on a world eight hundred light-years from Earth. The whirring of a small computer and the tiny hands sweeping across each tube in an array of cathode-ray tubes (these last on the face of a toposcopic unit opposite the table itself) made the room an eerie place. Sayati Elk's voice droned on over the computer sound; his hands continued to wire, and probe, and snip, and hover, lingering now clinically, now out of something deeply unscientific. Before Elk could take note, I took my leave.

Upstairs, the boy's inert trees awaited, frozen in time, tangled in my own nascent memory.

XX

I have been at Stonelore two years. The sloak has not returned to Ongladred, and the beach bonfires have long since been allowed to go out. Maybe there's no such creature; maybe the Parfects—in their infinite, condescending wisdom—have granted us their penultimate reprieve. I don't care anymore, I live as if my fate were in no one's hands but my own. When I regard the night sky, I see only the Shattered Moons, nothing sinister, nothing quietly malign—and I hold my breath and genuflect before their mysteriously choreographed beauty.

The photon-directors that Sayati Snow and Master Gordon used against the Pelagans have still not come back to us. Our Shathra Anna and Chancellor Blaine have each been to Stonelore twice since the morning I

was granted my liberty at Grotto House, and they now assure us that Atarite scientists dismantled the weapons in Lunn. I don't know how we should accept this news. Gabriel Elk, for one, believes Blaine is lying.

As for our enemies, they have ceased to attack us even in the small reiving parties for which they are famed. For what purpose, then, can our rulers want a weapon like the photon-director? We know. We are not naive. But uncertainty about the disposal or purloining of the ones wielded by Sayati Snow and Master Gordon still plagues us. And how demand clarification of Our Shathra Anna.

Elk, however, has clarified a point that once deprived me of sleep. Why a place like Stonelore? Why the agony and frustration to which he seasonly subjects himself? "Because one day," he says, "I will make them weep, Ingram." Until that day, despite his and Lady Bethel's justified reproaches, his audience will continue to be maskers to me. Not Mansuecerians; maskers. But they will weep, that day is coming—I know it will. And when it does, the citizens of this island nation will cremate the dead when they die, and I, with no talent for dramaturgy or sculpture, will pace Stonelore's stage, the first living actor in all our history.

For, assuredly, the day is coming when they will weep.

TO
THE LAND
OF SNOW

Excerpts from *The Computer Logs of Our Reluctant Dalai Lama*

Years in Transit: 82 out of 106?

Computer Logs of the Dalai Lama-to-Be, age 7

Aboard *Kalachakra*, I open my eyes in Amdo Bay. Sleep still pops in me, yowling like a really hurt cat trying to well itself. I look sidelong out my foggy eggshell. Many ghosts crowd near to see me leave the bear sleep that everyone in a strut-ship sometimes dreams in. Why have all these somnacicles up-phased to become ship-haunters? Why do so many crowd the grave-cave of my Greta-snooze?

"Greta Bryn"—that's my mama's voice—"can you hear me, kiddo?"

Yes I can. I have no deafness after I up-phase. Asleep even, I hear Mama talk in her dreams and cosmic rays crackle off *Kalachakra*'s plasma shield out in front (to keep us all from going dead), and the crackle from Earth across the rolling ocean of all-around-us space.

"Greta Bryn?"

She sounds like Atlanta, Daddy says. To me she sounds like Mama, which I want her to play-act now. She keeps bunnies, minks, guineas, and many other tiny crits down along our sci-tech cylinder in Kham Bay. But hearing her doesn't pulley me into sit-up pose. To get there, I stretch my soft parts and my bones.

"Easy, baby," Mama says.

A man in white unhooks me. A woman pinches me at the wrist so I won't twist the fuel tube or pulse counter. They have already shot me in the heart, to rev its beating. Now I do sit up and look around, clearer. Daddy stands nearby, showing me his crumply face.

"Hey, Gee Bee," he says, but doesn't grab my hand.

His coverall tag is my roll-call name: *Brasswell*. A clunky name for a girl and not too fine for Daddy, who looks thirty-seven or maybe fifty-fifteen, a number Mama says he uses to joke his fitness. He does *whore-to-culture*—another puzzle-funny of his—so that later we can turn Guge green, and maybe survive.

I feel sick, like juice gone sour in my tummy has gushed into my mouth. I start to elbow out. My eyes grow pop-out big, my fists shake like rattles. Now Daddy grabs me, mouth by my ear: "*Shhhh shhh shh.*" Mama touches my other cheek. Everybody else falls back to watch. That's scary too.

After a seem-like century I ask, "Are we there yet?"

Everybody yuks at my funniness. I drop my legs through the eggshell door. My hotness has colded off, a lot.

A bald brown man in orangey-yellow robes comes up so Mama and Daddy must stand off aside. I remember, sort of. This person has a really hard Tibetan name: *Nyendak Trungpa.* My last up-phase he made me say it a billion times so I would not forget. I was already four, but I almost forgetted anyway.

"What's your name?" Minister Trungpa asks me.

He already knows, but I blink and say, "Greta Bryn Brasswell."

"And where are you?"

"*Kalachakra,*" I say. "Our strut-ship."

"Point to your parents, please."

I do, it's simple. They're wide-awake ship-haunters now, real-live ghosts.

He asks, "Where are we going?"

"Guge," I say, another simple ask.

"What exactly is Guge, Greta Bryn?"

But I don't want to think—only to drink, my tongue's so thick with sourness. "A planet," I at last get out.

"Miss Brasswell,"—now Minister T's being a smart-aleck—"tell me two things you know about Guge."

I sort of ask, "It's 'The Land of Snow,' this dead king's place off to the west in olden Tibet?"

"Excellent!" Minister T says. "And its second meaning for us *Kalachakrans?*"

I think again, harder: "A faraway world to live on?"

"Where, intelligent miss?"

Another easy ask: "In the Goldilocks Zone," a funny name for it.

"But where, Greta Bryn, is this so-called Goldilocks Zone?"

"Around a star called *Gluh*—" I almost get stuck. "Around a star called Gliese 581." *GLEE-zha* is how I say it.

Bald Minister Trungpa grins. His face looks like a brown China plate with an up-curving crack. "She's fine," he tells the ghosts in the grave-cave. "And I believe she's the 'One.'"

*

Sometimes we must come up. We must wake and eat and drink, and move about so we can heal from ursidormizine sleep and not die before we reach Guge. When I come up this time, I get my own nook that snugs in the habitat drum called Amdo Bay. It has a vidped booth for learning from, with lock belts for when the AG goes out. It belongs to only me, it's not just one in a common space like most ghosts use.

Finally I ask, "What did that Minister T mean?"

"About what?" Mama doesn't eye me when she speaks.

"That I'm the 'One.' Which 'One'? Why'd he say that?"

"He's upset and everybody aboard has gone a little loco."

"Why?" But maybe I know. We ride so long that anyone riding with us sooner or later crazies up: *inboard fever*. Captain Xao once warned of this.

Mama says, "His Holiness, Sakya Gyatso, has died, so we're stupid with grief and thinking hard about how to replace him. Minister T, our late Dalai Lama's closest friend, thinks you're his rebirth, Greta Bryn, his heaven-sent successor."

I don't get this. "He thinks I'm not I?"

"I guess not. Grief has fuddled his reason, but maybe just temporarily."

"*I am I*," I say to Mama awful hot, and she agrees.

But I remember the Dalai Lama. When I was four, he played Go Fish with me in Amdo Bay during my second up-phase. Daddy sneak-named him "Yoda," like from *Star Wars*, but he looked more like skinny Mr. Peanut on the peanut tins. He wore a one-lens thing and a funny soft yellow hat, and he taught me a song, "Loving the Ant, Loving the Elephant." After that, I had to take my ursidormizine and hibernize. Now Minister T says the DL is I, or I am he, but surely Mama hates as much as I do how such stupidity could maybe steal me off from her.

"I don't look like Sakya Gyatso. I'm a girl, and I'm not an Asian person." Then I yell at Mama, "I am I!"

"Actually," she says, "things have changed, and what you speak as truth may have also changed, kiddo."

*

Everybody who gets a say in Amdo Bay now thinks that Minister Nyen-dak Trungpa calls me correctly. I am not I: I am the next Dalai Lama.

The Twenty-First, Sakya Gyatso, has died, and I must put on his sandals, which will not fit. Mama says he died of natural causes, but too young for it to *look* natural. He hit fifty-four, but he won't hit Guge. If I am he, I must take his place in "The Land of Snow" as colony dukpa, Tibetan for shepherd. That job scares me.

A good thing has come from this scary thing: I don't have to go back up into my egg pod and then down again. I stay up-phase. I *must*. I have too much to learn to drowse forever, even if I can sleep-learn by hypnoloading. Now I have a vidped booth that I sit in to learn and a tutor-guy, Lawrence ("Larry") Rinpoche, who loads on me a lot.

How old has all my earlier sleep-loading made me? Hibernizing, I hit seven and learnt while dreaming.

People should not call me *Her Holiness*. I am a girl person—not a Chinese or a Tibetan. I tell Larry these things the first time he comes to my room in Amdo. I've seen him in spectals about samurai and spacers, where he looks dark-haired and chest-strong. Now, anymore, he isn't. He has silver hair and hips like Mama's. His eyes do a flash thing, though, even when he's not angry, and it throws him back into the spectals he once star-played in as cool guy Lawrence Lake.

"Do I look Chinese, or Tibetan, or even Indian?" Larry asks.

"No, you don't. But you don't look like no girl either."

"*A* girl, Your Holiness." Larry must correct me. Mama says he will teach me logic, Tibetan art and culture, Sanskrit, Buddhist philosophy; and medicine (space and otherwise). And also poetry, music and drama, astronomy, astrophysics, synonyms, and Tibetan, Chinese, and English. Plus cinema, radio/TV history; politics and pragmatism in deep-space colony planting, and lots of other stuff.

"No girl ever got to be Dalai Lama," I tell Larry.

"Yes, but our Fourteenth predicted his successor would hail from a place outside Tibet; and that he might re-ensoul not as a boy but as a girl."

"But Sakya Gyatso, our last, can't stick his soul in *this* girl." I cross my arms and turn in a klutz-o turn.

"O Little Ocean of Wisdom, tell me why not."

Stupid tutor-guy. "He died after I got borned. How can a soul jump in the skin of somebody already borned?"

"*Born*, Your Holiness. But it's easy. It just jumps. The *samvattanika viñ-ñana*, the evolving consciousness of a Bodhisattva, jumps where it likes."

"Then what about me, Greta Bryn?" I tap-tap my chest.

Larry tilts his ginormous head. "What do *you* think?"

Oh, that old trick. "Did it kick me out? If it kicked me out, where did *I* go?"

"Do you *feel* it kicked you out, Your Holiness?"

"I feel it never got in. Inside, I feel that I . . . *own myself*."

"Maybe you do, but maybe his *punarbhava*—his 're-becoming'—is in there mixing with your own personality."

"But that's so scary."

"What did you think of Sakya Gyatso, the last Dalai Lama? Did he scare you?"

"No, I *liked* him."

"You like everybody, Your Holiness."

"Not anymore."

Larry laughs. He sounds like he sounded in *The Return of the Earl of Epsilon Eridani*. "Even if the process has something unorthodox about it, child, why avoid mixing your soul with that of a distinguished man you liked?"

I don't answer this windy ask. Instead, I say, "Why did he have to die, Mister Larry?"

"Greta, he didn't have much choice. Somebody killed him."

Every "day" I stay up-phase. Every day I study and I try to understand what's happening on *Kalachakra*, and how the last Dalai Lama, at swim in my soul, has slipped his *bhava*, "becoming again," into my *bhava*, or "becoming now," and so has become a thing old and new all at once.

Larry tells me just to imagine one candle lighting off another (even though you'd be crazy to light anything inside a starship), but my candle was already lit before the last Lama's got snuffed, and I never even smelt it go out. Larry laughs and says His Dead Holiness's flame "never quenched, but did go dim during its forty-nine-day voyage to bardo." Bardo, I think, must look like a fish tank that the soul tries to swim in even with nothing in it.

Up-phase, I learn more about *Kalachakra*. I don't need my tutor-guy. I wander all about, between studying and tutoring times. When the artificial-gravity cuts off, as it does a lot, I swim my ghost self into nooks and bays almost anywhere.

Our ship has a loco largeness, like a tunnel turning through star-smeared space, like a line of railroad tank cars *humming* through the Empty Vast *without any hum*. I saw such trains in my hypnoloading sleeps. Now I peep them as spectals and mini-holos and even palm pix.

Larry likes for me to do that too. He says anything "fusty and fun" is OK by him, if it tutors me well. And I don't *need* him to help me twig when I snoop *Kalachakra*. I learn by drifting, floating, swimming, counting, and just by asking ghosts what I want to know.

Here's what I've learnt by reading and vidped-tasking, snooping and asking:

1. UNS *Kalachakra* hauls 990 human asses ("and also the rest of each bloke aboard"—Dad's dumb joke) to a world in the Goldilocks Zone of the Gliese 581 solar system, 20.3 lights from *Sol*, the assumed-to-be-live-on-able planet Gliese 581g.

2. Captain Xao says that most of us on *Kalachakra* spend our journey in ursidormizine slumber to dream about our colonizing work on Guge. The greatest number of *somnacicles*—sleepers—have their egg pods in Amdo Bay toward the nose of our ship. (These hibernizing lazybones look like frozen cocoons in their see-through eggs.) Those of us more often up-phase slumber at "night" in Kham Bay, where tech folk and crew do their work. At the rear of our habitat drum lies U-Tsang Bay, which I haven't visited, but where, Mama says, our Bodhisattvas—monks, nuns, lamas, and such—reside, up-phase or down-.

3. All must wriggle up-phase once each year or so. You cannot hibernize longer than two at a snooze because we human somnacicles go dodgy quite soon during our third year drowse, so Captain Xao tells us, "We'll need every hand on the ground once we're all down on Guge." ("Every *foot* on the ground," I would say.)

4. Red dwarf star Gliese 581, also known as *Zarmina*, spectral class M3V, awaits us in constellation Libra. Captain Xao calls it the eighty-seventh closest known solar system to our sun. It has seven

planets and spurts out X-rays. It will flame away much sooner than *Sol*, but so far in the future that no one on *Kalachakra* will care a toot.

5.   Gliese 581g, aka Guge, goes around its dwarf in a circle, nearly. It has one face stuck toward its sun, but enough gravity to hold its gasses to it; enough—more than Earth's—so you can walk on it without drifting away. But it will really hot you on the sun-stuck side and chill you nasty on its drear dark rear. It's got rocks topside and magma in its zonal mountains. We must live in the in-between stripes of the terminator, *not* some old spectal but safe spots for bipeds with blood to boil or kidneys to broil. Or maybe we'll freeze, if we land in the black. So two hurrahs for Guge, and three for "The Land of Snow" in the belts where we hope to plug in.

6.   We know Guge has mass. It isn't, says Captain Xao, a "pipedream or a mirage." Our onboard telescope found it twelve Earth years ago, seventy out from Moon-orbit kickoff, with maybe twenty or so to go before we really get there. Hey, I'm more than a smidgen scared to arrive, hey, maybe a million smidgens.

7.   I'm also scared to stay an up-phase ghost on *Kalachakra*. Like a snow leopard or a yeti, my life is in deep-doo-doo danger. I don't want to step up to Dalai Lamahood. It's got its perks, but until Captain Xao, Minister Trungpa, Lawrence Rinpoche, Mama, Daddy, and our security folk find out WHO kilt the twenty-first DL, Greta Bryn Brasswell, a maybe DL, thinks her young life worth one dried pea in a vacu-meal pack. Maybe.

8.   In the tunnels running between Amdo, Kham, and U-Tsang Bays, the ghost of a snow leopard drifts. It has cindery spots swirled into the frosting of its fur. Its eyes leap yellow-green in the dimness when it gazes back at two-leggers like me. It jets from a holo-beam, but I don't know how or where from. In my dreams, I turn when I see it. My heart flutter-pounds towards a shutdown . . . which I fear it will, truly.

9.   Sakya Gyatso spent many years as an up-phase ghost on *Kalachakra*. He never did the bear sleep more than three months at once, but tried to blaze at top alertness like a Bodhisattva. He hibernized (when he did) only because on Guge he must lead the 990 shipboard faithfuls and millions of Tibetan Buddhists, native and not, in their unjust exiles. Can an up-phase ghost, once it really dies, survive on a strut-ship as a ghost for real? Truly, I do not know.

10. Once I didn't know Mama's or Daddy's first names. Tech is a title not a name, and Tech Brasswell married my mama, Tech Bonfils, aboard *Kalachakra* (Captain Xao prompting the vows), in the seventy-fourth year of our voyage. Tech Bonfils birthed me the following fall, one of only forty-seven children born on our trip to Guge. Luckily, Larry Rinpoche told me my folks' names: *Simon* and *Karen Bryn*. Now I don't even know if they *like* each other. I do know, from lots of reading, that S. Hawking—a now-dead astrophysicist—once said, *"People are not quantifiable."* He was sure right about that.

I know lots more, of course, but not who kilt the Twenty-first DL, if anybody did, and so I pick at that worry a lot.

Years in Transit: 83
Computer Logs of the Dalai Lama-to-Be, age 8

In old spectals and palm pix, starship captains sit at helms where they can see the Empty Vast through windows or screens. Captain Xao, First Officer Nima Photrang, and their helpers keep us all going toward Gliese 581 in a closed cockpit in the upper central third of the big tin can strut-shipping us to Guge.

This section we call Kham Bay. Cut flowers in slender vials prettify the room where Xao and Photrang and crew do their jobs. This pit also has a woven wall hanging of the *Kalachakra* Mandala and a big painted figure of the Buddha wearing a body, both a man's and a woman's, with many faces and arms. Larry calls this window-free place a control room and a shrine.

I guess he knows.

I visit the cockpit. Nobody stops me. I visit because Simon and Karen Bryn have gone back to their Siestaville to pod-lodge for many months on Amdo Bay's bottom level. Me, I stay my ghostly self. I owe it to everyone aboard—or so I often get told—to grow into my full Lamahood.

"Ah," says Captain Xao, "you wish to fly the *Kalachakra*. Great, Your Holiness."

But he passes me on to First Officer Photrang, a Tibetan who looks manlike in her jumpsuit but womanlike at her wrists and hands . . . so gentle about the eyes that, floating near because our AG's down, she seems to have just pulled off a hard black mask.

"What may I do for you, Greta Bryn?"

My lips won't move, so grateful am I she didn't say, "Your Holiness."

She shows me the console where she watches the fuel level in a drop tank behind our tin cylinder as this tank feeds the antimatter engine pushing us outward. Everything, she tells me, depends on electronic systems that run "virtually automatically," but she and Captain Xao's other crew must check closely, though the systems have fail-safes that can signal them from afar even if they leave the control shrine.

"How long," I ask, "before we get to Guge?"

"In nineteen years we'll start braking," Nima Photrang says. "In another four, if all goes as planned, we will enter the Gliese 581 system and soon take a stationary orbital position about the terminator. From there we'll go down to the adjacent habitable zones that we intend to settle in and develop."

"Four years to brake!" No one's ever said such a thing to me before. Four years are half the number I've lived, and no adult, I think, feels older at their old ages than I do at eight.

"Greta Bryn, to slow us faster than that would put terrible stress on our strut-ship. Its builders assembled it with optimal lightness, to save on fuel, but also with sufficient mass to withstand a twentieth of a g during its initial four years of thrusting and its final four years of deceleration. Do you understand?"

"Yes, but—"

"Listen: It took the *Kalachakra* four years to reach a fifth of the speed of light. During that time we traveled less than half a light year and burned a lot of the fuel in our drop tanks. Jettisoning the used-up tanks lightened us. For seventy-nine years since then, we've coasted, cruising over sixteen light-years toward our target sun using our fuel primarily for trajectory correction maneuvers. That's a highly economical expenditure of the antimatter ice with which we began our flight."

"Good," I say—because Officer Photrang looks at me as if I should clap for such an "economical expenditure."

"Anyway, we scheduled four years of braking at one twentieth of a g to conserve our final fuel resources and to keep this spidery vessel from ripping apart at higher rates of deceleration."

"But it's still going to take so long!"

The officer takes me to a ginormous sketch of our strut-ship. "If anyone aboard has time for a stress-reducing deceleration, Greta Bryn, you do."

"Twenty-three years!" I say. "I'll turn thirty-one!"

"Yes, you'll wither into a pitiable crone." Before I can protest more, she shows me other stuff: a map of the inside of our passenger can, a hologram of the Gliese 581 system, and a d-cube of her living mama and daddy in the village Drak—which means *Boulder*—fifty-some rocky miles southeast of Lhasa. But—I'm such a doofus!—maybe they no longer live at all.

"My daddy's from Boulder!" I say to cover this thought.

Nima Photrang peers at me with small bright eyes.

"Boulder, Colorado," I tell her.

"Is that so?" After a nod from Captain Xao, she guides me into a tunnel lit by tiny glowing pins.

"What did you really come up here to learn, child? I'll tell you if I can."

"Who killed Sakya Gyatso?" I hurry to add, "I *don't* want to be him."

"Who told you somebody killed His Holiness?"

"Larry." I grab a guide rail. "My tutor, Larry Rinpoche."

Officer Photrang snorts. "Larry has a bad humor sense. And he may be wrong."

I float up. "But what if he's right?"

"Is the truth that important to you?" She pulls me down.

A question for a question, like a dry seed poked under my gum. "Larry says that a lama in training must seek truth in everything, and I must do so always and everyone else by doing likewise will empty the universe of lies."

"'Do as I say and not as I do.'"

"What?"

Nima—she tells me to call her by this name—takes my arm and swims me along the tunnel to a door that opens at a knuckle bump. She guides me into her rooms, a closet with a pull-down rack and straps, a toadstool unit for our shipboard intranet, and a corner for talking in. We float here. Nicely, or so it seems, Nima pulls a twist of brindle hair out of my eye.

"Child, it's possible that Sakya Gyatso had a heart attack."

"'Possible'?"

"That's the official version, which Minister T told all us ghosts up-phase enough to notice that Sakya'd gone missing."

I think hard. "But the *un*official version is . . . somebody killed him?"

"It's one unofficial story. In the face of uncertainty, child, people indulge their imaginations, and more versions of the truth arise than you can slam a lid on. But lid-slamming, we think, is a bad response to ideas that will come clear in the oxygen of free inquiry."

I shake my head. "Who do you mean, 'we'?"

Nima gives a small smile. "My 'we' excludes anyone who forbids the expression of plausible alternatives to any 'official version.'"

"What do you think happened?"

"I probably shouldn't say."

"Maybe you need some oxygen."

This time her smile grows bigger. "Yes, maybe I do."

"I'm the new Dalai Lama, probably, and I give you that oxygen, Nima. Tell me your idea, now."

After squinting at me hard, she does: "I fear that Sakya Gyatso killed himself."

"The Dalai Lama?" I can't help it: her notion slanders the man, who, funnily, now breathes inside me.

"Why *not* the Dalai Lama?"

"A Bodhisattva lives for others. He'd never kill anybody, much less himself."

"He stayed up-phase too much—almost half a century—and the anti-aging effects of ursidormizine slumber, which he often avoided as harmful to his leadership role, were compromised. His Holiness did have the soul of a Bodhisattva, but he also had an animal self. The wear to his body broke him down, working on his spirit as well as his head, and doubts about his ability to last the rest of our trip niggled at him, as did doubts about his fitness to oversee our colonization of Guge."

I cross my arms. This idea insults the late DL. It also, I think, poisons me. "I believe he had a heart attack."

"Then the official version has taken seed in you," Nima says.

"OK then. I like to think someone killed Sakya Gyatso, not that tiredness or sadness made him do it."

Gently: "Child, where's your compassion?"

I float away. "Where's yours?" At the door of the first officer's quarters, I try to bump out. I can't.

Nima must drift over, knuckle-bump the door plate, and help me with my angry going.

*

The artificial-gravity generators run again. I feel them humming through the floor of my room in Amdo, and in Z Quarters where our somnacicles nap. Larry says that except for them, AG aboard *Kalachakra* works little better than did electricity in war-wasted nations on Earth. Anyway, I don't need the lock belt in my vidped unit; and such junk as pocket pens, toothbrushes, and d-cubes don't go slow-spinning off like fuzzy dreams.

Somebody knocks.

Who is it?

Not Larry, who's already taught me today, or Mama, who sleeps in her pod, or Daddy, who's gone up-phase to U-Tsang to help the monks lay out rock gardens around their gompas. He gets to visit U-Tsang, but I—the only nearly anointed DL on this ship—must mostly hang with non-monks.

The knock knocks again.

Xao Songda enters. He unhooks a folding stool from the wall and sits atop it next to my vidped booth: Captain Xao, the pilot of our generation ship. Even with the hotshot job he has to work, he roams around almost as much as I do.

"Officer Photrang tells me you have doubts."

I have doubts like a strut-ship has fuel tanks, and I wish I could drop them half as fast as *Kalachakra*, "The Wheel of Time," dropped its anti-hydrogen-ice-filled drums in the first four years of its run toward our coasting speed.

"Well?" Captain Xao's eyebrow goes up.

"Sir?"

"Does my first officer lie, or do you indeed have doubts?"

"I have doubts about everything."

Captain Xao cocks his head. "Like what, child?" He seems nice but clueless.

"Doubts about who made me, why I was born in a big bean can, why I like the AG on rather than off. Doubts about the shipshapeness of our ship, the soundness of Larry Lake's mind, the realness of the rock we're going to. Doubts about—"

"Greta," Captain Xao tries to interrupt.

"—the pains in my legs and the mixing of my soul with Sakya's because of how our lifelines overlapped. Doubts—"

"Whoa." Xao Songda says. "Officer Photrang says you have doubts about the official version of the Twenty-first's death."

"Yes."

"I too, but, as your captain, I must tell you that this vessel cruises in ship-shape shape . . . with an artist in charge."

I gape at the man, then say: "Is the official story true? Did Sakya Gyatso really die of Cadillac infraction?"

"Cardiac infarction," the captain says, not getting that I just joked him. "Yes, he did. Regrettably."

"Or do you say that because Minister T told everyone that and he out-ranks you?"

Xao Songda looks confused. "Why do you think Minister Trungpa would lie?"

"Inferior motives."

"Ulterior motives," the stupid captain again corrects me.

"OK: ulterior motives. Did he have something to do with Sakya's death . . . for mean reasons locked in his heart, just as damned souls are locked in hell?"

The captain draws a noisy breath. "Goodness, child."

"Larry says that somebody killed Sakya." I climb out of my vidped booth and go to the captain. "Maybe it was you."

Captain Xao laughs. "Do you know how many hoops I had to leap through to become captain of this ship? Ethnically, Gee Bee, I am Han Chinese. Hardly anybody in the Free Federation of Tibetan Voyagers wished me to strut our strut-ship. But I was wholeheartedly Yellow Hat and the best pilot-engineer not already en route to a habitable planet. And so I'm here. I'd no more assassinate the Dalai Lama than desecrate a chörten, or harm his likely successor."

I believe him, even if an anxious soul could hear the last few words of his speech unkindly. I ask him if he likes Nima's theory—that Sakya Gyatso killed himself—better than Minister T's Cadillac-infraction hypothesis. When he starts to answer, I say, "Flee falsehood again and speak the True Word."

After a blink, he says, "If you insist."

"Yes, I do."

"Then I declare myself, on that question, an agnostic. Neither theory strikes me as outlandish. But neither seems likely, either: Minister T's because His Holiness had good physical health and Nima's because the stresses of this voyage were but tickling feathers to the Dalai Lama."

To my surprise, I begin to cry.

Captain Xao grips my shoulder balls so softly that his fingers feel like owl's down, as I dream such stuff on an Earth I've never seen, and never will. He whispers to me: "Shhh-shhh."

"Why do you shush me?"

Captain Xao removes his hands. "I no longer shush you. Feel free to cry."

I do. So does Captain Xao. We are wed in knowing that Larry my tutor was right all along, and that our late Dalai Lama fell at the hands of a really mean someone with an inferior motive.

Years in transit: 87
Computer Logs of the Dalai Lama-to-Be, age 12

A week before my twelfth birthday, a Buddhist nun named Dolma Langdun, who works in the Amdo Bay nursery, hails me through the *Kalachakra* intranet. She wants to know if, on my birthday, I will let one of her helpers accompany me to the nursery to meet the children and accept gifts from them.

She signs off, —*Mama Dolma.*

I think, Why does this person do this? Who's told her I have a birthday coming?

Not my folks, who sleep in their somnacicle eggs, nor Larry, who does the same because I've "exhausted" him. And so I resolve to put these questions to Mama Dolma over my intranet connection.

—*How many children?* I ask her, meanwhile listening to Górecki's *Symphony of Sorrowful Songs* through my ear-bud.

—*Five,* she replied. —*Very sweet children, the youngest ten months, the oldest almost six years. It would be a great privilege to attend you on your natal anniversary, Your Holiness.*

Before I can scold her for using this too-soon form of address, she adds, —*As a toddler, you spent time here in Momo House, but in those bygone days I was assigned to the nunnery in U-Tsang with Abbess Yeshe Yargag.*

—*Momo House!* I key her. —*Oh, I remember!*

Momo means "dumpling," and this memory of my caregivers and my little friends back then dampens my eyelashes. Clearly, during the Z-pod rests of my parents and tutor, Minister Trungpa has acted as a most thoughtful guardian.

The following week goes by even faster than a fifth of light-speed.

On my birthday morning, a skinny young monk in a maroon jumpsuit comes for me and takes me down to Momo House.

There I meet Mama Dolma. There, I also meet the children: the baby Alicia, the toddlers Pema and Lahmu, and the oldest two, Rinzen and Mickey. Except for the baby, they tap-dance about me like silly dwarves.

The nursery features big furry balls that also serve as hassocks, blowuppable yaks, monkeys, and pterodactyls, and cribs and learning booths, with lock belts for AG failures. A system made just for the Dumpling Gang always warns us of an outage at least fifteen minutes before it occurs.

The nearly-six kid, Mickey, grabs my hand and shows me around. He introduces me to everybody, working down from the five-year-old to ten-month-old Alicia. All of them but Alicia give me drawings. These drawings show a monkey named Chenrezig (of course), a nun named Dolma (ditto), a yak named Yackety (double ditto), and a python with no name at all. I ooh and ah over these masterpizzas, as I call them, and then help them assemble soft-form puzzles, feed one another snacks, go to the toilet, and scan a big voyage chart that ends (of course) at Gliese 581g.

But it's Alicia, the baby, who wins me. She twinkles. She flirts. She touches. At nap time, I hold her in a vidped booth, its screen oranged out and its rockers rocking, and I nuzzle her sweet-smelling neck.

Alicia tugs at my lips and pinches my mouth flat, so set on reshaping my face that she seems a pudgy sculptor elf. All the while, her agate irises, bigger than my thumb tips, play across my face with cross-eyed puppy love. I stay with Alicia—Alicia Paljor—all the rest of that day. Then the skinny young monk comes to escort me home, as if I need him to, and Mama Dolma hugs me goodbye.

Alicia wails.

It hurts to leave, but I do, because I must, and even as the hurt fades, the memory of my outstanding birthday begins, that very night, to sing in me like the lovely last notes of Górecki's *Third*.

I have never had a better birthday.

*

Months later, Daddy Simon and Mama Karen Bryn have come up-phase at the same time. Together, they fetch me from my nook in Amdo and walk with me on a good AG day to the cafeteria above the grave-caves of our strut-ship's central drum, Kham. I ease along the serving line between them, taking tsampa, mushroom cuts, tofu slices, and the sauces to make them palatable. The three of us end up at a table in a nook far from the serving line. Music by J. S. Bach spills from speakers in the movable walls, with often a sitar and bells to call up for some voyagers a Himalayan nostalgia to which my folks are immune. We eat fast and talk small.

Then Mama says, "Gee Bee, your father has something to tell you."

O God. O Buddha. O Larry. O Curly. O Moe.

"Tell her," Mama orders.

Daddy Simon wears the sour face proclaiming that everybody should call him Pieman Oldfart. I hurt to behold him. But at last he says to me that before I stood up-phase, almost three years ago, as the DL's disputed Soul Child, he and Mama signed apartness documents that have now concluded in an agreement of full marital severance. They continue my folks, but not as the couple that conceived, bore, and raised me. They remain friends, but will no longer wish to cohabit because of incompatibilities that have arisen over their up-phase years. It really shouldn't matter to me, they say, because I've become Larry Lake's protégée with a grand destiny that I will no doubt fulfill as a youth and an adult. Besides, they will continue to parent me as much as my odd unconfirmed status as DL-in-training allows.

I do not cry, as I did upon learning that Captain Xao believes that somebody slew my only-maybe predecessor. I don't cry because their news feels truly distant, like word of a planet somewhere whose people have brains in their chest. However, it does hurt to think about why I absolutely must cry later.

Daddy gets up, kisses my forehead, and leaves with his tray.

Mama studies me for a long moment. "I'll always love you. You've made me very proud."

"You've made me very proud," I echo her.

"What?"

We push our plastic fork tines around in our leftovers, which I imagine rising in damp squadrons from our plates and floating up to the air-filtration fans. I wish that I, too, could either rise or sink.

"When will they confirm you?" Mama asks.

"Everything on this ship takes *forever*: getting from here to there, finding a killer, confirming the new DL."

"You must have some idea."

"I don't. The monks don't want me. I can't even visit their make-believe gompas over in U-Tsang."

"Well, those are sacred places. Not many of us get invitations."

"But Minister T has declared me the 'One,' and Larry has tutored me in thousands of subjects, holy and not so holy. Even so, the under-lamas and their silly crew think less well of me than they would of a lame blue mountain sheep."

"Don't call their monasteries 'make-believe,' Gee Bee. Don't call these other holy people and their followers 'silly.'"

"Oh, rot!" I actually say. "I wish I were anywhere but on this bean can flung at an iceberg light-years across the stupid Milky Way."

"Don't, Greta Bryn. You've got a champion in Minister Trungpa."

"Who just wants to bask in the reflected glory of his next supposed Bodhisattva—which, I swear, I am not."

Mama lifts her tray and slams it down.

Nobody else seems to notice, but I jump.

"You have no idea," she says, "who you are or what a champion can do for you, and you're *much* too young to dismiss yourself or your powerful advocate."

One of the Brandenburg Concertos swells, its sitars and yak bells flourishing. Far across the mess hall, Larry Lake shuffles toward us with a tray. Mama sees him, and, just as Daddy did, she kisses my forehead and abruptly leaves. My angry stare tells Larry not to mess with me (no, I won't apologize for the accidental pun), and Larry veers off to sit with some bio-techs at a faraway table.

Years in transit: 88
Computer Logs of the Dalai Lama-to-Be, age 13

Today marks another anniversary of the *Kalachakra*'s departure from Moon orbit on its crossing to Guge in the Gliese 581 system.

Soon I will turn thirteen. Much has happened in the six years since I woke to find that Sakya Gyatso had died and I had become Greta Gyatso, his premature reincarnation.

What has not happened haunts me as much as, if not more than, what has. I have a disturbing sense that the "investigation" into Sakya's murder resides in a secretly agreed-upon limbo. Also, that my confirmation rests in this same misty territory, with Minister T as my "regent." Recently, though, at First Officer Nima's urging, Minister T assigned me a bodyguard from among the monks of U-Tsang Bay, a guy called Ian Kilkhor.

Once surnamed Davis, Kilkhor was born sixteen years into our flight of Canadian parents, techs who'd converted to the Yellow Hat order of Tibetan Buddhists in Calgary, Alberta, a decade before the construction of our interstellar vessel. Although nearing the chronological age of sixty, Kilkhor—as he asks me to call him—looks less than half that and has many admirers among the female ghosts in Kham.

Officer Nima fancies him. (Hey, even I fancy him.)

But she is celibacy-committed unless a need for childbearing arises on Guge. And assuming her reproductive apparatus still works. Under such circumstances, I suspect that Kilkhor would lie with her.

Here I confess my ignorance. Despite lessons from Larry in the Tibetan language, I didn't realize, until Kilkhor told me, that his new surname means "Mandala." I excuse myself on the grounds that "Kilkhor" more narrowly means "center of the circle," and that Larry often skimps on offering connections. (To improve the health of his "mortal coil," Larry has spent nearly four of my last six years in an ursidormizine doze. I go to visit him once every two weeks in the pod-lodges of Amdo Bay, but these well-intended homages sometimes feel less like cheerful visits than dutiful viewings.) Also, "Kilkhor" sounds to me more like an incitement to violence than it does a statement of physical and spiritual harmony.

Even so, I benefit in many ways from Kilkhor's presence as bodyguard and stand-in tutor. Like Larry, Mama and Daddy spend long periods in their pods; and Kilkhor, a monk who knows *tai chi chuan*, has kept the killer, or killers, of Sakya from slaying me, if such villains exist aboard our ship. (I have begun to doubt they do.) He has also taught me much of history, culture, religion, politics, computing, astrophysics and astronomy that Larry, owing to long bouts of hibernizing, has neglected. Also, he weighs in for me with the monks, nuns, and yogis of U-Tsang, who feel disenfranchised in the process of confirming me as Sakya's successor.

Indeed, because the Panchen Lama now in charge in U-Tsang will not let me set foot there, Kilkhor intercedes to get high monks to visit me in Kham. The Panchen Lama, to avoid seeming either bigot or autocrat, permits these visits. Sadly (or not), my sex, my ethnicity, and (most important) the fact that my birth antedates the Twenty-first's death by five years all conspire to taint my candidacy. I doubt it too, and fear that fanatics among the "religious" will try to veto me by subtraction, not by argument, and that I will die at the hands of friends rather than enemies of the Dalai Lamahood.

Such fears, alone, throw real doubt on Minister T's choice of me as Sakya's only indisputable Soul Child.

Years in transit: 89
Computer Logs of the Dalai Lama-to-Be, age 14

"The Tibetan belief in monkey ancestors puts them in a unique category as the only people I know of who acknowledged this connection before Darwin."
  —Karen Swenson, 20th-century traveler, poet, and worker
  at Mother Teresa's Calcutta mission

Last week, a party of monks and one nun met me in the hangar of Kham Bay. From their gompas (monasteries) in U-Tsang Bay, they brought a woolen cloak, a woolen bag, three spruce walking sticks, three pairs of sandals, and a white-faced monkey that one monk, as the group entered, fed from a baby bottle full of ashen-gray slurry.

An AG-generator never runs in the hangar because people don't often visit it, and the lander nests in a vast hammock of polyester cables. So we levitated in a cordoned space near the nose of the lander, which the Free Federation of Tibetan Voyagers has named *Chenrezig*, after that Buddhist disciple who, in monkey form, sired the first human Tibetans. (Each new DL instantly qualifies as the latest incarnation of Chenrezig.) Our lander's nose is painted with bright geometries and the cartoon head of a wise-looking monkey wearing glasses and a beaked yellow hat. Despite this simian iconography, however, everyone on our strut-ship calls the lander the *Yak Butter Express*.

After stiff greetings, these high monks—including the venerable Panchen Lama, Lhundrub Gelek, and Yeshe Yargag, the abbess of U-Tsang's only nunnery!—tied the items that they'd brought to a utility toadstool in the center of our circle ("kilkhor"). Then we floated in lotus positions, hands palms-upward, and I stared at these items, but not at the pale monkey now clutching the PL and wearing a look of alert concern. From molecular vibrations and subtle somatic clues—twitches, blinks, sniffles—I tried to determine which of the items they wished me to select . . . or not to select, as their biases dictated.

"Some of these things were Sakya Gyatso's," the Panchen Lama said. "Choose only those that he viewed as truly his. Of course, he saw little in this life as a 'belonging.' You may examine any or all, Miss Brasswell."

I liked how my birth name (even preceded by the stodgy honorific Miss) sounded in our hangar, even if it did seem to label me an imposter, if not an outright foe of Tibetan Buddhism. To my right, Kilkhor lowered his eyelids, advising me to make a choice. OK, then: I had no need to breast-stroke my way over to the pile.

"The cloak," I said.

Its stench of musty wool and ancient vegetable dyes told me all I needed to know. I recalled those smells and the cloak's vivid colors from an encounter with the DL during his visit to the nursery in Amdo when I was four. It had seemed the visit of a seraph or an extraterrestrial—as, by virtue of our status as star travelers, he had qualified. Apparently, none of *these* faithful had accompanied him then, for, obviously, none recalled his having cinched on this cloak to meet a tot of common blood.

The monkey—a large Japanese macaque (*Mucaca fuscata*)—swam to the center of our circle, undid the folded cloak, and kicked back to the Lama, who belted it around his lap. Still fretful, the macaque levitated in its breech-clout—a kind of diaper—beside the PL. It wrinkled its brow at me in approval or accusation.

"Go on," Lhundrub Gelek said. "Choose another item."

I glanced at Kilkhor, who dropped his eyelids.

"May I see what's in the bag?" I asked.

The PL spoke to the macaque: a critter I imagined Tech Bonfils taking a liking to at our trip's outset. It then paddled over to the bag tied to the utility toadstool, seized the bag by its neck, and dragged it over to me.

After foraging a little, I extracted five slender books, of a kind now rarely made, and studied each: one in English, one in Tibetan, one in French, one in Hindi, and one (I'm guessing now) in Esperanto. In each case, I recognized their alphabets and point of origin, if not their subject matter. A bootlace linked the books. When they started to float away, I caught its nearer end and yanked them all back.

"Did His Holiness write these?" I asked.

"Yes," the Panchen Lama said, making me think that I'd passed another test. He added, "Which of the five did Sakya most esteem?" Ah, a dirty trick. Did they want me to read not only several difficult scripts but also Sakya's departed mind.

"Do you mean as artifacts, for the loveliness of their craft, or as documents, for the spiritual meat in their contents?"

"Which of those options do you suppose most like him?" Abbess Yeshe Yargag asked sympathetically.

"Both. But if I must make a choice, the latter. When he wrote, he distilled clear elixirs from turbid mud."

Our visitors beheld me as if I had neutralized the stench of sulfur with sprinkles of rose water. Again, I felt shameless.

With an unreadable frown, the PL said, "You've chosen correctly. We now wish you to choose the book that Sakya most esteemed for its message."

I reexamined each title. The one in French featured the words *wisdom* and *child*. When I touched it, Chenrezig responded with a nearly human intake of breath. Empty of thought, I lifted that book.

"Here: *The Wisdom of a Child, the Childishness of Wisdom*."

As earlier, our five visitors kept their own counsel, and Chenrezig returned the books to their bag and the bag to the monk who had set it out.

Next, I chose among the walking sticks and the pairs of sandals, taking my cues from the monkey and so choosing better than I had any right to expect. In fact, I chose just those items identifying me as the Dalai Lama's Soul Child, girl or no girl.

After Kilkhor praised my accuracy, the PL said, "Very true, but—"

"But what?" Kilkhor said. "Must you settle on a Tibetan male only?"

The Lama replied, "No, Ian. But what about *this* child makes her miraculous?"

Ah, yes. One criterion for confirming a DL candidate is that those giving the tests identify "something miraculous" about him . . . or her.

"What about her startling performance so far?" Kilkhor asked.

"We don't see her performance as a miracle, Ian."

"But you haven't conferred about the matter." He gestured at the other holies floating in the fluorescent lee of the *Yak Butter Express*.

"My friends," the Panchen Lama asked, "what say you all in reply?"

"We find no miracle," a spindly, middle-aged monk said, "in this child's choosing correctly. Her brief life overlapped His Holiness's."

"My-me," Abbess Yargag said. "I find her a wholly supportable candidate."

The three leftover holies held their tongues, and I had to admit—to myself, if not aloud to this confirmation panel—that they had a hard-to-refute point, for I had pegged my answers to the tics of a monastery macaque with an instinctual sense of its keepers' moody fretfulness.

Fortunately, the monkey liked me. I had no idea why.

O to be unmasked! I needed no title or any additional powers to lend savor to my life. I wanted to sleep in my pod and to awaken later as an animal husbandry specialist, with Tech Karen Bryn Bonfils-Brasswell as my mentor and a few near age-mates as my fellow apprentices.

The PL unfolded from his lotus pose and floated before me with his feet hanging. "Thank you, Miss Brasswell, for this audience. We regret we can't—" Here he halted, for Chenrezig swam across our meeting space, pushed into my arms, and clasped me about the neck. Then the astonished monks and the shaken PL rubbed shoulders as if to ignite their bodies in glee or consternation.

Abbess Yargag said, "There's your miracle."

"*Nando*," the lama said, shaking his head: No, he meant.

"On the contrary," Abbess Yargag replied. "Chenrezig belonged to Sakya Gyatso, and never in Chenrezig's sleep-lengthened life has he embraced a child, a non-Asian, or a female—not even me."

"Nando," the PL, visibly angry, said again.

"*Rha* (Yes)," another monk put in. "*Om mani padme hum* (Hail the jewel in the lotus). *Ki ki so so lha lha gyalo* (Praise to the gods)."

I kissed Chenrezig's white-flecked facial mane as he whimpered like an infant in my already weary arms.

Years in transit: 93
Computer Logs of the Dalai Lama-to-Be, age 18

—*A Catechism: Why do we voyage?*

At age seven, I learned this catechism from Larry. Kilkhor often has me say it, to ensure that I don't turn apostate to either our legend or my long-term charge. Sometimes Captain Xao Songda, a Han who converted and fled to Vashon Island, Washington—via northern India; Cape Town, South Africa; Buenos Aires; and Hawaii—sits in to temper Larry's flamboyance and Kilkhor's lethargic matter-of-factness.

—*Why do we voyage?* one of them will ask.

—*To fulfill,* I say, *the self-determination tenets of the Free Federation of Tibet and to usher every soul pent in hell up through the eight lower realms to Buddhahood.*

From the bottom up, these realms include *1)* hell-pent mortals, *2)* hungry ghosts, *3)* benighted beasts, *4)* fighting spirits, *5)* human beings, *6)* seraphs and such, *7)* disciples of the Buddha, *8)* Buddhas for themselves only, and *9)* Bodhisattvas who live and labor for every soul in each lower realm.

—*Which realm did* you *begin in, Your Probationary Holiness?*

—*That of the bewildered, but not benighted, human mortal.*

—*As our Dalai Lama in Training, to which realm have you arisen?*

—*That of the disciples of Chenrezig:* Om mani padme hum! *I am the funky simian saint of the Buddha.*

—*From what besieged and bludgeoned homeland do you pledge to free us?*

—*The terrestrial "Land of Snow": Tibet beset; Tibet ensnared, ensorcelled, and enslaved.*

—*As a surrogate for that land gone cruelly forfeit, to which* new *country do you pledge to lead us?*

—*"The Land of Snow," on Guge the Unknowable, where we all must strive to free ourselves again.*

The foregoing part of the catechism embodies a pledge and a charge. Other parts synopsize the history of our oppression: the ruin of our economy; the destruction of our monasteries; the subjugation of our nation to the will of foreign predators; the co-opting of our spiritual formulae for greedy and warlike purposes; the submergence of our culture to the maws of jackals; and the quarantining of our state to anyone not of our oppressors' liking. Finally, against the severing of sinews human and animal, the pulling asunder of ties interdependent and relational, only the tallest mountains could stand. And those who undertook the khora, the sacred pilgrimage around Mount Kailash, often did so with little or no grasp of the spiritual roots of their journeys. Even then, that mountain, the land all about it, and the scant air overarching them, stole the breath and spilled into the pilgrims' lungs the bracing elixir of awe.

At length, the Tibetans and their sympathizers realized that their over-lords would never withdraw. Their invasion, theft, and reconfiguration of the state had left its peoples few options but death or exile.

—*So what did the Free Federation of Tibet do?* Larry, Kilkhor, or Xao will ask.

—*Sought a United Nations charter for the building of a starship, an initiative that we all feared China would preempt with its veto in the Security Council.*

—*What happened instead?*

—*The Chinese supported the measure.*

—*How so?*

—*They contributed to the general levy for funds to build and crew with colonists a second-generation antimatter ship capable of attaining speeds up to one-fifth the velocity of light.*

—*Why did China surrender to an enterprise implying severe criticism of a policy that it saw as an internal matter? That initiative surely stood as a rebuke to its efforts to overwhelm Tibet with its own crypto-capitalistic materialism.*

Here I may snigger or roll my eyeballs, and Lawrence, Kilkhor, or Xao will repeat the question.

—*Three reasons suffice to explain China's acquiescence,* I at length reply.

—*State them.*

—*First, China understood that launching this ship would remove the Twenty-first Dalai Lama, who had agreed not only to support this disarming plan but also to go with the Yellow Hat colonists to Gliese 581g.*

—*Ki ki so so lha lha gyalo (Praise to the gods),* my catechist says in Tibetan.

—*Indeed, backing this plan would oust from a long debate the very man whom the Chinese reviled as a poser and a bar to the incorporation of Tibet into their program of post-post-Mao modernization.*

Here, another snigger from a bigger poser than Sakya, namely, me.

—*And the second reason, Your Holiness?*

—*Backing this strut-ship strategy surprised the players arrayed against China in both the General Assembly and the Security Council.*

—*To what end?*

—*All these players could do was brand China's support a type of cynicism warped into a low-yield variety of "ethnic cleansing," for now Tibet and its partisans would have one fewer grievance to lay at China's feet.*

With difficulty, I refrain from sniggering again.

—And the third reason, Miss Greta Bryn, our delightfully responsive Ocean of Wisdom?

—Supporting the antimatter ship initiative allowed China to put its design and manufacturing enterprises to work drawing up blueprints and machining parts for the provocatively named UNS Kalachakra.

—And so we won our victory?

—Om mani padme hum (Hail the jewel in the lotus), I reply.

—And what do we Kalachakrans hope to accomplish on the sun-locked world we now call Guge?

—Establish a colony unsullied by colonialism; summon other emigrants to "The Land of Snow"; and lead to enlightenment all who bore that dream, and who will bear it into cycles yet to unfold.

—And after that?

—The cessation of everything samsaric, the opening of ourselves to nirvana.

—Hallelujah, Ian Kilkhor always concludes: *Hallelujah.*

Years in transit: 94
Computer Logs of the Dalai Lama-to-Be, age 19

For nearly four Earth months, I've added not one word to my Computer Log. But shortly after my last recitation of the foregoing catechism, Kilkhor pulled me aside and told me that I had a rival for the position of Dalai Lama.

This news astounded me. "Who?"

"A male Soul Child born of true Tibetan parents in Amdo Bay less than fifty days after Sakya Gyatso's death," Kilkhor said. "A search team found him almost a decade ago, but has only now disclosed him to us." Kilkhor made this disclosure of bad news—it is bad, isn't it?—sound very ordinary.

"What's his name?" I had no idea of what else to say.

"Jetsun Trimon," Kilkhor said. "Old Gelek seems to think him a more promising candidate than he does Greta Bryn Brasswell."

"Jetsun! You're joking, right?" My heart did a series of arrhythmic lhundrubs in protest.

Kilkhor regarded me then with either real, or expertly feigned, confusion. "You know him?"

"Of course not! But the name—" I stuck, at once amused and appalled.

"The *name*, Your Holiness?"

"It's a ridiculous, a totally ludicrous name."

"Not really. In Tibetan it means—"

"—'venerable' and 'highly esteemed,'" I put in. "But it's still ridiculous." And I noted that as a child, between bouts of study, I had often watched, well, "cartoons" in my vidped booth. Those responsible for this lowbrow programming had purposely stocked it with a selection of episodes called *The Jetsons*, all about a space-going Western family in a gimmick-ridden future. I had loved it.

"I've heard of it," Kilkhor said. "The program, I mean." But he didn't twig the irony of my five-year-younger rival's name, or pretended not to. To him, the similarity of these two monikers embodied a pointless coincidence.

"I can't do this anymore without a time-out," I said. "I'm going down-phase for a year—at least a quarter of a year!"

Kilkhor said nothing. His expression said everything.

Still, he arranged for my down-phase respite, and I repaired to Amdo Bay and my eggshell to enjoy this pod-lodging self-indulgence, which, except for rare cartoon-tinged nightmares, I almost did.

Now, owing to somatic suspension, I return at almost the same nineteen at which I went under.

When I awake this time amid a catacomb vista of eggshell pods—like racks in a troopship or a concentration-camp barracks—my mother, Minister T, the Panchen Lama, Ian Kilkhor, and Jetsun Trimon attend my awakening.

Grateful for functioning AG (as, down here, it *always* functions), I swing my legs out of the pod, stagger a step or two, and retch from a stomach knotted with a fresh anti-insomniac heat. The Tibetan boy, my rival, comes to me unbidden, slides an arm around me from behind, and eases me back toward his own thin body so that I don't topple into the vomit-vase Mama has given me. With his free hand, he strokes my brow and tucks stray strands of hair behind my ear, a familiarity that I hugely resent.

Although I usually sleep little, I do take occasional naps, for I *deserve* a respite.

I pull free of the presumptuous young imposter.

He looks about fifteen, and if I've hit nineteen, his age squares better than does mine with the passing of the last DL and the transfer of Sakya's bhava into the material form of Jetsun Trimon.

Beholding him, I find his given name less of a joke than I did before my nap and more of a spell for the inspiriting that the PL alleges has occurred in him. Jetsun and I study each other with mutual curiosity. Our elders look on with darker curiosities. How must Jetsun and I regard this arranged marriage, they no doubt wonder, and what does it presage for everyone aboard the *Kalachakra*?

During my year-plus sleep, maybe I've matured some. Although I want to cry out against the outrage—no, the *unkindness*—of my guardians' conspiracy to bring this fey usurper to my podside, I don't berate them. They warrant such a scolding, but I refrain. How do they wish me to view their collusion, and how can I see it as anything other than their sending a prince to the bier of a spell-afflicted maiden? Except for the acne scarring his forehead and chin, Jetsun is, well, cute, but I don't want his help. I loathe his intrusion into my pod-lodge and almost regret my return.

Kilkhor notes that the lamas of U-Tsang, including the Panchen Lama and Abbess Yargag, have finally decided to summon Jetsun Trimon and me to our onboard stand-in for the Jokhang Temple. There, they will conduct a gold-urn lottery to learn which of us will follow Sakya Gyatso as the Twenty-second Dalai Lama.

Jetsun bows. He says his tutor has given him the honor of inviting me, my family, and my guardians to this "shindig." It will occur belatedly, he admits, after he and I have already learned many sutras and secrets reserved in Tibet—holy be its saints, its people, and its memory—for a Soul Child validated by lottery.

But circumstances have changed since our Earth-bound days: The ecology of the *Kalachakra*, the great epic of our voyage, and our need on Guge for a leader of heart and vision require fine tunings beyond our forebears' imaginations.

Wiser than I was last year, I swallow a cynical yawn.

"And so," Jetsun ends, "I wish you joy in the lottery's Buddha-directed outcome, whichever name appears on the slip selected."

He bows and takes three steps back.

Lhundrub Gelek beams at Jetsun, and I know in my gut that the PL has become my competitor's regent, his champion. Mama Karen Bryn holds her face expressionless until fret lines drop from her lip corners like weighted ebony threads.

I thank Jetsun, for his courtesy and his well-rehearsed speech. He seems to want something more—an invitation of my own, a touch—but I have nothing to offer but the stifling of my envy, which I fight to convert to positive energies boding a happy karmic impact on the name slips in the urn.

"You must come early to our Temple," the PL says. "Doing so will give you time to pay your respects at Sakya Gyatso's bier."

This codicil to our invitation heartens me. Lacking any earlier approval to visit U-Tsang, I have seen the body of the DL on display there.

Do I really wish to see it, to see *him*?

Yes, of course I do.

We've lost many Kalachakrans in transit to Guge, but none of the others have our morticians bled with trochars, painted with creams and rouges, or treated with latter-day preservatives. Those others we ejected via tubes into the airless cold of interstellar space, mere human scraps for the ever-hungry night.

In Tibet, the bereaved once spread their dead loved ones out on rocks in "celestial burial grounds." This they did as an act of charity, for the vultures. On our ship, though, we have no vultures, or none with feathers, and perhaps by firing our dead into unending quasi-vacuum, we will offer to the void a sacrifice of once-living flesh generous enough to upgrade our karma.

But Sakya Gyatso we have enshrined; and soon, as one of only two applicants for his sacred post, I will gaze upon the remains of one whose enlightenment and mercy have plunged me into painful egocentric anguish.

At the appointed time (six months from Jetsun's invitation), we journey from Amdo and across Kham by way of tunnels designed for either gravity-assisted marches or weightless swims. Our style of travel depends on AG generators and on the rationing of gravity by formulae meant to benefit our long-term approach to Guge. However, odd outages often overcome these formulae. Blessedly, Kalachakrans now adjust so well to gravity loss that we no longer find it alarming or inconvenient.

Journeying, we discover that U-Tsang's residents—all Bodhisattvas, allegedly—have forsworn all use of generators during the 72-hour Festival of the Golden Urn, with that ceremony occurring at noon of the middle day. This renunciation they regard as a gift to everybody aboard our vessel—somnacicles and ghosts—and no hardship at all. Any stress we spare the generators, our karmic economies tell us, will redound to everybody's benefit in our voyage's later stages.

My entourage consists of my divorced parents, Simon Brasswell and Karen Bryn Bonfils; Minister T, my self-proclaimed regent; Lawrence Lake Rinpoche, my tutor and confidant, now up-phase for the first time in two years; and Ian Kilkhor, security agent, standby tutor, and friend. We walk single-file through a part of Kham wide enough for the next Dalai Lama's subjects to line the walls and perform respectful *namaste* as he (or she) passes. Minister T tells us that Jetsun Trimon and his people made this same journey eighteen hours ago and that their well-wishers in this trunk tunnel were fewer than those attending our passage. A Bodhisattva would take no pleasure from such a petty statistical triumph. Tellingly, I do. So what does my competition-bred joy say about my odds in the coming gold-urn lottery? Nothing auspicious, I fear.

Eventually, our crowds dwindle, and we enter a deck area featuring a checkpoint and a sector gate. A monk clad in maroon passes us through. Another dials open the gate admitting us, at last, to U-Tsang.

I smell roast barley, barley beer (*chang*), and an acrid tang of incense that makes my stomach seize. Beyond the gate, which shuts behind us like a stone wheel slotting into a tomb groove, we drift through a hall with thin metal rails and bracket-like handholds. The luminary pins here gleam a watery purple.

Our feet slide out from under us, not like those of a fawn sliding on ice, but like those of an astronaut trainee rising from the floor of an aircraft plunging to create a few seconds of pedagogical zero-g.

The AG generators here shut down a while ago, so we dog-paddle in waterwheel slow-motion, unsure which tunnel to enter.

Actually, I'm the only uncertain trekker, but because neither Minister T nor Larry nor Kilkhor wants to help me, I stay mute, from perplexity and pride: another black mark, no doubt, against my lottery chances.

Ahead of us, fifteen yards or so, a snow leopard manifests: a four-legged specter with yellow eyes and frost-etched silver fur. Despite the lack of gravity, it faces us as if standing on a rock ledge and licks its coal-colored beard as if savoring again the last guinea-pig-like chiphi that it crushed into bone bits. Stymied, I startle and sway. The leopard switches its tail, turns, and leaps into a tunnel that I would not have chosen.

Kilkhor laughs and urges us upward into this same purplish chute. "It's all right," he says. "Follow it. Or do you suspect a subterfuge from our spiritually elevated hosts?" He laughs again . . . this time, maybe, at his inadvertent nod to the Christian sacrament of communion.

Larry and I twig his mistake, but does anybody else?

"Come on," Kilkhor insists. "They've sent us this cool cat as a guide."

And so we follow. We swim rather than walk, levitating through a Buddhist rabbit hole in the wake of an illusory leopard . . . until, by a sudden shift in perspective, we feel ourselves to be "walking" again.

This ascent, or fall, takes just over an hour, and we emerge in the courtyard of Jokhang Temple, or its diminished *Kalachakra* facsimile. Here, the Panchen Lama, the Abbess of U-Tsang's only nunnery, and a colorful contingent of Yellow Hats and other monks greet us joyfully. They regale us with *khata* (gift scarves inscribed with good-luck symbols) and with processional music played by flutes, drums, and bells. Their welcome feels at once high-spirited and heartfelt.

The snow leopard has vanished. When we broke into the courtyard swimming like ravenous carp, somebody, somewhere, ceased projecting it.

So let the gold-urn ceremony begin. Put me out of, and into, my misery.

But before the lottery, we visit the shrine where the duded-up remains of Sakya Gyatso lie in state, like those of Lenin in the Kremlin or of Mao in the Forbidden City. Although Sakya should not suffer mention in the same breath as mass murderers, nobody can deny that we have preserved him as an icon, just as the devotees of Lenin and Mao mummified them. And I must trust that a single Figure of Peace weighs more in the karmic justice scales than does a shipload of bloody despots.

Daddy begs off. He has seen the dead Sakya Gyatso before, and traveling with his ex-wife, the mother of his Soul Child daughter, has depressed him beyond easy repair. So he retreats to a nearby guesthouse and locks himself inside for a nap. Ian Kilkhor leaves to visit several friends in the Yellow Hat gompa with whom he once studied; Minister T, who has often paid homage at the Twenty-first's bier, has business with Lhundrub Gelek and others of the confirmation troupe who met with me in Kham in the shadow of the *Yak Butter Express*.

So, only Mama, Larry, and I go to see the Lama whom, according to many, I will succeed as the spiritual and temporal head of the 1000 or so Tibetan colonizers aboard this ship. The shrine we approach does not resemble a mausoleum. It sits on the courtyard's edge, like an exhibit of amateur art in a construction trailer.

Two maroon-clad guards await us beside its doors, one at each end of the trailer, now graffitified with mantras, prayers, and many mysterious symbols—but no one else in U-Tsang Bay has come out to view its principal attraction. The blousy monk at the nearer door examines our implanted, upper-arm IDs with click-scans, smiles beatifically, and nods us in. Larry jokes in Tibetan with the guy before joining us at the DL's windowed bier, where we three float: ghosts beside a pod-lodger who will not again arise, unless he has already done so in yet another borrowed body.

"He is not here," I say. "He has arisen."

Larry, who looks much older than at his last brief up-phase, laughs in appreciation or embarrassment: the latter, probably.

Mama gives me a blistering "cool-it" glare.

And then I gaze upon the body of Sakya Gyatso. Even in death, even through the clear but faintly dusty cover of his display pod, he sustains about his face and hands a soft amber aura of serene lifelikeness that startles, and discomfits. I see him smiling sweetly upon me when I was four. I imagine him displeasing his religious brethren and sisters by going more often into Amdo and Kham Bays to interact with his secular subjects than our under-lamas thought needful or wise, as if such visits distracted him from his obligations and sabotaged his authority in both realms, profane and holy. And it's definitely true that his longest uninterrupted sojourn in U-Tsang coincides with his years lying in state in this shabby trailer.

Commoners aboard ship loved him, but maybe—I reflect, studying his corpse with both fascination and regard—he angered those practitioners of Tantra who viewed him as their highest representative and model. Certainly, during his life he moved from external *Kalachakra* Tantra—a concern with the lost procession of solar and lunar days—to the internal Tantra, with its focus on the energy systems of the body, to the higher alternative Tantra leading to the sublime state of *bodhichitta*, perfect enlightenment for the sake of others.

Thus reflecting, I cannot conceive of anyone aboard ever wishing him harm or of myself climbing out of the pit of my ego to attain the state of material renunciation and accepting comprehension of emptiness that Sakya Gyatso reached and embodied through so many years of our journey.

That I stand today as one of two Soul Children in line to follow him defies logic; it offends reason and also the 722 deities resident in the *Kalachakra* Mandala as emblems of reality and consciousness. I lack even the

worth of a dog licking barley-cake crumbs from the floor. I put my palm on
the Twenty-first's pod cover and erupt in sobs. These underscore my unsuit-
ability to succeed him.

Mama's glare gives way to a look of fretful amazement. She lays an arm
over my shoulder, an intimacy that keeps me from drifting blindly away from
either her or Larry.

"Kiddo," she murmurs, "don't cry for this lucky man. We'll never cease to
honor him, but the time for mourning has passed."

I can't stop: All sleep has fled and the future holds only a scalding wake-
fulness. Larry lays his arm over my other shoulder, caging me between them.

"Baby," Mama says. "Baby, what's going on?"

She hasn't called me "baby" or "kiddo" since, over seven years ago, I had
my first period. I twist my neck just enough to tell her to glance at the late
DL, that she *must* look. Reluctantly, it seems, she does, and then looks back at
me with no apparent hesitancy or aversion. Her gaze then switches between
him and me until she realizes that I won't—I simply can't—succeed this saint
as our leader. Moreover, I intend to withdraw from the gold-urn lottery and
to throw my support to my rival. Mama remains silent, but her arm deserts
me and she turns from the DL's bier as if my declaration has acted as a ver-
nier jet to change her position. In any case, she drifts away.

"Do you understand me, Mama?"

Mama's eyes jiggle and close. Her chin drops. Her jumpsuit-clad body
floats like that of a string-free marionette, all raw angles and dreamily rafting
hands.

Larry releases me and swims to her. "Something's wrong, Greta Bryn."
I already suspect this, but these words penetrate with a laser's precision. I
fumble blurry-eyed after Larry, clueless about what to do to help.

Larry swallows her with his arms, like the male hero in an anachronistic
spectal, and then pushes her away to study her more objectively. Immediately,
he pulls her back in to him, checks her pulse at wrist and throat, and pivots
her toward me with odd contrasting expressions washing over his face.

"She's fainted, I think."

"Fainted?" My mother, so far as I know, never faints.

"It's all the travel . . . and her anxiety about the gold-urn lottery."

"Not to mention her disappointment in me."

Larry regards me with such deliberate blankness that I almost fail to
recognize the man, whom I have known seemingly forever.

"Talk to her when she comes 'round," he says. "Talk to her."

The blousy monk who ran click-scans on us enters the makeshift mausoleum and helps Larry tow my rag-doll mama outside, across the road, and into the battened-down Temple courtyard. The two accompany her to a basket-like bower chair that suppresses her driftability. They attend her with colorful fake Chinese fans.

I go with them, looking on like a gawker at a mess-hall accident.

Our post-swoon interview takes place in the nearly empty courtyard. Mama clutches two of the bower-chair spokes like a child in a gravity swing, and I maintain my place before her with the mindless agility of a pond carp.

"Never say you're forsaking the gold-urn lottery," she says. "You bear on your shoulders the hopes of a majority, my hopes highest of all."

"Did my decision to withdraw cause you to faint?"

"Of course!" she cries. "You can't withdraw! You don't think I *faked* my swoon, do you?"

I have no doubt that Mama didn't fake it. Her sclera clocked into view before her eyelids fell. But, before that, her gaze cut to and rested on Sakya's face just prior to her realizing my intent. Feelings of betrayal, loss, and outrage triggered her swoon. Now she says I have no choice but take part in the gold-urn drawing, and I regard her with such a blend of gratitude, for believing in me, and loathing, for her rigidity, that I can't speak. Do Westerners carry both me-first genes and self-doubt genes that, in combination, overcome the teachings of the Tantra?

"Answer me, Greta Bryn: Do you think I faked that faint?"

Mama knows already that I don't. She just wants me to assume the hair shirt of guilt for her indisposition and to pull it over my head with the bristly side inward. I have just enough Easterner in my being to deny her that boon and the pinched ecstasy implicit in it.

I hold her gaze, and hold it, until she begins to waver in her implacability.

"I didn't swoon solely because you tried to renounce your rebirth right, but also because you tried to humiliate me in front of Larry." Mama stands so far from the truth on this issue that she doesn't even qualify as wrong.

And so I laugh, like an evil-wisher rather than a daughter. "Not so," I say. "Why would I want to humiliate you before Larry?"

"Because I've always refused to coddle your self-doubts."

I recall Mama beholding Sakya's death mask and memorizing his every aura-lit feature. "What else caused you to 'fall out'?"

Her voice drops a register. "The Dalai Lama. His face. His hands. His body. His inhering and sustaining holiness."

"How does his 'sustaining holiness' knock you into a swoon, Mama?"

She peers across the courtyard road at the van where the DL lies in state. Then she pulls herself upright in the bower chair and tells this story:

"While married to your father, I began an affair with Minister Trungpa. He lived wherever Sakya lived, and Sakya chose to live among the secular citizens of Amdo and Kham rather than in the ridiculously scaled-down model of the Potala Palace in U-Tsang. As one result, Minister T and I easily met each other; and Nyendak—Neddy, I call him—courted me under the unsuspecting noses of both Sakya and Simon."

"You cuckolded my daddy with Minister T?" I need her to say it again.

"Oh, that's such an ugly word to label what Neddy and I still regard as a sacred union."

"I'm sorry, Mama, but it's the prettiest word I know to call it."

"Don't condescend to me, Gee Bee."

"I won't. I can't. But I do have to ask: Who fathered me, the man I call Daddy or Sakya's old-fart chief minister?"

"Your father fathered you," Mama says. "Look at yourself in a mirror. Simon's face underlies your own. His blood runs through you, almost as if he gave his vitality to you and thus lost it himself."

"Maybe because you cuckolded him."

"That's crap. If anything, Simon's growing apathy and addiction to pod-lodging shoved me toward Neddy. Who, by the way, has the eggs, even at his age, to stay on the upright outside of a Z-pod."

"Mama, please."

"Moreover, Neddy loves you. He cherishes you because he cherishes me. He sees you as just as much his own as Simon does. In fact, Neddy was the first to—"

"I'll stop saying 'cuckold' if you'll stop calling your boyfriend 'Neddy.' It sounds like filthy baby talk."

Mama closes her eyes, counts to herself, and opens them again to explain that when Sakya Gyatso at last figured out what was going on between Mama and Minister Trungpa, he called them to him and urged them to break off the affair in the interest of a higher spirituality and the preservation of shipboard harmony.

Minister T, ever the tutor, argued that although traditional Buddhism stems from a slavish obeisance to the demands of morality, wisdom cultivation, and ego abasement, the Tibetan Tantric path channels sexual attraction and its drives into the creation of life-force energies that purify these urges and tie them to transcendent spiritual purposes. My mother's marriage had unraveled; and Minister T's courtship of her, which culminated in consensual carnality and a principled friendship, now demonstrated their mutual growth toward that higher spirituality.

I laugh out loud. "And did His Holiness give your boyfriend a pass on this self-serving distortion of the Tantric way?"

"Believe as you will, but Neddy—Minister Trungpa's—take on the matter, and the thoroughness with which he laid out everything, had a great effect on the DL. After all, Minister T had served as his regent in exile in Dharmasala, as his chief minister in India, and finally as his minister and friend here on the *Kalachakra*. Why would he all at once suppose this fount of integrity and wise counsel a scoundrel?"

"Maybe because he was sleeping with another man's wife and justifying it with a lot of mystical malarkey."

Mama squints with thread-thin patience and resumes her story. Because of what Minister T and Mama had done, and still do, and what Minister T told His Holiness to justify their behavior, the Dalai Lama fell into a brown study that finally edged over into an ashen funk. To combat it, the DL hibernated for three months, but emerged as low in spirits as he'd gone into his egg. All his energies had diminished, and he told Minister T of his fears of dying before we reached Guge. Such talk profoundly fretted Mama's lover, who insisted that Sakya Gyatso tour the nursery in Amdo Bay. There he met me, Greta Bryn Brasswell, and fell in love, often returning over the next few weeks and always singling me out for attention. He told Mama that my eyes reminded him of those of his baby sister, who had died very young of rheumatic fever.

"I remember meeting His Holiness," I tell Mama, "but not his coming to see us so often in the nursery."

"You were four," Mama says. "How could you?"

She recounts how Minister T later took her to Sakya's upper-deck office in Amdo to talk about his long depression. With the AG generators running, they shared green tea and barley breads.

The DL again voiced his fear that even if he slept the rest of our journey, at some point in transit he would surrender his ghost in his eggshell pod and we his people would arrive at Guge with no agreed-upon leader. Minister T rebuked him for this worry, which he identified as egocentric, even though the DL took pains to articulate it as a concern for our common welfare.

Mama had carried me to this meeting. I lay sleeping—not like a pod-lodger but as a tired child—across her lap on a folded poncho liner that Simon had brought aboard as a going-away gift from a former roommate at Georgia Tech. As the adults talked, I turned and stretched, but never awakened.

"I don't recall that either," I say.

"Again, you were sleeping. Don't you listen to anything I tell you?"

"Everything. It's just that—" I stop myself. "Go on."

Mama does. She says that the DL walked over, leaned down, and placed his lips on my forehead, as if decaling it with a wet rose petal. Then he mused aloud about how fine it would be if, as an adult, I assumed his mantle and oversaw not only our voyagers' spiritual education but also our colonization of "The Land of Snow." He did not think he had the strength to undertake those tasks, but I would never exhaust my energy reserves. This fanciful scenario, Mama admits, rang in her like a crystal bell, a chime that echoed through her recurrently, as clear as unfiltered starlight.

Later, Mama and Minister T talked about their meeting with His Holiness and the tender wish-fulfillment musing with which he'd concluded it: my ascension to the Dalai Lamahood and eventual leadership on Guge. Mama asked if such a scenario could work itself out in reality, for if His Holiness died and Minister T championed me as he'd once stood behind Songsten Chodrak (later Sakya Gyatso), lifting him to his present eminence, then surely I, too, could rise to that height.

"'I'm too old for such fatiguing machinations again,' he told me," Mama says, remembering, "but I told him, 'Not by what I know of you, Neddy,' and just that simple expression of admiration and faith turned him."

I find Mama's account of this episode and her conspicuous pleasure in relating it hard to credit. But she has actually begun to glow, with a coppery aura akin to that of the DL in his display casket.

"At that point," she adds, "I grew ambitious for you in a way that once never would have crossed my mind, your ascension was just so far-fetched and prideful a thing for me to contemplate." She smiles adoringly, and my stomach shrinks upon itself like new linen applied wet to a metal frame.

"I've heard enough."

"Oh, no," Mama chides. "I've more, much more."

In blessed summary, she narrates a later conversation with Minister T, in which she urged him to carry to Sakya—now more a moody Byronic hero than a Bodhisattva in spiritual balance—this news: that she had no objection, if any accident or fatal illness befell him, to his sending his migrating bhava into the vessel of her daughter. Thus, he could mix our subjective selves in ways that would propagate us both into the future and so assist in our all arriving safely at Gliese 581g.

Bristling, I try to parse this convolute message. In fact, I ask Mama to repeat it. She does, and my deduction that she's memorized this nutty formulae—if you like, call it a "spell"—sickens me.

Still, I ask, as I must, "Did Minister T carry this news to His Holiness?"

"He did."

"And what happened?"

"Sakya listened. He meditated for two days on the metaphysics and the practical ramifications of what I'd told him through his minister."

"Finish," I say. "Please just finish."

"On the following day, Sakya died."

"*Cadillac infraction*," I murmur. Mama's eyes grow wide. "Forgive me," I say. "What killed him? You used to tell me 'natural causes, but at too young an age for them to *seem* natural.'"

"That wasn't entirely a lie. Sakya did what came natural to him. He acted on the impulse of his growing despair and his burgeoning sense that if he waited much longer to influence his rebirth, you'd outgrow your primacy as a receptacle for the transfer of his mind-state sequences and he'd lose you as a crucible for compounding the two. So he called upon his mastery of many Tantric practices to drop his body temperature, heart rate, and blood pressure. And when he irreversibly stilled his heart, he passed from our illusory reality into bardo . . . until he awoke again wed to the *samvattanika viññana*, or evolving consciousness, animating you."

Here I float away from Mama's bower chair and drift a dozen meters across the courtyard to a lovely, low cedar hedge. (In a way that she's never fully understood, Nima Photrang was right about the cause of Sakya Gyatso's death.) I want to pour my guts into this hedge, to heave the burdensome reincarnated essence of the late DL into its feathery silver-green leaves.

Nothing comes up. Nothing comes out. My stomach feels smaller than a piñon nut. My ego, on the other hand, fills the entire tripartite passenger drum of our starship, *The Wheel of Time*.

Later, I meet Simon Brasswell—Daddy—in a back-tunnel lounge near Jokhang Temple for chang and sandwiches. To make this date, of course, I must visit his guesthouse and ping him at the registry screen, but he agrees to meet me at the Bhurel—or The Blue Sheep, as the place is called—with real alacrity. In fact, as soon as we lock-belt into our booth, with squeeze bottles for our drinks and mini-spikes in our sandwiches to hold them to the small cork table, Daddy key-taps payment before I can object. He looks better since his nap, but the violet circles under his eyes lend him a sad fragility.

"I never knew—" I begin.

"That Karen and I divorced because she fell in love with Nyendak Trungpa? Or, I suppose, with his self-vaunted virility and political clout?" Speechless, I gape at my dad. "Forgive me. Ordinarily, I try not to go the spurned-spouse route."

I still can't speak.

He squeezes his bottle and swigs some barley beer. Then he says, "Do you want what your mama and Minister T want for you—I mean, really?"

"I don't know. I've never known. But this afternoon Mama told me why I ought to want it. And because I ought to, I do. I think."

Daddy studies me with an unsettling mixture of exasperation and tenderness. "Let me ask you something straight up: Do you think the bhava of Sakya Gyatso, the direct reincarnation of Avalokiteshvara, the ancestor of the Tibetan people, dwells in you as it supposedly dwelt in his twenty predecessors?"

"Daddy, I'm not Tibetan."

"I didn't ask you that." He unspikes and chomps into his *Cordyceps*, or synthetic caterpillar-fungus, sandwich. Chewing, he manages a quasi-intelligible, "Well?"

"Tomorrow's gold-urn lottery will reveal the truth, one way or the other."

"Yak shit, Greta. And I didn't ask you that, either."

I feel both my tears and my gorge rising, but the latter prevails. "I thought we'd share some time, eat together—not get into a spat."

Daddy chews more sedately, swallows, and re-spikes his "caterpillar" to the cork. "And what else, sweetheart? Avoid saying anything true or substantive?" I show him my profile. "Greta, forgive me, but I didn't sign on to this mission to sire a demigod. I didn't even sign on to it to colonize another world for the sake of oppressed Tibetan Buddhists and their rabid hangers-on."

"I thought you *were* a Tibetan Buddhist."

"Oh, yeah, born and raised . . . in Boulder, Colorado. Unfortunately, it never quite took. I signed on because I loved your mother and the idea of spaceflight at least as much as I did passing for a Buddhist. And that's how I got out here about seventeen light-years from home. Do you see?"

I eat nothing. I drink nothing. I say nothing.

"At least I've told you a truth," Daddy says. "More than one, in fact. Can't you do the same for me? Or does the mere self-aggrandizing idea of Dalai Lamahood clamp your windpipe shut on the truth?"

I have expected neither these revelations nor their vehemence, but together they work to unclamp something inside me. I owe my father my life, at least in part, and the dawning awareness that he has never stopped caring for me suggests—in fact, requires—that I repay him truth for truth.

"Yes. I can do the same for you."

Daddy's eyes, above their bruised half-circles, never leave mine.

"I didn't choose this life at all," I say. "It was thrust upon me. I want to be a good person, a Bodhisattva possibly, maybe even the Dalai Lama. But—"

He lifts his eyebrows and goes on waiting. A tender twinge of a smile plays about his mouth.

"But," I finish, "I'm not happy that maybe I want these things."

"Buddhists don't aspire to happiness, Greta, but to an oceanic detachment."

I give him my fiercest Peeved Daughter look, but do refrain from eye-rolling. "I just need an attitude adjustment, that's all."

"The most wrenching attitude adjustment in the universe won't turn a carp into a cougar, pumpkin." His pet name for me.

"I don't need the most wrenching attitude adjustment in the universe. I need a self-willed tweaking."

"Ah." Daddy takes a squeeze-swig of his beer and nods that I should eat.

My gorge has fallen, my hunger reappeared. I eat and drink and, as I do, become unsettlingly aware that other patrons in the Bhurel—visitors, monks—have detected my presence. Blessedly, though, they respect our space.

"Suppose the lottery goes young Trimon's way," Daddy says. "What would make you happy in your resulting alternate life?"

I consider this as a peasant woman of an earlier era might have done if a friend, just as a game, had asked, "What would you do if the King chose you to marry his son?" But I play the game in reverse, sort of, and can only shake my head.

Daddy waits. He doesn't stop waiting, or searching my eyes, or studying me with his irksome unwavering paternal regard. He won't speak, maybe because everything else about him—his gaze, his patience, his presence—speaks strongly of what for years went unspoken between us.

Full of an inarticulate wistfulness, I lean back. "I've told you a truth already," I tell my father. "Isn't that enough for tonight?"

A teenage girl and her mother, oaring subtly with their hands to maintain their places beside us, hover at our table. Even though I haven't seen the girl for several years (while, of course, she hibernized), I recognize her because distinctive agate eyes in an elfin face identify her at once.

Daddy and I lever ourselves up from our booth, and I swim out to embrace the girl. *"Alicia!"* Over her shoulder, I say to her mama in all earnestness, "Mrs. Paljor, how good to see you here!"

"Forgive the interruption," Mrs. Paljor says, ducking her head.

"Certainly, certainly," I say.

"We've come to U-Tsang for the Gold Urn Festival, and we just had to wish you well tomorrow. Alicia wouldn't rest until Kanjur found a way for us to attend."

Kanjur Paljor, Alicia's father, had served since the beginning of our voyage as our foremost antimatter-ice specialist. If anyone could get his secular wife and daughter to U-Tsang for the gold-urn lottery, Kanjur Paljor could. He enjoys the authority of universal respect. As for Alicia, she scrunches her face in embarrassment, as well as unconditional affection. She recalls the many times that I came to Momo House to hold her, and later to her family's Kham Bay rooms to take her on walks or on outings to our art, mathematics, and science centers.

"Thank you," I say. "Thank you."

I hug the girl. I hug her mother.

My father nods and smiles, albeit bemusedly. I suspect that Daddy has never met Alicia or Mrs. Paljor before. Kanjur, the father and husband, he undoubtedly knows. Who doesn't know that man?

The Paljor women depart almost as quickly as they came. Daddy watches them go, with a deep exhalation of relief that makes me hurt for them both.

"I was almost a second mother to that girl," I tell him.

Daddy oars himself downward, back into his seat. "Surely, you exaggerate. Mrs. Paljor looks more than sufficient to the task."

Long before noon of the next day, the courtyard of the Jokhang Temple swarms with levitating lamas, monks, nuns, yogis, and some authorized visitors from our other two passenger bays.

I cannot explain how I feel. If Mama's story of Sakya Gyatso's heart attack is true, then I cannot opt out of the gold-urn lottery. To do so would constitute an insult—the supreme insult—to his *punarbhava*, or karmic change from one life vessel to the next, or from his body to mine. Mine, as everyone knows, established its bona fides as a living entity years before the DL died. Also, opting out would constitute a heartless affront to all believers, of all who support my candidacy. Still . . .

Does Sakya have the right to self-direct his rebecoming or I the right to thwart his will . . . or only the obligation to accede to it? So much self will and worry taints today's ceremony that Larry and Kilkhor, if not Minister T, can hardly conceive of it as deriving from Buddhist tenets at all.

Or can they? Perhaps a society rushing at twenty percent of light-speed toward some barely imaginable karmic epiphany has slipped the surly bonds not only of Earth but also of the harnessing principles of Buddhist Tantra. I don't know. I know only that I can't opt out of this lottery without betraying a good man who *loved* me in the noblest and the most innocent of senses.

And so, in our filigreed vestments, Jetsun Trimon and I swim up to the circular dais to which the attendants of the Panchen Lama have already fastened the gold urn for our name slips.

In staggered vertical ranks, choruses of floating monks and nuns chant as we await the drawing. Our separate retinues hold or adjust their altitudes behind us, both to hearten us and to keep their sight lanes clear. Small flying cameras, costumed as birds, televise the event to community members in all three bays.

Jetsun's boyish face looks at once exalted and terrified.

Lhundrub Gelek, the Panchen Lama, lifts his arms and announces that the lottery has begun. Today he blazes with the fierce bearing of a Hebrew seraph. Tug-monks keep him from rising in gravid slow motion to the ceiling. Abbess Yeshe Yargag floats about a meter to his right, with tug-nuns to prevent her from wandering up, down, or sideways. Gelek reports that name slips for Jetsun Trimon and Greta Bryn Brasswell already drift about in the oversized urn affixed to the dais. Neither of us, he proclaims, needs to swim forward to reach into the urn and pull out a name-slip envelope. Nor do we need stand-ins to do so. We will simply wait.

We will simply wait . . . until an envelope rises on its own out of the urn. Then Gelek will seize it, open the envelope, and read it aloud for all those watching in the Temple hall or via telelinks. Never mind that our wait could take hours, and that, if it does, viewers in every bay will volunteer to rejoin the vast majority of our population in ursidormizine slumber.

And so we wait.

And so we wait . . . and finally a small blue envelope rises through the mouth of the crosshatched gold urn. A tug-monk snatches it from the air, before it can descend out of view again, and hands it to the PL.

Startled, because he's nodded off several times over the past fifty-some minutes, Gelek opens the envelope, pulls out the name slip, reads it to himself, and passes it on to Abbess Yargag, whose excited tug-nuns steady her so that she may announce the name of the true Soul Child.

Of course, that the Abbess has copped this honor tells everybody all that we need to know. She can't even speak the name on the slip before many in attendance begin to clap their palms against their shoulders. The upshot of this applause, beyond opening my tear ducts, is a sudden propulsion of persons at many different altitudes about the lottery hall: a wheeling zero-g dance of approbation.

Years in transit: 95
Computer Logs of Our Reluctant Dalai Lama, age 20

The Panchen Lama, his peers and subordinates in U-Tsang, and secular hierarchs from Amdo and Kham have made my parents starship nobles.

They have bestowed similar, if slightly lesser honors, on Jetsun Trimon's parents and on Jetsun himself, who wishes to serve us colonizers as Bodhisattva, meteorologist, and lander pilot. In any event, his religious and scientific educations proceed in parallel, and he spends as much time in tech training in Kham Bay as he does in the monasteries in U-Tsang.

As for me, I alternate months among our three drums, on a rotation that pleases more of our up-phase ghosts than it annoys. I ask no credit for the wisdom of my scheme, though; I simply wish to rule (although I prefer the verb "preside") in a way promoting shipboard harmony and reducing our inevitable conflicts.

Years in transit: 99
Computer Logs of Our Reluctant Dalai Lama, age 24

I've now spent nearly five years in this allegedly holy office. Earlier today, thinking hard about our arrival at Guge, in only a little over seven Earth years, I summoned Minister Trungpa to my quarters.

"Yes, Your Holiness, what do you wish?" he asked.

"To invite everyone aboard the *Kalachakra* to submit designs for a special sand mandala. This mandala will commemorate our voyage's inevitable end and honor it as a fruit of the Hope and Community"—I capitalized the words as I spoke them—"that drove us, or our elders, to undertake this journey."

Minister T frowns. "Submit designs?"

"Your new auditory aid works quite well."

"For a competition?"

"Any voyager, any Kalachakran at all, may submit a design."

"But—"

"The artist monks in U-Tsang, who will create the mandala, will judge the entries blindly to determine our finalists. I'll decide the winner."

Minister T does not make eye contact. "The idea of a contest undercuts one of the themes that you wish your mandala to embody, that of Community."

"You hate the whole idea?"

He hedges: "Appoint a respected Yellow Hat artist to design the mandala. In that way, you'll avoid a bureaucratic judging process and lessen popular discontent."

"Look, Neddy, a competition will amuse everyone, and after a century aboard this vacuum-vaulting bean can, we could all use some amusement."

Neddy would like to dispute the point, but I am the Dalai Lama, and what can he say that will not seem a coddling or a defiant promotion of his ego? Nothing. (Chenrezig forgive me, but I relish his discomfiture.) Clearly, the West animates parts of my ego that I should better disguise from those of my subjects—a term I loathe—immersed in Eastern doctrines that guarantee their fatalism and docility. Of course, how many men of Minister Trungpa's station and age enjoy carrying out the bidding of a woman a mere twenty-four-years old?

At length he softly says, "I'll see to it, Your Holiness."

"I can see to it myself, but I wanted your opinion."

He nods, his look implying that his opinion doesn't count for much, and takes a deferential step back.

"Don't leave. I need your advice."

"As much as you needed my opinion?"

I take his arm and lead him to a nook where we can sit and talk as intimates. Fortunately, the AG has worked much more reliably all over the ship than it did before my investiture. Neddy looks grizzled, fatigued, and wary, and although he doesn't yet understand why, he has cause for this wariness.

"I want to have a baby," I tell him.

He responds instantly. "I advise you not to, Your Holiness."

"I don't solicit your advice in that area. I'd like you to help me settle on a father for the child."

Neddy reddens.

I've stolen his breath. He'd like to make a devastatingly incisive remark, but can't even manage a feeble Ugh. "In case it's crossed your mind, I haven't short-listed you . . . although Mama once gave you a terrific, unasked for, recommendation."

Minister T pulls himself together, but he's squeezing his hands in his lap as if to express oil from between them.

"I've narrowed the candidates down to two, Jetsun Trimon and Ian Kilkhor, but lately I'm tilting toward Jetsun."

"Then tilt toward Ian."

"Why?"

And Mama's lover provides me with good, dispassionate reasons for selecting the older man: physical fitness, martial arts ability, maturity, intelligence, learning (secular, religious, and technical), administrative/organizational skills, and long-standing affection for me. Jetsun, not yet twenty, has two or three separate callings that he has not yet had time to explore as fully as he ought, and the differences in our ages will lead many in our community to suppose that I have exercised my power in an unseemly way to bring him to my bed. I should give the kid his space.

I know from private conversations, though, that when Jetsun was ten, an unnamed senior monk in Amdo often employed him as a drombo, or passive sex partner, and that the experience nags at him now in ways that Jetsun cannot easily articulate. Apparently, the community didn't see fit, back then, to exercise its outrage on behalf of a boy not yet officially identified as a Soul Child. Of course, the community didn't know, or chose not to know, and uproars rarely result from awareness of such liaisons, anyway. Isn't a monk a man? I say none of this to Neddy.

"Choose Ian," he says, "if you must choose one or the other."

Yesterday, in Kham Bay, after I extended an intranet invitation to him to come see me about his father, who lies ill in his eggshell pod, Jetsun Trimon called upon me in the upper-level stateroom that I inherited, so to speak, from my predecessor. He fell on his knees before me, seized my wrist, and put his lips to the beads, bracelet, and watch that I wear about it. He wanted prayers for his father's recovery, and I acceded to this request with all my heart.

Then something occurred that I set down here with joy rather than guilt. I wanted more from Jetsun than gratitude for my prayers, and he wanted more than my prayers for his worry about his father or for his struggles to master all his many studies. Like me, he wished the solace of the flesh, and as one devoted to forgiveness, contentment, and the alleviation of pain, I took him to my bed and divested him of his garments and let him divest me of mine. Then we embraced, neither of us trembling, or sweating, or flinching in discomfort or distress, for my quarters hummed at a subsonic frequency with enough warmth and gravity to offset any potential malaise or annoyance. Altogether sweetly, his tenderness matched mine. However—

Like most healthy young men, Jetsun quickly reached a coiled-spring readiness. He quivered on *Go*.

I rolled over and bestrode him above the waist, holding his arms to the side and speaking with as much integrity as my gnosis of bliss and emptiness could generate. He calmed and listened. I said that I begrudged neither of us this tension-easing union, but that if we proceeded, then he must know that I wanted his seed to enter me, to take root, to turn embryo, and to attain fruition as our child.

"Do you understand?"

"Yes."

"Do you consent?"

"I consent."

"Do you further consent to acknowledge this child and to assist in its rearing on the planet Guge as well as on this ship?"

He considered these queries. And, smiling, he agreed.

"Then we may advance to the third exalted initiation," I said, "that of the mutual experience of connate joy."

I slid backward over the pliable warmth of his standing phallus and kissed him in the middle of his chest. He reached for me, tenderly, and the AG generators abruptly cut off—suspiciously, it seemed to me. I floated toward the ceiling like a buoyant nixie, too startled to yelp or laugh. Jetsun shoved off in pursuit, but hit a bulkhead and glanced off it horizontally.

It took us a while to reunite, to find enough purchase to consummate our resolve, and to do so honoring the fact that a resurgence of gravity could injure, even kill, both of us. Nonetheless, we managed, and managed passionately.

The "night" has now passed. Jetsun sleeps, mind eased and body sated.

I sit at this console, lock-belted in, recording the most stirring encounter of my life. Every nerve and synapse of my body, and every scrap of assurance in my soul, tell me that I have conceived: Alleluia.

Years in transit: 100
Computer Logs of our Reluctant Dalai Lama, age 25

Some history: Early in our voyage, when our AG generators worked reliably, our monks created one sand mandala a year. They did so then, as they do now, in a special studio in the Yellow Hat gompa in U-Tsang. They kept materials for these productions—colored grains of sand, bits of stone or bone, dyed rice grains, sequins—in hard plastic cylinders and worked on their designs over several days. Upon finishing the mandalas, our monks chanted to consecrate them and then, as a dramatic enactment of the impermanent nature of existence, destroyed them by sweeping a brush over and swirling their deity-inhabited geometries into inchoate slurries.

These methods of creating and destroying the mandalas ended four decades into our flight when a gravity outage led to the premature disintegration of a design. A slow-motion sandstorm filled the studio. Grains of maroon, citron, turquoise, emerald, indigo, and blood-red drifted all about, and recovering these for fresh projects required the use of hand-vacs and lots of fussy hand-sorting. Nobody wished to endure such a disaster again. And so, soon thereafter, the monks implemented two new procedures for laying out and completing the mandalas.

One involved gluing down the grains, but this method made the graceful ruination of a finished mandala dicey. A second method involved inserting and arranging the grains into pie-shaped plastic shields using magnets and tech-manipulated "delivery straws," but these tedious procedures, while heightening the praise due the artists, so lengthened the process and stressed the monks that Sakya Gyatso ceased asking for annual mandalas and mandated their fashioning only once every five years.

In any case, today marks our one-hundredth year in flight, and I am fat with a female child who bumps around inside me like those daredevils in old vidped clips who whooshed up and down the sloped walls of special competition arenas on rollers called skateboards.

I think the kid wants out already, but Karma Hahn, my baby doc, tells me she's still much too small to exit, even if the kid does carry on like "a squirrel on an exercise wheel." That metaphor endears both the kid and Karma to me. Because the kid moves, I move. I stroll about my private audience chamber, aka "The Sunshine Hall," in the Potala Palace in U-Tsang. I've voluntarily relocated here to show my fellow Buddhists that I am not ashamed of my fecund condition.

Ian announces a visitor, and in walks First Officer Nima Photrang, whom I've not seen for weeks. She has come, it happens, not solely to visit me, but also to look in on an uncle who resides in the nearby Yellow Hat gompa. She has brought a khata, a white silk greeting scarf, even though I already have enough of those damned rags to stitch together a ship cover for the *Kalachakra*. She drapes it around my neck. Laughing, I pull it off and drape it around hers.

"Your design contest spurs on every amateur-artist ghost in Amdo and Kham," Nima says. "If you wish your mandala to further community enlightenment by projecting an image of our future Palace of Hope on Guge, well, you've got a lot of folks worrying away at it—mission fully goosed, if not yet fully cooked."

I realize that Sakya Gyatso, my predecessor, his eye on Tibetan history, called the world toward which we relentlessly cruise Guge partly for the g in Gliese 581g. What an observant and subtle man.

"Nima," I ask, "have you submitted a design?"

"No, but you'll probably never guess who intends to."

No, I never will. I gape cluelessly at Nima.

"Captain Xao Songda, our helmsman. He spends enormous chunks of time with a drafting compass and a pen, or at his console refining design programs that a monk in U-Tsang uploaded a while back to Pemako."

Pemako is the latest version of our intranet. I like to use it. Virtually night-ly (stet the pun), it shows me deep-sea sonograms of my jetting squid-kid.

"I hope Captain Xao doesn't expect his status as our shipboard Buzz Lightyear to score him any brownies with the judges."

Nima chortles. "Hardly. He drew as a boy and as a teenager. Later, he de-signed maglev stations and epic mountain tunnels. He figures he has as good a chance as anyone in a blind judging, and if he wins, what a personal coup."

"Mmm," I say.

"No, really, you've created a monster, Your Holiness—but, as one of the oldest persons aboard, he deserves his fun, I guess."

We chat some more. Nima asks if she may lay her palm on the curve of my belly, and I say yes. When the brat-to-be surfs my insides like a ber-serk skateboarder, Nima and I laugh like schoolgirls. By some criteria, I still qualify.

Years in transit: 101
Computer Logs of Our Reluctant Dalai Lama, age 25-26

I return to Amdo to deliver my child. Early in the hundred and first year of our journey, my water breaks. Karma Hahn, my mother, and Alicia and Emily Paljor attend my lying-in, while my father, Ian Kilkhor, Minister Trungpa, and Jetsun perform a nervous do-si-do in an antechamber. I give the guys hardly a thought. Delivering a kid requires stamina, a lot of Tantric focus, and a cooperative fetus, but I've got 'em all and the kid slams out in less than four hours.

I lie in a freshly made bed with my squiddle dozing in a warming blanket against my left shoulder. Well-wishers and family surround us like sentries, although I have no idea what they've got to shield us from: I've never felt safer.

Mama says, "When will you tell us the ruddy shrimp's name? You've kept it a secret eight months past forever."

"Ask Jetsun. He chose it."

Everyone turns to Jetsun, who at twenty-one looks like a fabled Kham warrior, lean and smooth-faced, a flawless bronze sculpture of himself. How can I not love him? Jetsun looks to me. I nod.

"It's . . . it's Kyipa." Like the sweetheart he is, he blushes.

"Ah," Nyendak Trungpa sighs. "Happiness."

"If we all didn't strive so damned hard for happiness," Daddy says, "we'd almost always have a pretty good time."

"You stole that," Mama rebukes him. "And your timing sucks."

From behind those crowded about my babe-cave, a short, sturdy, gray-haired man edges in. I know him as Alicia Paljor's father, Emily Paljor's hus-band—but Daddy, Ian, and Neddy know him as the chief fuel specialist on our strut-ship and thus a personage of renowned ability. So I assume he's come—like a wise man—to kneel beside and to adore our newborn squiddle. Or has he come just to meet his wife and daughter and fetch them back to their stateroom?

In his ministerial capacity, Neddy says, "Welcome, Specialist Paljor."

"I need to talk to Her Holiness." Kanjur Paljor bows and approaches my bed. "If I may, Your Holiness."

"Of course."

The area clears of everyone except Paljor, Ian Kilkhor, Kyipa, and me. A weight descends—a weight comprising everything that's ever floated free of it moorings during every AG quittage that our strut-ship has ever suf-fered—and that weight, condensed into one tiny spherical mass, lowers itself onto my baby's back and so onto me, crushing this blissful moment into dust and slivered glass. Ian edges to the top of my bed, but I already know that his strength and his heavy glare will prove impotent against whatever message Kanjur Paljor has brought.

Paljor says, "Your Holiness, I beg your infinite pardon."

"Tell me."

He looks at Ian and then, in petition, at me again. "I'd prefer to deliver this news to you alone, Your Holiness."

"Regard my agent's simultaneous presence and absence as an enacted mystery or koan," I tell Paljor. "He speaks a helpful truth."

Paljor nods and seizes my free hand. "About fifteen hours ago, I found a serious navigational anomaly while running a fuel-tank check. Before bringing the problem to you, I ran some figures to make sure that I hadn't made a calculation error; that I wasn't just overreacting to a situation of no real consequence."

He pauses to touch my Kyipa's blanket. "How much technical detail do you want, Your Holiness?"

"Right now, none. Give me the gist."

"For a little over one hundred and twenty hours, the *Kalachakra* traveled at its top speed at a small angle off our requisite heading."

"How? Why?"

"Before I answer, let me assure you that we have since corrected for this deviation and that we'll soon run true again."

"What do you mean, 'soon'? Why don't we 'run true' now?"

"We do, Your Holiness, in the sense that First Officer Photrang has set us on an efficient angle to intercept our former heading to Guge. But we don't, in the sense that we still must compensate for the unintended divergence."

Ian Kilkhor says, "Tell Her Holiness why this 'unintended divergence' constitutes one huge fucking threat."

Totally appalled, I look back at my bodyguard and friend. "I thought you weren't here! Or did you leave behind just that part of you that views me as an unteachable idiot? Go away, Mr. Kilkhor. Get out."

Kilkhor has the decency and good sense to do as I command. Kyipa, unsettled by my outburst, squirms fretfully on my shoulder.

"The danger," I tell Kanjur Paljor, "centers on fuel expenditure. If we've gone too far off course, we won't have enough antimatter ice left to reach Guge. Have I admissibly described our peril?"

"Yes, Your Holiness." He doesn't fall to one knee, like a magus beside the infant deity Christ, but crouches so that our faces are nearly at a level. "I believe—I think—we have just enough fuel to complete our journey, but at this late stage it could prove a close thing. If there's another emergency requiring an additional course correction—"

"We might not arrive at all."

Paljor nods, and consolingly pats Kyipa's playing-card-sized back.

"How did this happen?"

"Human error, I'm afraid."

"Tell me what sort."

"Lack of attention to the telltales that should have prevented this divergence from our heading."

"Whose error? Captain Xao's?"

"Yes, Your Holiness. Nima says his mental state has deteriorated badly over these past few weeks. What she first thought eccentricities, she now views as evidence of age-related mental debilities. He stays awake so long and endures so much stress. And he puts too much faith in the alleged reliability of our electronic systems."

Also, he came to feel that creating a design for my Palace of Hope mandala took precedence over his every other duty on a strut-ship programmed to fly to its destination, with the result that he put himself on auto-pilot too.

"Where is he now?" I ask Paljor.

"Sleeping, under medical supervision—not ursidormizine slumber but bed rest, Your Holiness."

I thank Paljor and dismiss him.

Clutching Kyipa to me, I nuzzle her sweet-smelling face.

Tomorrow, I'll tell Nima to advise her flight crew that they must remain up-phase ghosts until we know for sure the outcomes of Xao's inattention and our efforts to correct for its potential consequences: a headlong rush to nowhere.

Without benefit of lock belts, my daughter, Kyipa kicks in her bassinet. I seldom worry about her floating off during AG outages because she loves such spells of weightlessness. She uses them to exercise her limbs—admittedly, with no strengthening resistance—and to explore our stateroom, which boasts Buddha figurines, wall hangings, filigreed star charts, miniature starship models, and other interesting items. At five months, she thinks herself a big finch or a pygmy porpoise. She undulates about, giggling at the currents she creates, or, the AG restored, inches along with her pink tongue tip between her lips and her bum rising and falling like a migrating molehill.

As Dalai Lama (many argue), I should never have borne this squiddle, but Karen, Simon, Jetsun, and Jetsun's mama might disagree, and all contribute to her care. Even Minister T acknowledges that conceiving and bearing her has confirmed my sense of the karmic correctness of my Dalai Lama-hood more powerfully than any other event to date. Because of this happy squiddle girl, I do stronger, better, holier work.

To those who tsk-tsk when they see Kyipa squirming in my arms, I say:

"This child is my Wheel of Time, my mandala, who has as one purpose to further my evolving enlightenment. Her other purposes she will learn and fulfill in time. So set aside your resentments so that you may more easily fulfill yours."

But although I don't fret about Kyipa during gravity outages, I do worry about her future . . . and ours.

Will we safely arrive at the Gliese 581 system? Of the fifty antimatter-ice tanks with which (long before my birth) we started our journey, we've used up and discarded thirty-eight, and Paljor says that we have exhausted nearly half of the thirty-ninth tank, with over five and a half years remaining until our ETA in orbit around Guge. From the outside, our ship begins to resemble a skeleton of its outbound self, the bones of a picked-clean fish. And if the *Kalachakra* makes it at all, as Paljor has speculated, it will slice the issue scarily close.

I stupidly assumed that our eventual shift into deceleration mode would work in our favor, but Paljor cautioned that slowing our strut-ship—so that we do not overshoot Guge, like a golf putt running up to but not beyond its cup—will require more fuel than I thought. Later he showed me math proving that reaching Guge will require "an incident-free approach"—because our antimatter reserves, the fail-safe reserves with which we began our flight, have already dissolved into the ether slipstreaming by the magnetic field coils generating our plasma shield out front.

Still, I don't believe in shielding our human freight from issues bearing on our survival. Therefore, I've had Minister T announce the fact of this crisis to everyone up-phase and working. Thankfully, general panic has not ensued. Instead, crew members brainstorm stopgap strategies for conserving fuel, and the monks and nuns in U-Tsang pray and chant. Soon enough, when we begin to brake, everyone will arise again, shake off the fog of hibernizing, and learn the truth about our final approach. Then every deck will team with ghosts preparing to orbit Guge; to assay the habitable wedges between its sun-stuck face and its bleaker sides; and to decide which of the two wedges is better suited to settlement.

Years in transit: 102
Computer Logs of Our Relucant Dalai Lama, age 27

Xao Songda, our deposed captain, died just twelve hours ago. Although Kyipa celebrated her first birthday last week, the man never laid eyes on her.

Xao's "bed rest" turned into pathological pacing and harangues unintelligible to anyone ignorant of Mandarin Chinese. These behaviors—symptomatic of an aggressive type of senility unknown to us—our medicos treated with tranqs, placebos (foolishly, I guess), experimental diets, and long walks through the commons of Kham Bay. Nothing calmed him or eased the intensity of his gibbering tirades. I had so wanted Kyipa to meet our captain (or the avatar of the self preceding this sorry incarnation), but I could not risk exposing her to one of his abusive rants.

It bears stating, though, that everyone aboard *Kalachakra*, knowing the sacrifices that the captain made for us, forgives him his navigation error. All showed him the honor, courtesy, and patience that he deserved for these sacrifices. Nima Photrang, who assumed his captaincy, believes he and Satya Gyatso suffered similar personality disintegrations, albeit in different ways. Sakya used Tantric practices to end his life and Xao Songda fell to an Alzheimer's-like scourge, but the effects of sleep deprival, suppressed anxiety, and overwork ultimately caused their deaths.

Xao created designs for my mandala competition, I think, as a way to decompress from these burdens. During the last hours of his illness, Ian Kilkhor searched his quarters for anything that could help us fathom his disease and preserve our memory of him as the intrepid Tibetan Buddhist who carried us within three lights of our destination. However, Ian returned to me with two hundred hand-drawn sketches and computer-assisted designs for my Palace of Hope mandala.

These "designs" appalled and saddened us. The ones Xao hand-drew resemble big multicolored Rorschach blots, and those stemming from his cyber-design programs look like geometrically askew fever dreams. All are pervaded with interlocking claws, jagged teeth, vermiform bodies, and occluded reptilian eyes. None could serve as a model for the mandala of my envisioning.

"I'm sorry," Ian said. "The old guy seems to have swallowed the pituitary gland of a Komodo dragon."

So, given our fuel situation and Captain Xao's death, I've declared a moratorium on mandala-design creation.

Now there is a strong movement afoot—a respectful one—to eject Captain Xao Songda's corpse into the void, one more human collop for the highballing dark. As I've already noted here, we've used this procedure many times before, as a practice coincident with Buddha Dharma and, in this case, as one befitting a helmsman of Xao's stature. But I resist this seeming consensus in favor of a better option: taking the captain to Guge and setting his sinewy body out on an escarpment there, to blacken in its gales and scale in its thaws, our first sacrificial alms to the planet.

One work cycle past, Captain Photrang began to brake the *Kalachakra*. We are four years out from Gliese 581g, and Kanjur Paljor tells me that unless a meteorite penetrates our plasma shield or some other anomalous disaster befalls us, we will reach our destination. Ian notes that we will coast into planetary orbit like a vehicle with an internal combustion engine chugging into its pit on fumes. I don't altogether twig the analogy, but I do get its gist. Alleluia! If only time passed more quickly.

Meanwhile, I keep Kyipa awake and ignore those misguided ghosts advising me to ease her into grave-cave sleep so that time will pass more quickly for her. Jetsun and I enjoy her far too much to send her down. More important, if she stays up-phase most of the rest of our journey, she will learn and grow; and when we descend to the surface of Guge with her, she will have a sharper mind and better motor skills at five or six than any long-term sleeper of roughly similar age.

Every day, every hour, my excitement intensifies. And our ship plows on.

Years in transit: 106
Computer Logs of Our Reluctant Dalai Lama, age 31

Maintenance preoccupies nearly everyone aboard. In less than a week, our strut-ship will rendezvous with Guge and orbit its oblate, sun-locked mass. Then we will make several sequential descents to and returns from "The

Land of Snow" aboard our lander, the *Yak Butter Express*.

Jetsun will serve as shuttle pilot for one of these first excursions and as backup on another. He and others perform daily checks on the vehicle in its hangar harnesses, just as other techs strive to ensure the reliability of every mechanical and human component. Our hopes and our anxieties contend. At my urging, the Bodhisattva of U-Tsang go from deck to deck assisting in our labors and transmitting positive energies to every bay and to all those at work in them.

Twelve hours after Captain Photrang eased *Kalachakra* into orbit around Guge, Minister T comes to me to report that the Yellow Hat artists in U-Tsang have finished a mandala based on a design that they, not I, chose as our most esteemed entry. Eagerly, I ask whom these Bodhisattva selected.

Lucinda Gomez, a teenager from Amdo Bay, has taken the laurel.

Neddy asks the monks to transport the mandala in its pie-shaped shield to Bhava Park, a commons here in Kham Bay, and they do. A bird camera in the park transmits the mandala's image to public screens and to vidped units everywhere. Intricate and colorful, it sits on an easel amid a host of tables and many happily milling Kalachakrans. Because we're celebrating our arrival, I don't watch on a screen but stand in Bhava Park before the thing itself. Banners and prayer flags abound. I hail the excited Lucinda Gomez and all the artist monks, congratulate them, and also speak to many onlookers, who heed my words smilingly.

The Yellow Hats chant verses of consecration that affirm their fulfillment of my charge and then extend to everyone the blessings of Hope and Community implicit in the mandala's labyrinthine central Palace. Kyipa, almost six, reaches out to touch the bottom of the encased mandala.

"This is the prettiest," she says.

She has never before seen a finished mandala in its full artifactual glory.

Then the artist monks start to carry the shield from its easel to a tabletop, there to insert narrow tubes into it and send the mandala's fixed grains flying with focused blasts of air—to symbolize, as tradition dictates, the primacy of impermanence in our lives. But before they reach the table, I lift my hand.

"We won't destroy this sand mandala," I announce, "until we've planted a viable settlement on Guge."

And everyone around us in Bhava Park cheers. The monks restore the mandala to its easel, a ton of colored confetti drops from suspended bins above us, music plays, and people sing, dance, eat, laugh, and mingle.

Kyipa, holding her hands up to the drifting paper and plastic flakes, beams at me ecstatically.

In our shuttle-cum-lander, we glide from the belly of Kham Bay toward Gliese 581g, better known to all aboard the *Kalachakra* as Guge, "The Land of Snow."

From here, the amiable dwarf star about which Guge swings resembles the yolk of a colossal fried egg, more reddish than yellow-orange, with a misty orange corona about it like the egg's congealed albumin. I've made it sound ugly, but Gliese 581 looks edible to me and quickly trips my hunger to reach the planet below.

As for Guge, it gleams beneath us like an old coin.

In our first week on its surface, we have already built a tent camp in one of the stabilized climate zones of the nearside terminator. Across the tall visible arc of that terminator, the planet shows itself marbled by a bluish and slate-gray crust marked by fingerlike snowfields and glacier sheets.

On the ground, our people call their base camp Lhasa and their rugged territory all about it New Tibet. In response to this naming and to the alacrity with which our fellow Kalachakrans adopted it, Minister T wept openly.

I find I like the man. Indeed, I go down for my first visit to the surface with his blessing. (Simon, my father, already bivouacs there, to investigate ways to grow barley, winter wheat, and other grains in the thin air and cold temperatures.) Kyipa, of course, remains for now on our orbiting strut-ship—in Neddy's stateroom, which he now shares openly with the child's grandmother, Karen Bryn Bonfils. Neddy and Karen Bryn dote on my daughter shamelessly.

Our descent to Lhasa won't take long, but, along with many others in this second wave of pioneers, I drop into a meditative trance and focus on a photograph that Neddy gave me after the mandala ceremony at the arrival celebration. Indeed, I recall his words as he presented it:

"Soon after you became a teenager, Greta, I started to doubt your commitment to the Dharma and your ability to stick."

"How tactful of you to wait till now to tell me," I said, smiling.

"But I never lost a deeper layer of faith. Today I can say that all my unspoken doubt has burned off like a summer meadow mist." He gave me the worn photo (not a hardened d-cube) that now engages my attention.

In it, a Tibetan boy of eight or nine faces the viewer with a broad smile. He holds before him, also facing the viewer, a baby girl with rosy cheeks and eyes so familiar that I tear up in consternation and joy. The eyes belong to my predecessor's infant sister, who didn't live long after the capture of this image.

The eyes also belong to Kyipa.

I meditate on this conundrum, richly. Soon, after all, the *Yak Butter Express* will set down in New Tibet.

THE GOSPEL ACCORDING TO GAMALIEL CRUCIS;

or, THE ASTROGATOR's TESTIMONY

CHAPTER I

Gamaliel's prologue.

1 In that eventful year, O Humanity, the Twentieth Expeditionary Force, having been gone from our solar system nearly two decades, flung itself back through the empty substratum of outer space carrying aboard its vanguard vessel, *Pilgrim*, the kidnapped Redeemer of another race.

2 Gamaliel Rashba, chief astrogator for the Twentieth, later self-christened Crucis, here sets forth his testimony as witness to the transuniversal Mantic truth, to the shameful treachery of his people's response, and to the Hope that yet abides and in whose promise we sustain our myriad private hopes.

3 At the homecoming of the Twentieth, the peoples of Earth and all her proximate satellites and colonies rejoiced; for only five of our earliest expeditions to much closer suns had returned, and those so long ago that the memory of their success had inevitably begun to fade.

4 Four other caravans to distant stars were yet en route, but the ten remaining fleets of humanity's most hopeful and arrogant outreach had altogether perished, saddening the vigilant human populations of their original solar system.

5 The rejoicing of the peoples at the homecoming of the Twentieth, then, briefly united us. Celebration triumphed over longstanding blood hatreds, territorial disputes, politico-religious conflicts, and many newer disagreements that those on the *Pilgrim* and her sister ships had neither foreseen nor imagined.

6 But these fragile reconciliations did not endure, for what is fragile must at length break, and with the resumption of old feuds and enmities, a glare like nova-light illuminated the astonishing nonhuman cargo brought to Earth aboard the *Pilgrim*.

7 To the hallowed disagreements, old and new, inflaming the passions of humankind, was added the disruptive power of a Savior stolen from the insectile peoples of the fifth planet of the far-off Alpha Crucis binary.

8 Stolen, indeed, with their blessing, kidnapped with their connivance; for they had other Redeemers in plenty, and, by what the crew of the Twentieth told them about conditions Earthward, it occurred to the intelligences of this world that humanity had need of one of their troublesome surplus.

The alien Messiah introduced.

9 This was the one whom Gamaliel and the others called *Lady Mantid, Gottesanbeterin, prie-Dieu, God-horse, Mistress*—a host of names redolent of awe or respect, depending on their birthplaces and the idioms of their native tongues—

10 a being that some aboard the *Pilgrim* came to know as an alien essence consubstantial with the Second Person of the long-discredited Nicene Trinity. (That Gamaliel adopted this particular view surprised him as much as, or even more than, it unsettled those who knew his background and personal history.)

11 This was the Alphacrucian Christ, a female mantid of untoward delicacy and strength, easily as large as the largest Russian wolfhound, in hue a lovely avocado, in movement a clockwork ballerina, gracefully strange, strangely graceful, and ever glittering at the eye.

12 "Call me Mantikhoras," she had said in the hold of the *Pilgrim*. "For I am the man-eater whose appetite means not death but regeneration, and you, Gamaliel, are he who must satisfy your people's hunger by satisfying mine."

13 This saying frightened more of Gamaliel's crew and passengers than it comforted or converted; and, from that day on, he championed the salvific mission of this six-legged being at his own wary discretion, and always at his peril.

Presentation to the press.

14 Into Cleveland, Ohio, capital of North America's Multipartite Union,

the officers of the Twentieth took their alien charge to a colloquy with the superstars of the Pan-Solar Press. (Eighty-odd years earlier, the opening salvos of the Cobalt Galas had obliterated Boston, New York, Philadelphia, Baltimore, and Washington.)

15 At sight of Mantikhoras, all these personages fell back in awe, and many fainted, but among the first to recover was CABLE-STAR holocaster Rachelka Dan, who pressed to the fore to machine-gun the mantid with questions.

16 She directed most of these at Captain H. K. Bajaj, leader of the Twentieth: "How did you come to take the creature from its world? Does it know of the geopolitical standoff on Earth or of the intercolonial relationships underlying Sunspace politics? What does it think of Cleveland?"

17 And Ms. Dan also asked, "Has the alien consented to this interview? Why have you chosen this time and forum to introduce it to humanity? Does it speak?" And an array of similar questions too numerous to try to echo.

18 Captain Bajaj said, "This meeting takes place here and now by order of the Interstellar Diplomatic Instrument for Outreach, Trade, and Study, the very global authority that has mounted every extrasolar expedition to date."

19 Whereupon Gamaliel the Astrogator spoke, saying, "Never fear. The mantid learned human languages, history, and cultural lore en route from Acrux V. She indeed speaks, friends, but her hour is not yet come."

20 "Her hour for what?" asked the holocasters, amazed that Gamaliel had identified the mantid as female. "She is a big green bug, but you imply that she carries an apocalyptic message for our worlds."

21 "M. religiosa crucensis," Gamaliel corrected. "Family Mantidae, order Dictyoptera, substance Divine. Not a 'big green bug.' And those of you who swooned a moment ago have unaccountably acquired courage in the wake of Rachelka's questioning."

22 Chastened, some of the throng mumbled crankily, thinking to repay the astrogator by ridiculing his belief in the insect's supernatural origins. "Are you the bug's disciple?" one asked. "Do you wish our immediate conversion

to High Buggery?"

23 These questions instigated so much belligerent laughter and raillery that Captain Bajaj threatened an abrupt termination of the interview.

24 "I am indeed the Alphacrucian's disciple!" Gamaliel shouted above the din. "I confess it to every nation, satellite, and colony!"

25 When the noise abated, Rachelka Dan asked the captain, "Has the mantid made other disciples among the officers and crew of the Twentieth? Or is your astrogator alone in his startling declaration of faith?"

26 Said Captain Bajaj, his eyes downcast, "At least two others on the *Pilgrim* share his perspective: medical officer Andrew Stout and assistant xenologist Priscilla Muthinga. How many others share their view I cannot say." And he strode from the dais to escape further probing.

Mantikhoras calms the throng.

27 Bedlam ensued. Neither Gamaliel Crucis nor any of the remaining five officers could re-impose order on the chaos. And when the mantid on the platform began to stalk from side to side, she added to the dismay of many and thus to the noise.

28 In a voice of porcelain purity and authority, she cried, "Give heed to Gamaliel!" This unexpected command draped silence on the throng, and everyone gazed up at the creature in thunderstruck awe.

29 And Gamaliel, the way having been prepared for him, stepped to the middle of the platform and in impassioned tones addressed the peoples of every nation, satellite, and colony, declaring:

CHAPTER 2

Planetfall on Acrux V.

1 "This mantid is the Messiah, the Anointed One long ago promised the

Jews, and though I have come to believe in her as a child of Abraham, I recognize that even those in Peter's church and its schismatic heirs may also believe, for she and the problematic Jesus are of the same essence as The One.

2 "On Acrux V, we happened to put down during the messianic mission of Lady Mantid and her sibling saviors, an accident that The One, in loving repudiation of the attribute of all-knowingness, did nothing to prevent.

3 "The people of this world are thinking insects, self-aware Mantidae, but like us fallen from the primeval Garden into Sin and Death: for which reason The One sent unto them a Holy Family of vermiform larvae.

4 "Each of these hatchlings emerged from the same encompassing egg case, or *ootheca*, which itself was extruded by a virgin mantid blessed with fecundity by the inspiriting touch of the Transuniversal Holy Ghost.

5 "Acrux V crawls with sentient creatures, and all reproduce in immemorial orthopteran fashion. For the Daughter of Mantid, Mantikhoras, to appear among them as the *solitary* issue of an egg case would violate the covenant of their biology and the expectations of their culture."

Rachelka Dan interrupts.

6 Here, Rachelka Dan broke in, saying, "Do you mean to tell us that God— or The One, if you prefer that designation—sent a SWAT team of Messiahs to the Alphacrucians?" And this inquiry provoked another minor uproar among the Pan-Solar Press.

7 Having returned to the platform from the corridor, Captain Bajaj lifted a hand and said, "This is matter a Hindu such as I may easily explain, and if the lady from CABLE-STAR does not object, I will do so."

8 With Ms. Dan's ready consent, the captain resumed: "The avatars of Vishnu are many. Although they are not as many as the avatars of divinity sent as egg-case siblings to the Alphacrucians, even Mahatma Ghandi once asked a Christian missionary why God, if He had one son, did not have another and another."

9 The captain ended, "On Acrux V, God had so many children that like the old woman in the nursery rhyme he didn't know what to do." The press howled gleefully at this remark, and Captain Bajaj, shaking his head, stepped aside for Gamaliel.

The astrogator's narrative resumed.

10 Thus bolstered, the astrogator continued his story: "Some of the hundreds of nymphs emerging from the holy ootheca, there in the rocky desert of their homeland, fell upon and devoured one another, an orthopteran biological impulse that reduced their number to a couple of hundred or so.

11 "If you wish, call this postnatal feast a celebration of the Eucharist, the First Supper, Unruly Communion, or any other term that seems appropriate.

12 "But remember that if The One wished Its insectile offspring to be both fully mantid and fully divine, these teeming nymphal incarnations were altogether necessary; hence, The One accomplished them."

13 ("Yecch," said a holocaster near the dais, whose colleagues at first shushed and then snidely ridiculed him.)

14 Gamaliel continued: "We arrived while Mantikhoras and her surviving egg-mates, grown from wingless nymphs to adults capable of flight, whirred from one Alphacrucian town to another, preaching the gospel, healing the afflicted, and doing other miracles that we of the Twentieth were not always privileged to witness.

15 "Their evangelism enraged the duly established queens and councils of that world. It openly challenged the status quo and seemed to threaten their authority. These actions the rulers deemed crimes of a religious as well as a secular cast.

16 "Our advent further confused the situation: but because many of the male saviors gave in to mantid lust only to suffer decapitation at the jaws of their sated brides, day by day the ranks of the divine siblings thinned, leaving only females to continue the program on which The One had dispatched them.

17 "Disturbed by the ongoing mission of these last rabbis, down now to a mere sixty or seventy, the most powerful Alphacrucian rulers enlisted the aid of some of us from the Twentieth in curbing their evangelical activity;

18 "For we were often at court with the rulers, observing their ways and exchanging data, and they supposed us sympathetic to their position vis-à-vis the disruptive influence of the barnstorming redeemers.

19 "Intellectually keen but technologically backward, the Alphacrucian rulers may have seen us as harbingers of their own material evolution . . . *if* the evangels were prevented from plunging the citizenry at large back into the toils of superstition by encouraging in it a hopeless egalitarianism."

20 Cried one holocaster, "This is getting thick, Gamaliel! Come to the point!"

21 The astrogator replied, "The point is that after half a revolution of Acrux V around its primary, we determined that our presence itself was an anomalous factor in the life of the world, and so made plans to depart, symbolically washing our hands of any complicity in the fate of either the rulers or the evangels.

22 "Said the preeminent elder of the preeminent Alphacrucian council, 'If you don't take one of the self-proclaimed Daughters of Mantid with you as an object of study, she will die with the others when, for the crimes of cultic blasphemy and civil agitation, we arrest and devour them.'

23 "His wide-set eyes aglitter, this elder added, 'We are glad to let a people as advanced as you but so poor in offspring per couple borrow one of our redeemers,' and around the word *redeemers* it was totally impossible," Gamaliel said, "not to hear a set of scornful quotation marks.

24 "This elder, you see, had once visited Andrew Stout's surgery aboard the *Pilgrim* and assumed that we would subject our messianic passenger to vivisection, dismemberment, and microscopic examination, the end result being her death.

25 "Instead we accepted the offer as a way to preserve the creature's life and to fulfill our tripartite responsibility as sturdy concessionaires of the Interstellar Diplomatic Instrument for Outreach, Trade, and Study.

26 "And, on our voyage home from the Alpha Crucis binary, the insect we now call Lady Mantid or Mantikhoras convinced me of her godhood by her fierce serenity, her mighty intellect, and a modest array of signs and wonders."

27 Cried Rachelka Dan, "Details, please! Details!"

Lady Mantid buttresses the emptiness.

28 And Gamaliel replied, "Once on our voyage through the empty substratum beneath the vacuum proper, Mantikhoras stretched forth a forelimb and healed a tiny rent in an outer bulkhead through which the lethal force of nothingness had begun to seep."

29 A holocaster upbraided the astrogator, saying, "A patch would have done as well. In many cases miracles give birth to faith, but here, I fear, your own faith has given birth to a miracle."

30 "On another occasion," Gamaliel said, "pleased that I had pledged to her discipleship, Lady Mantid granted me a glimpse of the deathly void that belief in The One through the mediation of her person would vanquish utterly.

31 "This she did by standing alone with me in an aft compartment of the *Pilgrim* and saying to the ship's inanimate constituent parts, '*Away!*'

32 "Whereupon every bulkhead disappeared, and every crew member was visible to me as a living marionette hanging in the dark, seemingly without support and unaware of the vast self-centered emptiness in which they danced.

33 "Frightened and cold, I collapsed: but Mantikhoras picked me up. 'This is the realm of death,' she said, 'for which the empty transdimensional realm of the substratum beneath the void is only an elegant allegory.

34 " 'Here, however, not even an astrogator has power to move, for no stars shine. And what meaning resides in changing places within an emptiness that is everywhere the same and everywhere inhospitable?

35 " 'Just as you plot the *Pilgrim*'s course through the spatial substratum to

the light, I guide those who deliver themselves to me, for I Am that which shapes the formless: the bone in the body, the struts in the solar sail.'

36 "And Mantikhoras said another word, restoring the walls of the vessel and putting a deck beneath my feet again: so that I knew this miracle for a parable as well as a prodigy, and I straightway handed myself over."

37 Then Captain Bajaj mounted the podium to announce that all questioning must cease, and the holocasters shouted in one voice, "Is your astrogator lying? Did others experience this? What is *your* explanation of the matter?"

38 To which the captain answered, "A hallucination, my friends. The substratum is the very province of hallucinations."

39 Neither Gamaliel nor Lady Mantid could counter the captain's remark, for the party from the Twentieth was ushered from the room, the mantid stalking in her monarchial, clockwork way and the astrogator hurrying to remain abreast of her.

40 Whispered a colleague to Ms. Dan, "What do you think Thaddeus Thorogood and the New Testament Revivalists are going to make of this development? Not one among us had sense enough to raise the question, but it may be the most important one there is."

41 "Amen," said Rachelka quietly. "This adventure is only beginning. Mark my words, mark my words."

CHAPTER 3

1 After this introduction, the Interstellar Diplomatic Instrument set Mantikhoras apart from both humanity and the Pan-Solar Press, and not even Captain Bajaj or Gamaliel the Astrogator knew where; for it had been decided that the mantid must undergo more study and swear earthly allegiance to the disarranged government of the Multipartite Union of North America.

2 This she apparently did without delay or qualm, resting her spirit in the

saying (perhaps apocryphal), *Render unto temporal powers the inconsequential but unto The One all that truly counts.*

Mantikhoras's cross-country flight.

3 In some wise, the mantid obtained release and flew under her own power to the West Coast amusement park to which she knew Andrew Stout, Priscilla Muthinga, Nicholas Morowitz, and Gamaliel Crucis, disciples all, had repaired from the mothballed *Pilgrim* for some hard-earned R & R.

4 During this flight, Mantikhoras beheld the ruined cities, cratered farms, polluted rivers, slumped mountains, blighted forests, scarred hills, and pale dead lakes of the M.U.N.A., marveling that amid such desolation the people continued to support—over and above all other enterprises—professional sports stadia and thousands of gaudy playlands.

5 A squadron of obsolescent scoopjets escorted Mantikhoras from her place of detention (Pelee Island, Lake Erie) to Kansas City, Missouri, where simple curiosity induced her to descend to observe the people enjoying roller-coasters, parachute drops, and whirligigs in the restored ruins of an ancient theme park.

6 Upon seeing her, its agitated patrons pointed, ran, and cat-called her; for they knew her from holocasts, while she in turn felt pity for their deformities and bitter bewilderment in the face of such afflictions.

7 There in the park, she took several small children for brief flights, and talked with their parents, and answered the hatred of each and every vocal bigot with kindness and humor, but refrained from performing miracles.

8 At last, park officials asked her to go, saying that she'd taken profits from ice-cream and soft-drink sellers and led hundreds of frightened children to believe that a monster had beset the grounds: an accusation with only a slender margin of truth.

9 Undismayed, Mantikhoras bade her new friends adieu and left, taking care to continue her westward journey at a tree-top height that, by thwarting radar detection, enabled her to elude the clamor and pomp of her unasked-for scoopjet escort.

10 And so she whirred over wheat fields and cattle lots, through arroyos and diseased stands of cottonwoods; frequently along her route she registered radioactive hot spots, and always was struck by the numbers of malformed people and animals dwelling in the blasted continent.

11 Over Oklahoma's panhandle, a rancher in a buckboard knocked her from the sky with a double-barreled discharge from a 12-gauge, peppering her right wing with birdshot: so that she tumbled into a gulley reeking of alkali but so high-banked and twisty that it kept her from being discovered for the coup de grace.

12 "I am the coup de grace," said Mantikhoras to the cloudless heavens; "I am the stroke of mercy. Indeed, I am the hopeful death that opens a gate into paradise." But no one was near to hear her.

13 Nor could she depart by air, for her wing was broken, and she settled in for the night, asking forgiveness for her assailant on the grounds that to him she must have resembled the vanguard of a prodigious plague of locusts.

The temptation in the wilderness.

14 Thus commenced her sojourn in the wilderness, where she stayed forty days, praying continually, hallucinating pleasant Alphacrucian landscapes, and slaking her thirst on the brackish moisture in various succulent cacti and discarded diet-cola cans.

15 At last there appeared to Lady Mantid, in the flesh or a fever dream, a figure in greasy khaki, unshaven and ill-shod, whose eyes were shriveled raisins, an apparition who asked her into his rattletrap vehicle and put to her many disheartening proposals:

16 "Come with me to Vegas, baby, and we'll split the take sixty-forty, me on the up side for providing the transportation; or maybe fifty-fifty if it looks like you'll prove a *really* big hit."

17 And hustling Mantikhoras out of Oklahoma into New Mexico, the driver named the probable rewards to them of a night-club routine at Nero's Bistro on the Strip, if she, the Mantid Queen, did not disdain to do wonders.

18 Said the wannabe impresario, "You know, make the whole goddamn hotel disappear the way you did that spaceship. Then, just when everyone's good and scared, slap it back around them and keep them from crapping their drawers.

19 "Or maybe we could push a battery of slot machines up there on stage and you could pray up a jackpot on every one of them, which management would like because it'd make the suckers believe the same thing's possible out there in the casinos."

20 Mantikhoras, mesmerized by the heat waves dancing on the asphalt and the baffling incantations on her driver's lips, made no reply.

21 Noting this, the huckster said, "There's more than just silver to corral. There's booze, and baubles, and whatever turns you on. We could round up a bug box of dragonflies and just sort of shake them out in your bed, you know?"

22 "Stop!" Mantikhoras commanded. "This isn't my mission": so that, thus rebuked, the driver shoved her out without stopping and sped off down the deserted highway into the next sun-baked adobe town.

The calf.

23 As she rolled into yet another gulley, Lady Mantid realized that her tempter had been a living creature, not a dream, and she hungered mightily for solace as well as for food;

24 Whereupon a blind calf with two heads stumbled into the arroyo, bleating tenderly and nuzzling her thorax; and she stroked it with her forelimbs, saying,

25 "Because of the evil done against you by your masters, who are themselves blind, I bequeath unto you with this benediction a *rational soul,* and all the responsibilities and perquisites attending that gift."

26 By this speech the calf's tongues were loosed, and it said, both heads speaking as one, "If I am now in honorary possession of a rational soul, I beseech you to consume me for thy name's sake, that I may inherit the

kingdom"; for the calf had at once perceived the deeper identity of the Alphacrucian.

27 Mantikhoras wept.

28 And said to the two-headed calf, "I must first restore your sight," which she did in a trice: so that the calf beheld the first stars glimmering in the dusk and bleated at them in heartrending admiration and gratitude.

29 Embracing the creature, Mantikhoras fed her hunger, leaving the hides and hooves as offerings to The One (whose proxies were now a host of circling vultures); and the spirit of the ennobled calf ascended straightway into heaven.

Reunion with the disciples.

30 The forty days were ended, a period during which helicopters, highway patrolmen, and units of the Civil Air Patrol had crisscrossed the western half of the continent in search of her; and Mantikhoras, having escaped both discovery and rescue, took flight again.

31 Yet farther to the west, in the opulent park called Magic Kindgom VII, Gamaliel and his fellow believers from the Twentieth had grown weary of the rigors of their protracted R & R.

32 Groused Priscilla Muthinga, "I've enjoyed just about all of this I can stand," at which remark an employee in the get-up of an ill-tempered Dwarf poked her in the ankle with a stick designed for retrieving litter.

33 Seeing this attack, Gamaliel made Priscilla put forth her other leg so that the Dwarf could poke it in the ankle, too: whereupon he and his comrades-in-faith disarmed the park employee and warned him of the consequences of his ever again abusing their turn-the-other-ankle piety.

34 "I'm sick of this place, Gamaliel," said Andrew Stout after the Dwarf had slunk away. "Why don't we flick over to Hawaii for a round of Frisbee golf or maybe a bit of out-of-body surfing in etheric wetsuits by Bloomingdale & Sears?"

35 Shouted the others, "I'm for that!" and even Gamaliel doubted the survival of their Mistress and wavered in his allegiance to the code of discipleship.

36 But at the moment of consenting to the others' frivolity, they all heard a buzzing of wings and Mantikhoras came swooping down upon them from over the pseudo-glacial peak of a fiberglass mountain three hundred feet high.

37 Said Lady Mantid, landing near her followers, "The task is at hand. Come, let's get to work."

CHAPTER 4

On the air.

1 Soon thereafter, Mantikhoras appeared on a pan-solar broadcast of the holo program *Parsecs Ahead,* hosted by Rachelka Dan before a live studio audience in a dilapidated CABLE-STAR facility in Burbank, California.

2 The topic of the evening was the alleged divinity of the visitor from Acrux V, and the producers of the program had assembled not only Lady Mantid but also the scientists who had studied her on Pelee Island during her confinement after the holocast conference in Cleveland.

3 Although Gamaliel and many others advised their Mistress to refrain from appearing on *Parsecs Ahead,* fearing the debate would turn into a sideshow staged and manipulated by the skillful Ms. Dan, Mantikhoras rebuked them, saying,

4 "Isn't it likely that the Daughter of Mantid, having seen manipulations of much greater magnitude than anything you'll encounter here, knows exactly what she's up to?"

5 And in her opening interview with Rachelka Dan, while steadfastly refusing to identify herself as anything other than a large intelligent insect, she astonished everyone with the precision and poetry of her speech.

6 Ms. Dan pursued her, saying, "But the astrogator of the Twentieth claims greater things for you, and on your journey from Cleveland to Anaheim, which took a suspiciously long time, it's rumored that you stopped in several small communities to demonstrate your, uh, well, your *powers.*"

7 To which Lady Mantid replied, "The only nonhuman power I've demonstrated to date is that of unassisted flight, a capability I share with every other educated, self-aware adult on my distant world of origin."

8 And the host of *Parsecs Ahead* said, "A world, Lady Mantid, whose leadership rejected you and sent you home with the Twentieth as an insidious revolutionary, a bad seed they wanted planted in the exhausted but well-turned soil of *our* Good Earth.

9 "Is it any wonder that some of us suspect your intentions and regard your most ardent supporters as dupes of the ruling Alphacrucians? Perhaps you've come to undermine the very foundations of our lives."

10 And, much to the uneasiness of her disciples on the premises, Mantikhoras said, "If I've come to undermine lives, I've done so only to buttress your humanity and elevate your questing spirits."

11 On this pronouncement, Ms. Dan pounced: "So subversion *is* your mission! At last you admit it. And you also hint at a superhuman—indeed, a *supernatural*—motive that earlier you denied."

12 Mantikhoras's antennae quivered in gnomic acknowledgment, but otherwise she held her peace.

13 After some commercial messages (for a round-trip vacation package to Ganymede, a do-it-yourself bioengineering kit, and a pocket Geiger counter), Rachelka introduced a panel of scientists and another of theologians, all of whom professed to grok the mantid's genetic and spiritual makeup.

14 Dr. Millard Crews, an alien anatomist (who had never visited the Galapagos Islands), declared that Lady Mantid had an outsized orthopteran body and a tripartite brain whose like he had never seen before; nevertheless, he felt certain that the creature was a creature indeed and not an avatar of divinity.

15 Dr. Scheherezade Tabataba'i, late of the University of Isfahan, scoffed at the notion that our guest represented the long-awaited Shiite *mahdi*, saved from her "occultation" by the crew of the Twentieth; the Islamic scholar also rejected as unconvincing the mantid's impersonation of the Judeo-Christian Messiah.

16 Dr. Joe Bob Newcombe, of West Texas New Testament Revivalist College in El Paso, told the show's pan-solar audience that the mantid's very existence was an insult to God and that her manifold blasphemies on *Parsecs Ahead* warranted, at the least, deportation and probably a good deal worse.

17 Other experts testified that the Alphacrucian was a) a special effect, b) an argument for either atheism or credulity, c) an extraterrestrial analogue of the scarab beetle sacred to the ancient Egyptians, d) an orthopteran moron foisted upon us by her own evil people, or e) a genius banished from Acrux V for her innovative social ideas.

The L. G. Glauber psychoscope.

18 At last, Dr. Felipe Novello, a licensed psychoscopist and moderately famous depth-oneiromancer, overrode the others by declaring that he for one accepted the divine nature of Lady Mantid and that, in fact, he possessed what amounted to credible scientific proof of her divinity.

19 Rachelka Dan accosted Dr. Novello with a microphone: "All right, then, sir, let's have it: the worlds are waiting."

20 Said her guest, "The unconsciousness of an entity identical with God in almost every respect but that of spiritual ubiquity would present an unparalleled challenge to a depth-oneiromancer, wouldn't you agree? Well, it does, and I accepted the challenge."

21 "What Dr. Novello is trying to say," Rachelka Dan interpreted, "is that a peek inside the dreaming mind of a creaturely projection of the Supreme Being, or The One, would be a small assault on the mind of God itself."

22 Dr. Novello nodded his qualified assent to this paraphrase of his argument, and two mechanical stagehands rolled a gleaming L. G. Glauber psychoscope onto the ramshackle set of *Parsecs Ahead*.

23 Said Dr. Novello, going to the machine, "I will now replay for you a holotape of the Uncon dimension of Mantikhoras's mental activity during a four-hour sleep period at our research facility on [site *bleeped*]. I'll run the tape at twenty times our original recording speed to stay within stipulated programming limits."

24 And the video well of the psychoscope filled with fog, a formlessness as deep and all-pervasive as that of the substratum beneath the interstellar void; and this inchoate miasma began to shimmer and quake in basso-profundo registers of silence that every viewer felt in his or her bones.

25 And all that followed afterward no one watching could chronicle or synopsize, for to some it seemed that nothing had occurred; whereas to others the psychoscope revealed a pageant of cosmogenesis so rapid and minutely detailed that different images leapt out and fully overcame different people.

26 Gamaliel found himself stirring inside the sticky skin of a terrestrial *M. religiosa* just prior to its intermediate molt, stalks of grass towering around him like sequoias and every clod of dirt a miniature Gibraltar.

27 Andrew Stout waltzed in lunar orbit around a planetary gas giant in another galaxy; and Priscilla, somewhere in the Pacific Ocean, darted here and there over the gleaming hide of a hammerhead shark, cleansing it of microscopic parasites.

28 What other onlookers excerpted and felt only they could say, but it was everywhere as singular as it was vivid: a kaleidoscope of images, an infinitely grand smorgasbord from which to pick and choose.

29 At last the video well of the Kroeber psychoscope incandesced, radiating a powerful white light that united the audience of *Parsecs Ahead* in an overwhelming conflagration of phosphor dots and motile phosphenes.

30 And Mantikhoras spoke into this light, saying, "Remember what blinds you, and look through it, and on its other side you will certainly find that which has been there from the beginning."

31 Voices cried out in alarm, the psychoscope exploded, showering sparks,

and Ms. Dan cried, "Cut to a test pattern!" *Parsecs Ahead* went off air in a roar of incandescence that ruined the holosets of three quarters of CABLE-STAR's clientele.

Escape from the studio.

32 Said Felipe Novello, "See what I mean?" But the uproar in the studio among both his colleagues and the audience rendered his question inaudible; and the Daughter of Mantid hitched her way unmolested from the building to the parking lot, where Gamaliel and the others had taken refuge.

33 It was twelve-thirty in the morning, and clear, but none of Lady Mantid's followers could see the stars for the nimbus of celestial brightness lingering on their retinae from the blown-out psychoscope: so that the disciples felt themselves floating along as if in a perfusing billow of squid ink.

34 When they complained of this, Mantikhoras said, "Out of blindness, sight," and led them from Burbank into the desert, where the stars reemerged, and they spent the night talking of eternity, suffering, discipleship, and the mutability of holocast ratings.

CHAPTER 5

Rachelka Dan converted.

1 After this Mantikhoras went everywhere on the habitable continent, visiting hospitals, amusement parks, sports stadia, gambling casinos (even Nero's Bistro), military bases, zoos, and other mutant reservations.

2 Her successful appearance on *Parsecs Ahead* made her instantly recognizable, and welcome, wherever she went (excluding only the heartland of Thaddeus Thorogood's New Testament Revivalists); and she dispensed comfort or miracles as each site and situation warranted.

3 Rachelka Dan became the mantid's most zealous convert; indeed, she and Gamaliel often acted as the Alphacrucian's advance team, preceding their winged Mistress to each fresh venue to arrange both interviews and lodging.

4 Jews by birth and upbringing, Rachelka and Gamaliel together reached the conclusion that Lady Mantid was not necessarily a new incarnation of the God-in-man esteemed by the tattered remnants of latter-day Christendom, but the Suffering Servant prophesied in the fifty-third chapter of Isaiah.

5 For the verses of this chapter say of the servant, "he hath no form or comeliness; and when we shall see him, there is no beauty we should desire him," which descriptions had some seeming reference to the image of the alien redeemer in the eyes of a narrow-souled humanity.

6 Or, if not the Suffering Servant of Isaiah, then perhaps the Son of man in the visionary seventh chapter of Daniel, whose "dominion is an everlasting dominion, which shall not pass away."

7 For these constituted the Messianic likelihoods that did not rub against the faith of their childhoods, and that conformed both to the portrait of the Suffering Servant in Isaiah and to that in Daniel of the Son of man riding to glory on a heavenly thundercloud.

8 Said Gamaliel to Rachelka, "I never expected to escort the Messiah to Earth aboard the *Pilgrim,* but I infinitely prefer that sort of mundane arrival to the Messiah's advent in an apocalyptic blitzkrieg signaling all-out warfare between, well, Good and Evil."

9 "Although I never put my faith in a warrior Messiah or in a Levite priest-king come to cleanse us of our sins," replied Rachelka, "the mind of Lady Mantid is obviously that of God, and I must commit to her, as both captive and lover."

10 Uncertainty and bashfulness stayed Gamaliel's tongue (shore leave on Acrux V had not improved his social graces), and, for weeks during these exciting travels, he went to bed in motel rooms next to Rachelka's fighting to square his lust with his admiration for her and with his devotion to the Cause.

11 He hoped that Rachelka would become *his* captive and *his* lover, for he wanted her to go forward with him in their common ministry not merely as a fellow disciple but as his wedded helpmeet.

Miraculous cures.

12 Meanwhile, Mantikhoras toured the radiation-sickness wards of special sanatoria for fallout victims, held audiences with cancer patients whose malignancies were inoperable, and sought, on every medical front, sufferers whose physicians had numbered their days and despaired of ever curing anyone similarly afflicted.

13 Gamaliel saw the Daughter of Mantid pray with a man whose bone marrow showed up on thermoscans as fiery rivers of strontium 90. But an hour later the radioactivity had departed, and the blood-cell count had stabilized at a normal level.

14 The astrogator also witnessed the Alphacrucian drive a cancer that had metastasized through the liver and lights of a two-year-old girl into a lump of phlegm, which the child promptly disgorged and the doctors just as promptly doused with alcohol and burned in a chromium bedpan.

15 On another occasion, in a hovel on the wolf-ridden periphery of Tacoma, Washington, Mantikhoras hugged a woman in the last stages of rabies and, before the day was out, had her cheerfully eating and planning a visit to Tucson.

16 Everywhere that the mantid and her entourage went, people pressed forward with their misshapen bodies, their unlikely diseases, and their hungry spirits, looking for physical grace, or remedy, or nourishment; for those she'd healed since her appearance on *Parsecs Ahead* were legion.

17 But some supplicants she turned away, saying, "Your people have the knowledge and wherewithal to cure you"; whereupon Andrew Stout would come forward with a referral to the appropriate specialist or clinic, and Priscilla Muthinga with money to pay for the treatments.

The ungrateful petitioner.

18 Once, a young double-amputee advised to apply for lifelike prosthetics from a Swiss bioengineering firm, and funded on the spot for these devices, berated Mantikhoras for her heartlessness, shouting,

19 "You don't give a damn about my disability, do you? You've got wings! That I've been without legs almost my entire life doesn't mean shit to you, does it, you goddamn overgrown *grasshopper?*"

20 Andrew, who wished to dump the petitioner from his wheelchair, grew red-faced pointing out to this young man the powerful likelihood that his missing limbs were a visible sign of his spiritual poverty.

21 But Mantikhoras silenced Andrew. She lifted her papery wings and spoke to the bitter one: "I'd give these to you, young man, if they would do you any good. However, it's not upon fleshly wings that you'll mount from your affliction to fulfillment, but instead upon the wings of your faith in my ministry."

22 Yelled the man in the wheelchair, blatantly sneering his contempt and scorn, "What a crock of bullshit!"

23 Mantikhoras asked her followers to wrench her wings from her body and give them to the man as an offering of both love and commitment, which dreadful deed Gamaliel and the others could not bring themselves to perform.

24 Angry with their refusal, the mantid appealed to the crowd, at last prevailing upon two bikers from Birmingham, Alabama, to tear her wings from her prothorax. As they did so, the bikers wore nervous grins, for each one doubted the propriety of this duly-authorized mutilation.

25 Then said Mantikhoras to the man, "I give you my wings not to replace your legs, but as tokens of my willingness to share your suffering."

26 Still unrepentant, he said, "I couldn't ever fly, and I'm won't ever walk, so what good will the sacrifice of your freaking wings do me or anybody else?"

27 Turning to the bikers, Mantikhoras asked them to pull her praying forelimbs from her body, which request, although Gamaliel and the others cried out in warning, the two men appeared ready to honor.

28 Then the young man in the wheelchair cried, "Keep your goddamn legs, goddammit! You're not going to stick me with a guilt trip too!" And he rolled

out of the crowd, taking with him Andrew's referral and Priscilla's cashier's check.

29 And Priscilla said, "Mistress, your sacrifice was wasted. He'd rather have the entire world in wheelchairs than walk again himself. He spared your forelimbs not from love but from fear of having your loss of them forever on his conscience."

30 And the mantid said, "A judgment that confirms that he has one."

On conscience.

31 Later, after Mantikhoras and her disciples had walked apart, she said, "Conscience is God's greatest gift to rational souls, and I say to you that there is *no* rational soul upon whom The One has failed to bestow it.

32 "Some may put the gift in a drawer, or shove it into a closet and cover it with coats, toys, and board games: but when the drawer is opened or the closet set to rights, the gift is still there, cobwebbed perhaps but usable."

33 For every disciple attracted by Lady Mantid's miracles of healing, unselfishness, or wordless aura of authority, her occasional commentaries on them (see *Gamaliel 5:31-32*) often led one or two other converts to backslide or defect.

34 Repelled by parabolic statement or embarrassed by what they perceived as pious talk, these followers drifted away; therefore, Mantikhoras sometimes questioned the faithful about the efficacy of her approaches and so earned the mistrust of others by appearing to doubt herself.

35 "Maybe I'm going about this wrong," she said. "This just doesn't seem to be an age for beatitudes or parables."

36 Once, Rachelka Dan, to justify Lady Mantid's periodic bouts of self-questioning, reminded a group of adherents grumbling amongst themselves at poolside in a hotel in Omaha that humanity had borrowed its Messiah from another sentient species in another solar system.

37 Said Rachelka to the grumblers, "It's often hard for her. Allowances must be made."

38 Said one of the throng, "Room allowances, you mean! Mantikhoras always takes the bridal suite or some other plushy pad, and we get stuck in second-class accommodations five or six blocks down the street. My room doesn't even have a holoset."

39 Mantikhoras, overhearing this gibe from a balcony, revealed herself and said, "Don't begrudge me the temporal comfort of a bridal suite. I'm not with you for long, and the rooms I go to prepare for you when I depart, not even your fabled Conrad Hilton could duplicate for plushness."

40 And suffering from no uncommon homesickness, she retired, leaving them abashed and penitent.

CHAPTER 6

A wedding in Escambia County.

1 Not long after this, in Pensacola, Florida, M.U.N.A., Gamaliel asked Rachelka to marry him; and she consented on the condition, promptly met, that Mantikhoras herself preside over their exchange of vows.

2 Because Lady Mantid appeared in haste to bestow legitimacy on the astrogator's ardor, the couple abjured a full-blown ceremony with ushers, bridesmaids, flower girls, and the obligatory three-tiered cake, almost inevitably stale.

3 They would marry that evening, and the next morning Mantikhoras would announce the event as a *fait accompli,* at a breakfast gathering of the disciples in the restaurant of the Gulf Sands Budget Resort.

4 Tooling along in a rented dune buggy, Gamaliel and his passengers kept their eyes open for a roadside synagogue, of which there seemed to be, in this long coastal neighborhood, a disheartening dearth.

5 Satisfied that the couple would not soon find what they were seeking, Mantikhoras told the astrogator to turn and drive inland until they arrived at any cleanly structure dedicated to the remembrance and the service of The One.

6 This proved to be a Neutester church of reinforced cinder blocks and polarized glass tinted a shade of purple. Fenced about by palm trees, it sat in the shadow of a multistory condominium whose top floors loomed in the dusk like a shelf of storm clouds lit from within by sheet lightning.

7 Said Gamaliel, "This won't do," but Rachelka put a finger to his lips; and Mantikhoras said, "If we were in Cairo, it would be a mosque; if in Tokyo, a shrine; if on Acrux V, a verdant meadow with neither pillars nor canopy. We're going in."

8 The door was unlocked; and the dusk of the interior was deeper than that of the falling night, and on the wall behind the altar a sad effigy of the Crucified hung like a lynched horse thief in an old movie.

9 Rachelka murmured, "I've always thought the sight of a human God nailed to a cross would steal away the faith of the faint-hearted"; but she neared the altar with Gamaliel, and Mantikhoras married them before The One by taking them together in her clasp and praying wordlessly.

The transfiguration.

10 When this was done, the Alphacrucian released the newlyweds and climbed the cinder blocks behind the altar like a fly going up a wall, stopping at length beside the effigy of the Crucified.

11 When Mantikhoras sidled atop the plaster Christ's body, that end of the Neutester chapel shone as brightly as the flash of a fusion bomb, and the organ in the choir loft rumbled in the bass registers, faultlessly mimicking human speech:

12 "This is another of my beloved issue, in whom I renew my covenant with the lost, the sick at heart, the broken in body. I anoint her in Female guise to straighten what has been made crooked and in alien flesh to prepare the worlds for a wider love."

13 The light above the altar abated; and when Rachelka and Gamaliel next looked, the figure of Jesus Messiah stirred and carne down from its oaken crucifix to congratulate the newlyweds. However, Mantikhoras had vanished, and her disappearance greatly alarmed the human couple.

14 Rachelka retreated from this vivified Christ, saying, "Tell us where our Mistress has gone; we didn't come here to disturb you." And Gamaliel was no braver than his bride, backpedaling as fast, gaping in horror and disbelief at the blood oozing from the wound in the effigy's side.

15 And the plaster Christ, in Lady Mantid's womanly voice, said, "I'm with you yet, and this The One does to seal my authority and to exchange among the three of us the vows that wed us all. Behold, I am at once human, mantid, universal rational soul, and abiding compassion of God."

16 To which Rachelka replied, "And you're bleeding all over the carpet": so that even Mantikhoras, turning aside to seize a chalice from the altar cloth, could not suppress an impious chuckle.

17 And the living effigy said, "Wine for the wedding feast," held the chalice beneath her punctured side, and filled the vessel with a most excellent vintage.

18 Soon the flow had stopped, and the three convivially toasted one another and partook of a spontaneous sacrament that was also a simple human celebration.

19 Squinting over his cup at the transfigured mantid, the astrogator opined that matters would go better for them all if Mantikhoras retained this poignant human shape, trimmed her beard and tresses, and put on clothing, particularly if her ability to perform wonders remained unimpaired by the change.

20 Rachelka said, "If you did wish to keep this body, Mistress, I'd gladly style your hair and buy you a serviceable wardrobe."

21 "I'm surprised and disappointed," Mantikhoras replied, "to find that you tempt me to the impossible, for *this* is for you alone. I came as I came to widen rather than to delimit the circle of love.

22 "Sanctity for life the Hindus teach, often refraining from slapping an insect that has stung them; and although I honor that teaching, my concern is for rational souls, whatever their shape or element. All such must have the chance to affirm or to deny their kinship *with* The One and *in* The One.

23 "Therefore I return this plaster body to its place, and those who can resurrect it in their hearts are welcome to do that, and those who cannot are welcome to seek another way, in spirit and in truth."

24 The church filled with a new annihilating brightness, which briefly put out the sight of the newlyweds, but, soon after, they beheld Mantikhoras before them in her Alphacrucian body and the still effigy of Christ back upon its cross.

The newlyweds sworn to silence.

25 Said the mantid, "I charge you never to reveal what tonight you have witnessed; not, that is, until I have been taken from you": a charge that filled the couple with a painful foreboding.

26 "How will that happen?" Gamaliel asked, and Mantikhoras replied, "Do not fret, my astrogator. All I can say is that you've exchanged your vows in one of the few Neutester chapels east of the Mississippi, and that my death will be accountable to all who worship under Neutester auspices and guidance."

27 And thinking *Thaddeus Thorogood* and *Joe Bob Newcombe,* Gamaliel shuddered and wondered aloud if Lady Mantid would return to them after a certain time to grant them the right to testify to her wondrous transfiguration.

28 To their surprise, the Daughter of Mantid laughed. "In a sense I've already come back, haven't I?" But noting their confusion, she added, "I may not, Gamaliel. And, at this late date, my failure to rise again must not dishearten you. You already well know what must be done."

29 And she led them out to their dune buggy so that they could go back to the Gulf Sands Budget Resort before incurring any additional rental fee.

CHAPTER 7

Mantikhoras and the cetaceans.

1 After this, in Miami, the Alphacrucian and her followers visited Marine Merrymakers Amusement Park, a playland set amid the desolation of the rubble-strewn city; and, in a small painted rowboat, Mantikhoras went out upon the salt waters of the main pool with Gamaliel, Damaris Brown, and Nicholas Morowitz, there to commune with the porpoises and a rambunctious trio of killer whales.

2 When the snouts of these smiling, warm-blooded fish rose beside the boat, Lady Mantid spoke to the creatures in their own languages, squeaking in tones that her human disciples found alternately musical and ear-splitting.

3 Unable to follow this medley of cetacean homilies, Gamaliel asked, "Mistress, what are you saying to them?" Meanwhile, the porpoises and whales cavorted about them like big sea-going puppies.

4 And Mantikhoras replied, "The same as I say to you and yours, Gamaliel, for they have rational souls akin to yours, and they know in innocence what you, in your sophistication, must often remember with both pain and struggle."

5 This was a hard saying, and Nicholas Morowitz took exception: "Their innocence isn't all that wonderful, is it? I mean, wouldn't they be as prone to error and sin as any of us if they had hands?"

6 To which the Daughter of Mantid replied, "Blessed are they who have neither hands nor feet, for they cannot employ them to do evil. But doubly blessed are they who have both hands and feet and yet *refrain* from doing evil."

7 This saying led Nicholas to conclude that The One perceived human beings as superior to cetaceans, but Mantikhoras rebuked him for this error with a further remark: "Those who have hands likewise have an obligation, but only a few of the handed have chosen to pick it up."

8 From a pail of white fish and flounder segments in the prow of the little boat, Damaris fed the skylarking porpoises and whales, amazed that even though she had been throwing fish to them for a long time the pail was not yet empty.

9 At last the manager of the Marine Merrymakers Amusement Park came to poolside and said that Lady Mantid's talk with his animals had gone on too long, and that feeding them so many fish would spoil their next public performance.

10 When Mantikhoras said, "But I've *come* to feed them," the manager beckoned to a hireling to approach the pool in an antique fire truck with a turret-mounted water cannon. This the hireling did, and soon the water cannon was shooting powerful jets of salt water at the little boat.

11 Gamaliel and Nicholas were hurled overboard; porpoises rescued and deposited them, drenched but unharmed, on the far bank of the pool, and from there they witnessed the unexpected conclusion to the battle.

12 Shielding Damaris, Lady Mantid withstood a noisy stream of water ricocheting from her prothorax like a ruffle of lace. Then, lifting a forelimb, she deflected this spray back at the fire truck, which capsized and spun away across the damp concrete.

13 The boss and his unhurt hireling retreated; and with no further hindrance, Mantikhoras communed with the cetaceans until Venus was up in the west and a fresh evening breeze from the Carolinas had begun to blow.

Setting free the primates.

14 Soon afterward, in Atlanta, Rachelka accompanied Mantikhoras to the zoo, where some few people supposed the mantid an otherworldly critter imported for the purposes of display.

15 But these people were in the minority, for the Alphacrucian's reputation had preceded her; and her fame everywhere incited the envy, suspicion, and enmity of mean persons in the manifold ruling councils of the Multipartite Union.

16 Of late, in fact, Mantikhoras had often spoken with her followers about the imminence of her departure from them and the course they must lay out and cleave to once she had left them.

17 Neither Rachelka nor Gamaliel nor any of the others appreciated this kind of talk, and Rachelka, in particular, was happy to be walking with Mantikhoras along the paths of the Grant Park Zoo.

18 At last they came to the monkey house, where many primates from a local research institution resided now that their usefulness as experimental subjects had concluded; and Mantikhoras insisted on going inside.

19 The building's interior stank, and in cages apart from those of the spider monkeys and capuchins dwelt research-center apes: gorillas, chimpanzees, gibbons, and orangutans. They peopled this darkness as prison inmates people the shadowy tiers of a correctional facility, and Rachelka felt their sad and resentful eyes upon her.

20 "What are we doing here?" she asked the Daughter of Mantid. "Are you taking your ministry not only to articulate smooth-skinned cetaceans, but also to these mute shaggy beasts?"

21 And Mantikhoras said, "A soul may be rational even if it lacks a capacity to speak in tongues. These guiltless prisoners 'speak' with their hands and eyes, a speech to which they bring a talent surpassing that of even the cleverest holocasters."

22 "Touché," said Rachelka, blushing, and went deeper into the monkey house with the mantid, the two providing a focus for the frustrations of the apes, which at last began to pelt them with fruit rinds and feces.

23 Cried Rachelka, "Come, Mistress, let's run!" But Mantikhoras preferred to let each outraged simian screech at and bombard them as they passed along the row, ostensibly helpless against the onslaught.

24 Between her teeth, Rachelka whispered, "You deflected the stream of water from the fire truck at Marine Merrymakers Amusement Park. Why in tarnation can't you protect us from these disgusting missiles?"

25 "You may first blunt the enmity of the wronged," Mantikhoras said, "by letting them express it. But later you cannot root out what remains of this hatred without righting the wrong that created and sustains it."

26 Rachelka started to say, "How do we do that?" but the mantid turned and led her back down the row of cages, pausing to open each one's door and urge its puzzled occupants to emerge. Soon, many of the freed apes were knuckle-walking along behind their crap-bedizened emancipators.

27 Outside the monkey house, Mantikhoras bade the former inmates go in peace or else cast their lot with her human disciples: a choice that to Rachelka seemed hardly a choice at all, especially since liberty in the fallen human world might eventually bring the apes to either renewed confinement or death.

28 She said as much to her Mistress, who reminded her that the apes were also free to return to their cages, and that many would do so. And Mantikhoras added, "Those who stay with us will have demonstrated by that action the spiritual rationality that redeemed them. It's a kind of test."

29 It therefore came to pass on the travels of the Alphacrucians about the continent that Andrew Stout took an orangutan for a roommate, and Priscilla Muthinga a young gibbon; further, from thenceforward, reserving motel accommodations became a major hassle and an ever-mounting expense.

CHAPTER 8

Erotic spirituality.

1 By nights on their beds in a dozen different cities or playlands, Gamaliel and Rachelka sought each other's soul, speaking in the gardens of this nightly ceremony with both their mouths and their bodies.

2 The places in which they recited their liturgies of love were perfumed (it seemed) with Lebanese colognes and Lysol, with cinnamon-scented lotions and factory-strength floor waxes, with instant coffee and commercial bug spray.

3 The fluorescents in the bathrooms winked with every unpredictable power surge; and some of these surges were in the astrogator's blood, and the winking of the fluorescents illumined him within.

4 And Rachelka's eyes were like the fish ponds in Heshbon, by the gate of Bathrabbim, more limpid than the pools in the Marine Merrymakers Amusement Park in Miami, albeit as festively a-splash with a salt-water ardor.

5 Night after night in the inns of their itinerancy, his left hand was under her head, and his right hand embraced her; and when the dews in his brain were spent, and his hand drawn back from the hole in the door, and the mountains of spices thoroughly plundered, Gamaliel and Rachelka would chatter like children.

The newlyweds converse.

6 *Gamaliel:* Have I ever told you how happy I am that I'm not rooming, like Andrew, with an orangutan?

7 *Rachelka:* Or I you that I'm not the suitemate of a gibbon? Bless Priscilla's heart. She's bearing up, but Lady Mantid's latest converts—cetaceans, simians, pets with genetically augmented minds—aren't doing us much good at the grass-roots level.

8 *Gamaliel:* From the beginning, the fundamentalists murmured that Mantikhoras was the Antichrist, but now the murmurs grow stronger, and even some liberal theologians in the more moderate Protestant denominations have taken it up. That's scary.

9 *Rachelka:* Ah, yes, the ones who congratulate themselves on boldly admitting primates to the evolutionary family tree of *Homo sapiens,* but who balk at sitting down to tea with them. Well, I'm afraid I sympathize. I balk, too.

10 *Gamaliel:* But, Rachelka, Muggeridge has delicate manners for a chimp, Edward's the sweetest little gibbon you could ever hope to meet; and Bonzo, why, Bonzo, the scamp, he—

11 *Rachelka:* He utterly ruined that original Guy de Froissart jumpsuit I wore

into the Grant Park monkey house back in Atlanta, and it's a real bitch trying to forgive the little bugger.

12 Gamaliel: Well, for Mantikhoras's sake, you've got to *try*. She keeps saying that her time among us grows shorter, and if that's so, my Shulamite, we must strive very hard to obey her commandments to us.

13 *Rachelka:* I swear, Gamaliel, I think she's deliberately hastening her passion. This mandated fraternizing with nonhuman life forms appears *designed* to lose friends and alienate fundamentalists, no matter how bright and perky the converts.

14 *Gamaliel:* It's part of her ministry. How can we establish meaningful relationships with alien intelligences in other star systems if we can't reach a humane accord with the more rational species here on our own planet?

15 *Rachelka:* Kiss a porpoise for Christ, huh? Well, the absurdity of that, Mr. Worldly Wiseman, is that four generations after the Cobalt Galas, we find coreligionists sniping at one another, agnostics at agnostics, atheists at atheists, and devout dialectical materialists at anyone in a pair of well-soled shoes.

Erotic spirituality.

16 And Gamaliel said, "Mantikhoras never promised us . . . uh, what are you doing? . . . never promised us a rose garden . . . even if the joints of your thighs are like jewels . . . and, well, the bud of your navel like the whorl of a rose."

17 "Be quiet," Rachelka said. "Very soon we'll be proselytizing those who would convert or kill us, and I'm no traitor to the faith. So tonight make haste, my beloved, and be like a hart on a hill of fragrant spices."

18 Which Gamaliel eagerly did; and, from the inn's lowermost bowels, the astrogator and his Shulamite heard, but did *not* hear, the unceasing *thump thump thump* of the bass notes from the jukebox in the motel bar.

19 Meanwhile, cockroaches scuttled in the dark, and, in an upstairs room, the Daughter of Mantid contemplated her fate.

CHAPTER 9

The Neutesters.

1 Now on the Great Plains of North America, centered in eastern Colorado but ranging northward into Canada and southward into Old Mexico, there dwelt several bellicose enclaves of Christian sectarians known in the aggregate as Neutesters, a neologism for New Testament Revivalists.

2 Their leader was the Right Reverend Thaddeus Thorogood, D. D.; their headquarters was near Lamar, Colorado; and their most distinctive dwellings were the networks of underground tunnels built, years and years ago, for shuttling warhead-bearing missiles back and forth beneath the plains.

3 Not long into Mantikhoras's Earthly mission, Thad Thorogood told every Neutester stronghold from Four Buttes, Montana, to Brownsville, Texas, and far beyond, that Lady Mantid was the Antichrist, while Joe Bob Newcombe, his chief lieutenant, pounded this same inflammatory message as Rachelka Dan's replacement on *Parsecs Ahead*.

4 Anyone giving aid and comfort to the Daughter of Mantid's deluded followers, both these men proclaimed, would either forfeit resurrection altogether or else enjoy its most poignant perquisites in Hell.

5 Thorogood quoted at length from the Olivet Discourse in *The Gospel of Mark:* "'For false Christs and false prophets shall rise, and shall show signs and wonders, to seduce, if it were possible, even the elect'"; but as many Neutesters as denounced the mantid, just that many or more hurried to embrace her.

6 When Mantikhoras began to travel not only with Catholics, Jews, and Unitarians, but also with primates, porpoises, and evolved talking dogs, the tide of Neutester defections to the ranks of the Alphacrucians noticeably abated.

7 Remarking this, Thorogood mounted a counterattack, via the CABLE-

STAR program *Parsecs Ahead*, emphasizing the implied New Testament doctrines of "man's essential uniqueness" and "the permanent significance of human nature."

8 As the House of Representatives of the Multipartite Union of North America now had only fifty-four members, and as the Senate had adjourned even before its decampment to Cleveland, Ohio, and as most of the members of both the executive branch and the quasi-Supreme Court still moldered in prison somewhere near Moscow;

9 Thaddeus Thorogood and his Neutester church constituted the nearest thing to a stable temporal authority (excepting perhaps the Union of Amusement Park Managers, the Pan-Solar Press Guild, and the Interstellar Diplomatic Instrument for Outreach, Trade, and Study) still extant in North America.

10 Therefore, when Thorogood dispatched to Gamaliel Crucis, the astrogator, a decree insisting that his Alphacrucian Mistress make a pilgrimage to his subterranean holdings outside Lamar, so that he, the Right Reverend, could quiz Mantikhoras about her activities,

11 Gamaliel feared a trap, and told his Mistress so, and urged her, at all costs, to avoid going docilely into a Neutester stronghold *anywhere* in the country and most especially that of Thaddeus Thorogood himself.

12 Indeed, even Rachelka, who had recently learned that she was with child, sought to dissuade Mantikhoras from answering the Right Reverend's arrogant summons, saying, "That bastard sincerely believes you're the great antagonist, Lady Mantid: he's gunning for you in the name of God."

13 But Mantikhoras said, "A sincere belief is not overcome without a struggle. If I flee or sidestep this man, I will only confirm him in the notion that I am an imposter."

14 Rachelka expostulated, "Must *everyone* come to see you for Who you really are? Why not condemn this priggish villain? His piety is a disguise for his own self-worship."

15 Said Mantikhoras, "And that's the ultimate blasphemy, even for those

who believe in Unguided Chance. Indeed, I must tell him so. His name is an allegory whose informing irony every thinking creature must one day acknowledge."

16 "Feh," said Gamaliel, who believed this exegesis needlessly explicit; but Lady Mantid was determined not to let anyone slip through her clutches via murky doctrine or abstruse pedagogy, and she waved her antennae almost gaily.

Sister Salvation & so forth.

17 The Alphacrucian set off from Richmond, Virginia, for Lamar, Colorado, in a caravan of methane-powered buses and two water-filled tank trucks for the cetaceans: a rattletrap assemblage of multihued vehicles.

18 One Pan-Solar Press reporter dubbed Mantikhoras and her entourage "Sister Salvation & Her Traveling Technicolor Menagerie & Medicine Show," a name that stuck because, gleefully, Gamaliel and the others started using it themselves.

19 In St. Joseph, Missouri, once a jumping-off place for the Oregon Trail, another press person asked Lady Mantid why she and her disciples traveled in such a gaudy caravan to see the authoritarian leader of the Neutesters.

20 And Mantikhoras said, "If the mountain won't come to Mohammed, then Mohammed will go to the mountain"; and this off-hand recitation of a hallowed cliché was interpreted by analysts as everything from a cryptic earthquake prediction to an oblique self-denial of the alien's own divine mandate.

21 The journey itself was a rowdy inchmeal affair, during which the mantid performed several semimiraculous cures, talked the caravan's way past a dozen illegal roadblocks, and faced down any number of adolescent hecklers (whatever their age) with soft words and earnest good humor;

22 And at last the buses, tank trucks, and motor cars achieved their destination; and the mantid and her retinue, minus the porpoises and orcas, disembarked to the strains of an old cowboy ditty, "Home on the Range."

An audience underground.

23 It was snowing outside Lamar, but in the vast subterranean prairie-dog village of the Neutesters, the temperature was balmy, downright spring-like; and Mantikhoras, along with Gamaliel, Rachelka, Andrew, and Priscilla, rode a pump-powered handcar to their audience with Thaddeus Thorogood.

24 A tall, cadaverous man whose receding hairline and blotchy age spots gave his head the look of a freshly unearthed skull, Thorogood greeted the Alphacrucians with notable effusiveness, welcoming them to his carpeted lair at the heart of the complex.

25 To counter his facial resemblance to a death's-head, Rachelka saw, Thorogood rouged his lips and kept his pale-blue eyes constantly in motion, as if by darting his glances here and there he would avoid being mistaken for a corpse.

26 After certain preliminaries (Mantikhoras declined a bowl of tea), the chief Neutester asked, "Why have you confined your ministry to the continental Multipartite Union when there are sinners abroad, out among our Solar System's colonies and surely on your home planet, too?"

27 "Surely," Mantikhoras replied. "The answer to your question, however, is that this is where I'm most needed. Here you have amusement parks, sports stadia, and radiation-treatment centers; casinos, massage parlors, and mutant reservations; monkey houses, Holiday Inns, and brothels; military bases, drag—"

28 *Thorogood:* You've made your point, Lady Mantid. But you've neglected to mention that media coverage isn't bad in this part of the world. I'm sure that was a consideration, too, was it not?

29 *Mantikhoras:* I was taken against my will from Acrux V, Your Right Reverendship. What I've done in your contaminated homeland, I've done in the name of The One who permitted my kidnapping for purposes self-disclosed in my ministry.

30 *Thorogood:* "*For many shall come in my name, saying I am Christ; and shall deceive many.*" Mark 13:6. But you don't deceive us Neutesters, Lady

Mantid, and certainly not their democratically ordained shepherd, Thaddeus Thorogood, D. D.

31 *Mantikhoras:* A verse or two later, you should note, Jesus is quoted to the effect that nation shall rise against nation, that earthquakes and famines shall occur, and that such signs shall signal *"the beginnings of sorrows."*

32 *Thorogood:* Ah. You're familiar with The Book. But even Satan can quote Scripture, Lady Mantid, and what you've quoted has come to pass in these very days of tribulation. As the poet wrote, *"Surely the Second Coming is at hand."*

The debate grows heated.

33 Rachelka murmured, *"What rough beast . . . slouches toward Bethlehem'"*; and the Right Reverend, hearing, turned his head and smiled condescendingly.

34 *Thorogood:* If you'll forgive the observation, Rachelka, your Mistress qualifies as a *"rough beast."* Although Yeats was a visionary heretic, I almost believe that your Lady Mantid has arrived on earth as a portent of the *true* Second Coming.

35 *Mantikhoras:* Your Right Reverendship, the passage from Mark suggests that you and your people, without yet witnessing the Messiah's return, have lived *through* the epoch of sorrows. The Cobalt Galas are over, the California Earthquake has already occurred, and humanity lives on.

36 *Thorogood:* What are you driving at? That we've outlived the conditions that should have foretokened the Second Coming?

37 *Mantikhoras:* Exactly. Things are bad today, I'll grant you, but they're *usually* bad, in one way or another; and the wars and rumors of war alluded to in your Olivet Discourse are things of the past. Albeit in aimless remnants all about the globe, the peoples of Earth are finally at peace.

38 *Gamaliel (unable to hold* his *peace):* Mostly because they're too exhausted or sick to wage war. [But both Mantikhoras and the chief Neutester ignored him.]

39 *Thorogood:* Let me get this straight. We've outlived the Time of Trials; therefore you *can't* be the Antichrist, because the Antichrist should already have come. By that very token, you can't be *Christ* because the Antichrist has not preceded you. Is that the gist of your argument?

40 *Mantikhoras:* Only to the extent that I decline to be identified with your problematic Antichrist. On the other hand, your second deduction is faulty.

41 The significance of this last remark sank into Thorogood's understanding slowly; but when he encompassed it, his lips drew in so that prim little crow's-feet bracketed them at the corners.

42 *Thorogood:* Who do you say you are?

43 *Mantikhoras:* Although I have indeed come again, this is not *the* Second Coming. By the grace of The One whose compassion and mercy are limitless, it's but an extension—an addendum, if you like—to my first meta-historic visit. I'm renewing in this dramatic fashion, sir, what you Neutesters *claim* to revive, in spirit and in truth.

44 *Thorogood:* The impudence of your self-aggrandizement is almost as reprehensible as its sacrilege! It represents bad theology and even worse manners! Jesus would never say *anything* like that, and it condemns you utterly!

45 *Gamaliel (interrupting):* How do you account for the cures she's effected, the miracles she's performed, the converts she's made, and the love among both kindred and strangers she has successfully inspired?

46 *Thorogood:* Telepathic suggestion, telekinetic trickery, deceitful promises, the satanic perpetration of mass hysteria! People do it all the time! Why, *I've* been known to do it!

47 *Mantikhoras:* Then I don't understand what—

48 *Thorogood:* You've had media help. The presence of Rachelka Dan in your entourage is telling. It wouldn't be so intolerable if you didn't try to pass yourself off as a ridiculous *orthopterization,* so to speak, of the Living Christ!

The audience ends.

49 And Thorogood stormed from the chamber, abandoning his lieutenants within glaring range of those of the Alphacrucian mantid, whose forelimbs at once assumed an attitude of prayerful contemplation.

50 But Gamaliel's heart misgave him, for they were now at the mercy of the outraged Neutesters, and Mantikhoras had just said, "I don't understand," a phrase he had never before heard escape her mouth.

51 Brandishing a weapon called a lanceflame, one of Thorogood's jackbooted warders said, "Too bad you didn't bring one of them snot-slick, fat-headed fish down here. I could fry it on the spot, and your six-legged Jesus would have something to eat when she comes back from the dead."

52 Laughing, the warders led her and her disciples back into the tunnel to the handcar on which they'd earlier arrived at this private silo. Gamaliel realized that they were prisoners and would not soon be returning to the surface.

CHAPTER 10

And what of Judas?

1 And that night Mantikhoras resided with Gamaliel, Rachelka, Andrew, and Priscilla in an underground room belonging to their enemies, who had not allowed them to return to the Traveling Technicolor Menagerie & Medicine Show, the members of which awaited them at a commercial campground outside Lamar.

2 The walls of their room sweated a rust-colored condensation; and taking this as a sign, no one imprisoned with Lady Mantid could sleep.

3 Also, all about the cell, Gamaliel found small bowls containing crisped locust bodies, which the Neutesters had left them as scornful suppers before their Mistress's inevitable Passion, whenever it might occur.

4 Neither Gamaliel nor any of the others wished to partake of this meal, but

Mantikhoras bade them eat what they could and then sponge from the walls enough of the ferruginous condensation to slake their powerful thirsts, for they had had no food or water since early that morning.

5 The disciples expected their Mistress to relent and eat with them, or else to explain the ritual significance of the meal supplied them by the Neutesters; but she prayed in troubled silence over the repast and declined any food for herself.

6 Surprisingly, their crisped locusts had a pleasant taste and the dampness from the walls was also potable; and an angry guilt stole upon Gamaliel because Mantikhoras continued to observe both her silence and her fast.

7 At last, then, Gamaliel threw his bowl against the wall, crying, "It's easy to see what's happening here, Lady! Which of us will betray you further? Which of us have you chosen for your Judas? Is it I, Lady Mantid? If so, tell me this very moment! I'll kill myself now instead of later!"

8 Rachelka tried to comfort Gamaliel, but Andrew and Priscilla also began to petition the mantid, demanding to know if she had selected one of them as her Iscariot and pleading exemption on the grounds of their great love for and service to her cause.

9 Mantikhoras said, "This clamor doesn't become you, friends. If there were to be a Judas this time, it would not be as a result of *my* selection that you—or *you*—or *you*—fulfilled that role. It would follow instead from the purblind dictates of your own heretofore loyal hearts."

10 The astrogator cursed, and beat on the sweating walls, and raged that if there *were* to be a Judas this time, one of them would surely fall into the role, and he, for one, did not like the odds: the original Twelve had been far better off.

11 Mantikhoras said, "Gamaliel, restrain your fear and your anger. Have you not noted that, on this occasion, I worked *to betray myself?* In mortal eyes, even The One may err; and although I don't embrace that sad notion, I *do* understand its ineradicable popularity among you."

12 She continued: "My self-betrayal is a sop to your ignorance and a mercy

to those close enough to me to fall into the *potential* danger tormenting the four of you tonight. If I am only a reminder of the covenant forged during Caesar's time, then I may gladly forgo the drama inherent in the traitorous act of Iscariot."

13 Rachelka said, "Lady Mantid, although you have spared us a Judas, you still have not excised villains from your Story. The Neutesters seem to be surrogates for your powerful Pharisaical adversaries in the Original Version, and I fear they'll also to stand in for your Roman executioners."

14 "It's impossible to excise villainy from this Story," the mantid said, "because it's hard to excise villainy from the self-aware condition. No segment of a self-aware population has either a corner on or immunity from it."

15 Priscilla said, "And this time you've chosen the Neutesters to demonstrate that fact?"

16 And Mantikhoras answered, "They've chosen themselves. That they assume the role in the mistaken belief that I am the Antichrist illuminates their grandiose self-corruption but in no way mitigates it."

17 Andrew ended this metaphysical discussion by saying that members of the Traveling Technicolor Menagerie & Etc. would storm their underground Bastille and free them, as Mantikhoras had freed the great apes from the monkey house in Atlanta.

18 But the Alphacrucian said, "I assembled you for discipleship, not guerrilla warfare. You're proposing a pipedream of your own, but at least it recommends to me the strength and indomitability of your hope." Hearing these words, Andrew crept into a corner and wept.

The disciples poisoned.

19 An hour later, all four of Lady Mantid's human disciples fell ill, and she understood that a henchman of Thorogood's had poisoned the locusts left in the room for them. To find that she had let those whom she loved act as her expendable food tasters enraged as well as saddened Mantikhoras.

20 Quickly, she cast the maleficent chemicals from her friends' bloodstreams,

beginning with the astrogator's wife (to reverse at once any harm that had been wrought against not only the woman herself but also the nascent soul in her womb) and concluding with Gamaliel.

21 Gamaliel said, "This is the Neutesters' 'humane' substitute for crucifixion. Clearly, it never crossed their minds that one might construe the taking of five other lives"—he was counting the unborn child—"as a small blot on the humanity of their methods."

22 And because Mantikhoras's rage was kindled against Thorogood and the Neutesters, she took all the empty bowls in the cell and shattered them on the walls as the astrogator had earlier done with his own.

23 "Mistress, had you no idea of what they'd done to the food?" Priscilla asked. "It seems to me that—"

24 Rachelka interrupted, saying, "Mantikhoras isn't *completely* coincident with The One, Priscilla. Her knowledge is finite, like our own, even if her wisdom far exceeds that of us imperfect mortals."

25 But even Gamaliel, now that the danger had passed, was outraged that his wife and unborn child had been placed in jeopardy: he asked why the wisdom of the Alphacrucian had not allowed her to deduce the likelihood of the food's having been "lethally tampered with."

26 Mantikhoras rounded on him: "Had the Neutesters presented you with *tempting* meats or succulents, my suspicions would have awakened instantly; but because they gave you *insects*, I was lulled to the danger.

27 "Now, I expect only the worst from our captors, and I will make it exceedingly hard for them to carry out the deed that their ignorance and prideful piety compel them to do.

28 "As for you, Gamaliel, the words you have uttered are a small betrayal that serves to legitimize my Passion. Fortunately, it's a betrayal of the vain and venial, rather than the mortal, kind, and I forgive you."

29 Hearing this, the astrogator hung his head, shut his eyes, and eased to his knees before his Mistress.

The disciples admonished to survive.

30 Mantikhoras found a speaker switch near the door, threw it, and informed Thorogood (wherever he was) that he must instantly release her followers if he hoped for success in physically obliterating her.

31 Gamaliel and the others bewailed this announcement, assuring her that they wished to stay with her to the end, and arguing that to coerce Thorogood to liberate them would be no kindness but a bereaving cruelty.

32 But Lady Mantid said, "You must survive this, friends, and go out from this continent to others, from this planet to others, from this solar system to others, and even from this galaxy to others, to proclaim the gospel to every creature with brains enough to hear and accept it."

33 Because Gamaliel still begged to go with her to the place of her Passion (to atone for his lapses of faith and gratitude), Mantikhoras granted him this boon, stipulating only that afterward he immediately return to Rachelka and the others.

More treachery.

34 Whereupon Thorogood's disembodied voice spoke, saying, "Woe to gravid serpents, and to every snake that slithers in the Great Serpent's wake, for they shall die in the pit with the Viper that seduced them!"

35 Before Gamaliel could make this serpentine metaphor jibe with his Mistress's insectile form, the door flew open. In rushed a host of Neutester warders in uniforms emblazoned at the breast with the classic fish insignia, each warder firing a weapon.

36 Screaming, Mantikhoras's disciples sought cover by dropping to the floor, while the Alphacrucian, opting for a more decisive measure, waved a forelimb and stopped time, at least within the cell's tight walls.

37 As in holographic tableau, every armed warder froze. In the air before them hung harmless streaks of multicolored light and interwoven parabolas marking the paths of rays, bullets, or birdshot (for some bore weapons older than lanceflames).

38 And then the mantid lifted the spell from her disciples so that they could ease past the frozen warders into a nearby tunnel. She went with them and, activating another speaker switch she had hit upon, told Thorogood, "If you want my life, sir, let my people go or I will never cooperate in its sacrifice."

39 But the foremost Neutester released a cyanide gas into the corridor, sent electrical fire running along the floor, and directed at them through the sprinkler system a lethal rain of hydrochloric acid.

40 Each such attack, the Alphacrucian thwarted by speaking a word or raising a forelimb; and at last Thaddeus Thorogood himself appeared at the end of the damp, burnt-smelling corridor striding toward them like an upright corpse.

41 Angrily he told her, "You've hypnotized my warders and jimmied the death-dealing systems on which we've based our internal security. Because you've stymied me to this point, Sister Salvation, I'll cut a deal with you.

42 "No more tricks! Yield to the fate you deserve. If you agree, I'll let all but Gamaliel the Astrogator return to the chaos of your Traveling Technicolor Menagerie, et cetera."

43 With great alacrity, Mantikhoras said, "Done!"

CHAPTER 11

Thorogood tries again, and again, and again.

1 But even after Rachelka, Andrew, and Priscilla had found safety aboveground, the Alphacrucian resisted the Neutesters' efforts to kill her; and Thorogood in mounting hatred and frustration accused her of reneging on her promise.

2 Mantikhoras countered that she wished to die in the sun, not in the bowels of a human ant-farm; but privately she told Gamaliel that she was giving Thorogood and his minions every chance to abjure an evil act that would condemn and stigmatize them forever.

3 To that end, she sidestepped two more attempts to shoot her, one to poison her, and a series of more exotic assaults: bludgeoning, burning, decapitation, drowning, garroting, hanging, overfeeding, smothering, starvation, induced cardiac infarction, electrocution, telemetrically activated organ failure, and vivisection to the point of no return.

4 Gamaliel was also at risk, but because Mantikhoras wrapped him in a protective cloak, in the end he was only a horrified witness to these inept enormities: failures that did not convert or discourage Thorogood but that stimulated in him an even more fanatical desire to obliterate the mantid.

The journey.

5 At length, the Neutesters put Mantikhoras and Gamaliel into a railroad car with barred windows; and, for three days, its subterranean train traveled northwestward beneath the Great Plains and Rocky Mountains toward the Sarcee Indian Reserve in Alberta, Canada, M.U.N.A.

6 Gamaliel was often delirious during this trip, for the tunnel walls hurtling past triggered in him memories of the undifferentiated corridors of the interstellar substratum; and he dreamed that he was practicing his occupation as an astrogator aboard a ship altogether unresponsive to his skills.

7 "We'll escape," he murmured, "as soon as I get a transdimensional fix on the stars. Why can't I find the stars? Where are the damned stars?" And Mantikhoras eased his distress by whispering into his delirium heartening words of solace.

8 Denver, Casper, Billings, Great Falls (each with its own level of lingering radioactivity) passed by above, until the Neutester train reached the contaminated barrens of the Sarcee Reserve, a place of little strategic value that during the Cobalt Galas had suffered four—count 'em, four—misdirected or wholly senseless nuclear strikes.

Calgary.

9 The countryside around Calgary was a glowing moonscape, long since quarantined; and into this hot desolation, Thorogood and his minions, clad

for its persistent peril, escorted the unprotected Alphacrucian and her lone attending disciple.

10 "Give Gamaliel a suit like yours," Mantikhoras thundered, "or I will people this hell with demons you'll recognize as former companions, and you, Your Right Reverendship, will be their everlasting Lucifer."

11 Gamaliel had never heard Lady Mantid threaten anyone before, nor had Thorogood, and soon the astrogator was submitting to decontamination protocols in a nearby structure fabricated for that purpose and, later, donning the kind of insulated gear and air-filtration system that the Neutesters wore.

12 And Mantikhoras said, "As soon as he's witnessed the abuses and abominations you inflict upon me in the name of one of my hypostases, take him well away from this site. My strength is utterly gone."

13 The sky shone red, the mountains lay about the plain like huge, caries-riddled teeth, and the waters of the Elbow River crept by like molten copper. Over the Calgary Tower, two-headed vultures circled in silent flights.

14 Thorogood prodded Lady Mantid with a gloved finger. "If your strength's gone, we will do with you as we like, and your astrogator will fare no better once your protection's withdrawn, I must warn you." (To his chagrin, Gamaliel had been fretting about this very possibility.)

15 Mantikhoras replied, "My strength is renewed through suffering, and in defense of my people, let me clue *you* in, sir: I am a retributive power that disdains even the barrier of death."

16 Here, Thorogood appeared to waver in his resolve to slay the alien Redeemer: but the visored faces of his warders searched his for guidance, and, ultimately, he chose to cast himself as a defender of the faith.

17 Commanded Thorogood, "Let it begin!"

18 More like insects than Mantikhoras herself, the Neutesters besieged her with torments in the shadow of the spindly metal tower whose purpose Gamaliel still had not plumbed. Although he fought to aid his Mistress, the arms of two of Thorogood's beefiest warders prevented him from doing so.

19 The warders blinded Mantikhoras in one of her multifaceted eyes, tore from her body two legs from one side and one from the other (so that, as they scourged her, she almost toppled), and strapped to the chitinous saddle behind her head a nuclear device wired for detonation from afar.

Mantikhoras climbs the tower.

20 And the Neutesters forced her to climb the struts of Calgary Tower with this device on her back, jeering and laughing from within their muffling helmets, and at last she reached the flimsy, riveted lookout over a hundred feet from the ground;

21 And, here, the nimble warder who had followed her aloft, catcalling and prodding, put out many of the drupelets in her remaining eye and fastened her with heavy chains to the platform.

22 These tasks finished, the man pulled off his helmet, cried, "Behold the Alphacrucian god!" and, after covering his head again, climbed down to ground zero to the tumultuous (muffled) cheers of his coreligionists and the piteous (muffled) lamentations of Gamaliel Crucis, the Astrogator.

23 Then, with an arctic wind howling over the Sarcee moonscape from the Pole, they withdrew to a bunker north of Calgary and from there triggered the device on the helpless Lady Mantid's back.

24 Said Thaddeus Thorogood, who appeared in the bunker at Gamaliel's side, "That's a relatively clean fission unit, friend. Your mantid savior will be flash-liberated from the snares of corporeality, and there won't be much fallout at all."

25 Gamaliel, who knew there would be more fallout than the chief Neutester could ever imagine, said nothing.

26 An immense dome of light, like a gigantic globe of mirrors, surrounded the tower on the plain, dazzling both eyes and mind; then the tower was swept away in an enormous priapic updraft of phosphorescent debris, a column that arose, and arose, and arose; and Gamaliel could watch no more.

CHAPTER 12

Gamaliel rejoins the others.

1 And when the Neutesters, fearing to defy the final words of Mantikhoras, freed the astrogator, he quickly ascertained the whereabouts of the other disciples and hurried to join them.

2 A remnant of faithful disheartened Alphacrucians had gathered in South Bend, Indiana, to raise their spirits (if possible) at a football contest between Notre Dame and the Rock City Rabbinical Institute of Rock City, Tennessee, the winner of this little-known rivalry to play Southern Methodist University two hours later in the same stadium.

3 Unhappily, the game proceeded in a raging acid snowfall, and Gamaliel could not reach his wife and fellow disciples until just a few minutes before halftime.

4 Said Rachelka, embracing her husband on a drifted upper tier, "It's zero to zero, honey, and I'm sorry there's no body to reclaim. That's why Thorogood did it as he did, isn't it? To deny us any chance to tender her corpse our last respects."

5 Gamaliel agreed, sat between Rachelka and a knobby homunculus in a raccoon coat (Muggeridge the Chimp, in his very own hair), and, glancing about, shook hands with Andrew Stout, Nicholas Morowitz, Damaris Brown, and Muggeridge the Chimp, all of whom seemed glad to see him again.

6 And he placed his hand on Rachelka's belly (beneath two cardigans and a goose-down parka) and whispered in her ear, "The kid's got the best seat in the house."

7 And Priscilla Muthinga, edging near with rapidly chilling coffee for the astrogator, told everyone that the snowflakes eddying about the stadium were "eucharistic particles of the comminute essence of the Redeemer," and that they must all stick out their tongues and take her in.

8 The disciples did so, and Gamaliel sipped his ice-cold coffee, and they were all zero at the bone there above the boring zero-to-zero combat between Notre Dame and Rock City Rabbinical.

9 And Andrew, hugging himself, said, "I thought she'd return to us in the orthopteran body we knew, not in these damned 'eucharistic particles' of some goddamn 'comminute essence'!" And he booed the Irish's quarterback for handing off to a snowdrift that had gone in motion to his right.

10 Rachelka noted that it had been over a week since the fission blast near Calgary, and that the odds of a real resurrection grew slimmer with every passing day. (Meanwhile, her undelivered baby did a backflip for RCRI, and she clutched her sides in spasms of agony and wonder.)

11 The game dragged on as the eucharistic particles of the comminute essence continued to swirl; and the talk, as well as the hope, of a more palpable resurrection faded to zero as zero-to-zero loomed as the likely final score, and in fact prevailed.

A messenger.

12 As the mantid's disciples filed from the stadium, a peanut vendor in a white fur coat and a Jiminy Cricket mask approached and said, "Don't be so down in the mouth, gang. You'll see her again in various guises. Here, have some peanuts."

13 And he tossed them several complimentary bags, most of which Muggeridge managed to intercept.

14 Before the disciples could thank the man, he vanished in an eddy of gusting whiteness; and Priscilla vouched that they'd beheld an angel from the interstellar substratum, which assertion Andrew pooh-poohed and Gamaliel dismissed as pipedream buncombe.

Counterpoint.

15 Many months passed, and, contrary to the masked vendor's prophecy, Lady Mantid did not appear to any of them again.

16 At last, in the obstetrics ward of a hospital for families of the Interstellar Diplomatic Instrument for Outreach, Trade, and Study, in Port-au-Prince, Haiti, Rachelka Crucis was brought to her confinement.

17 Gamaliel was there for the labor, which was long and difficult. When it became clear that the baby would not come for several more hours, an attending doctor took Gamaliel into an antechamber with a cot and told him to sleep.

18 Said this solicitous woman, "We'll wake you when it's time. Rachelka doesn't need to worry about both you *and* the baby, you know." And she left him there.

19 Against his will and better judgment, Gamaliel obeyed. Sleep stole upon him like the spirit of *gnosis,* and in this slumber he had a dream of such shameful implications that he thrashed futilely about to escape the toils of sleep.

20 Meanwhile, Rachelka's labor resumed, and the doctor who had led Gamaliel to the antechamber had no time to wake him and fetch him back to the delivery room, so busy was she doing what her heart and training required.

21 Mantikhoras entered the room in which Gamiliel lay by the door opposite Rachelka's place of confinement; and the musky pheromone wafting its scent to Gamaliel from the alien's ovipositors conveyed a summons impossible to ignore.

22 Aroused and frightened, Gamaliel stood and walked toward the mantid; and she said, "My husband."

23 Gamaliel circled the insect, whose body was entire again, even to the replacement of the gouged-out drupelets in her compound eyes; he kissed her forehead, held her praying forelimbs, and, at her silent urging, went abaft to consummate their union.

24 Said the doctor to Rachelka, "Push, dear": she obeyed, grimacing into the lights, and the tiny passenger in her womb slid headfirst into the doctor's gentle hands.

25 But the astrogator, spent, was in the throes of a weird postcoital ritual, two-stepping like a sleepwalker in the mantid's embrace and staring into the green cavern of her jaws. And Lady Mantid said, "The better to devour you, my worshiper-spouse, to make you mine forever and also me your everlasting own."

26 Her jaws closed on his skull, and in grave peristaltic gulps he was borne upward bone by bone into a disembodied consciousness where blooming bowls of light and the blurred aureoles of stars melded in a grand orgasmic knowledge that obliterated time.

27 Said the doctor to Rachelka, lifting the infant into the sheen of the chrome-encircled fluorescents, "It's a boy! And he's perfect perfect perfect!"

28 And a nurse sped to Gamaliel, found him lying beside his fallen cot, and escorted him sleep-stoned into the incandescent delivery room, where he smiled at Rachelka and took into his arms the luminous, bawling midge that was his son.

Afterbirth, afterdeath.

29 And later H. K. Bajaj came—also Priscilla Muthinga, Andrew Stout, and many more members of the Twentieth, along with Damaris and Muggeridge and Edward and so on; and the captain brought word that two expeditions assumed lost had lately arrived home from the stars.

30 Aboard one returning ship, the captain said, there was an adept who, even before the expedition's arrival on Earth, had predicted the birth of Rachelka and Gamaliel's child by means of the headachy mental flashes that had plagued her during the last stages of their approach.

31 "Over and over again," said Captain Bajaj, "the gift is life, and that is what the adept experienced during the pain of her reading. She wishes mother and infant health, wealth, and happiness, and sends heartfelt congratulations to the father, too."

32 And the captain presented the family a bouquet of towering sunflowers that the adept had sent from her vessel's hydroponic garden.

33 Aboard the second of the returning ships, Captain Bajaj said, was a hitchhiking energy being, a plasmoidal intelligence scooped from the skin of a gas giant in the Alphard solar system, and this bodiless entity was insistently proclaiming itself a visible fragment of the "soul" of The One.

34 Asked Rachelka, cradling her baby, "Is it possible for God to *possess* a soul? I would have thought that The One was nothing *but* soul: a transcendent spiritual being by its very nature synonymous with . . . with soulfulness."

35 Said Captain Bajaj, picking a sunflower for a boutonniere, "Even so, the Alphardic Plasma wishes to enlist the self-aware species of every world in a revival of the recent Mantic crusade, arguing via energy pulses to the ship's computer that

36 "A) the Son of Man and the Daughter of Mantid are its own sibling soulmates and evangelical forerunners, and B) the arrival of itself as a kind of Holy Ghostling may be the historical act that at last begins to get its message across here on Earth. What say you to these revelations?"

37 In unison, the astrogator and his wife cried, "*Hallelujah!*"

38 Elsewhere at that moment, to commemorate this Day of Days and all the days yet to come, apes in the jungles of Borneo waltzed, while orcas and porpoises off the coast of Yucatán leapt like living streaks of lightning.

39 And the spirit of Lady Mantid reigned. And he who testifies to these wonders says, "Come, Lady Mantid, come." *Amen.*

AUTHOR'S AFTERWORD:
A Long Tale Cut Short?

i / backstory

Not quite a decade ago, Patrick Swenson, the publisher, editor, and art director of Fairwood Press, and I agreed that his press would republish my then out-of-print novel *Brittle Innings*. It would appear in a new edition, with a new cover, a new introduction by Elizabeth Hand, and a revised text that I would designate, officially, my preferred version of the novel.

Since then, Patrick and I have worked to release seven more of my out-of-print novels in revised editions, along with two original works: a novel for young persons in 2016, *Joel-Brock the Brave and the Valorous Smalls* (with fine black-and-white art by Orion Zangara), and a collection in 2017 of primarily mainstream short fiction, *Other Arms Reach Out to Me: Georgia Stories*, for a total of nine books . . . *if* we add in a late 2017 title, a thoroughgoing recasting of my novel *Transfigurations*, whose first edition appeared in—dare I say it?—1979.

To my glee, after publishing our second Fairwood Press title in 2013, *Ancient of Days*, Patrick allowed me to create my own imprint, Kudzu Planet Productions, for any future titles that we undertook. Much of my writing, even if marketed as science fiction, takes place in Georgia, where kudzu abounds, rather than in deepest space or anywhere remotely near Patrick's home in Bonney Lake, Washington. And, if you're wondering, I chose *Productions* as the final word in this new imprint to avoid repeating *Press* and to acknowledge the fact that Patrick habitually releases *all* of his titles as e-books, not solely as ink-on-paper artifacts.[1]

All right, then: What book, or books, would we do together in 2018? At first, we thought to rerelease my Nebula Award-winning novel, *No Enemy but Time*, which has been available as an e-book with a cover by my son Jamie Bishop since 2000 through Bob Kruger's ElectricStory.com—albeit long out of print as an honest-to-God book. My desire to do *No Enemy but Time* began to shift, though, when a sarcoma in my right thigh, the reemergence of an old idea for a new novel, and Bob's announcement that he would soon shut down ElectricStory.com converged to persuade me that I could not juggle these three unexpected developments in one year, especially if I hoped to do a purposeful revision of *No Enemy but Time*.

So I asked Patrick, "What if we do an original book rather than a reprint?" We might have to cheat a little and assemble a volume featuring four stories, two not yet collected long fictions, "The Sacerdotal Owl" and "To the Land of Snow," and two long tales, *And Strange at Ecbatan the Trees* and "The Gospel According to Gamaliel Crucis," a novella from the November issue of *Isaac Asimov's Science Fiction Magazine* early in Shawna McCarthy's three-year editorial reign.

I figured that Patrick and I would one day do a spiffed-up version of *And Strange at Ecbatan the Trees*, which would make an awfully thin addition to my Fairwood Press/Kudzu Planet Productions shelf, and even thinner for the cuts I meant to inflict upon it. We could fatten it by adding three more long tales—"The Sacerdotal Owl," "To the Land of Snow," and a newly revised "Gospel According to Gamaliel Crucis"—but the *Ecbatan* title alone could deter readers from picking it up, if they'd read it in its first (Harper & Row), second (DAW), and third (Tor) versions, and even the presence of three unfamiliar stories might not offset their sales resistance.

And so we set aside the Archibald MacLeish-derived *Ecbatan* title and seized on the frankly pulpish *The Sacerdotal Owl* as our overall moniker, appending to it *and Three Other Long Tales* to hint that this once uncollected tale and the three longer stories in its company would repay any buyer's investment.[2] Does that sound devious? I hope not. The earliest published and/or collected stories, *Ecbatan* and "Gospel," have *never* appeared in these texts before, and their last appearances in unrevised versions occurred in 1990 and 1986 respectively. Anyway, pairing them with "The Sacerdotal Owl" and "To the Land of Snow," long tales of twenty-first-century origin, seemed a justifiable, and satisfactory, way of offering them to a new audience.

To change tacks, a major perk of working with Patrick at Fairwood Press/Kudzu Planet Productions is his willingness to consult with writers on issues like cover design and text layout. Early on, we had a cover in mind for this collection that struck us as ideal for *And Strange at Ecbatan the Trees and Three Other Long Tales*, but its creator, whose work Patrick had located online at Deviant Art, had just sold exclusive rights to it to a rock band for an album cover.

This development required us to rethink, and some of our rethinking resulted in our settling on *The Sacerdotal Owl*, etc., as our title. Tentatively, I suggested some online photos of Mayan dancers clad as various Mayan deities, including one dancer costumed as the Owl God, but the site in question wanted more than we cared to pay—one pitfall of working as an independent publisher. And so we rethought again, or at least *Patrick* did, creating through his own intuitive mix-and-match method the fine Maya-themed design that graces the cover of this Kudzu Planet Productions title.

Heartfelt thanks, Patrick.[3]

ii / long tales I've liked

As a teen, I liked long stories, or short novels, more than I did *War and Peace*-length epics, no matter the amount of swashbuckling or high-jinks those Tolstoy-sized doorstops put, or failed to put, on display. I devoured Voltaire's *Candide*, Melville's *Billy Budd*, Wells's *The Time Machine*, Heinlein's "Universe," Maugham's "Rain," Steinbeck's *The Red Pony*, Kuttner and Moore's "Vintage Season," Bradbury's "The Fireman" (a forerunner of *Fahrenheit 451*), Faulkner's *The Bear*, and Styron's *The Pistol*, among many other novellas or short novels, long before I essayed tomes as hefty as *Of Human Bondage* (Maugham), *Lie Down in Darkness* (Styron), or *Stranger in a Strange Land* (Heinlein). Further, the first hardcover book I bought with my own pocket money—at a bookstore in Utica Square in Tulsa, Oklahoma—was an illustrated, gold-tipped edition of Hemingway's *The Old Man and the Sea*.[4] It cost five bucks.

My point?

Just that short novels and novellas have bolstered the literary granaries and the popularity of sf from the beginnings of the genre. (Who presumes to know when ghost stories, horror, or dark fantasy first reared their gnarly heads? Maybe around muddy veldt oases, antelope kills, or antique campfires. Wherever and whenever they began, these types of storytelling strike me as elemental.) In any case, editors of sf, horror, and weird-story pulps called for and bought *many* long tales—to the delight of writers making at best a penny a word—to fill their magazines with exciting material for often overlapping readerships.

These longer stories got cover treatments, built the reputations of their creators, and statistically, going by reader polls, more often gratified the expectations of readers seeking plot, fabulous characters, exotic action, and mind-blowing payoffs than did short stories, even those with a witty twist. Some such shorts, like Damon Knight's "To Serve Man," have eyebrow-lifting punch lines that make them golden to literary anthologists or TV script writers like Rod Serling of *Twilight Zone* fame—but longer tales usually better feed readers set for a more immersive experience than your average short story provides. After all, good longer tales, even the detailed ones, tend to cut a lot of the flapdoodle and padding of a full-bore novel.

Here are seven science-fiction-related titles, which I have accessed in editions on my own shelves and obsessively endnoted, that consist of *nothing* but novelettes and/or novellas[5]:

> *More Than Human* by Theodore Sturgeon, a bona fide novel that nonetheless *consists of* three interlocking novellas, "The Fabulous Idiot," "Baby Is Three," and "Morality"[6] ;

> *Four for Tomorrow* by Roger Zelazny, which features the long tales "The Furies," "The Graveyard Heart," "The Doors of His Face, the Lamps of His Mouth," and "A Rose for Ecclesiastes," stories that Theodore Sturgeon characterizes in this small paperback's introduction as "fabulous," not in the modish 1960s sense of "fab," but in the way of a work, a *fable* for example, that "says more than it says, is bigger than its own parameters"[7] ;

> *The Science Fiction Hall of Fame, Volume Two A & Volume Two B*, edited by Ben Bova, each of which contains ten novellas, by such strong late sf eminences as John W. Campbell, Jr., Walter M. Miller, Jr., Isaac Asimov, James Blish, Algis Budrys, Clifford D. Simak, Jack Vance, and four other sf talents noted in the first

paragraph of part ii of this Afterword, for every story in these two volumes was chosen for inclusion by the Science Fiction Writers of America (now the Science Fiction and Fantasy Writers of America, but still known as SFWA) to recognize their merit, given that every selected novella first appeared before the creation of SFWA or the Nebula Awards, which laud speculatively imaginative work in four different length categories—short story, novelette, novella, and novel—every year in the sf and fantasy fields[8];

The Fifth Head of Cerberus by Gene Wolfe, an even more subtle example than Sturgeon's *More Than Human* of a bona fide, but sophisticatedly unorthodox, novel consisting of three novellas, the title piece followed by " 'A Story,' by John V. Marsch" and "V. R. T.," and concluding with an Afterword, unacknowledged except on the copyright page, by sf writer/anthologist Pamela Sargent, who details thoughtfully many of the cunning connections among the three tales and thus their camouflaged unity as an insightfully complex novel[9];

Four Ways to Forgiveness by Ursula K. Le Guin, a collection of four long tales, later augmented with a fifth ("Old Music and the Slave Woman") and published, albeit only as an e-book, as *Five Ways to Forgiveness*, consisting of "Betrayals," "Forgiveness Day," "A Man of the People," and "A Woman's Liberation," yet another group of interlocking fictions that Le Guin herself liked to term a "story suite," and that she felt she could have fashioned into a novel had she not chosen to give voice to so many different characters[10];

and, finally, at least for my purposes here,

The Found and the Lost: The Collected Novellas of Ursula K. Le Guin, a career-spanning 803-page volume gathering thirteen long tales first published between 1970 and 2002, starting with "Vaster Than Empires and More Slow," moving on to include the entire contents of *Five Ways to Forgiveness*, and concluding with "Paradise Lost," a collection that I mention here because it stands not only as a massive doorstop for folks with disobedient doors, but also as a formidable brick in the formidable monument of her life's work, her incomparable oeuvre, a legacy unlike any other writer's to readers everywhere.[11]

If I pushed it, a catalogue like the foregoing could fill many more pages, and by compiling it, I don't intend to suggest that the stories in *The Sacerdotal Owl and Three Other Long Tales* rise to the heights of the best longer tales of Sturgeon, Zelazny, Wolfe, Le Guin, or of the stories in the two volumes of *The Science Fiction Hall of Fame* given over to novellas, only that we have these works before us as seas to cross and bourns to travel toward. And who among us doesn't like a reading list that points us to fresh vistas and mind-expanding new voyages?

As Emily Dickinson wrote, "There is no frigate like a book." [12]

iii / four stories

1: "The Sacerdotal Owl"

This story would not exist but for the fact that writer and editor Brian A. Hopkins solicited a contribution from me for an anthology honoring thirteen years of the World Horror Convention.[13] His invitation resulted from the fact that I, like all the other twelve contributors to the anthology, had attended a past WHC as a Writer Guest of Honor. In 1999, I had gratefully accepted that role in Atlanta, Georgia, at Convention IX—with fellow Writer Guest of Honor John Shirley, Artist Guest of Honor Lisa Snellings, Master of Ceremonies Neil Gaiman, and Grandmaster Ramsey Campbell, company in which I felt like a bit of an imposter.

My output of horror or dark fantasy hardly equals in quantity or quality that of the other writers attending WHC that year, or even my own output as an sf writer and fantasist. (Darker elements of the human experience infiltrate my work in every field, but my only "horror" novel also features impudent parodies of horror clichés and a bestseller by Stephen King, whom, on the whole, I admire.) So I couldn't help wondering if my invitation in 1999 owed as much to my living in close proximity to the convention site as to my kindly alleged horror-writing skills.[14]

Whatever the case, I found Brian Hopkins's invitation—challenge, I'd call it—to write a tale for *13 Horrors* deliciously provocative and Hopkins a person of commitment and talent whom I did not want to disappoint. He had emerged from the small presses in the mid-1990s, editing an anthology series called *Extremes* and writing at least three novels, one of which—*El Dia de los Muertos*, or *The Day of the Dead*—my insightful colleague James Morrow called "a searing journey into the mythic soul of Mexico and the intolerable heart of loss."

How could I ignore Brian's invitation and live with myself? Anyway, I had been looking for a (paying) project and turned to *Twentieth Century Latin American Poetry: A Bilingual Anthology*, edited by Stephen Tapscott, for inspiration, and to books, magazine articles, and Internet sites about the Maya and twentieth- and twenty-first-century slash-and-burn depredations to the rainforests of Central and South America. These researches ended in my writing "The Sacerdotal Owl." Brian accepted it, and my effort also resulted in a surprise sale to *Weird Tales*, then edited by George Scithers and Darrell Schweitzer. Jeffrey Ford read the story in that venue and wrote me an email congratulating me for hopping with both galoshes into a steamy pulp-fiction milieu and ruthlessly exploiting it for all it was worth. I misplaced that email a decade or more ago, so you'll have to take my word for what Jeff said. If I don't have his reaction verbatim, I'm pretty sure I've remembered its congratulatory gist. [15]

2: *And Strange at Ecbatan the Trees*

The earliest long tale here, *And Strange at Ecbatan the Trees*, eschews quotation marks around it in the Acknowledgments or the Afterword of this FP/KPP collection. Why? Because it first appeared as a stand-alone book and its title thereby warranted italics. Indeed, I can reassure myself to this fact by going downstairs, finding that slim little book, and pulling it from its bookcase. [16]

I wrote *Ecbatan*, just as I did my first novel, *A Funeral for the Eyes of Fire*, under the influence of Le Guin's *The Left Hand of Darkness* and her earlier Ekumen novels, *City of Illusions*, *Planet of Exile*, and *Rocannon's World*. But its "otherworldly" setting owes a lot to my private image of seventeenth- or eighteenth-century England, if only Earth had boasted three moons and its people mysterious ancestors who had genetically engineered them to vitiate but not eliminate their inbred bent for one-on-one mayhem and intercommunity war.

On its surface, *Ecbatan* presents itself as science fiction, but goes only a small way toward granting its human characters a coherent mix of technologies, giving them historical knowledge, electricity, recording devices, and laser-style weaponry, but when it comes to transport, relegating them to boots, horses, and masted sailing ships. In fact, this aspect of my short novel reminds me of Mary Shelley's *The Last Man*, wherein people of the twentieth century, and later, still go to war a-horseback and no one knows a rat's rear about auto repair or computers. In that regard, *Ecbatan* skates by as self-aware pseudo-sf, gliding on the atmospheric lyricism of Jack Vance-style science fantasy.

Or not.

That doesn't mean that I dislike *Ecbatan* or rue writing it. It was the work of a fledgling genre writer, and I had half-, or maybe three-quarters-, hoped that my agent at that time, Virginia Kidd, who also represented Ursula Le Guin, Gene Wolfe, and R. A. Lafferty, would place it, possibly as a two-part serial, with *Fantasy & Science Fiction*, *Galaxy*, or *Analog*—although even to me that last market loomed as a pipe-dream long shot. What instead happened surprised me almost as much as a sale to John W. Campbell, the editor at *Analog*: Virginia placed my skinny manuscript with Harper & Row, where sf editor Buz Wyeth and his staff did not blink, much less balk, at my highfalutin literary title. Moreover, the art department asked if I wanted a "design element" on and/or in the book's hardcover edition. I suggested the silhouette of an exotic-looking tree, and, *voilà*, that's just what appeared at various places in my slender hardcover. Moreover, they thought it clever that the poem providing my novel's epigram, "You, Andrew Marvell," in synopsizing, without rhythmic surcease or punctuation, the fall of every dynasty ever to arise, also gave me *Ecbatan*'s plot and theme: the action of calamity in human history and the impermanence of human civilizations.

Truth is, I was *always* more interested in literature than I was science, although science does fascinate me, whether I understand it or ape understanding it so as to avoid appearing less evolved than, say, Mighty Joe Young. Hence, the maskers of Ongladred, when dead but neurologically revived, became surrogates for those Elizabethan actors who acted the roles of women in dramas of that period, for live maskers are forbidden, not so much by law as by their own psychology and physiology, to act the parts of people still hag-ridden by antique instinct and raw emotion. For which excellent reason, William Shakespeare's avatar in *Ecbatan* appears in the guise of a 63- (read 75-) year-old cadaver re-animator and neuro-drama creator yclept Gabriel Elk.

At thirty, I loved that name. I guess I still do.

Donald A. Wollheim, an editor at Ace Books for twenty years and the founder in 1972 of DAW Books, bought paperback rights to *Ecbatan* and released it in June 1977 with a DAW Books-style cover by H. R. Van Dongen: a slain masker woman, Bronwen Lief, dancing in a pink-chiffon dress before her own dead self prostrate on a bier as well as before the enormous background image of a Pelagan warrior holding a knife in front of his sinisterly shadowed face.

Wollheim, of course, objected to my consternating literary title and asked me to change it. I was ready for him and gave him one that I knew he'd like. And, so, for all its paperback appearances until paired in a Tor Double Novel with James Tiptree, Jr.'s "The Color of Neanderthal Eyes" in January 1990, *And Strange at Ecbatan the Trees* became *Beneath the Shattered Moons*, with a bow to Edgar Rice Burroughs and a nod to the die-hard legacy keepers of the dead or dying pulps.

3: "To the Land of Snow"

This long tale—an accidental companion to an earlier novella of mine, "Cri de Coeur," about a multi-decade starship voyage—had its genesis in an invitation from my friend and fellow sf-writer Jack McDevitt to write a piece for an anthology that he and Les Johnson, Deputy Manager of NASA's Advanced Concepts Office, were assembling for Baen Books about traveling to the stars, *Going Interstellar*.

Fortunately, the editors provided me with some background on the configurations and power sources of the types of ships that could, and might, make such perilous future voyages, as well as with the names of some recently discovered extra-solar planets that have slim-to-acceptable chances of supporting human life. The *Kalachakra* in my story is an anti-hydrogen-fueled starship with twenty-four drop tanks that it sheds over the course of its interstellar migration, and the planet to which its crew has directed the ship is a real planet called Gliese 581g circling a red dwarf star called Gliese 581. The lower-case *g* clinging to its appellation signifies the planet, a sun and a world approximately twenty light-years from Earth. For that reason, the novella appeared in Les and Jack's anthology as "Twenty Lights to 'The Land of Snow.'" We've renamed it for its appearance here to get rid of its discomfiting single quote marks inside double quote marks, and because the voyagers themselves regard their destination as a hopeful counterpart to their ideal home, a kind of Buddhist Eden, The Land of Snow.

In their intro to the piece, the editors declare, "The first thing most American readers will have to do when reading [this story] is put aside their preconceived notions of what the crew and culture of an interstellar space-craft must emulate—western culture. And with the current pace of space exploration in the West, new notions of how it might actually happen are certainly worth considering."[17]

In conceiving my story, I had two controlling notions. The first was that I wanted the crew and passengers of my ship to consist of Buddhists, or committed Buddhist allies, fleeing persecution in Tibet but also, in the case of their supporters, seeking a world and a homeland entirely their own. The second idea was that I wanted an unusual girl-woman as my narrator, specifically a Buddhist person of hidden potential who would mature over the century or so that it would take for the *Kalachakra* to reach its destination. And, having just read Canadian writer Emma Donoghue's remarkable novel *Room*, narrated by a five-year-old boy in a weird, isolate environment all his own, I chose to take the voice of seven-year-old Greta Bryn emerging from a profound drug sleep and confronting the common plight, or opportunity, of her shipmates—and then to follow her growing up all the way to planetfall on Guge, *aka* Gliese 581g.

Later, Gardner R. Dozois chose "To the Land of Snow," under its original title, for his thirtieth annual best-of-the-year volume from St. Martin's, and a society devoted to promoting space travel nominated it for one of its literary awards. Still later, John Joseph Adams republished it online in *Lightspeed Magazine*. And it appears as well in Neil Clarke's anthology *The Far Frontier*, a volume about future spacefarers published almost concurrently with this collection.

4. "The Gospel According to Gamaliel Crucis"

In 2015 or so, an editor of a publishing house in England devoted to left-leaning philosophical screeds, novels, etc., approached me with the idea of reprinting this 1983 novella as a stand-alone book, with a new introduction of his own. He would not put it out, though, until he could acquire two or three more science-fiction novellas of similar quasi-radical content. I took that as an excuse—and a good one—to revisit the text of the testimony of this Gamaliel Rashba fellow, *aka* G. Crucis, and to rework it for publication in the United Kingdom. I did so. Nothing happened on the publisher's end . . . except that I was advised a time or two to upload my manuscript to their email server for editing, etc. I remained certain that I had already done so, through the auspices of the editor who had first approached me.

And nothing happened, and went on not happening, except for the tardy arrival of the editor's promised intro and an apology for the time that had passed since his initial query. I wrote an email stating that I was almost ready to abandon our agreement—no money had changed hands—and received an apology and a muted plea to hang fire a while longer. I did, but still nothing happened. Then, fatigued, I withdrew "Gospel" from the British firm and received another apology and the explanation that the editor had not yet found three other quasi-radical novellas to fulfill his plan for a quartet—a suite?—of long stories to come out together close in time. I sympathized with the editor's situation, but immediately began to think of a vehicle for showcasing Gamaliel's revised "Gospel," to wit, *The Sacerdotal Owl*, etc.

I wrote "Gospel" in 1982, while Mutually Assured (Nuclear) Destruction seemed a likely end-time fate for the United States and the Soviet Union (the mirror image U.S. and S.U.), but I had conceived of writing a story in scriptural form in 1962 or '63 while taking a typing class at the dependent school in the housing enclave for U.S. Air Force personnel and their families, Santa Clara, seven or eight miles south of Seville, Spain. I was a senior, the editor of our school literary magazine, *El Toro*, and a wannabe Ernest Hemingway, a fan of "The Snows of Kilimanjaro," "Hills Like White Elephants," and "Today Is Friday."[18]

So it was at least twenty years on before I actually sat down and wrote, in chapter and verse, my own apocryphal gospel as a satirical science fiction tale. As noted earlier, Shawna McCarthy acquired the story for *Isaac Asimov's Science Fiction Magazine*, and it upset a number of readers as blasphemously offensive, even though I had written not to satirize religionists as a whole, or Christians in particular, but rather our built-in human proclivities for enmity, violence, and war. One reader wrote the magazine—indeed, Isaac himself—

saying that he was "strongly displeased" and that my story was "a burlesque of the scriptures."[19]

Fortunately for me, in the lead editorial in the June 1984 issue of *Asimov's*, which Asimov later revised as an introduction to my collection *Close Encounters with the Deity*, Isaac took on the reader's argument and defended accepting my novella for publication. He wrote that *Asimov's* was "a serious science fiction magazine" featuring, presumably, "stories of literary merit"[20], adding that serious sf cannot ignore topics as crucial as religion is to us, even if we reject it as vital component of our lives. Toward the essay's end, he states, "We put the story's literary quality and thematic importance ahead of a chance that it might offend,"[21] and he concludes,

> We hope that our angry correspondent will reconsider the matter and come to see that "The Gospel According to Gamaliel Crucis," like nearly all the other stories with theological themes in this collection [*Close Encounters with the Deity*], is far more than a burlesque. He might even give Bishop points for skill and courage.[22]

Those words were balm for any wounds that the words of the "angry correspondent" had inflicted on me, and I was grateful I had not had to write them myself, for I would have most likely met outrage with outrage and self-righteousness with disdain. And that would have undercut one of the points of my long—but less long in this version—tale and cursed me with ashes to roll on my tongue.

(Endnotes)

[1] My two sole Fairwood Press titles and their dates of publication are *Brittle Innings* (Aug 2012) and *Ancient of Days* (Sept 2013), whereas my seven, now eight, Fairwood Press/Kudzu Planet Production titles include *Who Made Stevie Crye?* (Aug 2014), *Count Geiger's Blues* (Nov 2014), *A Funeral for the Eyes of Fire* (May 2015), *Philip K. Dick Is Dead, Alas* (Nov 2015), *Joel Brock the Brave and the Valorous Smalls* (June 2016), *Other Arms Reach Out to Me* (June 2017), *Transfigurations* (Nov 2017), and *The Sacerdotal Owl and Three Other Long Tales* (Aug 2018).

[2] Actually, the *full* title of this quartet of stories, after the words and *Three Other Long Tales*, concludes with the words *of Calamity, Pilgrimage, and Atonement*. But I should have inserted *Respectively* between *of* and *Calamity* to indicate that each of these other long stories does not deal with all three of these themes at once. Or maybe each does. Maybe I could make that case. Maybe.

[3] Heartfelt thanks as well to the original editors of the four stories herein, Brian Hopkins, Buz Wyatt, Les Johnson and Jack McDevitt, and Shawna McCarthy, as well as to Isaac Asimov, Gregory Frost, Nancy Kress, and Jane Lindskold for defending or blurbing this collection, and to Patrick Swenson and Michael Hutchins for their literary advice and proofreading skills.

[4] *The Old Man and the Sea* by Ernest Hemingway, illustrated by C. F. Tunnicliffe and Raymond Sheppard. New York: Charles Scribner's Sons, First Printing: September 1960; 140 pp, $5.00.

[5] Excepting, of course, front matter, intros, afterwords, and about-the-author notes.

[6] *More Than Human* by Theodore Sturgeon. New York: Ballantine Books, Fourth Printing: November 1968; 188 pp, 75¢.

[7]   *Four for Tomorrow* by Roger Zelazny (With an Introduction by Theodore Sturgeon). New York: Ace Books, Inc., First Book Publication, 1967; 192 pp, 45¢, 8.

[8]   *The Science Fiction Hall of Fame, Volumes Two A & Two B*, edited by Ben Bova. Garden City, New York: Doubleday & Co., Inc., SF Book Club editions, 1973; 527 and 529 pp respectively, prices not given and today lost to memory.

Authors in *Volume Two A* include Poul Anderson ("Call Me Joe"), John W. Campbell writing as Don A. Stuart ("Who Goes There?"), Lester del Rey ("Nerves"), Robert A. Heinlein ("Universe"), C. M. Kornbluth ("The Marching Morons"), Henry Kuttner and C. L. Moore, writing as Lawrence O'Donnell ("Vintage Season"), Eric Frank Russell (". . . And Then There Were None"), Cordwainer Smith ("The Ballad of Lost C'Mell"), Theodore Sturgeon, ("Baby Is Three"), H. G. Wells ("The Time Machine"), and Jack Williamson ("With Folded Hands").

Authors in *Volume Two B* include Isaac Asimov ("The Martian Way"), James Blish ("Earthman, Come Home"), Algis Budrys ("Rogue Moon"), Theodore Cogswell ("The Spectre General"), E. M. Forster ("The Machine Stops"), Frederick Pohl ("The Midas Plague"), James Schmitz ("The Witches of Karres"), T. L. Sherred ("E for Effort"), Wilmar H. Shiras ("In Hiding"), Clifford D. Simak ("The Big Front Yard"), and Jack Vance ("The Moon Moth").

[9]   *The Fifth Head of Cerberus: Three Novellas* by Gene Wolfe. (*Afterword* copyright © 1976 by Pamela Sargent.) New York: Ace Books, First Ace Printing: June 1976; 277 pp, $1.75.

[10]   *Four Ways to Forgiveness* by Ursula K. Le Guin. New York: HarperPrism, First Mass Market Printing: August 1996; 312 pp, $5.99.

[11]   *The Found and the Lost: The Collected Novellas of Ursula K. Le Guin*. New York: Saga Press [an Imprint of Simon & Schuster], First Published: October 2016; 803 pp, $29.95.

Ursula Kroger Le Guin (b Oct 21, 1929 – d Jan 22, 2018, age 88) was a major American novelist, story writer, and poet, who wrote beautiful, smart, anthropologically savvy, character-driven science fiction and fantasy. She became a significant influence of mine after I read her Hugo- and Nebula-Award-winning novel *The Left Hand of Darkness* in an Ace Science Fiction Special edition with a cover painting by Leo and Diane Dillon. At the time, I was a second lieutenant in the United States Air Force and teaching English to cadet candidates at the USAF Academy Preparatory School outside Colorado Springs, Colorado.

My first novel, *A Funeral for the Eyes of Fire*, grew out of my respect for *The Left Hand of Darkness* and my authorship of an inept novella that I called (forgive me) "A Far Galapagos, an Inward Heart." I scrapped the novella but to some extent cannibalized it for *Funeral*, which I began in the Air Force and finished while teaching freshman English at the University of Georgia. And to this day I revere Le Guin as a significant influence, even if much of my work, beyond *Funeral*, resembles hers only obliquely, if at all.

Even so, Ursula, farewell and peace abiding.

[12]   *Frigate* is not a euphemism seldom used in polite company, but "a light, fast boat that was rowed or sailed." At least, that was the earliest definition of the term, its 16th-century origin. Later, naturally, it came to mean "a warship with a mixed armament, generally heavier than a destroyer" (*The New Oxford Dictionary*, 679).

[13]   *13 Horrors: A Devil's Dozen Celebrating 13 Years of the World Horror Convention* edited by Brian A. Hopkins, Foreword by Joe Lansdale. Kansas City, MO: KaCSFFS (Kansas City Science Fiction and Fantasy Society, Inc.) Press, First Edition: Apr 17, 2003, 256 pp, $75.00.

[14]   In 1994, I was a writer Guest of Honor at the World Science Fiction Convention. Its venue that year was the Callaway Gardens Inn in Pine Mountain, Georgia. I was almost certainly the only sf writer in attendance *from* Pine Mountain, Georgia.

[15]   Okay, Jeff never used the words "hopping with both galoshes into a steamy pulp-fiction milieu and ruthlessly exploiting it for all it was worth." But I'm sure that's what he meant. And although I *am* subject to twinges of forgetfulness, an army of MDs at Emory University Hospital Midtown in Atlanta recently certified me "dementia-free."

16   Let me note that the title *on* the cover of a book or *on* its title page, is usually *not* italicized . . . unless the book designer has specified a font that *resembles* italics. It is in *referring to* the title of a book in a review, essay, or critical work that one italicizes the title of any book-length work—unless you write for *The New Yorker*, in which case you will put *quotation marks* around the titles of even book-length published works. And if these rules confuse you, think how hard they were to sell to freshman English students writing essays about William Faulkner's *A Rose for Emily* or Robert A. Heinlein's "The Moon Is a Harsh Mistress."

17   Introduction to "Twenty Lights to 'The Land of Snow' " in *Going Interstellar*, edited by Les Johnson and Jack McDevitt. New York: Baen Books, First Baen Printing, June 2012; 438 pp, $7.99, 263.
   Also, on 349, NASA scientist and Nebula Award-winner Geoffrey A. Landis provided an image of the mid-flight configuration of the anti-hydrogen-fueled starship *Kalachakra*, minus a good number of its storage tanks.

18   And, of course, *The Old Man and the Sea*.

19   "Foreword: Religion and Science Fiction" by Isaac Asimov in *Close Encounters with the Deity: Stories* by Michael Bishop. Atlanta: Peachtree Publishers, Ltd., 1st Printing, 1986; i-vi pp + 308 pp, $8.95, ii.

20   *Ibid.*

21   *Ibid.*, vi.

22   *Ibid.*

ABOUT THE AUTHOR

Michael Bishop is the award-winning author of *No Enemy But Time* and several other acclaimed novels, including *Ancient of Days* and *Brittle Innings*, and also such story collections as *At the City Limits of Fate*, *Brighten to Incandescence*, and *Other Arms Reach Out to Me: Georgia Stories*. He lives in Pine Mountain, Georgia, with his wife, Jeri, a retired elementary school counselor, who is now an avid gardener and a conscientious yoga practitioner.